D1109537

CHINESE CHECKERS

Carol Doumani is also the author of

UNTITLED. Nude.

CHINESE CHECKERS

a novel by

CAROL DOUMANI

Wave Publishing
Venice

Manufactured in the United States of America
First Edition
Published by WAVE PUBLISHING
Post Office Box 688
Venice, California

This is a work of fiction. While the author will be flattered if the reader believes that the characters and circumstances herein are real, they are not. Any similarities to actual people, places and predicaments is purely coincidental.

ISBN 0-9642359-7-8
Library of Congress Catalog Card Number 95-61683

Composed by ReadMe Interactive
Troy, New York
Printed and Bound by The Haddon Craftsmen
Scranton, Pennsylvania
Designed by John Deep
10 9 8 7 6 5 4 3 2 1

For Roy, who, trip by trip, has given me the world.

CHINESE CHECKERS

An ancient game of strategy and cunning,
the object of which is
to move across a given space
as quickly as possible,
to reach a designated goal
in advance of one's opponents.

FUCHOW, CHINA

Friday, December 30, 1985

A TWILIGHT FOG SETTLES over the ancient streets, weightless as the downy feathers of a Mandarin duck. The thick tufts obscure all but the newest buildings, rickety ten- and twelve-story structures, hastily erected after Mao's death to symbolize China's entry into the modern era.

Seen from the outlying countryside these modest skyscrapers resemble the first growth of spring tentatively sprouting through a March frost. The mist is lighter here, revealing primitive dirt roads that anticipate the dawn as they have for centuries. The only visible concessions to the twentieth century are the street lamps, whose evenly spaced glass globes, though unlit, are linked by a slack electric wire, like dusky pearls strung on a giant's necklace.

Up a steep and rutted path from the main road, two mean huts straddle a barren courtyard. One is dark, but in the other a kerosene lantern glows, casting shadows on the interior. A wooden chair, a small table, and a cot are all huddled in one corner under a calendar displaying the month of May in the year 1978 and a photograph of Disneyland. In startling contrast to this spartan decor, the rest of the room is filled with crude scientific apparatuses: tools, monitors, microscopes, and pumps, all jerry-built from spare bicycle parts and scrap iron, an improvised laboratory.

The architect of this incongruity putters about so intent on his work that he is oblivious to the pink and purple dawn breaking outside. He is a stooped old man, dressed in traditional peasant garb — a round-collared jacket of blue cotton buttoned to the throat, baggy pants draped loosely over his thin frame, and broad-strapped sandals with two-inch soles. A long, gray pigtail trails down his spine, and on his weathered chin, wisps of beard form the requisite goatee. He could be mistaken for a nineteenth-century coolie were it not for the maroon and gold USC Trojans baseball cap he wears backwards on his head.

Hands trembling, the old man removes the cap, and with great ceremony unfastens a tiny pin from it. The pin glows in his hand, an ember of light. With surprising deftness for a man of his age and frailty, in one jerking motion he pulls the pin apart, extracting a chip of metal barely larger than a grain of rice. This he inserts into the circuitry of a small black box on the work table. Outside, a rooster crows.

FIFTY FEET ACROSS THE COURTYARD, the occupant of the other hut shuffles to his doorway and squints into the dawning day, cursing the ever-present fog. Through the misty shroud he senses movement and strains to see. A fox in his chicken coop? An intruder stealing eggs? He relaxes. No, it is just his neighbor, Wan Lo, hurrying down the dirt road lugging a black box. Another of the crazy old man's foolish experiments, no doubt. He's seen many of them during the twelve years they have been neighbors, each one more ridiculous than the next.

Muttering to himself, he crosses the courtyard, his bare feet shuffling noiselessly in the soft dirt. He stoops and enters the coop, tossing feed to the Qing Yuan hen and the Zhusi rooster, calling them by name. As the birds peck at the grain, he peers through a slit in the wall and watches the old man open the electrical junction box at the base of the closest streetlight.

Theoretically this box links the two huts to the central power source. But electricity has never flowed through the wires, another promise of progress abandoned by the government.

Now, to his surprise, Wan Lo reaches in and snips the dead filament. Aha! He has suspected his neighbor of tampering with the dormant utilities in the past, but this is the first time he has caught him in the act. Won't their cadre leader be impressed when he identifies the culprit! The old man will surely be criticized, while his accuser will be commended for his keen observations.

The chicken farmer watches with curiosity as Wan Lo attaches one end of the wire to the circuitry of the black box. When it is secure, the old man flips a switch in the box, and suddenly, startlingly, the street lamps all along the road blaze with light, a thrilling sight. To create electricity without a power source, the contents of the black box must be magic, scientific magic!

And such magic must have a value that can be measured in Yuan.

Later, still marveling at this miracle as he eats his breakfast of congee and pickled beans, the chicken farmer sees the old man leave his hut and put the black box in the basket of his bicycle. Unaware of his observer, Wan Lo pulls some blue flowers off of his carefully nurtured wisteria vines and lays them over the box, covering it completely. With some difficulty, he mounts the rusted Shanghai Flyer and pedals off down the steep path.

As soon as Wan Lo reaches the main road, the chicken farmer runs from his house and jumps on his own bicycle. It is still early; his work shift at the Superior Eel Hatchery does not begin for several hours. He has time to follow the old man, and to think about who might offer a reward for news of this auspicious invention.

FATIGUE IS HEAVY in Wan Lo's legs as he pedals through the main gate of Wing On University and parks his bicycle next to the Science Building. He marvels at how modern the students are in their colorful clothes and contemporary hairstyles, at their relaxed manners and their con-

fident good cheer. In his day, the life of a student was serious business, a privilege and a duty. By the look of it, these young people know nothing of that responsibility.

"Hey, old man, what position you play?" taunts a student, knocking the Trojan baseball cap off of Wan Lo's head and tossing it to a friend. Wan Lo makes a futile effort to retrieve it.

"Bad catch, grandfather. You strike out," the other student laughs.

"Enough!" Dr. Zhou Ping rushes from his classroom. "Have you no respect?"

"For this old grandfather?" the first student scoffs. "He can't even speak English."

"Maybe not," Dr. Zhou replies. "But he understands more of science than you will ever learn. Move on now, or I'll report this to your cadre leader."

He turns to Wan Lo. "Forgive my ill-mannered students, Professor. This generation has no respect for their elders. He bends to pick up the cap and hands it to Wan Lo.

"In these times it is we who should respect the youth, "Wan Lo replies gently. "They are the blossoms; we are but the gnarled vines upon which they grow." He extends a wisteria flower to Dr. Zhou, who bows again and accepts the gift.

"And like blossoms, they soon wither when they are no longer supported by the vines."

The two men enter Dr. Zhou's classroom, and Wan Lo looks around with satisfaction. "I am reminded of my days as Head of the Department."

"That's because nothing has changed since you were here in 1968," replies Dr. Zhou. "How can we compete with the West when our equipment is twenty years behind the times?" he grumbles.

"The only equipment that counts is this," says Wan Lo, tapping his head.

"Perhaps in your day, learned Professor. But no more. The computers are the new geniuses. They make the great discoveries."

"Genius consists not in making great discoveries, but in finding the relationships of small ones." Wan Lo brushes the wisteria off of the black box and holds it up to Dr. Zhou. "I have made my breakthrough."

"The magnet?" Dr. Zhou's eyes glow with excitement.

Wan Lo nods. "With this I can illuminate the whole of Fuchow."

"It will revolutionize China!"

"It is not for China alone. It must be shared by the whole world." Wan Lo draws closer, his eyes glittering with paranoia. "The T'ung Yu Triad has been watching me. They will go to any lengths to control this invention. And our own political leaders — they too want to squander it to gain riches and power. This must not happen!

"You must take it to the Energy Symposium in Hong Kong and show it to the esteemed Dr. Kensington. In his hands I know it will be used for peace and the good of mankind." He thrusts the box at Dr. Zhou.

"But I could never carry this out of China," Dr. Zhou stutters nervously. "Public Security would take it from me at the border. I would be detained and interrogated."

"Then you must bring Dr. Kensington here, to Fuchow," Wan Lo says. "Tell him I will give the magnet to him, only to him."

中國
象棋

ONE

Evil has many faces— but I'd never expected it to be wearing a Vera Wang wedding dress.

When Peter insisted we attend Lauren Covington's marriage ceremony on New Year's Eve I'd thought he was kidding. It was the last thing on earth I wanted to do, and it had taken him all day to cajole me into going. As a final, subtle protest I'd taken my sweet time getting dressed, so we were late arriving.

We weren't the only ones. By the time we found the church, a parking spot, and seats in the crowded chapel, it was seventeen minutes after the appointed hour, and the string quartet was still playing filler music. The buzz around us was that the groom was a no-show.

Peter caught the eye of a passing usher. "What's the hold up?" he asked.

"Ferdy must've escaped," the man confirmed, clearly indicating his feelings about the bride-to-be.

"Ha!" The exclamation erupted from my mouth before I could stop it. Peter gave me a dark look, so I tried to stifle my triumphant smirk. As a distraction, I looked around the sanctuary to see if I could ferret out any familiar faces. The crowd was a mix of Hollywood has-beens and Peter's old college chums, no one we ever socialized with, unless you counted a "Hi, how are you?" to a waving pom-pom two tiers up at a Trojan football game.

That was partly why I was less than ecstatic to be here. But the main reason was that the bride was an old girlfriend of Peter's. Apparently they'd been the quintessential L.A. couple of the '70s, a match made in Hollywood — she the teen queen of ABC's top-rated sitcom, he the star quarterback of the university team in a winning season. I'd only learned about this liaison when we were moving to our new house a month ago. I was packing some files of Peter's and came across an old issue of *Life* magazine folded open to a full-page picture of a buxom blonde playing tonsil hockey with a handsome jock, and under it the caption:

> *California Dreamin' — USC Trojan quarterback Peter 'The Pied Piper' Matthews and dream girl Lauren Covington, star of the hit TV series "The Cheerleader" have found love on the fifty-yard line. Is marriage in their future, or is Matthews just trying to score? Well, the Pied Piper admits he's eager to give his honey a ring, a Super Bowl ring, that is — he hopes to play for the Rams next year.*

I'd tried not to let it get to me, but who wouldn't be a little startled, finding out that her husband's old flame, of whom he'd never spoken, had not only been poster girl to a whole generation of horny high school boys, but a rich and famous TV celebrity to boot?

Okay, we all have our romantic pasts. The question is, why hadn't Peter mentioned his to me? Miffed though I was, I might have let it go, except that Lauren had reared her bleached blonde head again just a few days later, when we received a hand-delivered invitation to her wedding.

Yes, Lauren had actually hired a messenger service to convey the gaudy, flower-bedecked, perfume-soaked, satin-lined indulgences to the invitees by hand, at a cost which must have been roughly equal to the national debt.

When I summoned up the courage to ask Peter why we'd been invited to Lauren Covington's wedding, he'd innocently admitted he'd 'known' her in school. But unaware that I'd already found the damning editorial evidence, he'd neglected to add the tag line 'in the biblical sense.' And then to make matters worse, he'd insisted that we attend the spectacle!

Now, usually I'm a big fan of weddings. They work for me as pure entertainment — costumes, music, pageantry, feasting, the spectacle of family ritual. And seeing two people bungee jump over the great matrimonial abyss does serve to strengthen one's belief in the triumph of hope over experience, doesn't it?

But going to this particular wedding was pushing the marriage-qua-compromise envelope, not only because Lauren had prior claim to Peter, but because New Year's Eve was *our* anniversary, Peter's and mine. Our first. It cut me to the quick, it really did, that he would rather spend Our Special Day toasting her than celebrating us. So I had gone to the mat over it.

Nevertheless, there we sat in the twelfth pew, awaiting the start of the sacred ritual. But we were barely speaking to each other, both smarting from the hot words we'd traded, hurtful accusations uttered for shock value, which were, hopefully, far from the truth.

Without appearing too obvious, I snuck a peek at Peter. His eyes were on the door off the right transept where the groomsmen would enter, riveted there as though he expected a band of Iraqi terrorists to burst in and spray the congregation with bullets. Was it just my imagination or were little sweat beads forming in the crease of his forehead and in the crescent-shaped hollow just below his mouth that give his face such character?

What was his problem? He was usually as imperturbable as a rock, a guy who delivered a litter of kittens in the back seat of a Toyota as it careened around the curves of the Pasadena Freeway on the way to the vet on a rainy night in March.

Maybe our argument had struck a nerve, and had thrown him off balance. We hardly ever fought. Peter was so even-tempered, and I . . . well, harmony was important to me, and I was generally willing to compromise in order to achieve it.

Oh, what the hell. I adored Peter. And after all, it was our anniversary. I'd wasted most of the day being angry, but if I called a truce now, we might still be able to salvage our anniversary and end the night on a happy note.

So I reached over and took one of Peter's powerful and dexterous hands in mine and gave it a squeeze. Not much, but Peter was fluent in body language.

His eyes met mine, but instead of returning my loving look, for a split second his expression was insultingly blank, like he couldn't remember who the hell I was. But then the curtain lifted, and his expression softened into one of affection and relief. He raised my hand to his lips, tickling my fingers with the bristly hairs of his mustache as he anointed them with a sweet, soft kiss. For the thousandth time in our marriage I was completely smitten with the man I love.

"You were right," he whispered, "we shouldn't have come."

"We could slip out the side door now," I suggested. But I guess I was pushing my luck, because I got a glimpse of another one of Peter's withering looks, which I quickly deflected by saying, "Just kidding. I wouldn't *dream* of leaving before we find out what happened to old Ferdy."

"What time is it?" It was about the tenth time he'd asked me in as many minutes. Peter hated to wear a watch himself, so as an engagement present he'd given me a beautiful gold Movado, which I cherished.

"6:43," I replied.

Peter rose. "I'll see if I can find out what's going on," he said, and I watched his powerful body squeeze past annoyed knees all down the pew.

The buzz of whispers around me had risen from a patient hum to an annoyed drone, drowning out the offerings of the string quartet, who had exhausted their repertoire and were repeating the same Bach Prelude over and over like a jammed CD. The guests were no longer even trying to be discreet about their conversations; they were leaning over the pews, kibbitzing with neighbors like sports fans at a Lakers' game.

"I *told* her this would happen," said the woman sitting in front of me. She was wearing a chic blue leather hat and dyed-to-match over-the-elbow gloves. "The man is simply too drop dead gorgeous to be real."

"Darling, didn't you know? He isn't real! He's had a complete lift. I saw the scars when she brought him in for a blow job," sneered the man on her right, a celebrity hairdresser from one of those chichi Beverly Hills salons.

"I knew there was something off about him," the woman in the hat whispered. "Fernando Ferrar, what kind of a name is that?" She rolled her eyes. "Imagine, leaving Lauren Covington at the altar. Army Archerd's here for heaven's sake!"

"Honest to god, Lucille, Ferdy's probably just stuck in traffic," said a smarmy man in his mid-fifties, who I semi-recognized as a retired game show host.

"Oh, Harold, really. Haven't you ever heard of a car phone? He would have called if he'd gotten gridlocked," Lucille continued.

"So where do you think he is if you're so smart?"

Lucille shrugged, causing her hat to tilt precariously. "Maybe he's met with foul play," she breathed.

Obviously forgetting where he was, Harold guffawed loudly. People turned to stare, and he glowered back at them, leaning close to Lucille to whisper, "Foul play! What do you think this is, 'Murder She Wrote'?"

It was more like "The Never-ending Story," I thought, and again looked at my watch. It was 6:51. To hell with it. I decided to make a quick trip to the ladies' room, then grab Peter out front and insist we leave. This wedding was not going to happen.

The hallway connecting the chapel to the main church building was empty, but at the far end I saw the neon glow of the generic female form above a doorway, and walked toward it. My hard-soled shoes tapped conspicuously on the slippery polished tile as I hurried past meeting rooms and Sunday school classrooms, trying not to see the ghosts of my childhood lurking within them.

I pushed open the door to the ladies' room and stopped dead in my tracks. There was nobody at the sinks; what halted me was the sight of the bridal bouquet, splayed in all its fragrant, wilting beauty on the tile counter, and the sounds of voices echoing from the toilet stall for the handicapped on the far side of the partitioned room.

A man's voice, angry, "You've gone too far this time."

A woman's voice, patronizing, "Never too far, dearest. I'm sorry if it took you by surprise, but we both knew it had to happen sooner or later."

I recognized both voices immediately. The woman's was familiar because I had heard it on television over the years. Also, the bouquet was a dead giveaway. It and the voice belonged to none other than Lauren Covington, the bride-to-be.

And I would have known who the man was even if I hadn't heard him speak; it was Peter. My Peter. Lauren's ex-Peter. Or so I'd thought. But as I listened to their conversation I began to question just how "ex" Lauren and Peter were to each other.

"You shouldn't have done this to me," I heard Peter say, his voice stretched taut as a guitar string.

"I didn't do it *to* you, darling," she replied. "I did it *for* you. And you know you love what I do for you . . ."

"That's bullshit," he snorted.

I certainly hoped so!

"Peter, how long have we been in this?"

In what?

"Too long. I'm tired of the sneaking around."

"This will make it so much easier. It's a perfect cover for us. It's protection. You know, like wearing a condom."

I was enraged! Whatever I'd thought was ancient history between Peter and Lauren was apparently current events. But would Lauren actually get married just as a cover for an affair with a married man?

"Lauren, listen to me. I can't live with this lie anymore. Karen suspects something. She's not as dumb as you think."

Just how dumb did Lauren think I was? Dumb enough to be shocked that a bride-to-be was making overtures to my husband at her own wedding? Dumb enough not to have known that she and Peter were still hot and heavy into the affair they'd begun ten years ago? Dumb enough to assume that she would honor her own marriage vows when she and Peter had obviously scoffed at ours?

"Petey —"

Petey! How dare she call my husband by my pet name!

" — the only way she's going to find out anything is if you get sloppy. You haven't gotten sloppy, have you dearheart?"

"No. But I want to face the music now and get on with my life."

"And risk destroying everything we've built together? Sorry, darling, but as you know, you're in it up to your gorgeous ass. We're a team, Peter. You can't just walk away. Besides, we both know you don't want to."

I was stunned, seething, and speechless with outrage. I felt as though I'd crashed into a wall of glass — it was invisible until it shattered, and then each little shard inflicted a painful cut. My agony was so intense that my body erupted, and I leaned over the nearest sink to heave my guts out.

Perfect timing. My retching was drowned out by an amplified voice announcing that 'due to unforeseeable circumstances' the wedding ceremony was being postponed.

I fled, out of the restroom, out of the building, out into the night. Since Peter had the keys to his Cherokee, I ran past the Jeep, through the parking lot and onto Mulholland Drive. It was cold and dark. Home was at least ten miles away, joggable in running shoes, but I was wearing my best pair of suede flats.

Still, fueled by adrenaline and oblivious to everything except the jackhammer of my heart and the cramp in my belly, I ran. Why hadn't I seen it coming? Was it possible I'd read Peter so wrong? All through our marriage I'd trusted him implicitly. Business trips to strange cities? Fine, honey, I'll be here waiting. Late nights at the office? Wake me up when you get home, darling. Two A.M. phone calls? No problem, dear, I'll just roll over and go back to sleep like a good, dumb wife.

Wait. Could I have misunderstood Peter and Lauren's conversation? It was conceivable. I had entered in medias res; was I taking what I'd heard out of context? Far-fetched as this possibility was, I clung to it. Anything rather than face the specter of Peter's infidelity.

A horn tooted beside me and I heard the crunch of wide tread tires on the gravel roadside. Peter pulled the Cherokee to a stop a few yards ahead of me and leaned over to throw open the passenger door. The moment of truth.

"Karen, what the hell? I'm surprised you didn't break an ankle," Peter called out.

What could I say? How should I act? I couldn't look at him, so I just stood there breathing hard, choking down the bile that was threatening to spew from my mouth.

"Look," he continued when I didn't move, "I know you're pissed off at me, and you have every reason to be."

An understatement.

"I never should have dragged you to this fiasco tonight."

Oh, he was only talking about the wedding.

"I'm sorry, Karen."

Not as sorry as I was.

"Come on and get in, please? I'll make it up to you, I promise."

I waited another minute, wondering how he could ever accomplish that. Then I got in.

ON THE DRIVE HOME Peter kept his eyes glued to the rearview mirror and said little. That in itself was not surprising. He'd always been the strong silent type, Gary Cooper in Docksiders and a polo shirt. In the past I'd always admired his reserve. But after what I'd heard at the church, I was suddenly suspicious of everything, especially his silence. What was going on behind those Foster Grants? I was afraid to find out.

Taking deep breaths to control my anger, I asked, "So what do you think happened to Ferdy?"

Peter's head whipped around à la Linda Blair in "The Exorcist." "What do you mean?" he demanded angrily.

I'd expected contrition, so the venom in his tone took me by surprise. "I mean, why do you think he got cold feet?" I stammered.

"Cold feet," Peter repeated, and broke into a peal of manic laughter, a reaction I'd never heard from him before. "A strange choice of words," he said.

I was beginning to think that Lauren Covington had the same effect on my hero that kryptonite had on Superman; there he was, crumbling before my very eyes. Unless I wanted to capsize the leaking boat that was our marriage, I knew I should avoid any subject related to Lauren. But an evil force had seized control of my vocal chords and I sailed on into the storm.

"Poor Lauren," I said with mask pity. "Supposedly she was crying her eyes out in the ladies' room."

The Jeep lurched forward, then swerved, barely missing an oil tanker which was merging into our lane. Peter, that rare California motorist with an unblemished record, was driving like a carjacker who'd just commandeered a Corvette. He slammed on the brakes, obsessed by that rearview mirror.

"I highly doubt it," he said.

I pulled my seat belt tighter across my lap and took a deep breath. "Why?" It was like picking at a scab — I knew forcing the issue right now might permanently scar our marriage, but I had to see what was underneath. "Did you see her at the church?"

He turned to me in surprise, sweat trickling down the side of his face. "No," he croaked in a voice I barely recognized. "I haven't seen or talked to Lauren since . . . "

"Look out!" I cried, and Peter braked again, this time to avoid running up the tailpipe of an ancient Volkswagen. Fortunately, we missed the VW, but the scream of metal against metal told me we'd nicked the bumper of a horse trailer on our right. And as we slowed, our headlights showed the dent our fender had made just under the frightened horse's swishing tail.

"Christ!" Peter muttered. It was a close call, and we were both shaken. The horse trailer pulled off to the shoulder and Peter pulled up behind it. Two large men in Levis got out of the cab to inspect the damage. One stooped to look at the trailer gate. The other swaggered up to Peter's window.

"Hey, buddy, what? Did ya have a few too many? He leaned on the door, his own beery breath coming out in polluted white puffs. "I hope t'hell you're insured."

"I am," Peter said, and reached over me to open the glove compartment. "By Smith & Wesson."

To my complete horror, he pulled out a handgun, black and gleaming, sinister in its polished potential. The man saw the gun and immediately backed away from the car with his hands in the air. Peter stepped on the gas and we merged back into the flow of traffic which quickly carried us past the horse trailer.

I was incredulous. And speechless. And getting more scared by the minute.

Peter glanced at me, then his eyes shifted back to the rear-view mirror. "That trailer was a wreck. One little dent more or less doesn't make a difference. We'd've been there all night, and I'd rather not celebrate our anniversary at the L.A.P.D., would you?"

Finally, I managed to whisper, "The gun."

"Don't worry, it's not loaded," Peter said, as though that explained why he had a gun in his glove compartment in the first place, and why he'd pulled it out over a minor fender bender in the second.

"Petey, is there something you aren't telling me?"

"What are you fishing for, Karen?"

"I don't know. But it's obvious something's bothering you, and I want to help if I can."

"You can't," he replied in a reassuringly calm voice. I wasn't reassured.

"Does it have to do with Lauren Covington?"

"Drop it, Karen. It's not your problem."

"Of course it's my problem. Anything that affects you affects me."

"I can handle it on my own," he replied.

"Please, I want to know."

"No you don't."

"But — "

"Mind your own fucking business!"

I was stunned. Peter had never spoken to me like that before. Not in those words, not in that tone. Within the space of twenty minutes I'd found out my husband had a mistress, a gun and the vocabulary of a longshoreman. It was a little over the top, even on New Year's Eve.

Peter steered the Jeep into our driveway and pushed the remote control for the garage door. I jumped out before we'd come to a complete stop, and charged into the kitchen through the connecting door. There, waiting with a smile of transcendent ecstasy at my arrival, was the true love of my life, my Ibizan hound, Hermanubis.

I named him for the Alexandrian dog-god pictured on the interior walls of the pyramids, because the breed originated in Egypt. Dear, sweet, gorgeous Hermie has been my sanity and my saving grace since the moment I saw him in the breeder's whelping paddock three years ago. And in all that time, he's never lied to me, carried a concealed weapon, or fallen in love with someone else.

He must have sensed that I needed comfort and a shoulder to

cry on, because by the time I'd charged up the stairs and into the bedroom Hermie had already leapt gracefully onto the bed and was waiting for me to lie down, so he could curl into the crook of my arm and blot my tears in his red-bronze coat.

When Peter came in a few minutes later, Hermie stood to greet him with a guardedly wagging tail and a lowered muzzle. His prominent prick ears rigid and angled backwards to signal submissive pleasure, he traversed the short distance between the foot of the bed where Peter stood, and the pillow on which my head rested, as though to bridge the gap between us with his own affection, forming a live conduit between us, slowly drawing the synapse closed. Soon Peter was stretched out on his side of the bed. He reached over Hermie, who lay between us, to embrace me. I felt love in his touch.

"I'm sorry," he said. "I didn't mean to say that, any of it. It just came out." He paused, and then he said in a voice so somber it broke my heart, "Sometimes I wonder why you and Hermie put up with me. But I'm glad you do. I love you, Karen."

"I know," I said, and in spite of everything I was sure of it. "I love you too."

中國象棋

TWO

Neither of us mentioned the incident on the freeway or Lauren's wedding again. And miraculously, life seemed to slip back into its comfortable routine. In hindsight I can see that, as was my way, I had numbed myself with denial — take two aspirin and avoid confrontation. All my life I'd had a problem facing reality, operating on the principle of retreat rather than attack, desperate to preserve the status quo at all costs. Maybe a therapist would blame my parents. They had come to this country as penniless Armenian immigrants fleeing Turkish persecution, and they had taught my brother and me to err on the side of caution, not to risk, not to challenge, but to accept and make the most of what we had. So that's what I did: I put it out of my mind and concentrated on preparing for my dental school finals, which were only days away.

It was strange to think that I would soon be a dentist. I certainly didn't start out on that career path. After graduating from college, I'd gone to work at my father's Oriental rug store on a temporary basis, which became permanent by default after a few years. The hours were good, the stress was minimal, and I could be pretty confident of job security. In fact it was too secure. My father Gordon was constantly pressing me to let him change the sign over the door to G.A. Kalderian and Daughter. I didn't mean to be ungrateful; he'd built the business from nothing, had poured his life into it and supported our family with it. Offering to make me a partner was the most profound gift of love he could offer. But the dim, dusty interior of a carpet warehouse was no place for a young unmarried woman. I wasn't brawny enough to haul rugs around, and my negotiating skills were hopelessly outclassed by the Persians and Israelis who came in to buy stock from us for their retail stores. Also, I had become increasingly allergic to the dankness in the air, manifest in an unsightly rash on my neck that wouldn't go away. The bottom line was that, with thirty staring me in the face, I needed a change.

My best friend Lily Pullen had similar family expectations foisted upon her, only she came from a long line of dentists. Supposedly an ancestor of hers had sailed to the U.S.A. from China to lay track for the transcontinental railroad. But on the boat, he'd discovered he had a talent for pulling teeth. Word-of-mouth (literally) did the rest. He soon earned the nickname Pull No Pain and went on to become the first Chinese dentist in America.

In the ensuing 150 years, Pull No Pain had been anglicized to Pullen, and the Pullens had been dentists ever since. Lily's father and brother currently ran an upscale practice in Brentwood, bonding and bleaching the teeth of the forty-something baby boomers who populated that yuppie suburb of Los Angeles. Her uncle was a wire-bender — orthodontist, that is — in Pacific Palisades, whose practice thrived on his brother's referrals. Lily had been slotted to join the uncle's shop, thereby cementing the link between the two practices into the next generation.

At least, that was the theory. In actuality, Lily had an abject fear of dentistry and had managed to avoid dental school for almost a decade, pursuing instead her vocation of choice, cooking; Lily was a chef. This infuriated her father, who had cut her off financially, thus making her all the more determined to stay out of the tooth business. After college, she'd worked at most of the trendy restaurants in Los Angeles, gathering experience and recipes, biding her time and building up capital to open a place of her own. But she was hopeless with money, notorious for taking every last penny she'd saved and on impulse flying off to remote outposts to study the local cuisine. A recent trip to Alaska comes to mind, where she ate what she called 'Eskimo ice cream,' an unappetizing concoction of sugar whipped into Crisco vegetable shortening.

When Lily first approached me with the idea that I go to dental school in her place and fill the cavity in her uncle's practice when I graduated, I was wary. But it made sense. We were like sisters after all, and I knew my parents would swoon with pride if their only daughter had the initials D.D.S. after her name, higher degrees being the ultimate currency of approval in our family. Why not make her family happy too, and have a good-paying job to boot?

The realization that I had been selling Oriental rugs for eight years was stupefying, and the thought that I might be doing it for the rest of my life was horrifying. But the idea of being a dentist held a certain appeal. I'd always had a fascination with minutia and an aptitude for handwork. The thought of poking around in someone's mouth, exploring crevices and cavities, and filling them with beautiful gold inlays and intricate miniature bridges, might have repulsed Lily, but to me it sounded more appealing than trying to scrub cat urine stains out of an antique Keshans. And the possibility of meeting a promising young dental student didn't sound so bad to me either.

The only hang-up was the pre-dent undergraduate requirement, but thanks to Dr. Pullen's pull, I was able to take a test and get it waived. So I plunged into the study of dentistry and, to my relief, found I had a real aptitude for it. Two years later I'd fallen madly in love with Peter and added an MRS. in front of my name. In a few weeks, I'd have a D.D.S. after it. According to my life plan, the next steps were to go into private practice with Lily's uncle, and to get pregnant, in that order.

But the week before Christmas, I'd started waking up with a queasy feeling in my stomach, and remembered that I hadn't bought a box of tampons since before Thanksgiving. Afraid I'd gotten the cart before the horse, I went to Sav-on and bought an early pregnancy test.

I hadn't used it right away; buying it was scary enough. Then the situation with Lauren Covington had raised its bleached blonde head, and the last thing I wanted to think about was the possibility of being pregnant and jilted simultaneously.

But then again, I wondered if announcing my pregnancy would defeat Peter's fascination with Lauren. It was possible; I'd seen it happen on TV.

I was mulling this over as I labored in my patient's mouth during lab, when suddenly the lights dimmed, and for an instant the hypnotic hum of thirty dental drills was stilled.

"This moment of silence is brought to you by Southern California Edison," quipped the student next to me.

And then, the electricity was restored.

"It's all right, people," our fearless leader Doctor Tak Noritoki called out, the pitch of his voice annoyingly higher than the whining decibel of the drills. "Just a power surge. Back to work now."

If I had known when I started school that I'd be relegated to spending four hours a day three times a week under the thumb of this self-styled Nipponese Napoleon, I might have rethought my commitment to dentistry. The class had nicknamed Noritoki 'the Tooth Fairy' because of his sexual persuasions; he liked to demonstrate his drilling techniques on susceptible male students at private tutorials, both in and out of the lab. As for the female students, he either ignored or harassed us, depending on his mood.

This day he must have been in one of his harassing moods, because I could see him coming my way, clenching and unclenching his right hand inside the pocket of his lab coat, around the two cloisonné balls he kept there. Supposedly it was some kind of ancient Oriental relaxation device, but it was more like stylized masturbation, if you ask me. When Noritoki fiddled with his balls, it was a dead giveaway that he was in a state of arousal, and it was better for people of the female persuasion to stay out of his way.

So I tried not to look at him and prepared to go on with my work. My patient was a homeless man named Sandy, a frequent visitor to the lab, known to the dental students as what we called a 'garbage dump' — a patient with truly bad oral hygiene. Life on the streets had taken its toll on Sandy. His eyelids sagged over his weary eyes, nearly obscuring the dilated pupils, and his nose was so misshapen that his breath had to fight its way out in snorts and gasps. His brain did work, but barely. Only once had I heard him utter a word of more than two syllables, and that was the time my drill accidentally hit a nerve and he called me a 'motherfuckingmaniac.'

The oddest thing about Sandy was that despite the disintegration of his facial features, all thirty-two of his rotted, yellow teeth still clung tenaciously to his gums. And each tooth offered the student a new and fascinating opportunity to practice dentistry. This day I was working on the chipped right canine, which was chartreuse with tartar, but still firmly rooted. My task was to shave down the jagged enamel, avoiding the nerve at all costs, and apply bondo to the stub to give it somewhat of an even bottom.

Then I would start work on the gum, scaling the soft tissue of the periodontal pocket with a Jacquette scaler number two. Afterward, I planned on using an Orban hoe number six to remove the calculus and finish the job.

I worked gingerly; once before I'd hit a hidden cache of abscess in Sandy's mouth. Pus had gushed out like a geyser, drenching the front of my lab coat in a foul, green mess. Despite the protection of gloves, clear plastic face mask and lab coat, it was not an experience I was eager to repeat, especially in my current, possibly pregnant state of queasiness.

But I didn't have to worry. When the five-second blackout ended, I found that old Sandy had clenched his decayed teeth together so tightly it would have taken a crowbar to pry them apart.

"Sandy, open up," I prodded, sensing Dr. Noritoki's imminent approach.

But Sandy shook his head fiercely, his eyes steely, his jaw iron.

"Come on, Sandy." It was only weeks away from the end of the semester and I was not above begging. "You don't want to blow it for me in front of the Tooth Fairy, do you?"

But Sandy refused to open up, cryogenically shutting me out. The only sign that he was still among the living was the tickle of his grungy fingers, stealing up under my lab coat to diddle my thigh. A swift application of the drill on his sleeve shocked some sense into him. But unfortunately, Noritoki noticed the gambit and scurried over to investigate and castigate.

"What's going on here?"

Noritoki's whine miraculously thawed Sandy's features, and he offered up his most winsome gap-toothed grin. "She's makin' sushi outta my mouth, Doc. And I ain't stickin' around to let her finish the job."

With that, he climbed out of the chair, and ambled out of the room, the white sanitation bib still chained around his neck. I could see him unwrapping a Snickers bar as he strode through the door.

Noritoki glared at me without speaking. The only sound was the clanking of the cloisonné balls in his pocket.

"His gums were bleeding when he came in," I tried to explain. "Severe gingivitis plus glossitis. You know what kind of shape Sandy's in."

"Your job is to repair the damage, not make it worse."

"If I could just work on a real mouth for a change — one with living teeth."

"You're welcome to work on anyone you like, provided they sign the proper release form. In fact, it will be up to you to find your own patient — or should I say victim — for the root canal tomorrow afternoon. I'm not going to risk allowing you to alienate another one of our regulars." And then Dr. Noritoki walked away.

Denial of the right to use the school's pool of volunteers might not sound like a big deal. But finding someone who a) needed a root canal; b) was willing to have the work done by a second-year dental student; and c) would be available with less than twenty-four hours' notice would be next to impossible.

I had two choices: I could cruise skid row and pray I found a willing, dentally challenged victim before I became a victim myself, or I could go home early, take Hermie for a run, prepare a romantic dinner for Peter and me, and forget the whole thing.

I was home in twenty-two minutes.

WHEN I PULLED INTO THE GARAGE, I was startled to see Peter's Jeep Cherokee in its spot — it was only three o'clock and normally he didn't get home until after five. Peter was a vice president of the Occidental Insurance Corporation, a medium-sized firm headquartered in Virginia. He was one of six people they'd installed in the offices they'd opened in downtown Los Angeles, mainly, I suspect, for the prestige of having a West Coast presence, because they never seemed terribly busy.

Personally, I thought Peter was wasted in the insurance business. He didn't talk much about his past, but he'd been on the short list for the Heisman Trophy and an Asian studies major at USC. No doubt those two facts alone would have brought him a ton of fast track post graduate opportunities. But instead, by the time we'd met, he'd mothballed his football jersey and his Mandarin dictionary in favor of actuarial tables, opting for a quiet life and a steady job out of the limelight.

On one hand it bothered me that a man as confident and accomplished as Peter was so devoid of ambition. But on the other, I'd been brought up to believe that a man's greatest achievement was to be an honest and capable provider for his family, and Peter was definitely that.

And he seemed content enough in his work. The job entailed a little travel, short trips which seemed to crop up like flash fires, and were just as quickly over. I'd offered to go with him when my class schedule permitted, but Peter had discouraged the idea, preferring to get his work done quickly and come home, rather than prolong a business trip and pretend it was a vacation.

Peter's Jeep in the garage mid-afternoon was a sign that he was probably going off again. Stifling an urge to look in the glove compartment to see if the gun was still there, I let myself into the house.

"Peter?" I called as I dumped my purse and books on the kitchen table. I hoped he was still packing. It always made me heartsick when he had to leave without saying good-bye, but since I couldn't be reached in the lab, and airline schedules were immutable, Peter would sometimes be in the air before I even knew a trip was in the offing.

Apparently this was one of those times. Instead of Peter's answering voice, I heard Hermie's delighted yip and the click of his toenails on the hardwood floors. Hermie was thrilled to have me home early and greeted me as though I'd been gone for three months instead of three hours. In a canine imitation of Peter's affection, he jumped up on his hind legs, placing his front paws delicately on my shoulders so that we were face to face, and gave me a sloppy kiss on the end of my nose.

I kissed him back and gave his lovely erect ears a scratch before heading up the stairs. If Peter was in the closet packing or in the shower he might not have heard me come in. "Petey?" I called again.

But the bedroom and the bathroom were both empty. A glance at Peter's side of the closet confirmed my suspicions: his Sportsac garment bag and Lark carry-on were missing from the upper shelf.

I hated for Peter to leave with things so unsettled between us. Since the verbal pas de deux I'd overheard at Lauren's aborted wedding, things hadn't been the same. Yes, we'd kissed and made up, but clearly, our relationship had suffered some damage. It was like a broken mirror we'd tried to piece back together — you could use it, but the crack still showed, and the resulting image was distorted.

In a moment of weakness, I allowed my heart to ambush my mind with the dread question: If Peter was having an affair with Lauren Covington, was he flying off to be with her at this very minute?

The thought unleashed the flood of odious sentiments I'd been trying to keep at bay since the wedding — rage, resentment, fear, curiosity, helplessness and hope. Hope? Yes, hope that I was wrong to doubt Peter. I'd always believed implicitly in his faithfulness; I think you have to for a marriage to work. Doubt undermines everything the partnership is about, to say nothing of what it does to a wife's self-esteem. Right now, mine was at an all-time low.

But now that my eyes were open, I could see that I had been tuning out the obvious clues as a form of self-preservation. I remembered the time I'd needed to reach Peter when he'd been on a business trip to Minneapolis, and found he wasn't registered at the hotel whose name and number he'd given me. When I'd called his office to ask where he was staying, the secretary had been vague, saying she didn't know, but would tell him to call home when he checked in.

But I hadn't wanted to wait. So although I'd promised Peter when we got married to keep my compulsion for neatness to myself and never mess with his papers, I rifled through the things on his desk to find his phone number in Minneapolis. It wasn't as though I was prying. I just needed to talk to him.

I never did find the number. What I did find was an odd receipt from someplace called Rodney's in Langley, Virginia, and, even more strange, two passport-size photos of Peter, with the signature "P. Linden" inscribed in the border. Linden is Peter's mother's maiden name. We use it sometimes when we're making dinner reservations we aren't sure we're going to use. But why would he write that name on his passport pictures?

Still, I wasn't suspicious, not even when I found a scrap of paper in the pocket of a bunched up T-shirt I'd never seen before, with a phone number scrawled across it. I wasn't upset, just curious enough to dial the number.

"Operations. Enter code now," a computerized voice intoned. Code? What code? I waited. "Enter code now," the voice repeated. Then it added, "Please be advised this call is being traced." I hung up.

Why hadn't I confronted Peter when he got home? Why hadn't I asked him where he'd been, and about the T-shirt and phone number? Why had I conveniently dismissed the whole episode and never even thought about it again until this moment? Because, as Lauren Covington assumed, I was just plain dumb.

Fortunately the phone rang, and I was temporarily spared from my savage self-reproach. Instead of picking up, I listened to the answering machine click on, and heard my recorded voice tell the caller to please leave a message after the beep.

"Hey, Karen, it's me, Lily. I just bought this new holistic cookbook and it's got some great recipes I want to try out on you and Peter. Can I come by tonight and use your kitchen? I'd use mine except my stove's on the blink again. I can't get the damn pilot light —"

"Hi, Lily," I interrupted, picking up the receiver.

"Karen? What are you doing there?" Lily sounded surprised, almost indignant.

"I live here, remember?"

"But you've got lab this afternoon."

"Then why did you call?"

"To leave a message on your machine."

"You'd rather talk to the machine than me?"

"Well, the machine can't tell me you're busy tonight. And I figured by the time you got the message, I'd already be on my way to your house, so you couldn't say 'no.'" She was manipulative, but at least she was honest.

"Gosh, Lil, you sound a little desperate for company."

"Tell me about it. You know those Lebanese cousins who were going to back 'Ah-So Schwarma?'" Ah-So's was Lily's latest restaurant concept, combining Japanese and Middle Eastern cuisines, dishes such as sushi kebabs and seaweed tabuli. "They folded up their tents and went back to Beirut. I should have known better than to trust someone named Omar. At least I haven't signed the lease yet. Then I really would have been up shit creek without a Cuisinart."

"Bummer," I said. Lily's life was a soap opera of prime time proportions. She seemed to live from crisis to crisis with short lulls of normalcy in between. I think that's one reason why we're friends — she provides the drama and I the audience. "You'll find another backer," I said, trying to sound more optimistic than I felt.

"Yeah, hopefully before I'm too old to read a recipe without a magnifying glass. So what do you say, are you and Peter up for a little nouvelle à la Lily?"

"Peter's gone on a business trip."

"Again? Boy, I'd love to have his frequent flyer miles. Where to this time?"

"I don't even know."

"Well, not to take advantage of you in your distressed state, but how about I come over and fix dinner for us?"

中國象棋

THREE

To distract myself from worrying about Peter while I waited for Lily, I decided to take Hermie to the park. The fresh air would do us both good. But when I arrived at El Rancho Recreation Center, I realized I'd tricked myself, because it was the place where Peter and I had met, and instead of driving thoughts of him from my mind, being there flooded me with memories.

El Rancho Park is a mecca for dog lovers, with its unique combination of a grassy, fenced-in field, and an officially sanctioned moratorium on the city's leash law during the hours of seven to nine in the morning and four to six in the afternoon.

The park had been a godsend for me. Ibizan hounds are running dogs, swift, lean and energetic. They love nothing more than sprinting across open spaces, as their ancestors had run across the deserts of northern Africa. So since the first week I got Hermie, we have been regulars at El Rancho.

East of the fenced dog park was another grassy area with a dirt track around it — a football field. Joggers frequently used the track, but they were mostly plodding housewives and shuffling seniors. El Rancho wasn't what you'd call a high-profile fitness hangout.

We in the dog park didn't pay much attention to the track scene. Mostly we congregated under a tree, swapping pet stories, every once in a while pointing out some cute thing one of our own was doing, ever alert to that tone of bark which signified danger or a dog fight.

That particular day there couldn't have been more than a half dozen people and pets at play. It was mid-week and Santa Ana wind season. Since the Ibizan breed originated in Egypt, they are able to endure extremes of temperature, so despite the heat, Hermie was raring to go, looking for someone to play his favorite game: chase. Unfortunately, his options were limited to a Samoyed/shepherd mix aptly named Sloth, an ancient half-blind cocker spaniel, and a bulldog who must have tipped the scales at 125 lbs. Try as he might, Hermie couldn't interest any of them in meaningful activity. So he had resigned himself to running circles around Sloth, every so often loping to my side and nudging me as though to say 'pretend you're a rabbit and let's race!'

Then a jogger appeared, doing wind sprints along the length of dirt track that paralleled the fence. To my frustrated four-legged friend the man must have seemed like an answered prayer. Hermie just watched until the jogger followed the angle of the track as it curved eastward, so that he was running away from us. Then it was as though his retreating figure had sparked a genetic memory of the hunt in Hermie, because my boy suddenly shot out after the man, covering the fifty-some yards across the grass in the blink of an eye, and hurling his body up and over the five-foot chain link fence which surrounded the dog park. He soared through the air with such grace that my first emotion was awe — how beautiful he was!

Then my fear mechanism kicked in. Hermie was loose in an open field, only yards away from a busy intersection.

"Hermie! Stay! Hermie!" I screamed at the top of my lungs, and when that didn't work, I whistled the four-note signal I'd taught him to obey. It was plenty loud enough — I have a world class whistle I spent years perfecting — but even if Hermie heard me, endorphin-crazed as he was to at last have something to chase, he ignored the command, and bore down on the running man as he would a hare fleeing for its life across the sandy Sahara.

He drew up alongside the man and they ran in tandem for a moment, until Hermie playfully went for the jugular of the man's bright yellow shorts. With horror I saw the runner stumble. Graceful as a gymnast, he tucked into a neat ball to deflect what he must have thought were the vicious fangs of a rabid killer, and rolled off the track onto its grassy side, where he remained protectively crouched.

"He won't hurt you!" I cried out, climbing over the fence as fast as I could. "He just wants to play!"

Sure enough, Hermie was standing over the downed jogger, wagging his tail victoriously, and grinning down at him, a large swatch of the man's jogging shorts clutched between his teeth.

Unaware of the gaping hole in his trunks, the jogger jumped to his feet and struck a defensive Bruce Lee pose. He flashed me a look so withering it singed my eyelashes, then he turned his full attention back to Hermie. "Restrain your dog, lady," he barked.

Having won the game, Hermie was now on his most cordial behavior, his right paw raised, offering a handshake to his new friend. But the man would have none of it. He remained frozen, hands poised to strike, eyes riveted on Hermie, until I snapped the lead on Hermie's collar, and knelt down to encircle his neck with my arm. Then I saw relief soften the man's face and the tension drain from his body, which, I had noticed, despite all that was going on, was impressively exposed by the hole in his shorts. I tried not to look as I pried the shredded fabric from Hermie's mouth and held it out to him. Wordlessly, he tucked it into his waistband, so it hung like an Indian's loincloth over the hole. It didn't hide everything, but at least he wouldn't be arrested for indecent exposure on his way home, unless the wind came up.

Then I started to cry. Now I hate it when women do that. I especially hate it when I do it, because tears make me look and feel like a silly child, not a mature feminist who is in charge of her own life. Not the granddaughter of Hadji Kalderian, who survived the Turkish massacres and lived to start a Kalderian dynasty. But I knew the law. If this man made a complaint against Hermie, the Department of Animal Regulation could take my boy away from me, even put him to sleep!

"I'm so sorry," I blubbered. "I hope he didn't hurt you. I know he didn't mean to hurt you."

"How can you be so sure?" the man snapped. "Did he tell you, or can you just read his mind?"

At least the guy was speaking to me. "It's in his blood," I explained, stroking Hermie's golden coat. "They were bred by the Egyptians to hunt rabbits and deer, anything that runs."

The man just watched me silently and without expression, so I babbled on, "He's an Ibizan hound. They're one of the oldest breeds of dogs. You've probably seen pictures of them in the Egyptian hieroglyphics, you know, like in King Tut's tomb?"

As if on cue, Hermie dropped to the ground, his haunches tucked under him, his forepaws thrust straight out in what I call his sphinx position. His magnificent pear-shaped ears were pricked up, and his eyes danced with friendliness. I looked at the man, hoping Hermie's magnificence was melting his icy reserve, but his face remained impassive. For a tense moment, we stared at each other.

"What does that make you, Cleopatra?"

His wisecrack caught me off guard, but then I saw the hint of a smile peeking out from behind his mustache. That's when it hit me that this guy was absolutely oozing with animal magnetism, which is probably why Hermie went for him in the first place.

"Maybe in a past life," I replied with relief. "My name's Karen in this one."

"I'm Peter," he said, and then he knelt down to stroke Hermie. "This is the most beautiful dog I've ever seen."

With that Peter won my heart. And now, wherever it was he'd gone, he'd taken it with him.

IT WAS PAST SIX when I got home, and Lily was already cooking with both burners. To look at a kitchen when Lily was at work in it, you would think her primary objective was to create chaos, not haute cuisine. Like most chefs, Lily only cared what the food tasted like, not what the kitchen looked like after she used it.

When I walked in she was poring over an artichoke-green loose-leaf notebook, its pages already decorated with the overspray from my Waring blender, which whirred a mixture the clotted texture of buttermilk and the color of rotten bananas. Predominant among the aromas wafting through the house was that of overripe gorgonzola cheese.

"Whatever it is, it looks —" I tried to think of something positive to say about the cauldron roiling with green slime on the stove. "— fresh."

"It is," Lily replied, cheerfully going back to her chopping. "The one drawback to this kind of cooking is that finding the ingredients takes almost as long as cooking them." She held up what looked like a bunch of beets, only they were egg yolk yellow, not red. "These guys, for example. I had to drive all the way out to Chino Farms to get them."

Only Lily would drive seventy miles to buy a bunch of freak mutant beets. "What do you care, you're color-blind," I pointed out.

"That's not the point. It's a matter of aesthetics."

I pushed up the sleeves of my sweatshirt and reached into the sink for the sponge. Speaking of aesthetics, I didn't like the look of the yellow stains in the chopping block. Better to scrub them out now before they set. "Dare I ask what's for dessert?"

Lily stared at me in mock annoyance. "I haven't even finished cooking dinner and already you're thinking about dessert? I'm telling you, Karen, you need to face it. You're addicted to refined sugar and saturated fat. Sooner or later it's going to take its toll."

"Can I worry about nutrition tomorrow, please? Peter's gone and I need to binge."

Lily beamed with a self-satisfied smile. "Well, knowing you as intimately as I do, and sympathizing with your predicament, I did take pity. But you've got to swear you won't eat them until after we eat this meal I've been slaving over."

"What did you bring me?" I was starting to salivate.

"Promise?"

"I promise."

Lily reached into one of her ecologically correct reusable canvas shopping bags and pulled out a slightly crushed but still beautiful bag of Mrs. Field's cookies. Like a true pal she had remembered that Peter and I had fallen in love at a Mrs. Field's, when we discovered our mutual passion for chocolate chip cookies. It had been a touchstone of our relationship ever since.

I took the bag from her. It was still warm.

"Lily, you're the best! What kind did you —?"

"Even though I personally prefer the semisweet with macadamia nuts, they're milk chocolate, no nuts, of course." She rolled her eyes, "Just like the one you and Mr. Wonderful shared on your first date. How long is he going to be gone this time?"

"Who knows? He didn't even tell me where he was going." This thought depressed me so much I decided to hell with it and broke open the bag. "He didn't even leave a note."

"Yes he did," Lily called, her voice muffled because now her head was buried in the vegetable bin of our old Philco refrigerator. She must have heard the crinkling of the waxed paper, because she suddenly looked up and caught me in the act of inhaling a cookie whole.

"He did?" I chewed guiltily.

"Yeah." She stepped back and let the door of the Philco swing open so I could see. There on the second shelf, propped up against some leftover pasta primivera, was a note in Peter's handwriting.

It was a thing we did, leaving each other notes in the refrigerator, ever since he'd proposed by putting an out-of-season Valentine on the shelf against some chocolate mousse with the message,

"Dear Karen, I love you more than chocolate itself. Will you marry me?"

If indeed I was pregnant, for my note I was planning to put a baby bottle filled with Dom Perignon on the top shelf, no words necessary.

Now, swallowing and brushing the crumbs from my hands, I reached for Peter's message. It read,

Dear Kar — Hong Kong this time. Sorry to leave without goodbye — only one United nonstop a day. I'll call later. P.

The words were as flat and cold as the paper they were written on. I crumpled the note and slam-dunked it into the trash compactor. Then on impulse, I ran out to the garage and got into Peter's Jeep. I took a deep breath and opened the glove compartment. The gun was gone.

COMPASSIONATE FRIEND THAT LILY WAS, she didn't mention Peter's name again until we were sitting at the dining room table, eating. Or rather Lily was eating. The emotions ricocheting around inside me had manifest themselves physically in the form of a knot the size of Pittsburgh in my stomach. So I was only toying with my dinner, three piles of glop varying in color and consistency, none even remotely resembling anything edible. Finally, I shoved my plate away and reached for the cookies, chocolate being the only known antidote for emotional trauma.

Lily eyed me ruefully. Then she pushed her plate away too. "I agree, this stuff stinks. Back to the old chopping block." She watched me chew for a second. I could see a transparent bubble of drool forming at the edge of her mouth, so I held out the bag of cookies. With a sigh she reached in and drew out a big chunk. "Don't you dare tell anyone you saw me eat this. I swear I'll deny it."

I nodded, too overcome with worry and dazed by the sugar rush to tease her about being the closet junk-food junkie I knew she was.

"So come on, he's always flying off on a moment's notice. What's the big deal this time?"

Normally, I bared my heart to Lily. She was a good listener and closer than a sister to me. And I knew she lived vicariously through my relationship with Peter, since she was, it seemed, terminally single. But I was afraid that verbalizing my suspicions about

Peter's affair with Lauren Covington would somehow make them more real. And how could I ever broach the subject of the gun?

"Oh, it's not Peter's trip," I hedged. "It's, you know, school. The Tooth Fairy's on my case again." It was, after all, also causing me stress.

"Don't mention teeth," Lily groaned, and stuck her finger into her mouth, probing the gingiva around her right rear molar.

"What's wrong?" I asked.

"I don't know. Something major, no doubt. I'm afraid to let my father look at it. He'd just love to get me in his chair and inflict a little agony, pay me back for not going to dental school."

"Why don't you see someone else?"

Lily shrugged noncommittally. "I did, a friend of my brother's from school. But when he tried to give me a shot of Novocain, I sort of . . . bit him."

"How do you 'sort of' bite someone?"

"I guess it was a real bite. Four stitches and a bruised knuckle. Word got around, and now no one I trust will see me. God, I hate dentists."

A little light flashed on in my brain. It was a long shot, but the only shot I had. I tried to sound nonchalant. "I'll see you."

"What?"

"I'll take a look at your mouth. I'm practically through with school, you know. If you wait another month I'll have to charge you $75 for a consultation."

Lily eyed me long and hard. I knew she was considering whether or not she trusted my hands in her mouth. Strange as it seems considering how close we were, this wasn't an intimacy we had shared.

"Just let me look at it." I stood and walked to the hallway, hoping she would follow me out of habit. At first she didn't move.

"Look, if it's something major, I'll tell you and you can find a licensed dentist. It's as simple as that."

"Simple for you, maybe," she grumbled. But as she spoke she pushed back her chair and padded after me toward the spare bedroom I use as my office.

Lily hadn't seen the space since I'd set up my pseudo-Stickley work table, NEC computer, two tensor lights and dental tools, or the collaged smiles cut out from magazine ads and plastered on the walls, making it what Peter called my 'happy room.'

"What do you think?" I asked, trying to read a reaction in her face.

She studied it for a moment. "Don't hold your breath waiting for *Architectural Digest* to call," she said at last. "But maybe the *Dental Review* will bite."

"Why am I even asking you? Your idea of style is a soufflé made with quail egg whites and quinoa, topped with porcini puree."

Lily considered this. "I'll have to try it."

"Sit," I commanded, and pointed to my desk chair. Lily collapsed into it, allowing me to swivel her around so her head would be in the light. I powdered a pair of disposable plastic gloves and snapped them on. "Say ahh."

Despite a few stray green flecks left over from dinner, Lily's teeth were gorgeous, a testament to her dental lineage. But I could see the problem immediately: a chip in the left rear molar. A little bondo would be an easy though temporary solution to the problem, but left untreated, it could become infected and ultimately a root canal might be needed. Right now such drastic treatment would be overkill, like repainting your whole car to get rid of a couple of nicks around the wheel rim. But there was no reason I couldn't apply the Earl Scheib 'why-touch-up-one fender-when-you-can-paint-the-whole-car-for-the-same-price?' theory to dentistry. It would solve the problem permanently, and after all, I was desperate.

"You're in luck," I said brightly. "I have to do a root canal tomorrow in class, and that'll take care of this problem."

"A root canal! Thanks for breaking it to me gently."

I shrugged. "It'll only take a couple of hours to fix." The truth was closer to six, spread out over two or three days, but I wasn't going to tell her that now.

"A couple of hours! What do you think I am, a sadomasochist with a tooth fetish?"

"You're the one who's in pain. I'm only trying to help."

"Let me ask you this. Do I need a root canal?"

"Well, not exactly," I conceded, "but I'd consider it a huge favor, and it wouldn't hurt you to have one."

Lily leapt out of the chair. "You just said the magic word, hurt."

"Come on, Lily. It's not like I've never done stuff for you before."

"Such as?"

"How about that time I took care of your cat when you went to study at the Culinary Institute."

"The cat died."

"That wasn't my fault. She choked on a hairball. It could have happened even if you'd been home."

Lily narrowed her eyes. "Just think how you'd've felt if it had been Hermie."

My heart clutched at the thought. "It's not the same. Hermie is a part of me, he's my child. I'd die if something happened to him." Hermie had followed us into my study and was lying on his pillow in the corner. At the sound of his name, he pricked up his giant ears and looked at me, awaiting further instructions.

"Oh, so now you're insinuating that I didn't love Paté?"

"Of course you did. But cats are different than dogs. Besides, you'd only had her for a couple of months."

"Yeah, but she was all I had. You have Hermie and Peter."

That was it. That one sentence put me over the edge. My eyes filled with tears. "Who says I have Peter?"

"What's that supposed to mean?"

"I think he's having an affair."

There, I'd said it out loud. Instead of feeling worse, I felt like a great weight had been lifted off my heart.

"How do you know?"

"I heard them talking."

"You mean Peter and . . . his mistress?"

And then the weight came crashing back down.

"Oh Kar, don't cry."

Lily heaved one of her trademark 'men are scum' sighs, and listened to the whole sordid saga of Peter and Lauren. Instead of telling me I was crazy to worry about losing Peter to Lauren since she was marrying someone else, she urged me to confront my rival woman to woman. "Are you nuts? Get right in her face! Let her know she can't have him without a fight," Lily counseled. "The nasty bitch. If I were you, I'd give her a good excuse to visit the plastic surgeon of her choice!"

Her anger was soothing, but I kept crying, laying it on thick, knowing it wouldn't hurt to get Lily's sympathy ducts pumping. She went into the bathroom to get me a Kleenex.

When she came back with the tissue she had a prescient look on her face.

"What is it?" I asked uncomfortably.

"Not that I make a habit of rummaging through people's

medicine drawers, but what's this?" She held up the early pregnancy test box.

Instantly, I saw the chance to use my 'condition' to win her sympathy, and I grabbed it, promising to let her be the baby's godmother if and only if she consented to be my patient for the root canal final. Somewhat reluctantly, she agreed. "At the rate I'm going, godmother's probably the closest I'll ever get to having one of my own," she said with a surprising hint of longing in her voice.

Then, still enthralled with the vision of herself wielding a fairy wand and sifting stardust like powdered sugar over my unborn child, she made me promise to take the test first thing tomorrow morning. "This isn't something you can put off," she told me as I walked her to her car. "If you are pregnant you've got to start eating right immediately. The first three months are critical."

Leave it to Lily to bring it all back to food.

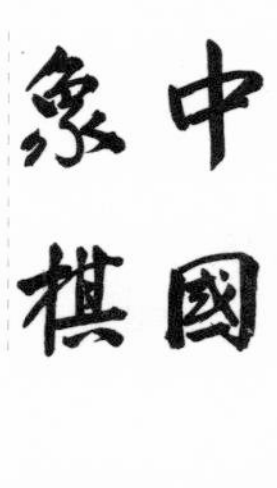

FOUR

Appropriately, the water turned baby blue.

I called Lily, despite the fact that it was barely 5 A.M, awakening her from a deep sleep. But she whooped with delight, giddy at the prospect of being a godparent, and we babbled for twenty minutes before her call-waiting beeped.

"Who's calling you at this hour?"

"Probably Omar," she grumbled. "It's got to be the middle of the afternoon in Beirut. I don't think he grasps the concept of time zones."

I reminded her of her promise to meet me at the dental lab. "Be there at two o'clock," I begged, and we hung up.

Lily's excitement about my pregnancy made me crazy to share the news with Peter. Only where was he? When I hadn't heard from him by 10:30, I decided to call his office.

"Occidental," the receptionist said with all the enthusiasm of a catatonic. I thought I remembered that her name was Inez, but it had been months since I'd called Peter at work, and for all I knew this could be a new girl. Embarrassed, I skipped the salutation all together. "This is Karen Matthews, Peter's wife."

"Yes, Mrs. Matthews, how may I help you?" Her voice was the aural equivalent of nonfat frozen yogurt — cold as ice, untextured and artificially sweet.

"Is Denise there?" Denise was the secretary Peter shared with the two other West Coast executives, a woman in her early thirties named Louise Winkler, and an older man named Jed Miller. I'd met them all exactly once, at our wedding reception a year ago. Peter didn't encourage me to make impromptu visits to his office, and that was fine with me. He didn't bring work home with him, and I didn't bore him with the daily routine at school. We had our separate careers, and then we had our life together.

"I'm sorry, Denise is in the field."

'In the field' I knew to be a euphemism for 'late to work.' Denise was notoriously 'in the field,' something Peter griped about whenever he spoke of her. I'd suggested he try to find a more reliable secretary, but he'd acted as though her employment was a force beyond his control, like the weather or the escalating national budget deficit.

"Oh, well, maybe you can help me." Humiliating as it was to admit that Peter had left home without telling me where he was staying, I was desperate. "I seem to have misplaced the phone number of Peter's hotel in Hong Kong. Could you give it to me?"

"I'm sorry, Mrs. Matthews, but I don't have that information. Shall I ask Denise to contact you when she gets in?"

"Is there a number where I can reach her now?"

"We're not allowed to give out an employee's private number," she replied.

I was annoyed, but not surprised. The staff at Peter's office were always monumentally unhelpful. They made me feel like they belonged to an exclusive club to which I was denied membership. "All right then," I snapped. "Ask her to call me when she gets in. She can leave Peter's hotel number on my machine if I'm not here."

"Thank you, Mrs. Matthews," she said, and hung up.

I still had three hours to kill before I was due at school to drill and fill Lily, and for want of a better way to spend them, I decided to reconnoiter Peter's desk to see if I could find the number or any other proof that he really was in Hong Kong on business. Admittedly, I was breaking a promise, but telling myself I only wanted to eradicate the vermin eating away at the foundation of our marriage, I sat down at Peter's swivel chair and flipped on the reproduction Tiffany lamp. A pool of yellow light spilled over the old rolltop desk. It had been with Peter longer than I had, and still bore scars from his days at USC. Although only a matter of months had passed since he'd swept its surfaces clean and packed the contents of its cubbyholes into boxes to move to our new house, the riot of paperwork and discarded clutter had spontaneously regenerated.

Sitting in Peter's chair, resting my arms on the frayed and soiled suede where his own arms so often rested, I was engulfed by guilt. What was I really looking for? Proof of Peter's fidelity, or a tawdry shard of evidence to press against the jugular of our marriage? What if I found something truly damning, a love letter, a photograph? What would I do then?

But curiosity won out, and I carefully slid open the top drawer of the desk. Nothing unusual there — pencil stubs and dried-up pens, yellow post-it pads, calculator, ruler, rubber bands, crumpled paper. There was a Xeroxed newspaper article by someone named Dr. Leo Kensington called "Energy Alternatives," and oddly enough, a map of China. Strange, but not damning, just evidence of Peter's eclectic interests. I was about to close the drawer when I saw a recognizable shape half-hidden at the back of the drawer. I pulled it out.

It was a pack of Marlboro cigarettes. This was truly bizarre. Peter didn't smoke. He abhorred tobacco with the disdain of a former athlete. So why on earth would he keep cigarettes, unless they belonged to a friend . . . Lauren? No doubt she smoked, and she was just the type who would refuse to buy her own butts, instead bumming them off her friends.

I heard a noise behind me and wheeled around, startling poor Hermie, who had tiptoed into the doorway to find out what I was doing. He cocked his head, silently reproaching me for invading Peter's private sanctum.

Guilty as charged, I pushed the chair away from the desk and stood, determined to keep my curiosity in check. But then the gaudy silk and sequined invitation to Lauren Covington's wedding caught my eye, and, at the same time, stabbed my heart. Propped against the frame that held a picture of me and Hermie, it virtually covered my face and most of my body. Why had he kept that tasteless memento? How dare she insinuate herself in Peter's private place, where even I was not allowed? Seized with righteous indignation, I grabbed it and tore it to shreds.

I picked up the wastebasket and swept the wounding tatters of paper into it. But trying to erase Lauren from my mind only embedded her there more deeply, like a tick burrowing in, sucking out the lifeblood of my marriage. Lily's suggestion of the night before rang in my ears. I should confront Lauren face to face and get the facts.

But did I have the guts?

I always write the bride's address on the back of the invitation, so when I go to buy the gift I have all the vital information at hand. (I'd bought Lauren a cheap silverplate hand mirror — appropriate, I thought, for a narcissist.) So I dumped the contents of the wastebasket onto the floor and started to sift through them, looking for the scrap that would have her address on it.

Hermie interpreted my being on the floor as a game and danced over to cover my face with affectionate doggie slobber.

"Good boy, sweet boy," I said, pushing him away. But he'd already picked up several of the paper scraps and now mocked me by holding them with his front paws and ripping them into tinier pieces with his front teeth. I was able to pry the damp shreds out of his mouth and was bent over, piecing them together on the floor, when I noticed a flat, square box hidden under the desk.

I pulled it out and stared at it for a moment. It was a game of Chinese Checkers — the marble game played on a board shaped like a six-pointed star. We'd had one as kids, but I didn't remember seeing one in Peter's things when we'd moved. And this one looked brand new. I opened it, and sure enough, there was the wooden board with six different colors of marbles in a leather pouch. It meant nothing to me, except, I thought wryly, that Peter was playing games. I put it back where I had found it, and went back to piecing together Lauren's address.

IT WAS ALMOST NOON by the time I'd dressed to confront my husband's mistress. Usually I don't waste a lot of time primping, but I couldn't face Lauren without mustering all my resources — emotional and physical, and cosmetic. Standing in front of the mirror, I took stock as dispassionately as I could in my highly passionate state:

Hair - Mediterranean brown, shoulder-length, wavy and in need of a trim. I tied it with a silk scarf to project seriousness and sophistication — I was trying for Jackie Kennedy, but she remained a distant goal.

Eyes - also brown, and almond-shaped, highlighted with enough shadow and liner to accentuate an expression of righteous indignation, without going all the way to Elizabeth Taylor in "Cleopatra."

Makeup - more than usual, so heavy it looked like I had slathered it on with a trowel. But since I hadn't slept well the last few nights, I needed serious coverage — foundation, two tones of eye-shadow, blush and mascara, lipstick and gloss. Imagine, most women do this every day.

Clothes - my favorite Ann Taylor blue blazer over a camel color pleated skirt and print blouse. On second thought, I traded the blouse (too frivolous) for a more serious gray turtleneck, and tied the scarf from my hair around my neck, a direct steal from Jane Pauley on the "Today Show."

Jewelry - I tried on a number of necklaces and bracelets, but ultimately opted to emphasize my wedding band by wearing no other jewelry, a technique I'd heard Raymond Burr suggest to a client falsely accused of murdering her husband on "Perry Mason."

Attitude - I perfected a look of hauteur: chin raised, eyes forward, shoulders squared. I was a woman with a mission, a wife, a mother-to-be. And I was ready, or at least I looked ready. Inside, I still had my doubts about pulling this off.

AS I MERGED into traffic on the San Diego Freeway, my blood was careening through my veins like a Formula One speedster in the Prix de Monte Carlo. To attempt a full frontal attack on Lauren was reckless and thoroughly unlike me. Maybe it was hormones that were causing this personality change. Or maybe it was desperation. But from what I'd seen of Lauren on TV and read about her in the tabloids, it appeared she was just the kind of fragile, flighty actress-type who could be intimidated by conviction. So I began to work on mine. I reminded myself that I had the weight of generations of oppressed Armenians on my side. They had stood tall in the face of their adversaries, and I should too. If nothing else, my ancestry had taught me to wield guilt like a weapon. For God's sake, this woman was trying to steal my husband, the father of my unborn child! True, Peter had been unfaithful, but if I could convince myself that it was all Lauren's fault, that he had been a hapless victim, then maybe I could start to forgive him.

I found Lauren's house just over the crest of Benedict Canyon, up a steep, winding drive that would be treacherous in bad weather. The location fit my impression of her: she thought she was better than the rest of us so she'd smugly bought a house that looked down on the city.

I parked on the street, carefully slanting my tires toward the curbless hillside, jammed the parking brake up tight, and walked to her driveway.

There was a tacky wrought iron gate protecting the entrance, and a buzzer for the intercom. I considered announcing myself, but rejected the idea. This was not a social call. What if she told me to go away? I'd have come all this way, wasted all this adrenaline for nothing. Since the gate was designed to keep out cars, not people, I easily slipped through the bars.

As I said, the drive was steep, and it was longer than it looked from the street. So I'd worked up a sweat by the time I reached the flat area where the pavement swung around to the front of the house. I stopped to catch my breath.

It was one of those ranch-style houses built in the '50s, long and low-slung, with plain wood siding and a sloped, shingled roof, unremarkable in every way, save for the view of the San Fernando Valley, spreading like spilt milk to the far reaches of the horizon. It was clear enough for the panorama to be impressive, but the price Lauren paid for the view was the treacherous driveway and the steep brush-covered hills on all sides, a pyromaniac's dream.

My sense of vertigo escalated when I turned to walk to the door and saw that the two cars in the drive were undercover police cars. You know the type, Dodge Darts in drab green or tan, with single yellow lights centered on the shelves behind the backseat. What in the world were they doing here?

In a flash of paranoia, I wondered if Lauren had called the cops in anticipation of my visit. But that was ridiculous. No one but Lily knew I'd planned to come here, and even Lily didn't know I was here now. Besides, Lauren had no idea I'd found out about her relationship with Peter. Nevertheless, I could hardly confront her in the presence of the L.A.P.D. Should I beat a hasty retreat and come back later?

I was standing there in a funk, trying to decide what to do, when the front door of the house opened, and out walked Herself, flanked by three men: two plainclothes policemen, recognizable by the holsters bulging under their windbreakers, and one officer in uniform blues.

On TV, Lauren was usually cast as the sexy young mother, or the executive whose bust always managed to spill out of her business suit. You got the feeling she wasn't so much acting as simply advertising her prodigious physical talents. So it was quite a shock when she stepped into the midday sun and I saw her for what she was: a lumpy, horse-faced, bottle blonde. Maybe I'm being cruel, or maybe I was prejudiced by my predicament, but those eyes the camera loved were ringed with circles as dark as the roots of her palomino hair, and her pale skin was freckled with broken capillaries and midlife acne. She was wearing old sweats which made her bulge in all the wrong places, and a pair of dirty Reeboks. And to my surprise, she wasn't even as tall as I was. She must have had to play every scene perched on an orange crate.

To put it bluntly, Lauren Covington, former finalist for Miss California, Emmy-nominated television actress and sex symbol to a generation now chronologically in their thirties and forties but emotionally eternally pubescent, looked like shit. I should have been ashamed how good this made me feel.

But my exultation was stifled mid-gloat by the officer in uniform, who noticed me standing at the edge of the drive and approached, his hand cautiously but dramatically slung over his gun.

"Can I help you ma'am?" he asked, his bulk blocking the spectacle of Lauren getting into one of the Dodges.

"I just came to talk to Lauren, er Officer Stratton," I said, reading his name off the badge on his chest.

"You a friend of hers?"

Was I? "Not exactly, I —"

"What are you then, a fan?"

How insulting. Did I look like a Lauren Covington groupie? "She knows my husband," I answered indignantly.

He cocked an eyebrow at me and put his hand on my arm to direct me out of the path of the car with Lauren in it. It pulled to a stop beside us. "Who's she?" one of the men inside asked Officer Stratton.

"Says her husband's a friend of Miss Covington." They traded looks that implied 'friend' was a euphemism for 'sex slave,' or so it seemed to me.

"What's she doing here?"

"Dunno. Says she just came to talk, or something."

The man in the car squinted at me with barely disguised boredom. "Find out what she knows about it and get her out of here," he mumbled, as though I couldn't hear.

"Yessir."

The car sped off down the drive, leaving Officer Stratton and me in a cloud of exhaust.

"What I know about what?" I asked.

"The murder of Fernando Ferrar."

"Ferdy's been murdered!" I was stunned. I'd never known anyone who'd been murdered. Not that I'd actually met Ferdy, but I had attended his aborted wedding. This was going to make a great story to tell Lily.

Officer Stratton nodded, removing a small pad and a pen from his uniform pocket. "You were a friend?"

"Not really. We, my husband and I, went to their wedding on New Year's Eve, but he didn't show up. Ferdy, I mean. Nobody knew what to make of it."

He nodded indifferently, slowly writing down my words in loopy, second-grade-style handwriting. "How about your husband?"

"What about him?"

"Was he a friend of the victim?"

I was about to tell him no, when it struck me that I had no idea if Peter knew Ferdy or not. Just one more unknown in the Peter Matthews mystery file. "Um, I doubt it, but I'm not sure."

"But he is a friend of Lauren Covington?"

"Sort of."

"Look, Mrs. . . .?"

"Matthews. Karen Matthews."

He looked at me with interest for the first time. "Is your husband by any chance Peter Matthews?"

I felt all the blood drain from my face. How on earth did he know Peter's name? And why was he looking at me like I was an ax murderer? "Yes, he is," I answered evenly. "Why do you ask?"

"We want to ask him some questions."

"About the murder?"

Officer Stratton nodded.

I was horrified and indignant. "He's out of town. He left yesterday. There's no way he could know — "

"Where did he go, Mrs. Matthews?" His voice was calm but professionally insistent.

"He's in the Orient on business."

"And he left yesterday?"

"Yes, so I'm sure he knew absolutely nothing about this. He was thousands of miles away when . . . whatever happened to Ferdy, happened."

"Mrs. Matthews, Fernando Ferrar was killed three days ago, at approximately 1 P.M. on Saturday, December 31st, the day he and Miss Covington were supposed to get married."

IT WAS A GOOD THING I didn't know where Peter was staying in Hong Kong, because I didn't even have to lie when Officer Stratton asked me that question. As it was, he took my address and phone number, and the address and phone number of Peter's office, as well as the name of his secretary (I could only tell him Denise, since I didn't know her last name. If he thought this was strange, he didn't say so.)

His last words to me were, "Don't go anywhere we can't reach you." And then he let me leave.

I was halfway down the canyon before I even remembered school. Ohmygod — Lily, the root canal final, Dr. Noritoki breathing fire down my neck. How was I going to concentrate, knowing the police wanted to question my husband in conjunction with a murder?

The worst part of it was, I couldn't say for sure where Peter had been at 1 P.M. on Saturday. Of course I knew my husband wasn't a murderer, but he had been gone all that day. I'd assumed he'd been serving hot meals at the Salvation Army center where he volunteered a few times a month, or hitting a bucket of balls at the driving range, because that's what he usually did on Saturdays. Or at least that's what he told me.

Then there'd been the scene at the wedding, and his very strange demeanor on the way home. And now his sudden business trip out of the country. But most of all, there was the gun in the glove compartment, which was now gone. Was it possible he'd been so jealous about Lauren's marriage that he'd . . .

Maybe I needed to talk to a lawyer. But I didn't have a lawyer. I didn't even know a lawyer. Except . . . Mitch. My brother Mitch! He was exactly the person I should talk to about Peter, because in addition to being my brother and Peter's brother-in-law, he was an Assistant in the District Attorney's office in Sherman Oaks. And finding him was as simple as going home to my parents' for dinner.

Lily was waiting for me outside the lab. I could tell she was about ready to bolt because she was chewing gum, an obsessive habit she resorted to in times of extreme stress when food wasn't available.

"It's about time!"

"Sorry," I panted, breathless from the dash across campus.

"I want you to know, you owe me big time," Lily said as I pushed her ahead of me through the double doors into the lab. "So big time it isn't funny."

"Anything you want," I said, spotting Noritoki's pointed little head across the room. Naturally, he'd stationed himself next to my chair, the only empty one in the lab. When he saw me coming, disappointment contorted his face.

"Dinner, at the restaurant of my choice," Lily was saying.

"What?"

"You said anything I want, and I want dinner at the restaurant of my choice."

"You got it." Knowing Lily's palate, it would set me back a bundle, but just then money was the least of my worries.

"Anywhere?"

"Anywhere."

"Okay, what's wrong?" Lily had stopped walking and was looking at me with concern.

"Why?"

"That was too easy. Something's really wrong." She searched my face. "You talked to Lauren!"

"I saw her, but I didn't talk to her," I replied evasively. "I'll tell you about it when we're finished."

We were almost to my chair when Lily stopped again. "You're going to give me Novocain, right?"

I nodded. "Of course. And lidocaine first so the shot won't hurt. For God's sake, this is dental work, not the Spanish Inquisition."

Lily remained rooted to the spot. "There's a difference?"

I heard the cloisonné balls clanking in Noritoki's pocket as he approached."Come on, Lily, let's get this over with. Just think about that dinner . . . anywhere in the world you want to go. My treat."

"Well, Karen?" Noritoki taunted. He always called the female dental students by their given names; it was a mild form of sexual harassment not to call us doctor, as he did the men, but nothing to go to court over. "So you found a patient after all." He considered Lily, staring at her the way he would a pickup in a gay bar.

Lily looked at him, then at me, then at the dental chair with the bracket of tools next to it. I could see the panic in her eyes.

"Yes, sir," I said before she could speak, or cry out or run away.

"She has signed the release papers?"

I nodded.

"Then what are you waiting for?"

I looked at Lily. She was about ready to pass out. Maybe it would be better for everyone involved if she did.

中國象棋

FIVE

When I got off the elevator on the fifth floor, I was broadsided by the aroma of steamed cabbage. Euphrates was making *dolmas* for dinner. Despite the turmoil in my brain, my body responded automatically to the stimulus of my mother's cooking — my stomach growled and saliva bubbled in my mouth.

"Hullo," I called, letting myself in the unlocked door. Both Mitch and I had tried without success to convince my parents that they were being foolhardy to rely on the token security system at the street entrance to the building, but Gordon and Euphrates stubbornly refused to lock their door. They had lived in this building on the fringe of West Hollywood (half a mile south of the gay area, west of Koreatown and just east of ritzy Hancock Park) for eleven years without incident, and despite evidence to the contrary, they adamantly persisted in seeing the United States through the rose-colored glasses of grateful immigrants.

"Karen, is that you, *anoush*?" my mother called from the kitchen. There was no way she could have heard me enter; the click of the closing door had been drowned out by the sound of the garbage disposal, and my footsteps muffled by the Tabriz runner in the hall. But she'd known I was there nevertheless; her old country maternal instincts were infallible.

She poked her head out of the kitchen and ignored my attempt at a breezy smile, assessing my state of mind in the bat of an eye. "You are worried," she said, her own brow furrowing in concern. "What'samatta?"

"Nothing, Mama, I'm just tired," I replied, ducking her eyes and giving her a quick hug and a kiss on the cheek. I tried to pull away, but she held me close, and I could feel her wordlessly trying to dissect the jumbled mess of my emotions through the press of our bodies. I was aching to tell her the lovely news of my pregnancy, but I had promised myself I would tell Peter first. "Smells good," I said to distract her. "What's for dinner?"

Euphrates didn't answer right away, letting me know I wasn't getting off the hook so easily. Later, after plying me with food and affection, she'd try in more subtle ways to ferret out the causes of my anxiety. "Cabbage *dolma* and leg of lamb. There was a sale at Ralphs, $1.29 a lb. I got a beauty — eight pounds, lean like you never saw. I cooked it with onions, no garlic, just the way Peter likes." She looked at me sternly. "So, what?"

I knew what she meant: where is Peter, why isn't he with you, are you having trouble in your marriage, is that why you look worried? Good old Mama, always jumping to conclusions, which nine times out of ten hit the bullseye.

"He's on a business trip. Hong Kong," I said, lifting the lid off the pot of rolled, meat-and-rice-filled cabbage leaves. The rich fragrance swirled about me in a comforting mist. I knew I'd stuff myself, and, since I only succumbed to eating red meat at my mother's table, I'd probably have indigestion tomorrow, on top of morning sickness. But it would be worth it. The *dolmas* smelled delicious.

"Hong Kong? What kinda insurance business they got there?"

Euphrates' grasp of Peter's work was limited, but she did have a point. When Peter traveled abroad for business, it was usually to places like Frankfurt or Geneva, European capitals where monster conventions were held for representatives of insurance companies from all over the world.

But Peter scheduled trips to these gatherings months in advance. Besides, the receptionist at his office would have told me if that were where he was, unless — I hated to admit this even to myself — he had specifically told her *not* to tell me where he was.

"There's your brother," Euphrates said, once again intuiting the opening and closing of the front door. "Go tell him dinner's on the table in ten minutes. I made fresh *madzoon*." She smiled, nodding at the bowl of custardy, fermented milk on the counter. "I used low fat, just for you."

"Mama, you didn't even know I was coming."

"I knew."

"*I* didn't even know. How could you know?"

"You always come when I make *dolma*," she replied.

"But —" What was the point? She had her own logic, and nothing I could say was going to change her mind.

I walked through the living room, past my father, who was dozing in the big wing chair, still wearing his white shirt and tie, the newspaper open on his lap, the television tuned to the six o'clock news, with the sound off. When Papa said he was watching the news, he meant it literally. When I asked him why he didn't turn up the volume he said it was because he didn't like to hear bad news. Then why not watch a game show, or a rerun of one of those sitcoms? Because it's important to keep up on what's happening, he'd explain.

Mitch wasn't in his room when I knocked, but through the bathroom door which was slightly ajar, I could hear his strong stream splashing against the porcelain toilet bowl my mother scrubbed twice daily. If I'm a little obsessive about cleanliness and order, I'm a slacker compared to Euphrates. She's been known to iron the newspaper to keep it neat.

"Hi, Mitch," I called.

"Karen? What brings you to the shrine of our youth?"

"You. I need to talk to you."

"My hourly rate is $200 per."

"That was before you joined the D.A.'s office. Anyway, this is strictly pro bono."

"I was afraid of that. Well, make yourself at home. I'll be right out."

I flopped down on Mitch's bed, and out of sheer perversity propped my feet up on the quilted bedspread. When we were growing up it was forbidden to sit, let alone lie, on our beds during the day. Whether Euphrates was afraid such actions would lead to sloth, or whether sitting on the bed fell in the same problematic category as a crinkled newspaper, she had nevertheless ingrained in me a respect for a made-up bed, which lasted until Peter and I were married and together made our own bedroom rules.

I looked around the room. Mitch had moved home about a year ago, after his wife Jae ran off with her martial arts teacher. Don't ask me why she left him. As far as I knew, he had been a model husband. Jae had worked as a surgical nurse; maybe she just needed to get away from sick people.

In any event, when she left him he moved back into his boyhood room which was still decorated with the model airplanes he'd glued together twenty-five years before. There were baseball and bowling trophies on the dresser, and a couple of years' worth of *National Geographics* and an outdated *Encyclopedia Britannica* in the bookcase over the pine desk. I still remember the day the *Britannica* salesman came to the house, offering Gordon and Euphrates an opportunity to give their children access to all the knowledge of civilization for only $7.98 a week. Such a deal; they were probably still paying for it.

The only evidence that an adult was living here was the fax machine, incongruously wedged onto the nightstand next to a Roy Rogers lamp. I flicked on the lamp, illuminating Trigger's palomino body, and tried to imagine how it would feel to live here again. It would be as impossible and uncomfortable as returning to the womb. Mitch had to be an emotional contortionist to do it.

He came out of the bathroom and stepped into his closet to change out of his suit. "Where's Peter?" he called. Although they were opposites in many ways, Mitch and Peter liked each other. They found common ground in typically manly topics — sports, politics, the stock market. The only time they ever got down home and dirty together was the night Jae walked out on Mitch. Mitch had appeared at our apartment with a bottle of Mezcal in one hand and Jae's good-bye letter in the other. He and Peter had already polished off the liquor by the time I got home from school, and they were good-naturedly fighting over who would get to eat the wizened worm at the bottom of the bottle. Although neither of them ever told me what they'd talked about that afternoon, it had bonded them, and I was glad of it.

"Hong Kong," I answered, wondering if I sounded as unsure of Peter's whereabouts as I felt.

Mitch stuck his head out of the closet. Neither of us needed to mention the irony: when Jae had run off with her Shing-Yi teacher they'd gone to Hong Kong. I'd taken classes with her once or twice in an effort to be sisterly, but I hadn't gotten it — her love of the sport, her fascination with her teacher, the lure of exotic Hong Kong, not even the sister part. Jae's reasons for deserting my brother were as obscure to me as if she had been a stranger.

"And you stayed home so you could have cabbage *dolma* with us?" he asked neutrally.

"I couldn't go. I have school," I replied, only a partial lie. Mitch and I had been conditioned all our lives to put education first, so it was plausible that I would forego a trip to complete my classes. But I knew in my heart of hearts that I would have gone with Peter in a nanosecond — if he'd asked me.

"My sister, the drill sergeant," Mitch teased, using the nickname he'd given me when I started dental school. He walked out of the closet in khakis and a T-shirt and sat in the straightback desk chair to tie the laces of his old Adidas tennies. When he bent over I could see a circle of scalp poking through the thinning hairs on the top of his head. Poor Mitch, he was so incongruous: a balding, thirty-something man in a twelve-year-old's room, a model husband whose wife came home one day and gave him a karate chop to the heart.

"What's he doing there?"

I shrugged. "Business?"

It was a question and Mitch answered it with a question, his own version of mother's. "Why would an insurance salesman from Los Angeles go to Hong Kong on business?"

"That, my dear brother, is what I want to talk to you about."

But then Euphrates called us to dinner, and by the time I'd

stuffed myself with two helpings of *dolma*, a token slice of the lamb, some salad, marinated eggplant, *madzoon* and pickled beets, my nagging fears about Peter had numbed somewhat. This was due, no doubt, to the fact that all the blood in my body had pooled in my stomach to aid in the digestion of the meal. In any event I decided not to unload on Mitch. There had to be a logical explanation. Probably a prenatal hormone surge had caused me to overreact to the day's revelations. Why wreck his evening over a string of stupid coincidences?

I was on my way out, hurrying because Hermie had been alone all day and would be waiting for his dinner, when Mitch caught my arm. "I'll walk you down," he offered. And closing the door behind us, he reminded me, "You did want to talk to me about something, didn't you?"

I sighed. "Yeah, I guess." I hated to burden him with my problems. Or maybe since I idolized him, I didn't want him to know I had any problems.

"It's about Peter, isn't it?" Mitch asked. He must have inherited ESP from my mother.

I nodded. "I think he's in trouble, and I don't know what to do about it."

"What kind of trouble?"

"I think he may be . . . seeing someone else." I had to take this a step at a time.

"Another woman?"

"No Mitch, a zebra. Yes, another woman, what do you think?"

Mitch held up his hands defensively. "Hey, don't jump all over me. I'm just trying to help."

"I'm sorry. I'm just really upset."

He put his arm around my shoulders and squeezed me with brotherly compassion. "You don't have to tell me, it's the pits. Do you know her?"

"Yeah." I didn't want to tell him that Peter had traded up, to a rich and beautiful celebrity — it made my predicament seem all the more hopeless and pathetic. He didn't press for details.

"How'd you find out?"

"At first it was just little things — inconsistencies in what he said and did, the fact that he takes trips and I never know how to reach him. This time his office won't even tell me what hotel he's staying in. Then, last weekend I overheard them talking." My eyes flooded with tears and I choked on my grief. Mitch waited until I composed myself.

"Is she with him in Hong Kong?" he asked gently.

"No."

"You're sure?"

"Yes I'm sure," I snapped.

He looked a little hurt at my tone, but remained patient. "*How* are you sure?" he asked softly.

"I went to see her today, to let her know I know." I hated to mention the second half of my dilemma about Peter. But the concern in Mitch's face was real, and he was the one person I could tell. "She was supposed to get married last weekend, but the groom never showed up at the wedding. It turns out he's dead."

"What kind of dead?" he asked with the calm of someone who had asked this question before.

"Murdered dead," I replied.

Mitch was silent for a long minute. I could almost hear the wheels turning in his Assistant D.A.'s brain. "Is Peter a suspect?"

"I don't know. Maybe. The police said they want to question

him, but I told them he'd already left town. Mitch, he could be in big trouble, and I don't even know where he is."

Mitch's expression was serious, professional. He was no longer just my brother. He'd become my legal representative. "It's imperative that we talk to him before they do. Did you try his secretary?"

I nodded, comforted by his use of the pronoun 'we.' "She wasn't in when I called this morning. Maybe she's left a message at the house by now."

"If she hasn't, you'd better go down to the office tomorrow. Confront her face to face and tell her it's an emergency. Don't let her put you off."

Funny, Mitch was giving me the same advice about Denise that Lily had given me about Lauren: Don't let her avoid you. Force the issue. In person. I guess it was obvious to everyone but me that I had been avoiding the crucial confrontations in my life for too long.

"Then call me and let me know what she says," he continued, never taking his eyes off me.

"What if she doesn't know?"

"Then we'll have to think of something else. This is critical, Karen. If the police get it into their heads that he's skipped town to avoid talking to them, it would start the momentum going in the wrong direction. I hate to imply that the system doesn't work, but once you get the wheels spinning, sometimes it's hard to stop the machine from mowing down the wrong person. Especially if he doesn't have an airtight alibi, which I presume Peter doesn't. Does he?"

I was thinking about the gun. "I don't think so," I admitted.

"I'll do some checking on the murder at my end. What was the victim's name?"

"Fernando Ferrar."

"Fernando like the bull, Ferrar like Jose the actor. Right."

I reached up to give him a hug. "Thanks, Mitch. You're the best."

"Hey, I'd do it for one of my friends." He kissed me on the forehead. "Try not to worry too much, but talk to Peter. Whatever it takes."

中國象棋

SIX

It was after nine when I got home. The house was dark, but when I put my key in the lock, a business card which had been wedged against the jamb floated to the ground. I picked it up and held it up to the porch light. It read, "Detective Larry Rivers, L.A.P.D. Homicide Division," and written in a childish scrawl were the words, "Please call A.S.A.P." Just what I needed.

I opened the door. A familiar voice was talking on the answering machine."... it's hard, but you just have to trust me. I love you."

I raced to the phone and grabbed it. "Peter?"

I was a second too late. The vacant hum of the dial tone taunted me. The number "3" blinked on the machine, so two other calls had come in before Peter's. The way the old machine worked I had no choice but to rewind the tape and start from the beginning.

While I listened, I fed Hermie the lamb scraps Euphrates had saved for him — a concession, since she didn't consider any food too scrappy for human consumption. But out of love for me she grudgingly treated Hermie like a member of the family.

"Hello, Mrs. Matthews, this is Denise Pressman from Occidental. I received a message that you called to find out where Mr. Matthews is staying in Hong Kong. I'm terribly sorry, he left on such short notice that we weren't able to secure a reservation for him, and he was going to have to find a room once he arrived. When I hear from him I'll let you know. Sorry I can't be of more help."

What bullshit, I thought, absently forgetting to give Hermie the morsel of meat in my hand. He reminded me by gently stepping on my foot with his right front paw, and I lowered the treat so he could take it. His mouth was soft and gentle. Strange that jaws designed to crunch through the bony skeletons of gazelles and rabbits could also be so yielding.

The second message was from Lily. Her voice sounded as though she were talking through a mouthful of Styrofoam. "Karen? It's me. Please pick up. Something's really wrong. I'm in agony. It started about an hour ago, when the Novocain wore off. God, how can you not be there! Call me as soon as you get home. If I don't answer it's because I'm dead."

Lily had been a model patient that afternoon, immobile and uncomplaining throughout the two-hour procedure, as I'd drilled and drained and temporarily filled her tooth. Considering all I'd had on my mind, plus the ache in my gut and the tremor in my hands, the whole thing had gone remarkably well. Or maybe it hadn't . . .

I put the last of the scraps of lamb into Hermie's dish and waited to hear Peter's voice on the machine.

"Hey, babe, it's me." His voice sounded faint and toneless. Was his remoteness geographical or emotional? "I'm sorry I had to go again. You know I hate it as much as you do. I shouldn't be here more than a week though, ten days tops. They're having some kind of a power problem here, so I'm calling from a phone at the reception desk. For the time being, they're down to basic services — no phones in the rooms, no elevators, no hot water. What a drag."

"What hotel?" I asked out loud, as though Peter could hear me, but of course he couldn't.

"I suppose I deserve it for leaving so suddenly. I'll explain when I get back. I know it's hard, but you just have to trust me. I love you."

I turned off the machine and sat there for a long time, staring at it. It was so frustrating to hear his voice and not be able to ask him what I wanted to know. Damn!

Somehow I had to find out where he was staying and let him know the police were looking for him. Or maybe they were the reason he'd left. But if so, I needed to be told. I was more than willing to lie to protect Peter, but I needed to know the truth in order to do it.

I dialed Lily's number. She answered in the middle of the first ring. "Karen?" she asked. Only it sounded more like "Kaauun?"

"Hi. What's wrong?"

"I don't know. But my tooth is killing me. You know that feeling, when there's a lot of static in the air and you touch someone and get a shock? That's what it feels like in my mouth every time I bite down."

"Gosh, Lil, I'm really sorry. I'll take care of it first thing tomorrow. If you can meet me —"

She cut me off mid-sentence. "What am I going to do tonight?"

"Well, try not biting down."

"How am I going to eat?"

"Can't you not eat for one night?" Before the words were out of my mouth I realized my mistake. It was like asking Fred Astaire not to dance or George Burns not to smoke cigars.

"No!" The horror in her voice confirmed it. "It's already after nine and I'm starving."

"Okay, okay. What do you want me to do? I can't get into the lab now."

"You can at least look at it. Anyway, you haven't told me about Lauren yet."

"I've really got a lot on my mind —"

"Good. I'll be there in ten minutes and you can tell me all about it." And she hung up before I could object.

JUST AS I SUSPECTED, until we could get into the lab there was little I could do for Lily except make her comfortable. It looked like a case of electrolysis, a chemical reaction between the sealing point I had cemented into the hole I'd drilled and the gold inlay she had in her second bicuspid.

As an interim measure, I loosened the temporary crown to ease the pressure. That seemed to help. Then I gave her some oil of clove to rub on the gum to deaden the nerve, an old dentist's remedy that worked surprisingly well for a homeopathic treatment. Her relief was immediate, and she extolled my talents, thinking she was cured. But I knew the pain would be back.

To distract her while I worked, I hit the high points of my visit to Lauren Covington, telling her about Fernando Ferrar's murder and the police wanting to talk to Peter. I showed her the card Detective Larry Rivers had left, and as a grand finale I played the message Peter had left on the answering machine.

Lily was stunned silent, no small feat. But sharing it all, even with my best friend, made me feel like a reporter for the *National Enquirer*. Hypothesizing about Peter's secret life, like talking about sex, was so intimate, it was as though I was being unfaithful to him. But I reminded myself that he was the one who had been unfaithful. That's what had started this whole sequence of events.

BY THE TIME I FINISHED spilling my guts, I'd finished with Lily's emergency treatment. I washed my hands and wiped up around the sink, then tossed the used towel down the laundry chute, which emptied out into a bin in the basement next to the washing machine.

"I bet I know how you could find out where he's staying," Lily said nonchalantly, stuffing her own towel down the chute after mine.

"How?"

"Well, he told you he couldn't use the phone in his room, so he must have had to call from the reception desk, right?"

"Right."

"And to call long distance from Hong Kong, he'd either have to carry a hell of a lot of change, or use a calling card. If you know his code you can get the phone number from AT&T."

I was impressed. "And here I thought you were just another short order cook."

"Looks are deceiving," she smiled, pleased with herself.

IT'S SCARY how easy it is to get confidential information if you know who to ask. I had Peter's AT&T number because I'd used it myself until he'd gotten me my own, saying his was a business expense, and my personal calls confused his tax records.

Miraculously, AT&T had a twenty-four-hour 800 number, and it was answered by a real person. The phone number the operator gave me, after I told him Peter's birthdate and his mother's maiden name, Linden, as identification, had eleven digits. I dialed, and held the receiver out so Lily could listen. It rang four times, and then a British accent said, "Peninsula Hotel."

As untraveled as I was, even I had heard of the Peninsula in Hong Kong. It was supposedly one of the finest hotels in the world. Could Peter's business be so important that he was staying in five-star grandeur?

The voice repeated, "Peninsula Hotel. How may I direct your call?"

I had to say something so I said, "Could you please connect me to Mr. Matthews, Mr. Peter Matthews."

"Just one moment."

Lily and I held our breath and waited.

"I'm sorry, Madam, we don't have anyone registered by that name."

I was disappointed, but not surprised. And then, out of nowhere, I remembered the passport photos I'd found in Peter's desk, and the words just formed themselves unbidden in my mouth. "Do you by any chance have a Linden there, a P. Linden?"

"One moment."

Another breathless moment, and then, suddenly, the line was ringing! Was there a real P. Linden staying at the Peninsula, or had I stumbled onto Peter's room?"

"Hello?" It was a woman's voice. My heart leapt with joy. It wasn't Peter after all. P. Linden was Paula or Patty or Peggy.

Or, was it a woman who was with Peter, someone so confident his wife wouldn't be calling that she would even answer his phone? "Hello, who is speaking?" Her words had a clipped, slightly British cadence.

"Is Peter there?" I asked hoarsely.

"Hold the line," she said at last. I could hear what sounded like some muffled conversation, or it could have been static.

"Who is this?" It was Peter's voice, but why did he sound so angry?

"It's Karen. Your wife." For some reason it seemed important to remind him of our marital status.

"Karen! What are you — how'd you —" He was obviously thrown, but recovered quickly, his voice much closer to normal. "Is everything okay?"

"Yes. No. Peter, I need to talk to you." Now that I had him on the line I was tongue-tied. I looked imploringly at Lily.

"Fernando. Tell him about Fernando."

"What is it babe?" Peter demanded. "Tell me quick because this phone may cut out. The lines have been down all morning. They just came back on a few minutes ago."

"Did you know Fernando is dead?" I blurted out, the words tumbling from my mouth in a rush. "He was murdered, Peter. The police are asking all sorts of questions, and they want to talk to you. Do you know anything about it? Is that why you went to Hong Kong? Peter, I'm afraid."

All I could hear was the static on the long distance line. "Did you tell anyone about this?" he asked finally.

"No," I lied, pulling the phone away from Lily so she couldn't hear. "What should I do?"

"Nothing," he replied, his voice strong and harsh. "You don't say a word. You don't tell them you talked to me at all. You don't know where I am."

"But Peter, you can't — you didn't have anything to do with it, did you?" I couldn't believe I was even asking him this question.

"You know me better than that," he replied. "But there are some problems, things I don't want to talk about on the phone. I'll explain when I see you. I won't be here long."

"Peter, this is an emergency! A homicide detective has already come to the house — he may be back any minute."

"Don't let him in!" he said urgently. "And don't talk to anyone."

"What if he has a search warrant?"

"Just don't answer the door. Better yet, go away for a few days. We have enough cash in the joint account. Use it. Go on a little trip. To Santa Barbara or something. By the time you get back it'll all have blown over. You'll see."

"Where should I —" Suddenly the line crackled and went dead. "Peter?" I shouted helplessly. "Peter?" When there was no answer I hung up and redialed. A different hotel operator answered. "I'm sorry. The line has a 'do not disturb' on it. Would you like to leave a message?"

"No message," I said, and hung up the phone.

"What are you going to do?" Lily whispered.

I sat there in stunned silence, mulling over the options. Despite my rage and hurt at Peter's duplicity, and my fear that he might have been involved in a crime of passion, I still loved him every bit as much as I had a week ago. And until he told me otherwise, I would continue to hold out a shred of hope that he still loved me, and do what I could to save our marriage.

Spontaneity wasn't my strong suit. But in light of the events of the past twenty-four hours, drastic action seemed warranted. I needed answers, and the only person who could give them to me was Peter.

"Peter told me I should take a trip. Well I'm going to. I'm going to go to Hong Kong," I replied.

THE ONLY THING stopping me from stuffing myself into the economy section of a 757 and flying to the other side of the earth was Hermie. I called my brother first thing the next morning.

"Mitch, will you do something for me?"

"I'm an attorney, Karen. It's against my religion to agree to anything before I know what it is."

"Will you stay at my house for a few days and take care of Hermie?"

"Where are you going?"

On the one hand, I was afraid if I told Mitch my plan, he'd try to talk me out of it. On the other, if something happened to me, someone in the family should know where I was. "I'm going to Hong Kong, to talk to Peter face to face."

"You found him, then."

"Yeah, he's at the Peninsula Hotel, or at least he was last night."

"Karen, listen to me." Mitch's voice was serious now. "I've done some checking on this murder. An actress named Lauren Covington was brought in for questioning yesterday." A pause. His voice dropped an octave. "Is she the one, the mistress?"

I nodded, then realizing he couldn't see me, whispered, "Yes."

"No charges have been filed against her or anyone else yet. The victim's car plowed into a tree on St. Andrews Place in Hollywood and then exploded."

"He wasn't shot?" I asked. That would be a good sign.

"I'm still trying to find out the cause of death. For some reason, they're keeping the investigation classified. But the Coroner's report should be out in a day or so, and I've got a buddy over there who owes me one."

"A homicide detective named Larry Rivers came by the house last night while I was at the folks. If he comes back with a search warrant —"

"Don't worry, I'll handle it," Mitch said.

"How?"

"What do you think they teach us in law school? Just a sec."

The line went dead for a moment, then Mitch came back on. "I'm going to give you Jae's number. She lives in Mon Kok, which is a suburb of Kowloon. She's studying medicine at the University in Hong Kong. If you get into any trouble —"

"Wait a minute. Jae, your estranged wife Jae? How do you know where she is?"

"We keep in touch."

I was shocked. "What do you talk about?"

"It's not the easiest thing, moving to a place like Hong Kong. Sometimes she gets homesick and needs a friend."

"You amaze me, Mitch you really do. The woman leaves you high and dry, practically rips your heart out, and you still feel obligated to be there for her? Either you're a saint, or you're the sorriest sucker in the world."

"It must run in the family," he replied dryly. "When did you say you're leaving?"

I PACKED QUICKLY, dumping a jersey dress and a couple of changes of slacks, sweats, toiletries and my running gear into one of Peter's old carry-on bags. Then I ran my errands, nearly cleaning out our joint account and buying traveler's checks, picking up my ticket at the travel agent, stopping by the market to stock up on ground turkey and kibble for Hermie. When I got home I had just enough time to call school and leave a message with Noritoki's office that I had a family emergency and wouldn't be able to complete my finals. Hopefully, he'd find it somewhere in his dark soul to let me make up the tests when I got back.

Euphrates was entertaining her bridge group when I called to say good-bye. I could tell because she repeated everything I said, in a tone that made it sound thrilling. In her peer group, you got status points whenever one of your children called. It counted more than the bridge score, I think.

"Hi, Mom, it's me," I said.

"It's Karen," she bragged. "Tsun hy es, anoush?" she asked me in Armenian for the benefit of Mrs. Unjian, Mrs. Mardigian and Mrs. Garabedian. "How are you, sweetheart?"

"I'm fine. I just wanted to tell you I have to go away for a few days."

"You have to go away for a few days? A vacation?" she repeated, and then louder, obviously for the benefit of Mrs. Garabedian who was hard of hearing. "Karen says she has to GO AWAY for a few days!" As though 'going away' were a major accomplishment, like getting a Ph.D., or winning the lottery. "*Ench bes es*? Where to, darling?"

"Hong Kong."

From the inflection in my mother's voice you'd have thought I'd said I had been chosen by NASA to be the first woman astronaut to ride the space shuttle to Venus. "You're going to Hong Kong! When? Today? She's going today, just on the spur of the moment. How wonderful, dear. Is Peter going with you? Oh, yes, Peter's already in Hong Kong. Isn't that nice, Karen's going all the way to Hong Kong to surprise Peter. He's there on business."

We could have gone on like that all afternoon, but I had a plane to catch. "Gotta run, Mom. I'll call you when I get back. Kiss Papa for me."

"I will, darling. Good-bye."

I knew she'd call me back the instant the bridge club left, to read me her shopping list of maternal fears: a woman shouldn't travel alone; those planes are dangerous, didn't one crash just last week; it will cost a fortune; what about school; what about your house; what about your father's birthday next week?

Hopefully, I'd be back in time to celebrate Gordon's 78th birthday. I made a mental note to bring him an exotic trinket from the Orient, some electronic gadget that would make him the envy of his friends.

L.A.X. WAS A MOB SCENE, and the flight was booked solid. By the time I got on board I was a sweaty, nervous wreck. The aisle was jammed with cranky passengers. "Is it always this crowded?" I asked a flight attendant.

She gave me a tolerant smile and nodded. "Remember, a quarter of the world's population lives in the Orient."

"Yeah, but I didn't think they'd all be on this plane."

The coach seats were configured three - five - three. In each row, passengers were settling in for the fifteen-hour flight, stocking up on pillows and blankets, magazines, foil-wrapped peanuts and headphones. Propelled down the aisle by the flow of passengers, I finally made it to my row, but I couldn't get in because a woman was standing on the middle seat, her back to me, trying to stuff her bag into the overflowing overhead bin.

I waited for a moment, but fearing I would be swept past the row by the unrelenting stream of passengers behind me, I finally called out, "Excuse me, may I get in? I've got the window seat."

"No problem."

She gave the bag one last shove and stepped down, turning to face me.

"Lily!"

Lily gave me a grin which was one part sheepish and two parts apprehensive. "Welcome aboard."

"What are you doing here?"

"What does it look like? I'm going to Hong Kong."

I stood there in the aisle staring at her, until finally an aggravated voice from behind me snarled, "Hey, lady, do you mind? Some of us want to get to our seats before the plane takes off."

I squeezed past Lily, stumbling over a large box on the floor at her feet, and plopped down into my seat next to the window. We sat in silence for a moment, watching the last frenzied passengers find their places. It was like a game of musical chairs, and nobody wanted to be left standing when the music stopped.

"Before you get upset, let me explain," Lily said.

"Oh, good, there's an explanation," I said sarcastically.

"Well I am part Chinese —"

"What? About one-sixteenth? Practically everyone on earth's got that much Chinese in them."

"You know I love Chinese food," she began again.

"You love all food," I corrected.

"Chinese is one of the oldest food cultures in the world, and I thought, here is a chance to learn about it firsthand, to get my creative juices flowing again. And since you promised me dinner at any restaurant in the world — your exact words by the way — I chose Gaddis."

"That was a figure of speech and you know it . . .What's Gaddis?" I asked.

"One of the most famous restaurants in Asia, and coincidentally, it's located at the Peninsula Hotel in Hong Kong."

"No kidding." I had no idea if she was making this up. Famous Restaurants of Asia was not a category I'd choose if I were a contestant on "Jeopardy."

"Anyway, I deserve a vacation after what I went through yesterday. It still hurts." She made a great show of uncapping the bottle of oil of clove, dabbing it on her tooth. "You could at least be a little grateful."

Truth be told, I was thrilled to have Lily's company, but I couldn't resist giving her a hard time. "Grateful? I'm surprised Noritoki didn't flunk me, with you sitting there reciting the recipe for crown roast of pork."

"I was delirious with pain. I still am."

"Then at least you won't be tempted to eat the airplane food."

"Not to worry," Lily said. She reached down and took the lid off the box squashed between our feet. It was filled with food. At least she was consistent.

2

FUCHOW, CHINA

Wednesday, January 4, 1986

THE SLUICE rises, and a seething mass of green-black bodies gushes into the tank. Chun Sok Lee repositions the Styrofoam container stamped with the logo of the Superior Eel Hatchery so that it abuts the tank. Then he picks up his net and begins sorting adult eels, separating the breeders from the males who will otherwise cannibalize the newly hatched young, nature's way of controlling the population. Normally, Chun is proficient at his work, automatically ferreting out the slender males from the darker, thicker females so they can be packaged and shipped live to other parts of China and Japan, where they are culinary staples.

But today he is distracted and his gloved hand refuses to wield the net with the speed necessary to isolate the slippery bodies. His mind is on his neighbor Wan Lo's invention. Three days ago, after he witnessed Wan Lo's experiment with the electric street lamps, he begged his supervisor to arrange an audience for him with Wo Fat, the owner of the hatchery and Dragonhead of the T'ung Yu Triad. He even gave the man one of his black-skinned Zhusi chickens as a bribe to ensure his compliance. Chun is certain that if he can only speak to the all-powerful Dragonhead and tell him about the magical properties of the black box, Wo Fat will reward him with 10,000 Yuan, security for life. Then he can retire from this menial servitude and raise chickens as his family did for generations before the Cultural Revolution.

But although the supervisor swears he passed the request on to his superiors, thus far it has been ignored. And with every day that passes, the likelihood increases that it is too late for Chun to profit.

Chun focuses on the tank, dipping his net into the water and flicking his wrist at just the right moment to capture one of the eels. But as he raises it dripping from the tank, an iron hand grasps his shoulder and he is pulled around to face one of Wo Fat's brutish thugs. The man is built like a water buffalo, massive through the body, his ugly head set on a neck as thick as the trunk of a lychee tree. At close range Chun sees that the base of the thug's shaved skull is branded with the three-legged moon toad, ancient symbol of wealth, logo of the Superior Eel Hatchery, and totem of the T'ung Yu Triad.

"Come," the thug grunts.

A hush falls over the workers, but no one dares look at Chun. It is unusual for one of them to be singled out in this fashion, and when someone is, it is generally a sign of censure, and no one wants to be associated with a troublemaker for fear of similar reprimand.

Chun's legs tremble as the thug leads him past the tanks of transparent, newly spawned eels, and the fresh water pools where the adolescent elvers live until they reach maturity, to a wooden staircase. They climb the stairs to a narrow catwalk. From here, Chun can look down into the largest salt water tanks where the exotic species are kept — the long-jawed snipe eels, whose pointed tails enable them to burrow backward into the sand, morays, and conger eels. Chun has never known why Wo Fat maintains tanks for these rare breeds; they are both dangerous and inedible. A vertiginous thrill of fear momentarily paralyzes him as he watches the deadly eels writhe thirty feet below.

"Move on!" The thug shoves Chun through a soundproof door into the glass-enclosed office which is perched at the end of the catwalk. In contrast to the bleak, putrid atmosphere of the hatchery itself, the office is pristine and smells of lotus. Thick carpets woven with dragons cover the floor, and the glass walls are draped in blue velvet for privacy.

Inside, a round table is laid with an immaculate white cloth. On it is a plain porcelain bowl containing the three fruits of plenty: the peach, the pomegranate, and the bergam, symbolizing long life, large family, and vast wealth. The venerable Wo Fat sits behind the table, his obese body resplendent in a richly embroidered Mandarin coat. To Chun, his face resembles an oversized cabbage that has been left to mold in the garden, his small beady eyes like maggots which have burrowed into the decaying leaves. But despite his looks, he is the most powerful man in the province.

At Wo Fat's right stands his cousin Liu, his partner and spokesman. By contrast, Liu is compact and elegant, dressed in a smartly tailored western suit. The two men are as dissimilar as yin and yang, but together they are formidable. Liu lends the cunning and the intelligence of the tiger to their partnership, and Wo Fat the savage cruelty of the shark.

"We are told that you have something of great import to tell our cousin Wo Fat," Liu says politely. "Please proceed."

"The information is worthy of a reward of 10,000 Yuan," Chun blurts out.

Anger burns in Wo Fat's eyes, but Liu smiles coolly. "We are most eager to hear your information. After we have heard it we will discuss the reward."

Chun describes what he saw the morning Wan Lo tested his invention on the electrical pole near their huts. "And by simply attaching the wire to his magical box, he was able to light up a thousand lamps, all the way to Fuchow!"

Liu ponders a moment, staring at Chun. "So this invention creates energy without electricity?" he asks.

Chun nods eagerly. "Yes, I have seen it with my own eyes."

"Stupid idiot!" Wo Fat hisses. "How can you expect us to believe the word of an ignorant peasant that such an invention exists?" He waves Chun away with a dismissive gesture of his hand. "Get out of my sight! How dare you waste my time with mere talk. You must bring us proof." He claps his hands and the thug drags Chun toward the door.

"But it is impossible! I cannot bring it to you," Chun stutters. "Wan Lo has given it to a professor at the University."

At a look from Liu, the thug releases Chun. "Go on."

"I followed him to Wing On University and watched him give the invention to Dr. Zhou Ping in the Science Pavilion." This is a lie. Wan Lo did indeed go to the University, but he did not leave the black box there. He brought it home and buried it under the wisteria tree. But seeing that he has the attention of both Liu and Wo Fat, Chun continues. "Wan Lo told the professor he must take it to Hong Kong, to present it to an esteemed scientist from the West."

Liu blinks impassively. "Do you know the name of this scientist from the West?" he asks.

Chun nods eagerly. "I wrote it here." He fumbles in his pocket and pulls out a scrap of paper. "His name is Dr. Leo Kensington."

HONG KONG

Friday, January 6, 1986

A STEADY STREAM OF PEOPLE pours into the Hong Kong Space Museum, a huge, pock-marked dome perched at the harbor's edge like a half-buried golf ball, under a banner announcing, "International Energy Symposium — Finding the Fuel of the Future — Guest Lecturer, Nobel Prize Winning Scientist, Dr. Leo A. Kensington."

Dapper in a charcoal gray pinstriped suit and sky blue shirt, Dr. Kensington himself admires the banner. He is bespectacled and portly, but projects the innate confidence of a man who knows he can affect the way the world works. Kensington is surrounded by an entourage of public relations officials and mobbed by Chinese reporters and conference attendees, all clamoring for his attention. In this milieu of technocrats, he is a celebrity, a god. Hands reach out as he passes, offering scraps of paper to be autographed, bits of food as tribute. He stops to accept the adoration of his public.

A bus pulls up to the curb in front of the museum and deposits a contingent of scientists dressed in traditional navy blue Mao jackets.

Professor Zhou Ping is one of the last off the bus. He is wearing a plastic tag which bears his name and the Wing On University insignia, a dragon holding a scroll. He joins the throng of reporters and fans around Dr. Kensington, burrowing like a rodent through the press of bodies to the front of the crowd. When his chance comes, he holds out an envelope. Misunderstanding, Kensington tries to scribble his name on it, but his pen has run out of ink.

"Do you have a pen?" he asks, looking up. But Dr. Zhou and his envelope have already been swallowed by the crowd. Exasperated, Kensington reaches for another paper to autograph.

A RED AND WHITE TAXI turns off Nathan Road and skids to a halt in front of the museum. An attractive Chinese woman in chic Western dress gets out. She is followed by a man carrying an aluminum camera case and two cameras slung over his shoulders bandoleer style. His dark features are chiseled, almost too perfectly formed, and his hair is slicked close against his head. He digs into his pocket and thrusts a few coins in the driver's outstretched hand. The driver responds with angry shouts.

"Ferdy, you haven't even given him enough to pay the tunnel toll," the woman remarks, assuming it is a mistake.

The man ignores her. He lights a cigarette and watches the commotion in front of the museum, distractedly running his thumb over the miniscule scars by his ear. "Hell of a crowd," he murmurs. "We have our work cut out for us."

Taking a last puff, he tosses the cigarette into the gutter. A deformed beggar pathetically splayed on the sidewalk plucks the prize out of the street, pocketing it for future use.

The man pins a plastic press pass to his jacket. "You go around to the back," he says to the woman. "I'll meet you there after." She nods, and he lifts the aluminum camera case and walks rapidly toward the museum.

The museum's vast auditorium is filled to capacity and buzzing with eager anticipation. The man moves unobserved toward the proscenium, keeping careful watch at his sides and rear. But all eyes are on Dr. Leo Kensington as he strides from the wings to the center of the stage. The man kneels beneath the footlights, watching and waiting, stroking his scars.

Suddenly the auditorium darkens, and a hush falls over the audience. For a long time nothing happens. Then whispers of confusion. Is this planned, or is it another power outage?

"Energy. One of the most important words in any language." Dr. Kensington's voice booms out of the void. "Without it we live in a world of darkness. With it, our lives are enriched by light."

A single spotlight appears over Dr. Kensington's head, bathing him in an ethereal glow. "Today our world is in danger of depleting known energy sources. Unless dramatic strides are made in the development of new energy sources, modern society will be plunged into another Dark Age. It's up to you, the scientists of the world, to work together to see that the light of civilization continues to burn brightly."

The lights of the auditorium come up, and the audience bursts into thunderous applause. The man kneeling by the stage has disappeared. But his aluminum camera case remains, unnoticed.

When the applause dies down Dr. Kensington continues. "For decades, the field of controlled nuclear fusion has been rocked by promise and problems. But we are now confident that within our lifetime we will be able to create a new generation of machines which will ignite fusion fuel for the first time, releasing controlled bursts of energy to harness the violent process that powers stars and hydrogen bombs."

Suddenly an explosion jolts the auditorium. Once again the audience is confused — is this part of the show? But when they see that Dr. Kensington has been thrown to the floor by the force of the detonation, they react as one body, in panic and fear, racing toward the exits.

Through the confusion, Dr. Zhou Ping strains to keep his eyes on Dr. Kensington. He scrambles up onto his chair and waves at the smoke swirling about him. Although his view of the stage is obscured, he thinks he sees four men in black on stage with Dr. Kensington. But then he is knocked from his chair, and by the time he climbs up on it again, the stage is empty.

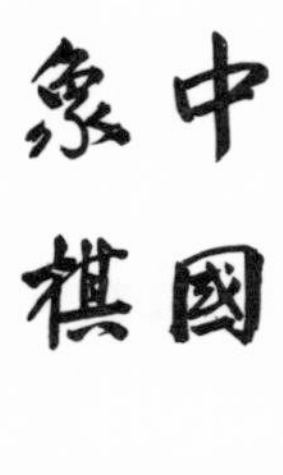

SEVEN

I'm a nervous traveler anyway, and raging prenatal hormones only made matters worse. So once we were airborne, I wasted no time locating the barf bag in the seatback pocket. I tried to ignore Lily, who was contentedly rummaging through her food box, unwrapping such enticing nouvelle edibles as herring with yogurt, squid ink pasta, and bean sprouts in pesto. She incanted the names of these delicacies as she ritualistically decanted them on her tray, unleashing pungent aromas in the close air of the cabin. The commingling of seafood, spices and fermented greens was more than my stomach could stomach. I closed my eyes and belched. A teaser of vomit burned the back of my throat.

"You okay?"

Lily must have noticed the chartreuse tinge on my cheeks because she didn't wait for me to answer, but once again plunged her hand into the gaping maws of her food box, and came up with a small vial of pills. "Maybe you'd better take one of these," she said, twisting off the top.

"What are they?"

"Cocculus Indicus — homeopathic dramamine," she replied, very proud of herself. "See here, it says 'safe for expectant mothers.'"

Later, the beast in my belly temporarily soothed, and Lily's sated with the food she'd brought, we reclined our seats as far as they would go and started discussing names for the baby. My choices were traditional: Peter, Jr. for a boy, Peter's mother's maiden name, Linden, for a girl.

Lily was more adventurous, suggesting a continuation of the 'river' theme begun by my grandmother, who named her daughter, my mother, Euphrates. "Nile would be a beautiful name for a girl with green eyes," she said, "Danube if they're blue."

"Or Amazon, if she's a big baby," I giggled.

What would Peter's reaction be to the news of little Amazon Matthews? As Lily dozed beside me, my mind ran rampant. The issue of children had come up between us a few times, but we'd never resolved it. The fact was, Peter acted spooky around kids. Once when I'd been late to meet him at the Santa Monica Mall, I'd found him waiting by the fountain, his back to me as I approached. Next to him, a four-year-old was balancing on the edge of the pool, trying to dip his tiny foot into the water. Suddenly the child slipped and fell into the water. He barely made a splash as he went under, disappearing beneath the surface with a thick whooshing sound.

Peter jumped up immediately, but rather than pull the boy out, which he could have done easily, he walked away, fast, without looking back.

The water wasn't deep and there were other people around. In an instant someone else had saved the child. But Peter had been the closest, and he had just walked away! I was horrified, and I had called him on it. To my surprise, he'd been remorseless.

"If you'd looked a little closer, you would have noticed that the kid was with a couple of gypsies," Peter had told me, his voice so cold even the memory of it sent chills up my spine. "It was a set up — the kid falls in the fountain, and while everyone's attention is distracted, they pick a few pockets."

"You don't know that for sure. What if he'd drowned?" I'd asked, shocked by his heartless indifference. But Peter had just shrugged it off.

"He wouldn't have. Trust me."

At the time, I'd let it go, rationalizing that he'd been an only child of a widowed, alcoholic mother who died when he was a freshman at USC, leaving him completely without relatives. He'd had no experience with children. More than anything I'd wanted to give him the joy of a loving family, the kind of secure, stable home I'd had myself. The fetus growing in my womb would provide my chance.

But, I thought grimly, timing was everything. Would I broach the subject before or after I asked Peter if he had murdered Fernando Ferrar?

The flight attendant announced that the in-flight movie would begin momentarily, and I pulled down the window shade, glad for a diversion from my troubling thoughts.

"What's playing?" I asked her, reaching for a headset.

"We're showing oldies this month," she replied. "It's the colorized version of 'The Bad Seed.'"

"I guess I'll pass," I said, handing back the headset. And I got up to go to the bathroom.

When I returned, Lily was awake. She was holding a small round object, rubbing its surface between her thumb and forefinger. "What's that?" I asked.

She put it in my hand. It was a beautifully carved cameo,

clearly very old, rubbed to a silken finish, no doubt by its passage through generations of hands. From the work I did carving bridges and inlays, I knew that the craftsmanship of this relic was exceptional.

"It's magnificent. Where did you get it?"

"My great-grandmother gave it to me before she died. It's been handed down through our family since the mid-eighteen hundreds, when our ancestor immigrated from China."

Lily rarely spoke of her heritage. After all, she was only about one-sixteenth Chinese. And she hardly looked Asian, with her henna-red hair permed into a froth of sloppy curls, her fair skin and dimpled body. In fact, I looked more Chinese than she did.

I examined the cameo. "It's too dark to be ivory. Is it some kind of stone?"

She shook her head. "Look closer."

I did. The face was Buddha-like, encircled by a halo of leaves which were accurately etched with veins and stems. The work was painstaking and impressively intricate, "Topaz?" I asked.

Lily shook her head and grinned triumphantly. "Peach pit."

"You're kidding."

She shrugged. "That's what my Amah said when she gave it to me. She told me I would some day return to the Middle Kingdom — that's what she called China — and there I would find the man who would become my husband."

"So that's why you're here? You thought you might as well give it a shot since nothing else has worked so far?"

Lily went through men like a Ferrari through a Jack-in-the-Box. And the analogy didn't stop there. The men she dated were like fast food — unhealthy choices from the bottom of the food chain, picked up on the run, ultimately leaving her with indigestion.

"What happened to that tall guy, Lionel? He was a chef too. I thought you two had so much in common."

"He was a *cook*. There's a big difference," Lily snorted. "It's like comparing tuna casserole to grilled ahi." She sighed. "That reminds me, we should eat the herring before it goes bad." She carefully put the cameo back in her pocket and reached for her box of goodies.

LILY SLEPT for most of the rest of the trip, but I stayed awake in growing panic. What would Peter say when I confronted him? If he admitted that he was having an affair with Lauren, what would I do? What would *he* do? To be so openly confrontational was wildly out of character for me, so I had no precedent to rely on. I was going out on a limb, and I had the feeling that any minute the bough would break — and down would go Karen, baby and all.

It was night when we arrived. The sky was black and impenetrable, with an equally dark ocean beneath it. But as the plane banked and made its final swooping dive to land at Kai Tak Airport, I saw out the window that a blanket of lights had magically appeared. And suddenly we were flying low, skimming the water like an ungainly seagull, between a gauntlet of high-rise buildings which thrust out of a blue-black harbor on either side of us.

I closed my eyes and waited to feel the thud of touchdown. When it came I added my silent thanks to the chorus of cheers that came from the passengers around me.

The arrival procedure at Kai Tak was in two parts: immigration and customs. Immigration was a long, slow process, a careful check of each person's passport number in a five-volume set of books, each as thick as the Unabridged Oxford Dictionary; customs was a breeze. Since we were carrying all our luggage with us we were among the first to approach the customs officers. Bored and unwilling to be bothered by actually doing their job, they merely glanced at our U.S. passports and waved us through.

"Amazing," Lily whispered, "we could have been smuggling drugs or diamonds."

"Mostly people smuggle stuff *out* of Hong Kong," I observed, "not in."

We slipped through the automatic exit doors and were released into a wide hallway where a horde of raven-haired people pressed forward, anxiously peering past us into the baggage area, looking for loved ones. Even though I knew it was completely impossible, I scoured the crowd hoping to see Peter's mustache and blonde head. But, of course, he wasn't there. And again I felt a wave of panic . Would he be at the Peninsula Hotel? Would he be angry that I'd come? Would he tell me the truth about Lauren? Did I really want to hear the truth?

We followed the signs directing us to "Hotel Transport," which led down a ramp and out of the terminal to an underground street. There, stretching as far as the eye could see, were cars, vans, and limousines of every imaginable color and description, honking and jockeying for position next to the curb, and emitting fumes so pungent that the air was practically unbreathable. All along the sidewalk were liveried attendants, whose jackets bore the insignias of the hotels they represented: the Hilton, the Mandarin, the Holiday Inn, the Shangri-La.

"What hotel you go?" demanded an unsmiling Chinese boy with *The Regent* embroidered on the pocket of his maroon jacket. He gripped a walkie-talkie in one hand and a clipboard in the other.

"The Peninsula," Lily told him. He pointed to a boy wearing an elegant gray and white striped tie. "Peninsula," he repeated, and hurried off to confront another arriving passenger.

Lily and I dragged ourselves the last few steps to the curb, and I smiled wanly at the Peninsula rep. "Peninsula?" I asked.

Wordlessly, he jerked the bag from my hand, and before I could object, stuffed it into the trunk of a forest green Rolls Royce. I must have looked stunned, because he frowned impatiently and repeated, "Peninsula?"

"Right, but — "

Lily gave me a push from behind. "Come on, it ain't gonna get any better than this." And she bent to get in the car.

I was too tired to object, so I followed her in and let myself sink into the plush interior of the Rolls. When the bags were stowed and the trunk shut with an expensive slam, the liveried boy gave us a receipt and closed the door.

"$400!" I read off the receipt. "That's impossible!"

"The conversion's eight to one, dummy," Lily said.

Even so, $50 was a lot to pay for a ride to the hotel, but I was too tired to fight.

The driver touched the brim of his cap in formal greeting. "Good evening," he said, making three distinct syllables out of 'evening.' "Welcome to Hong Kong."

"Thanks," Lily responded, "It's good to be here. How far is it to the hotel?"

"Yeah, yeah, yeah," the driver said agreeably, nodding his head. It was obvious he had exhausted his English vocabulary. All we could do was sit back and enjoy the ride.

Seeing Hong Kong through the tinted windows of a Rolls Royce gave me my first inkling of the dichotomy of the city. Around us was a jungle of neon lights and the cacophony of massed humanity — honking horns, blaring music, shouting people. No doubt the rich incense of oriental spices flavored the air. But insulated in the noiseless comfort of the Rolls Royce, we were spectators to the chaos, untouched by it, able only to watch the spectacle and dazedly wonder what lay ahead.

In minutes we were turning into a U-shaped drive in front of a stately moss-green hotel. I reached to open my door, but a small boy in a brass-buttoned white uniform, spotless white gloves, and a pillbox hat strapped beneath his chin beat me to it.

He bowed at the waist and tried to wrest my purse out of my hand. But no way was I letting go of my money and my identification. I saw that Lily had been similarly accosted and that she too, was hugging her purse to her chest. Undaunted, the two bellboys ran around to the trunk and hauled out our bags, dragging them up the steps and through a pair of enormous glass doors to the lobby.

"Should we tip the driver?" Lily asked as we trailed after our luggage.

"How should I know? It was your big idea that we take the limo. I hope you brought plenty of cash."

Inside, the Peninsula gave the same impression as the Rolls Royce — expensive, luxurious, exotic, sublimely insulated from external influences. Flanking the entry on either side were seating areas for the coffee shop, only it wasn't like any coffee shop I'd ever seen. Overhead, the ceiling was rococo gold leaf. Underfoot, the floor was pristine white marble. The chairs were tooled leather and brocade, and they were grouped around little marble-topped tables on carved rosewood bases, which were spread with immaculate, starched linen placemats, silver flatware, bone china and crystal goblets. On each table, a celadon vase held multiple sprays of flawless cymbidium orchids. I'd carried a single spray of cymbidiums as my bridal bouquet so I knew how expensive they were, and there were at least six on each table in this lobby. The roomful must have cost more than my whole wedding.

There was an army of uniformed employees. At one table two

waiters provided an audience for a third, who ceremoniously removed a silver dome from atop a plate and set what looked suspiciously like a tuna sandwich in front of a woman draped from head to toe in violet. She was wearing a hat with a gauzy veil, which covered her face and was clipped around in back with a purple-stoned jeweled pin the size of a small plum. Her companion, a dapper, bald-headed Asian, was ignoring the food, counting out his money on the table. The stack of bills was taller than his water glass.

"Occidental Insurance is footing the bill for this?" Lily whispered in awe. "No wonder Peter goes on so many business trips."

She had a good point, but I was sorry she'd made it.

"Checking in?" asked a handsome young man, one of four behind the reception desk. They were all identically dressed in immaculate black suits and gray and white striped ties, like ushers at a wedding. And their attitude was just as formal.

"No, my husband already checked in. I'm — we're — meeting him."

"I see. The name and room number, please?"

"His name is — " It suddenly occurred to me that I had no identification that I was "Mrs. P. Linden."

Lily came to my rescue. "Karen, what room did Peter say he was in, was it 502 or 205?" I looked at her blankly. "I knew you'd forget it if you didn't write it down." She turned to the reception clerk in feigned exasperation. "It's Mr. P. Linden. I *told* her she should write it down. Could you look it up, please? He came ahead of us, two days ago."

Without a word or a change of expression, the clerk turned to his computer and his fingers flew over the keys. Then he spent a long minute reading the information on the screen.

"Your name please?" he asked me unsmilingly.

"My name? I'm —" I stammered.

"His wife, Karen," Lily supplied.

To my surprise, the clerk beamed, suddenly responsive. "Ah yes, we had word that you were coming."

"You did?"

"It is my pleasure to welcome you to the Peninsula." He snapped his fingers for the luggage boys. "Mr. Linden is in Room 438. Shall I let him know you've arrived?"

"Oh, no, thank you. I wanted to surprise him."

"As you wish. Please allow me to show you the way."

"That won't be necessary. I'm sure we can find it."

Ignoring me, he came around the desk and bowed slightly. "Follow me, please."

We made a motley procession as we crossed the elegant lobby to the elevator: the clerk in his formal attire, Lily and I in our sleep-sodden sweat clothes, and the two small boys in their starched white uniforms, dragging our luggage. I knew people were staring at us, but I was preoccupied with anxiety. In mere seconds I would be face to face with Peter.

When the elevator doors opened on the fourth floor a bellman was waiting, standing as still as a flower arrangement. The clerk spoke to him in Chinese, and he jackknifed at the waist, then scurried off down the hall in a waddling, Chaplinesque shuffle. I dragged my feet, trying to postpone the inevitable.

The bellman rang the doorbell to 438, and without waiting for a response, turned his passkey in the lock. "No, wait!" I cried, as the door swung open. I didn't want to barge in on Peter like this. It was all wrong.

The boy stepped aside, eyes averted. "Anything you need Missy, my name T'ang." He bowed at Lily, then at the clerk. Then he shuffled away.

"T'ang is the room boy," the clerk explained. "He alternates with Zeng, on the night shift. You can call one of them twenty-four hours a day, for anything you need." He motioned to me to enter. "Please."

"Peter?" I called, my voice almost a whisper. There was no answer, so I stepped over the portal and into the room. "Hello?" my voice echoed emptily.

The suite was richly appointed, a far cry from the Hiltons and Holiday Inns I'd stayed in when I'd traveled, and huge — so large I could have run laps around it. A short hallway led to the living room, and I could see large bedrooms on either side. The furniture was antique, carved of rich red wood and covered in brilliantly colored silks. Everywhere I looked vases frothed with exotic flowers whose perfume scented the air, and even to my untrained eye the artwork looked authentic. Plus it had all of the modern conveniences — a two-line phone and fax machine, multiple televisions, a VCR, CD player and digital climate control panels. It had everything! Or did it?

No, something was missing. Specifically, *Peter* was missing. Nor was there any sign that this room had been occupied by Peter or by anyone else. It was cold and dark, with vacant air conditioned-air and drawn drapes.

"It doesn't look like anyone is staying here," I said to the clerk. "Are you sure this is Mr. Linden's room?"

"Yes, of course," he assured me. "He asked us to move him here, to the larger suite, this afternoon, in anticipation of your arrival."

"But how did he — " I began.

Lily cut me off. "I see. Well, thank you for your help." She opened her purse. "I'm sorry we haven't changed any money yet. Will you take — "

"It has been taken care of," he said, bowing his way out of the room. And then he was gone. Lily and I looked at each other in amazement.

"Something's wrong," I said. "This room must cost more per day than the monthly mortgage payment on our house."

"Maybe there's another P. Linden."

"You mean maybe this isn't Peter's room? She nodded. "There's one way to find out," I said, and headed for the bedroom. It was enormous and inviting. The luxurious bed was turned down, the pillows expectantly plumped, a Godiva chocolate on each immaculate white sham. I went to the closet and flung open the doors.

Hanging neatly on the brass rack were two familiar shirts, a pair of slacks, and the green suede jacket I'd given Peter for his birthday six months before. I stroked it lovingly.

"Well?" Lily asked, coming in behind me.

"Either this is Peter's room, or somebody's borrowed his clothes," I said.

We stared into the closet. "What do we do?" Lily yawned.

"What can we do? We wait for him to come back."

中國象棋

EIGHT

I woke with a start, dazed and disoriented, with no idea how long I'd been asleep or what time it was.The darkness of the room was suffocating and absolute, and I felt smothered by it. Where was I?

And then it came back to me. Hong Kong. Peninsula Hotel. Peter's room. I got out of bed quickly — too quickly obviously, because nausea hit me with the force of a blow to the gut. Whatever hour it was here, my biological clock was still on L.A. time, and my stomach responded accordingly with morning sickness. I groped my way to the bathroom and spent a good ten minutes barfing into the toilet.

By the time my nausea had dissipated, my eyes had become slightly accustomed to the dark, and the shapes and shadows around me began to make sense. Gradually, the events of the past evening came back to me. I must have fallen asleep waiting for Peter to return. Had he come yet? What time was it? Where was Lily? I got to my feet and stumbled through the bedroom until I found the door to the living room. When I opened it, I was hit with a blast of light so intense I had to shield my eyes with both hands.

"Good morning, sleeping beauty."

My heart stopped. With the sun ricocheting off my eyeballs I couldn't see him, but the voice was unmistakable. "Peter?"

His strong arms wrapped around me, crushing my exclamation into the soft cotton of his polo shirt, so that it came out more like "Prrr."

"Welcome to Hong Kong," he whispered in my ear, his mouth so close that his mustache tickled the nape of my neck. His body felt familiar and strong, his affection so natural and welcome, that for a second I forgot everything, and reveled in his nearness. As I leaned against his shoulder, my vision gradually cleared, and the beautiful room clicked into focus. The drapes were open, and the sunlight reflecting off the harbor exaggerated the dazzling brightness of the day. I saw that the glass-topped table by the window was covered with a white cloth and spread with a breakfast feast — fruits, breads, cereals, bacon, juice, coffee. My poor overstressed but empty stomach lurched uncomfortably.

"Is it morning?" I asked.

"11:02 A.M.," Peter replied. "You were dead to the world when I came in last night, so I thought I'd let you sleep."

I pulled back to look at him. He was so handsome, grinning at me with a smile that was both endearing and mischievous, his blonde hair tousled, his gray eyes twinkling with humor and expectation. I felt a jolt of longing. How could I even *think* this man might be capable of adultery, let alone be a party to murder? Whatever doubts were in my mind, my body had yet to be informed.

"You don't seem very surprised to see me," I said.

"I called home yesterday. Mitch told me you and Lily were coming."

But how had Mitch known Lily was coming with me? I hadn't know it myself until I'd gotten on the airplane.

"When I told you you should go away for a few days, coming

to Hong Kong wasn't exactly what I had in mind," Peter was saying, "but I'm glad you did. I got hung up at work or I would have met your plane. I couldn't even get to a phone. I'm sorry, Karen."

Why did it sound like he was apologizing for more than just getting hung up at work?

"We've got a lot to talk about." He took a step towards me.

I stepped back, strangely shy of my own husband, and unwilling to plunge into it all before I'd even brushed my teeth. "Where's Lily?" I asked, buying a little time.

"Still out like a light."

"She must really be tired if the smell of breakfast didn't wake her up." It was making my own stomach scream for mercy.

"Are you hungry? I waited for you."

I shook my head. "You go ahead. I'll check on her."

I opened the door to Lily's room and peeked in. It was dark, but the shaft of light streaming in behind me fell on her slumbering form, splayed diagonally across the bed. She was snoring lightly, her tangled curls framing her pale face like excelsior cushioning a piece of porcelain in a Tiffany box. I shut the door.

"Asleep?" Peter asked. He was layering smoked salmon on a piece of toast.

"Dead to the world," I replied. The oily orange translucence of the raw fish caught the light and my stomach tightened another notch. So I walked past Peter to the window and looked out. Beneath us was a huge round dome, an auditorium of some sort. Beyond, Hong Kong harbor bustled with maritime life: oil tankers sunk low in the water with cargo and ocean liners waving flags of many countries, tugboats and tramp steamers, double-deck ferries and sleek pleasure yachts. And interspersed among them, looking as though they'd sailed out of an earlier century, dozens of square rigged Chinese junks. I opened the window to get a better view.

Across the water, perhaps half a mile away, was the large land-mass I'd seen from the air — or was it land? From here it looked like solid skyscrapers, hundreds, maybe thousands of them thrusting upward, each an architectural miracle more impressive than the next, tributes to modern engineering and man's will to conquer nature. They blockaded the shoreline like a regiment of soldiers, pushing back from the harbor up steep slopes, to peaks where surprisingly lush greenery was thriving.

"You're looking at Hong Kong Island," Peter said, coming up behind me. "We're on Kowloon, which is part of the Mainland. The PRC is about fifty miles behind us." He put his arms around me from the back and rested his chin on top of my head.

I stiffened, torn between desire and dread of what would soon be coming.

"'Hong Kong' means 'Fragrant Harbor,'" Peter whispered close to my ear. I took a deep breath expecting to smell the exotic spice of Asia, and choked on rancid fumes rising from the street below.

"It smells like a sewer," I replied.

"That smell *is* the sewer." Peter pointed down to the street. Sure enough, a huge, ragged hole gaped in the pavement just below our window. The sprawling, unprotected construction site didn't seem to have any effect on the traffic which roared by in both directions, flirting dangerously with the edge of the open trench.

In fact, the traffic looked treacherous even without the added hazard of the open trench. As I watched, a taxi almost mowed down a pedestrian who was crossing against the light, causing the man to drop his shopping bags and leap to the curb. The taxi didn't stop, didn't even slow as it ran over a cantaloupe.

"Looks like traffic over here is a survival sport," I observed.

"Or population control."

"Peter!"

"I'm serious. Be very careful crossing the street. And remember, they drive on the English side."

"What's that thing?" I asked, pointing to the dome across the street, between us and the harbor.

"The Hong Kong Space Museum," Peter replied.

There was a pair of binoculars on the table. I picked them up and trained them on a banner strung across the entrance to the dome. "Finding the Fuel of the Future — Guest Lecturer, Nobel Prize Winning Scientist, Dr. Leo A. Kensington," I read aloud. "What's happening over there?"

"An energy symposium," Peter said. He reached past me to close the window and then drew the drapes. "It's over now. Anyway, I hope you didn't come all this way just to go to the museum." He put his hand at the small of my back and he ran it lightly up my spine to the base of my skull, clutching a handful of my hair to draw me into a kiss. Again I felt torn between wanting Peter and wondering what was going on in his heart. I'd traveled nearly seven thousand miles to find out the truth. That had to come first.

"We've got a lot to talk about," I said, pulling away.

"Could we start with some body language?"

I shook my head. "Peter, we need to . . ."

"Okay." He kissed me lightly on the forehead, then stepped back. "But not here. Let's go somewhere else."

WE BOARDED a double-deck green and white boat called the Star Ferry to cross the harbor to Hong Kong Island. The fare for the seven-minute trip was fifteen cents for first class and ten cents for second class. We splurged and went first class all the way.

As our boat plowed through the murky water Peter pointed out the sights, both of us avoiding any mention of why I'd come.

I listened to him speak, not really hearing the words, letting the rocking of the ferry lull me into temporary complacency. But in the back of my mind I realized that this might be the last time we sat side by side before the truth drove a wedge between us.

The ferry deposited us at a pier in the heart of the business district, and we walked through a forest of skyscrapers which were connected by a warren of covered overpasses and underground tunnels, insulating us from the traffic. Construction and renovation engulfed us. The city was like a living organism, sloughing off the old, building up the new, reinventing itself at breakneck speed. Workers in wicker hats mixed cement by hand, shoveled out foundations, and climbed thick bamboo stalks which were lashed together to form primitive, precarious scaffolding, creating new monoliths in every available square inch of space. Around them, men and women in business suits, tourists in tennis shoes and the local Chinese poured out of buildings in a continuous stream, drowning us in a liquid mass of humanity. The air was thick with their exotic conversation, isolating us, drawing us together.

We boarded a funicular tram which pulled us up a dramatic mountainside, The Peak. It was overgrown with vegetation, lush, almost tropical, and columned mansions as grand as any I'd seen in Beverly Hills were interspersed among the ferns, vines and flowers.

It was a long, steep ride up to the top, with abrupt stops on the way for passengers to board. Everyone else seemed to be enjoying the view, but I kept my eyes averted to quell my nausea, a reminder of the issue looming in my womb.

At the top, Peter led me to a wide jogging path. It was remarkably well-groomed, due no doubt to the crew of gardeners who were crouched in impossibly contorted positions, picking up bits of debris and fallen leaves by hand and stuffing them into ragged cloth bags. Their backs were hunched, some as rounded as the tops of candy canes. They wore conical straw coolie hats tied under their chins, and though I could not see their faces, I could feel their eyes staring at us from beneath the wide brims as we passed.

We stopped to catch our breath at a promontory which looked out over the harbor and across it to Kowloon. If my eyes had been good enough I probably could have seen all the way into the real China — it was that clear.

"We're almost there." Peter pulled me away from the view, and led me up some steep stone steps to a jagged outcropping of rock that rose forty feet high. It appeared to be a public shrine of some sort, festooned with tacky plastic flowers and tiny pinwheels which spun merrily in the breeze. Tourists of many nationalities as well as Chinese locals held hands and gazed out over the enormous jutting rock to the city far below.

"It's called Yan Yuen Shek," Peter told me. "Lovers' Rock. Supposedly it has magical properties that preserve love and marriage."

That got my interest. I followed Peter closer to the rock, hanging onto his every word.

"There's an old legend about a beautiful woman who was abandoned by her lover. In her grief she consulted a fortune teller. He advised her to offer prayers to this rock. She came up here and prayed, and as a result, her lover returned to her."

"Hooray for happy endings," I said aloud, wordlessly forming my own prayers.

An ancient, stooped soothsayer approached us offering his wares — incense, pictures of deities, more of the colored miniature pinwheels. There was only one green one, my favorite color. Peter gave the man some coins and handed it to me.

"I haven't seen one of those since I was a child," I said.

"It symbolizes the future. You hold it up to the breeze, and if it spins to the right, you will have good fortune. If it spins to the left, not so good." As we watched, a breath of air caught the spokes of the wheel and the toy whirled on its axis to the right. Then it caught another draft and switched directions, spinning to the left.

"I guess there's good news and bad news," I said with a lightness I did not feel.

"We'd better talk," Peter said. He had a strange serious expression on his face, the same one he'd had the night of Lauren Covington's aborted wedding.

"You first," I said. I wanted to hear his story before I told him mine. If he told me he was in love with Lauren, or that, God forbid, he had been involved in Fernando's murder, I would need to rethink whether or not I wanted him to know about the baby — or whether there would be a baby at all.

Peter led me to a stone bench, sat me down, and then settled beside me, throwing his leg over the seat to straddle it, facing me. "I might as well start at the beginning," he said, "back to when I first met Lauren."

The instant he said her name I stood abruptly. "I've changed my mind. I can't hear this," I said, prepared to bolt. I didn't know where I would go — back to the hotel, back to Los Angeles, as far as I could get from the sound of my husband's voice telling me he was in love with someone else.

But Peter shook his head and took my hands in his. "Please don't pass judgment on me until I've told you everything," he pleaded. "I need for you to hear me out. Then it's your call. Whatever you want to do, I'll understand. Deal?"

I couldn't look at him, so I watched a child crouch close — too close — to the ledge, and awkwardly throw one of the paper pinwheels over the side. Waiting to hear Peter's story, I felt as though I'd thrown my heart over the edge and it too was plummeting to the ground. But what choice did I have except to listen? I sat down again and tried to pretend that I could hear his confession without feeling that it signaled the end of our marriage.

"It started at USC, with that picture of me and Lauren in *Life*. I never told you how that came about, did I?"

I shook my head. "You just said it was a public relations stunt."

He nodded. "The press had been writing about me because the team was having a winning season and I was lucky enough to be quarterback."

Typical Matthews modesty, I thought. Peter was a gifted athlete, not a 'nerd who did sports,' which was the way he usually referred to himself.

"One day, Coach called me to the sidelines during practice, and told me to hit the showers, suit up in a clean uniform, and report to Tommy Trojan. He didn't say why, and I didn't ask." He shook his head. "I was conditioned to obey orders like a robot even back then.

"When I got to Tommy T., there was a crowd standing around watching a camera crew set up. And in the center of it all was Lauren Covington. I'd never met her or even seen her in person, but I knew who she was. Everyone knew who she was. Her sitcom was way up there in the ratings.

"Anyway, in person she was kind of disappointing, shorter and softer than she looked on TV. Her hair was sprayed as hard as my helmet and she had fat knees. Not my type at all, but then who asked me? I didn't even know what I was doing there."

I was relieved to hear Peter's description of Lauren. How could a man be in love with a woman he described as having fat knees? I felt a flutter of hopefulness.

He went on. "I just stood at the back of the crowd and watched the activity, until some jerk in a plaid sport coat spotted me. He introduced himself as Lauren's press agent and dragged me up to the line of scrimmage. 'Put your arm around her, it's just publicity,' they told me. 'Look at each other and say 'sex!' Before I'd even been introduced to Lauren they had us posed together in a clinch beneath Tommy Trojan, and the cameras started snapping.

"When they were through we joked around for a while, then she had to go. I thought that was the end of it, but after the picture came out in *Life*, her press guy called me, saying Lauren wanted me to escort her to a premiere. What was I going to say, no? At that point I was getting by on scholarship money. I would have gone just for the free food. Besides, she wasn't *asking* me to come, it was a command performance. Anyway, I went, and eventually we became friends." His voice dropped an octave. "Lovers even."

I wanted to put my hands over my ears and hum the Star Spangled Banner so I wouldn't hear anymore, but Peter kept on talking. "It wasn't serious. It was more of a fantasy to be with her — limos, Hollywood parties, movie stars, millionaires. When we were alone, we didn't have much to say to each other. Or at least I didn't. Lauren talked incessantly. I was the audience; that was my primary function, and I just accepted it. The truth is, I couldn't get close to her anyway because she was always afraid I was going to ruin her makeup or mess up her hair."

That was better. How passionate could you get without messing up someone's hair?

"I saw her pretty regularly for a couple of months. Then one night we went to a premiere of a low budget spy thriller she'd done during her show's hiatus, something called 'A.K.A. Poseidon.' It was typical Hollywood hype: photographers in front of the theater, second-rate stars jockeying for the status seats inside, a party afterwards with a loud, trendy band, tons of food and plenty of booze for everybody to hide behind.

"Lauren and I got pretty wasted, and when she suggested we drive down to the Santa Moncia Pier and ride the merry-go-round, it seemed like a good idea. I didn't stop to think that it was the middle of February and there would be no way the carousel would be operating.

"But oddly enough, it was. Lauren seemed to know her way around. She got me onto one of the carousel horses, then she disappeared, saying she was going to start the machinery.

"I sat there in the dark for a few minutes, realizing how truly drunk I was. I remember that it was a beautiful night, so still that I could hear the waves breaking on the beach and the tide lapping against the wooden pilasters beneath the pier. I could see the entire arc of Santa Monica Bay, Malibu to the north and Palos Verdes to the south. And I began to think about my future, laid out before me like the ocean, dark and silent, unfathomable."

I was mesmerized listening to Peter talk. In the years I'd known him, he'd never been so verbal. I didn't know where he was going with his monologue, but he certainly had my attention.

He continued. "Suddenly the carousel started to move, and with the motion, music came out of nowhere. The horse I was on drifted down, then rose in time with the calliope as the merry-go-round turned. It was probably partly the booze, partly the magic of the night, but I let myself go and just closed my eyes, leaning back, enjoying the air against my face and giving in to the sensation.

"And then a voice said, 'Mr. Matthews.' Just like that. A man's voice, someone on the carousel with me. I whipped around and there was this guy, tall, burly, wearing a three-piece suit.

"'Who are you?' I asked him.

"'I'm a friend of Lauren's,' he said.

"My adrenaline spiked, the way it did before a game. 'Where is she?' I asked him.

"'She's waiting in the car to give us a chance to get to talk.' He was calm, so deadly calm. It scared the shit out of me.

"'About what?'

"'Your future.'

"That freaked me out. How had he known I had been thinking about it myself? 'What the hell do you know about my future?'

"'I know that I'm offering you an opportunity to spend it serving your country.'

"'What are you, the local draft board? I didn't know you guys made house calls.'

"'I'm not from the Pentagon,' he said. 'But you're close. I work for the Central Intelligence Agency.'

"'You work for the CIA?' I repeated. He nodded.

"'Yeah, sure you do. And I suppose Lauren does too.'

"'That's right.'

"I laughed. I expected him to chuckle too, at the absurdity of the idea that Lauren Covington might be a spy. But he just looked me square in the eye, dead serious and as patient as a cat waiting for a mouse to make its move.

"'In case you hadn't noticed, Lauren is an actress on a sitcom,' I said to him. 'She has a pretty busy schedule. I don't think she has time to be a CIA spy.'

"'She's what we call a bird dog, a lookout for recruits. Being an actress is her cover. Quite a good one,' he added, 'don't you think?'

"'Her cover? That sounds like a line out of the crummy movie we saw tonight.'

"He shrugged. 'Art imitates life.'

"Then Lauren was back. She climbed onto the carousel horse behind me. I expected her to laugh and tell me it was all a big joke, smile, you're on "Candid Camera." But she didn't. She just sat there dead sober, looking mysterious and world-wise. And then she said, 'You'd be surprised how many people we know work for the company.'"

Peter stopped talking to search my face. I don't know what he saw there because my mind was numb. I'd come nearly seven thousand miles to ask my husband if he was involved with another woman. And he was telling me yes, they were involved, but not in a love affair, in espionage? "Go on," I said, disbelieving, but fascinated.

"The two of them took turns filling me in, trying to convince me to join up. I was stunned at how much they both knew about me, about my mother and my past. It was scary. But I have to admit I was blown away that all the time I'd spent with Lauren, all the months of seeing her, even the . . . you know, the sex, had been a build up to get me to join the CIA."

Peter stopped talking and just looked at the ground, waiting for me to say something. It seemed like it had been hours since I had spoken but my mouth was parched. "Let me just get this straight: you're telling me you're a spy, a secret agent for the CIA?"

Peter nodded.

"And you have been since college?"

"Just after. I trained the summer after graduation."

There were two ways I could look at it: either my husband had been duping me since we'd met by not telling me he was a CIA agent, or he was duping me now, trying to throw me off the track of his affair with Lauren, by making up this fantastic story. Neither alternative was appealing to me. All I wanted was for things to be the way they'd been — the way I'd *thought* they'd been — before Lauren's wedding.

"I've known you for three years. Why are you telling me this now?"

"Because I love you too much to keep on lying to you. When I told them I wanted to marry you they thought it was a good idea. It made a believable cover. But they were adamant that I not tell you what was really going on, and I was willing to go along with it. At the beginning I convinced myself it was okay, that I was protecting you by keeping you out of it. Lots of covert operatives, the majority, keep it secret from their spouses. But I never felt good about it. Never."

"Wait a minute. Back up. You had to *ask their permission* to marry me?"

"No, I told them we were going to get married."

"What else do they know about our private lives?"

Peter looked miserable. "Try to understand. It's what they do."

"Gosh, if I had known I was marrying you and the U.S. government, I would have insisted on a bigger wedding!"

Peter hung his head.

"So would you have told me all this if I hadn't followed you here?"

"I was planning to tell you when I got home. Because I'm getting out. I'm tired of being a pawn in someone else's chess game. The problem is, I'm good at what I do, and they don't want me to quit. But I've told them point blank this is my last assignment."

"You mean, you're here, on CIA business?"

Peter nodded.

"What is it?"

"I can't tell you."

"Oh, of course not. How foolish of me to think you might tell me the truth for a change."

"Karen, I am telling you the truth. I swear it."

"How am I supposed to know the difference?"

"You just have to trust me I guess."

"Don't you see, I did trust you. Silly me, I've been trusting you all along."

"That's why I was sure I could trust you now with the whole story."

That stopped me cold, but only for a minute."Then tell me how all this relates to Fernando Ferrar's murder."

Peter sighed. "Lauren was trying to recruit Ferdy. She'd been working on him for a few months. And then she found out he was undercover, deep cover, for the Central External Liaison Department. That's the foreign intelligence branch of the Chinese secret service. They keep watch on foreign agents and overseas Chinese."

"Fernando Ferrar hardly sounds like a Chinese name."

"It isn't. His real name was Pan Shu. He's a master of identities, the best they have."

I must have looked dubious because he continued, "This is serious stuff. People in this business will do anything to get information."

"Why was he killed?"

Peter shook his head. "He wasn't. It was a cacklebladder."

"A what?"

"A cacklebladder — a dummy corpse. Lauren had a plan to demote him maximally, but —"

"What? Speak English, God damn it."

Peter sighed. "To kill him. But he pulled a fast one. The guy she thought was Ferdy wasn't. He got away."

Now I was perplexed. "Then why did the police take Lauren in for questioning?"

Peter took both my hands in his. "It's better if you don't ask me any more specific questions. I'm not going to lie to you, but there are some things you're better off not knowing. Just believe me when I tell you I'm out after this. Finished. But I need for you to give me another couple of days. Can you do that? Can you wait for me? Karen, say something!"

My head was bursting with a million things to say but somehow only two words came out.

"I'm pregnant."

中國
象棋

NINE

Neither of us spoke on the way back on the ferry, but Peter held my hand tightly. In fact he hadn't stopped touching me in some form or other since I'd told him the news, telegraphing his emotional response to my pregnancy loud and clear through his touch and through the loving look in his eyes. If I could believe anything, this is what I wanted to believe.

"Tell me how you feel about what I told you," he said at last.

"Blown away, flabbergasted, frightened," I admitted. "And I don't know what to do about it."

He nodded, as though this was what he'd expected. "I feel the same way about what you told me," he said. "It's a lot to get used to."

"You're not kidding."

We lapsed into silence again, watching the boats around us in the harbor. If I accepted Peter's story it would certainly explain a lot of things about our marriage — the way he took off on sudden, unexplained business trips, his reticence about his work, his past, and his feelings, that stone-cold look in his eyes when I probed too deeply. And as much as I hated to admit it, I was relieved he hadn't confessed undying love for Lauren Covington. Anything but that. Well, almost anything.

But if Peter's story were true, what did it say about our relationship that he'd been able to keep such a monumental secret from me all this time? It would mean admitting that our marriage was part of a facade he'd built to hide the fact that his whole life was a lie.

"If this is true — and I'm not saying I believe it — how did you hide it from me all this time? Have I been asleep at the wheel, or are you just an incredibly good liar?"

Peter ignored the rancor in my voice. "The first test question a recruit is asked is 'Can you swear not to tell the person you are closest to that you are taking this test?' I guess I passed that one."

"Does anyone know?"

"Nobody who isn't in."

"You mean, there are other people we both know who are CIA agents?" I asked incredulously.

"Some."

"Who?"

"I can't tell you, Karen."

"Why not?"

"It would compromise their effectiveness."

"Oh, I see. You'd rather compromise the effectiveness of our marriage."

"Actually, I thought our marriage was pretty effective."

I ignored that one. "What made you such a good candidate for spy school?"

"I guess they felt I had a certain detachment that worked in my favor. Also my language skills and my athletic background played into it. It's surprisingly physical work."

The ferry docked and we got up to disembark. I was suddenly very weary. "Is there anything else you want to know?" Peter asked.

"What about your job? I suppose you don't really sell insurance."

"Occidental is what's called a 'proprietary' — it has real employees and goes through the minimum operations necessary to be functional. We do sell insurance, but most of our business is with 'notionals,' phony organizations that exist on company registration ledgers with letterheads and checking accounts, but produce no real product or service. 'Proprietaries' trade with and bill 'notionals' so they look good. Overseas CIA stations trade through them when they want transactions to be untraceable."

"Oh, that makes it all crystal clear!" I tried to pull my hand out of Peter's grasp, but he held it tighter.

"Karen, you love me, don't you?"

"It's not that I don't love you, but how can I trust you when you admit you've been lying to me virtually since the day we met?"

"Is that really it? Or is it the spy thing that bothers you?"

"Both! Obviously it doesn't make me happy that you're involved in a kind of secret, sleazy underworld —"

"It's not a sleazy underworld. It's very much the real world. It's simply a world you're not familiar with. That's one of the reasons I couldn't tell you about it."

"Some of the things the CIA has been involved in are horrifying."

"So is war, but do you hate soldiers too? What I'm doing for my country is just a variation of what a Marine does, or an Air Force pilot. And don't forget, our armed forces are voluntary these days. People get paid to fight in other countries, and they get paid well. What I do is based on putting a specially trained person in a situation where he has a goal to achieve, and certain obstacles in his path. I admit it's a rush. I have to be hyper-aware of myself and where I am and what I'm doing every single second. Success can depend on something as fragile as a change in the weather, or a whispered phrase caught in the wind."

"If you love it so much, why are you getting out?" I asked angrily.

"Because I love you more. Believe it, Karen."

I shook my head. "I don't know what to believe."

THE PENINSULA LOBBY looked like a stage set for a Noel Coward play. Schmaltzy music wafted down from the mezzanine balcony, and every table was occupied by women in silk dresses taking mincing bites of elegant petite fours, and men in immaculate three-piece suits smoking cigars and sipping brandy. I, on the other hand, was still wearing the grubby sweat clothes I had been wearing since I'd left Los Angeles thirty-six hours before. No wonder people stared and whispered as we passed; even the luggage porters were better dressed than I was.

Peter and I got on the elevator. "I suppose having a suite in this hotel is part of some big spy plan," I said.

"Right, just like in a James Bond movie," Peter said, and chuckled for the benefit of the other couple in the car with us, who I realized were listening. I shut up until they got off on the third floor.

"You're not going to tell me what's going on, are you?"

"Nope."

"Are you in danger?"

He squeezed my hand. "Not as long as my identity remains a secret. Do you understand what that means?" His expression combined love and concern in equal measure. "What I told you today is strictly between us. You can't talk about it. To anyone."

"Not even Lily?"

"Especially not Lily," Peter said. "I shouldn't even have told you." He squeezed my hand. "But I'm glad I did. I feel a helluva lot better. Like we're finally on the same team."

"Funny, I always thought we were."

The floor boy, T'ang, peeked out of his station by the elevator. Peter nodded to him and he scurried down the hall ahead of us in his peculiar duck-footed gait, sorting through his keys as he ran.

"What happens now?" I asked as we got out of the elevator.

"I'll get a call from the local contact and I'll do my job one more time. The last time. Then I'm out."

"Will they let you out? Just like that?"

Peter smiled indulgently. "This is the CIA we're talking about, not the Mafia. It's a government job, like being a mailman or a dog catcher."

"So why couldn't you be one of them instead?"

T'ang stood back from the open door and bowed at the waist as we passed. "You have laundry? You need towels? Soap?"

It wasn't a very subtle hint. "I'd love to get these washed," I said, motioning to my sweats, which looked and felt as though they could have walked to the laundry room under their own steam. I glanced at Peter to see if it was okay. The laundry charges in a hotel like this had to be exorbitant and he was normally frugal-minded.

"Sure, anything you want," he said. "It's on Uncle Sam."

T'ang nodded. "I come back," he said, bowing his way down the hall.

The comforting fragrance of bacon, eggs, and coffee hit me before I was all the way in the room. Sure enough, the small room service table we'd left that morning had been replaced by a much larger one near the window, and Lily was chowing down on an omelet the size of a deflated football. She was wearing one of the hotel's monogrammed white terrycloth robes and had a towel wrapped around her head turban style. A book was propped against her water glass and she was holding the fancy binoculars I'd found the night before. "Hey, you guys, where've you been? I ordered some food for you in case you didn't eat." She lifted two of the domed silver covers. "Asian style and American style, take your pick. They have the best soba noodles I've ever tasted."

"No thanks," I said, feeling my stomach churn at the sight of the congealed brown noodles. What I was craving was comfort food — cereal and sliced bananas, a bagel with cream cheese, or a cinnamon roll with thick white icing running down its sides.

"Sounds good to me," said Peter, sitting down opposite Lily. He picked up a pair of chopsticks and deftly isolated a particularly long, glutinous noodle which he sucked up with ease. Where had he learned to do that? Whenever we ate Chinese at home, he fumbled with the chopsticks like any good Presbyterian boy from the Valley.

"What're you reading?" he asked Lily.

"'*Chinese Nutrition for the '80s*,'" Lily recited off the cover. "'*Ancient Recipes for the Modern Palate*,' by chef Xiao Sang Ye. I can't believe some of these dishes." She leafed through the pages. "'Rice with Quince and the Tongues of Hundred Ducks.' I didn't even know ducks had tongues. I wonder if I can get them at Gelson's."

"Lily, could you tell us about that after breakfast?" I begged.

"That is breakfast," she said. "Listen to lunch, 'Scorpions with Tender Lotus Blossom, Turtle Meat Dumplings and Fried Milk.' I wonder how they fry milk."

"They freeze it, slice it, coat it in sugar, and toss it in a wok. They serve it at Gaddis. We'll go there tonight," Peter said.

"You've eaten at Gaddis?" Lily asked.

Peter nodded. "I try to go there whenever I come to Hong Kong."

My ears perked up. Peter never told me that he'd been to Hong Kong before. Was this a fabrication, or just another surprise revelation? "How many times is that?" I snapped.

"Three or four." Then he saw my face. "All before we met."

"You never talked about coming here," I said accusingly.

"No, Karen, I haven't told you everything I've done, every second of my life!" Peter's exasperation was building. We both knew we weren't talking about his trips to Hong Kong anymore.

"If you believed in our marriage you couldn't not tell me," I insisted. "That's what marriage is. You share things. You're on the same side, working together. How do you think I feel, knowing you were," I groped for a euphemism, "traipsing back and forth to Hong Kong all this time. God knows what might have happened to you on one of those trips!"

"I think we'd better talk about this later." Peter's tone had an edge to it, the way it did when his patience ran out.

"Why not now?" I prodded, ignoring the warning. "I'd really like to know, not just the easy things, but all the gory details." I curled my feet up on the couch and propped my head on my hand, staring intently at Peter. "Go ahead, tell me. I'm all ears."

Peter threw down his chopsticks and stared back at me, the fire in his eyes scorching the distance between us. "You know what your problem is, Karen? You refuse to see that the world doesn't orbit around you. There are other considerations here besides your ego and your life."

"Right," I said. "There's our child, beginning his or her life in my body right this very minute."

He sighed and shook his head, defeated. "I've got some calls to make," he said, and headed for the bedroom.

"Oh, I forgot to tell you," Lily piped up. "Someone phoned

for you, a woman named Cao. She wanted you to call as soon as you got back."

"Thanks," Peter said, and shut the bedroom door behind him.

"How did he take the news?" Lily asked.

"He was thrilled, can't you tell?"

"What did he say about Lauren?"

"Let's just drop it, okay?"

"Fine. As far as I'm concerned, it's dropped," she said, and went back to her breakfast, her book, and the binoculars.

I picked up the newspaper which had been delivered with Lily's feast and burrowed behind it. Normally I'm not much for the news. Reading about a fire in Philadelphia or an earthquake in Uruguay, news becomes digestible entertainment, like watching a movie on TV — the more disastrous the better. You become numb to the fact that these tragedies are actually happening to real people. But right now what I wanted was to become numb.

As I skimmed the *South China Morning Post* I imagined reading a story about myself: 'Woman Learns Husband Is a Spy' — Quote: He told me he was going away on business. Little did I know what kind of business. Unquote.

My mind was reeling. If Peter really was a spy, what kind of spying did he do? Was he smuggling secrets out of Communist countries? Was he shadowing state leaders or notorious international criminals?

Was he a hired killer?

I thought about the gun in the glove compartment of his Jeep. No way. Not Peter. He'd told me he'd never fired it. Then again, he'd told me he was an insurance salesman and that was a lie. What if he'd been sent to Hong Kong to assassinate someone? Could I love a man who killed for a living?

To make myself stop thinking about it I forced myself to read the lead article in the paper.

Explosion Halts Energy Symposium: A minor explosion rocked the auditorium of the Hong Kong Space Museum yesterday, during a lecture by Nobel Prize-winning scientist, Dr. Leo A. Kensington, forcing the audience to vacate the building. Although no official word has been received, sources at the Peninsula Hotel where Dr. Kensington was a guest, say that the esteemed scientist has not returned to his rooms, but is in the protective custody of the Hong Kong Police, until the culprit is caught and his safety can be assured.

THE DOOR TO THE BEDROOM flew open and Peter barreled through it, pulling on his green suede jacket. As angry as I was, something in me warmed. Whenever he wore the jacket, I knew he was thinking about me.

"I've got some business to take care of," Peter said coolly, his voice betraying neither anger nor remorse.

"What kind of business? Real business or funny business?"

"What about our dinner at Gaddis?" Lily asked.

"You'd better not wait for me," Peter said. "You two go ahead, and I'll meet you there if I can." And then he did something unexpected. He knelt beside me and kissed me square on the belly, just about the spot where the proof of our love was metamorphosing from a clump of cells into a person. I can't say I believe in embryonic intellect, but I know our baby felt Peter's fatherly love through the walls of my womb. I know I felt it.

"We'll wait and go to Gaddis with you tomorrow night," I said, "so you can pick up the tab."

Peter kissed me gently on the lips. "I love you," he said, and putting his hand on my belly added, "Both of you."

Tears sprang into my eyes. "We love you too." Wanting to

seal the tentative bond in some way, I pulled out the little green pinwheel he had bought me at Lovers' Rock, and tucked it in his pocket. "Here, make sure it keeps spinning to the right."

He squeezed my hand, and then he was gone.

"So if we're not going to Gaddis tonight, where d'you want to have dinner?" Lily asked as soon as the door shut behind Peter. Talk about a one-track mind.

"You just finished eating," I pointed out. "Don't tell me you're still hungry."

"It's not a matter of hunger," Lily said with exaggerated patience. "It's a matter of time. We only have so many nights in Hong Kong, and I don't want to miss a meal. I'm keeping a record of everything we eat, see?"

She showed me a notebook in which she'd entered what she'd just eaten under the heading 'Peninsula — R.S.'

"What's R.S.?" I asked.

"'Room service,' as applies to food, 'really slow' as applies to some people I know."

"I don't see here what flavor of toothpaste you used — or haven't you brushed your teeth today?"

"As a matter of fact, I have a special section for pills, medications and toiletries," Lily snapped. "Everything is important."

"Why don't you find us a good restaurant in one of your guidebooks," I said, gesturing to the pile of paperbacks stacked on the table.

"Those aren't guidebooks, they're cookbooks."

"You brought Chinese cookbooks with you from home?"

"Why not? I read them for pleasure, the way you read *The Journal of Dental Hygiene*."

"Very funny."

There was a knock at the door and before Lily or I could get up to answer it, T'ang let himself in with his passkey, nodding and bowing his way into the room. "I come laundry," he said.

"Oh, right." I jumped up. "Just a minute, I'll change." And to Lily I added, "Maybe T'ang can recommend some place for us to eat." She was eyeing him doubtfully as I shut the door.

中國象棋

TEN

Two hours later, we were negotiating our way up the gangplank of *The Dragonlady*, a wide, flat-hulled tourist boat featuring dinner cruises to Aberdeen Harbor. To say I was skeptical about this excursion was an understatement. Eating anything in my present state would be risky; attempting to dine on Chinese food of questionable quality (the $15 price included tax, tip, beverage, and the three-hour cruise), on a moving boat, seemed sure folly. But Lily was optimistic and excited, and I felt the least I could do was be a good sport. Anyway, it would help pass the time until Peter returned.

The gangplank was steep, and it pitched dizzily from side to side as we boarded with the other tourists. Even in the dimming light of evening, it was obvious that the boat was no luxury liner. She was a decrepit, oversized tug with a weathered prow and damp, peeling rails. The colored lights garishly strung above the deck reminded me that our Christmas tree was still up at home. I had planned to take it down after our anniversary, but by then I'd had other things to think about.

Like the Star Ferry, *The Dragonlady* had two classes of service. We were herded into the main cabin on the first class level. It was filled with rows of scarred, narrow tables, as though they'd raided an elementary school cafeteria. Ditto the silverware, china and glassware.

And either it was going to be a long, drawn out, multicourse event, or they just wanted to get it out of the way, because I hadn't even shrugged off my jacket before waiters began to file out of the kitchen with steaming trays of food.

Lest you envision a synchronized team of white-gloved butlers serving from silver salvers, let me be more specific. The waiters were a motley crew, adept at their work, but clearly untrained in the niceties of fine dining. Ours was a plain, stocky woman who, from a distance, looked like she was winking at us. When she got closer, I realized that her left eyelid was sewn shut with thick, red thread. Her bulk was amplified by the layers of sweaters and long underwear she wore beneath her shapeless uniform, making her look like a Chinese version of a bag lady.

If I'd had the presence of mind to speak when she plunked the first reeking dish down in front of me, I would have said 'nothing for me' and could then have managed to remain seated during the meal while my dinner companions poked at the variously textured clumps on their plates. But I was mesmerized by that red thread, and before I could open my mouth the plate was in front of me, and I'd made the mistake of glancing down at what had been euphemistically referred to as dinner.

"Some of the ingredients in these dishes don't look like they came from the four food groups," murmured Lily, pen poised above her notebook. She poked at a turgid lump with a chopstick. "I don't have a clue what to call this one."

We both watched as the diners around us attacked their meals with the gusto of hungry tourists who were going to eat no matter what they were served, for the simple reason that they had paid for it.

We watched the Asian woman across the table extract a stringy mass of chewed gristle from her mouth and set it on the table next to her. Not on the plate, mind you, on the table. Then she rooted around in there again and removed a jagged shard of bone, all the while keeping up a steady stream of conversation with the man sitting next to her, spitting little particles of food at him, which he seemed not to notice. "Have you ever noticed that with Chinese food, it's not what you put in your mouth that counts, it's what you take out?" Lily whispered.

"I think I'll get some air," I said, speaking as clearly as I could without breathing.

It was a great relief to stand and step away from the table, but my way out was blocked by a steward in a badly soiled uniform who objected loudly, and tried to bully me into sitting back down.

"No eat, no eat," I replied, holding my belly as though I was going to be sick, which wasn't far from the truth. He continued to shriek at me, but I stood my ground, staunchly refusing to return to my seat. Finally he relented and stepped aside, allowing me to pass, muttering loudly for the benefit of the other passengers, clearly insulted by my wastefulness and my lack of appreciation of *The Dragonlady's* hospitality.

The air on the deck was brisk and damp, and the view of Hong Kong Island, seen from the water at dusk, was thrilling. Although it was January 7th, you would have thought Christmas was still on the way. The buildings crowding the shoreline were emblazoned with displays of holiday lights that made Times Square look paltry. On one, a four-story high neon Santa was climbing up a chimney; on another, a twinkle-lit Christmas tree twice the size of a Sequoia was surrounded by multicolored gifts and toys. One whole building was wrapped with lights like an enormous Christmas present, bow and all. Another had motorized reindeer scampering across it, pulling what looked more like a '47 Chevrolet than a sleigh.

"This city must have one hell of an electric bill."

I turned to find an elderly American woman who had been sitting near us at dinner, staring out at the city. I guess I wasn't the only one with indigestion.

"Isn't it bizarre?" I agreed. "Especially since most of the people who live here aren't even Christian."

"It doesn't look to me like this has anything to do with religion," the woman observed. "Unless you consider commerce a religion."

I smiled. "I suppose to some people it is."

She let out a hearty chuckle, which suddenly turned into a dry heave, and she leaned over the rail to vomit. I felt my own stomach lurch.

"Are you all right?" I asked, trying not to look.

She nodded and waved me away, and I turned abruptly, before my body decided to play copycat. That's when I saw him, a short, stocky man, standing ghostlike in the shadows near the cabin, watching me. It was his hat that caught my eye, a black knit cap with a tassel on top, the kind American kids wear in the snow. But it wasn't snowing here. It had to be in the mid-60s. Even so, he had it pulled down all the way over his ears.

When he realized I was looking at him he ducked inside and disappeared. I walked around the bow to the other side of the boat and leaned on the rail, letting the salt spray tickle my face and the rocking movement lull me into a stupor. We plowed through the water at a slow speed, passing every kind of vessel imaginable. The shoreline ahead rose sharply from the water, as the city gave way to the outlying mountains, steep, jagged inclines upon which even the industrious Chinese couldn't erect a high-rise.

In the distance I could see the glow of a harbor; *The Dragonlady* was motoring toward it. Although we were still some distance away, music wafted through the air. In spite of everything, I felt, well, peaceful. Lily appeared at my side and we stood together, taking it all in.

"How was dinner?" I asked.

"I'm skipping the last seven courses," she replied, punctuating her pronouncement with a belch. "Maybe Hong Kong is going to be good for my diet."

She rooted around in her bag and pulled out the binoculars we'd found in the room. "These are infrared," she told me. "They even work in the dark. Why would Peter — "

"Don't ask me," I cut her off.

Together we gazed in awe at Aberdeen Harbor. A thousand or more junks were moored in rows along the coast. Like everything else I'd seen so far in Hong Kong, they were jammed close together. The waterways between them were filmy with oil and strewn with refuse, like streets in a bad part of town.

"Check that out." Lily handed me the binoculars and pointed in the direction of an enormous, elaborately illuminated boat in the middle of the harbor with the name *Jumbo* on the side. "That's where we should have eaten."

"It's a restaurant?" I asked, training the glasses on the boat.

"Yeah, a famous one," she said.

Sure enough, I could see white-clothed tables on each of three decks, and tuxedoed waiters scurrying between them carrying platters of food, as different from our own meal as Coq au Vin is from KFC.

"Supposedly they have phenomenal seafood," Lily said wistfully.

"You'd be crazy to eat anything that came out of this water." I handed her the binoculars — I was more interested in the local lifestyle than the tourist ship. Of course I'd seen poor and underprivileged people in the United States; we have more than our share of homeless in Santa Monica. But this was something different. The poverty here seemed to be culture unto itself, a culture in which the advances of the modern world didn't exist.

Each junk was a self-contained habitat. Laundry draped the wooden spars on which those curious moth wing sails would be rigged when and if the boats were used for transportation. The electric lights so abundant in the city were absent in this aquatic neighborhood. Kerosene lamps, small fires, and the rising moon provided illumination. Smells of cooking and trails of fragrant, garlicky smoke levitated above the decks of many of the junks; twangy music and the clipped inflection of Cantonese, both spoken and sung, seasoned the air.

Around and through the rows of moored junks, flat-bottomed sampans darted like bees pollinating a field of flowers, their owners the door-to-door salesmen of Aberdeen, offering vegetables, flowers, pots and pans, tools, and all manner of general household goods.

"That broker I dated, Jamie Walker, lived on his boat in Marina del Rey," Lily mused, trying to fit the scene before us into the framework of a world we knew — no small task.

"Girlie, girlie, you ride!"

A sampan bobbed next to *The Dragonlady*, and in it an old woman in a coolie hat clung to the rope ladder that dangled down from the deck where we stood. She was beckoning to us with a gnarled hand, smiling toothlessly. "Come, come," she begged. "Velly cheap."

I shook my head 'no' and tried to ignore her. But having caught my attention, she continued begging, "Come, come!"

Overhead a burst of light split the darkness and rained sparks on us. A fireworks display. Its brilliant and thunderous detonations drew the passengers of *The Dragonlady* to the far railing to watch, leaving Lily and me alone.

Lily was looking through the binoculars. "Karen, where did Peter say he was going tonight?"

"He didn't. He just said he had some business. Why?"

"On that junk over there. You won't believe it. There's a guy that looks just like him."

"No way," I said, taking the glasses from her. "Where?"

Lily positioned me facing a lone junk, one of few that wasn't moored to the others. Although it was dark, by using the special binoculars I could see it perfectly. On its forward deck a child squatted in a pot barely big enough to contain her little body while an older woman poured water over her. Next to them a father and son were mending nets. Or rather the boy was working, the man was smoking a long, thin pipe and staring back to the rear of the boat.

"I don't see him," I told Lily.

She grabbed the glasses from me, scanning the scene until she saw what she was looking for. Then she pulled me into position to see.

On the aft portion of the same junk two men were standing by a small fire. One of them was wearing a green suede jacket. I focused the binoculars on his face. It was Peter!

"Look there!" Lily pointed.

An elaborate motor launch powered by three outboard motors was speeding toward the junk, its flat bottom slapping angrily against the water as its hull severed the waves. Two men stood at the helm, the wind whipping back their hair. One of them held a machine gun. "Oh, my God! The guy in the launch has an Uzi!"

"Lemme see!" Lily tried to pull the glasses from me, but I jerked away and swung them back to the junk in time to see Peter and the other man duck out of sight.

The approaching launch cut its motors and drifted toward the junk. When another round of fireworks burst overhead, I saw the two boats side by side. It was surreal, like seeing a Ferrari parked next to a covered wagon. The dinner music from *Jumbo* faintly echoing "I *Left My Heart in San Francisco*" added to the Felliniesque atmosphere.

In L.A. it wasn't uncommon to encounter a scene like this — and a film crew filming it. I'd often stood behind police barriers and watched a robbery enacted, or a high speed chase. Once I saw a man free fall from a ten-story building. One moment he'd been chatting up the crew, coffee mug in hand, the next he was on the ledge of the building, hurling himself into space. It hadn't been all that scary, because I could see what was excluded from the camera's eye, the six-foot-high inflated pad he landed on.

But this was no movie — there was no camera or crew, no lights, no director, no inflated pad. Just the actors, playing out their roles for an audience of two, for Lily and I were the only people who could see, thanks to the night vision binoculars.

Suddenly machine gun fire pierced the air. It was so sharp and terrifying that I dropped the binoculars. Instinctively Lily and I both grabbed for them, but they disappeared over the rail.

I expected to hear a splash, but heard a thud instead. The binoculars had landed squarely in the lap of the old crone in the sampan. She gave a little cry of surprise and delightedly examined her windfall.

"Here, please," I stretched as far as I could over the side.

"Those are mine!" The old crone ignored me. Clearly, in her world, possession was 100 percent of the law. She stashed the glasses in a large straw basket and bent over the small outboard engine at the back of her boat to start it.

Across the water, the motor launch was now speeding away. The junk swayed in its wake, but on board there was no movement. Before I knew what I was doing, I was shimmying down the rope ladder, dangling in the air above the sampan. Relying on luck, I let go of the rope and dropped the last few feet, landing with a thud that rocked the shallow boat.

"What are you doing!" Lily called shrilly.

The old lady stared at me. I saw disappointment flicker in her eyes. Then she reached into the bamboo basket, removed the binoculars, and held them out to me.

"You take me there?" I pointed to the junk. "Fast!"

"You're crazy!" Lily shouted.

Apparently, the old crone didn't think so. She smiled at me and rubbed her fingers together, the universal gesture that compensation was expected. I jerked some bills out of my pocket, not bothering to check the denominations, and offered them to her. "Please hurry," I begged, gesturing toward the junk. "Hurry!"

She took the time to smooth the bills, examining them one by one, then folded them and stuffed them inside her shirt. Then she turned to her engine.

"Karen, you can't do this!" Lily cried.

"I have to," I replied. The old outboard sputtered to life, and at the same moment, Lily hurled her body over the railing, half climbing, half falling into the sampan.

"Well, you can't go alone," she said, brushing herself off.

We seemed to be moving in slow motion across the wet distance that separated us from the junk. I kept the binoculars trained on the junk. It was deathly still on board; there was no sign of life. At last the sampan butted against its rough wood bulwark. I looked around for a rope ladder, but saw instead foot-long slats of wood nailed horizontally to the hull. Apparently, it was the only way up. Well, if I could negotiate a rope ladder, I could do this.

"Wait here," I said to Lily, "so she doesn't split on us." Lily nodded uneasily, gripping the sides of the sampan.

"Be careful," she said.

Ignoring the splinters from the decayed wooden hull, I began to climb. It wasn't as hard as it looked, or as far up to the deck. The trick was not to think about what I was going to find on board. At the top I maneuvered my right leg over the rail, and then my left, looking around as I did. The deck was deserted.

Or so I thought. By now it was completely dark, and all I could make out were ominous and unfamiliar shapes. As long as none of them moved, I figured I was okay. I unhooked a kerosene lamp from the cabin wall and held it in front of me. In its dim light I could see evidence of the brief gun battle — bits of splintered wood, and, to my horror, a dark, wet stain. It could have been caused by any liquid, but as I calculated the equation, machine gun fire plus dark, wet stain equaled blood.

I followed its grisly trail into the cabin, moving slowly, foot in front of foot, until I stumbled and fell over something blocking my way.

I screamed and scrambled off it to one side, more surprised than anything. But when I saw what it was, I screamed again, this time from terror.

It was a body.

"Karen? Oh my God! Are you okay?" Lily called from the sampan. Her voice sounded distant, unreal.

I couldn't answer. The horror of tripping over a corpse was

bad enough, but the thought that it could very well be Peter immobilized me. All I had to do was move the lantern twelve inches closer to see the face, but I couldn't do it. I leaned against the wall, transfixed by fear that the dead man lying next to me was my husband, the father of my unborn child.

Suddenly, a chill ran up my back, and I knew the dead man and I were not alone. I dared to shift my eyes just slightly, and I saw them — the man and the young boy, the baby and the mother, all huddled together in the corner, eyes wide with fear.

A loud thud on the deck made me look away. "Karen? For God's sake, where are you?" Lilly called.

"In here," I replied in a loud whisper. "But don't come."

Ignoring my warning she barged into the cabin and tripped over the corpse just as I had, falling on top of it with a grunt of surprise.

As I instinctively reached to break her fall, I knocked over the lamp, and before I could right it, some of the kerosene leaked out on the rotting floor boards. I jerked the flame away from the dangerous puddle, unintentionally illuminating both Lily and the face of the body she was lying on. To my relief, I saw that the dead man was clearly Asian, not Anglo, definitely not Peter.

"Are you okay?" I asked Lily.

"Yeah, I guess," she mumbled, balancing herself on the man's torso, trying to get her bearings. Obviously she hadn't identified the nature of the soft cushion on which she was leaning.

"Don't freak out," I warned her, speaking calmly to lessen the impact of my words, "but you're lying on a body."

"Jesus!" she cried, and scuttled to my side.

"Don't worry. He's dead."

"That's supposed to make me feel better?"

"What I mean is, he can't hurt you."

"He who?" she asked, crowding behind me.

"I don't know." I took a deep breath and held the lantern out over the face so I could get a better view. The man's two most distinctive features were his thick black hair, now matted with the blood which had oozed from holes sprayed across his temple, and his horn-rimmed glasses, which were held together by a thick wad of tape at the bridge. Surprisingly, the frames were still on his face. But the lenses were shattered.

"It could have been Peter," said Lily. Then seeing my face, she added, "That guy we saw probably wasn't even him anyway."

"Yeah, right," I agreed. But I knew Peter had been on the junk, because when I'd seen the little boy huddled in the corner behind us, I'd noticed that he was clutching the bright green pinwheel Peter had bought me at Lovers' Rock.

中國象棋

ELEVEN

The sampan returned us to *The Dragonlady*, and we climbed on board. Outside of a few surprised looks from other passengers, no one seemed aware that we'd left the ship, let alone what we'd just witnessed. But then, it had been too dark to see with the naked eye, and the machine gun fire could easily have been confused with the noise of the fireworks display. If I hadn't seen the dead man with my own eyes I could have believed it was all a product of my imagination.

But I had seen the bloody holes in the man's head, and I'd inadvertently pressed myself against his inert but still warm body when I tripped over it. Someone had killed a man, and Peter had been a witness.

Or had he done more than witness the crime?

I reviewed my options. Peter hadn't seen me, and didn't know I had seen him. So when he got back to the hotel I could act as though nothing had happened. But what if he didn't mention that he had been in Aberdeen? Would I be able to, should I accept what I knew to be a lie?

Or, should I put him on the spot, tell him what I'd seen and ask him what I desperately needed to know — did his spy work involve killing? Peter was good with a gun, I knew that. Once he'd gone shooting with a couple of neighbors and come home with a bag full of doves, their tiny feathered bodies hardened to the touch. If he could target and shoot a bird in flight, then he must have the expertise to shoot a human being. The question was, did he have the cold-blooded detachment to commit murder? I could never, ever live with someone who killed for a living.

But maybe I had been doing just that for my whole married life without knowing it.

There was no message from Peter when we returned to the hotel, no sign of him in the room. The suite was immaculate, the drapes drawn for the night. The sight of it calmed me. I'd let my imagination get away from me. As soon as Peter got back he would explain what had happened on the boat, and it would all make the same perfect sense as this tranquil room.

Except for the dead man. He could not be explained away, and he certainly hadn't been a figment of my imagination. I realized I still had his blood on my hands, so I went to wash.

When I came out of the bathroom, Lily had reopened the curtains and was reading the room service menu, which for some reason set me off. "God, don't you have that memorized yet?"

She looked up at me, hurt. "I was just going to order something for you. You said you were hungry, and you've hardly eaten a thing since we left L.A. It can't be good for you, or the baby."

I flopped down beside her on the couch. "You're right," I said. "I'm sorry. Feed me." But how much would I have to eat to obliterate the picture of the dead man from my mind?

The phone rang, startling us both. I grabbed for it. "Peter?"

There was only static, then a man said, "Karen? Is that you?"

It was a familiar voice, but not Peter's. "Mitch? Is everything all right? Is Hermie okay?"

"Relax, everything is fine here. I just wanted to make sure you got there okay. You said you'd call when you got in, so when I didn't hear from you I got worried."

"Sorry, I've been . . . distracted. We got here with no problem. In fact, I'm glad you told Peter we were coming, because we didn't even have to hassle getting into his room."

"Wait a sec. I didn't tell Peter you were going to Hong Kong. I haven't spoken to him since Christmas Day. And who's 'we'? You keep saying 'we.'"

"Me and Lily. Oh, I forgot, you didn't know. She decided to come with me."

"Good, I'm glad you're not traveling alone. What did Peter say about the murder?"

"How did you know about it?" I asked, thinking about the man on the junk, amazed that word could travel so fast.

"You told me, don't you remember? Geez, Karen, what have you been doing, smoking opium? Don't you remember Fernando Ferrar?"

"Oh, oh, oh. Fernando. Peter said it wasn't him after all."

"Karen, this is all getting very complex."

"Well stay tuned, big brother, you haven't heard the half of it." And I told him what we'd just witnessed in Aberdeen.

"If Peter's not back by morning, call the American Embassy," he counseled. "If the local authorities have picked him up, you'll want to make sure our team gets into the act ASAP. After you call them, just stay put. I'm going to make some calls from this end."

"Thanks, big brother."

"There's something else," Mitch said. "I got the autopsy results. Fernando — whoever it was — didn't die when the car exploded. He was already dead, poisoned with a compound of lyophilized tiger snake venom and some obscure chemical that causes it to penetrate human tissue on contact."

It was a relief to know that Peter's gun had not been involved. "That's good news."

"What?"

"I mean, who poisoned him?"

"They don't know yet. Apparently someone painted the stuff on the steering wheel of his car. He got in and drove for a while. It took effect gradually, and when it did, it killed him. We're talking about a very sophisticated poison here, not something you can buy over the counter at Sav-On."

"So it was murder!"

"Definitely. Premeditated and professional. Whoever was responsible has access to some serious toys."

"Do they have any leads?" I asked, meaning anything that would lead them to Peter.

"Not that anyone will tell me. But I'll keep nosing around. I'm going to be in court all day tomorrow, so it may take me a couple of days to come up with anything," Mitch said, "but I'm on top of it."

"Did that homicide detective come back around?"

"Not yet. But don't worry about him."

The door buzzer sounded. Room service, I thought, or maybe the floor boy with some more towels. Lily got up to answer it.

"Call me when Peter gets back," Mitch was saying. "I want to talk to him."

"I'm sure he'll be here any minute," I said, trying to convince myself that neither of us had reason to be worried. "In fact, it might be him right now."

But Lily was ushering an attractive Chinese woman about my

age into the room. She was coolly stylish, with perfectly straight shoulder-length hair and a reed-slender size two figure. She followed Lily to the sofa and sat, or rather perched delicately on its edge like an exotic bird, looking at me.

"Mitch, I've got to go. I'll call you when I know something," I said. "Give Hermie a kiss for me."

"Don't forget to call Jae —" he was saying as I hung up.

"I will — I mean, I won't forget."

"Karen," Lily said, in a phony formal voice, "This is Cao. She called earlier for Peter. Remember, I told you?"

"Oh yes, sure. Nice to meet you." I hauled myself up off the couch and shook hands with the woman. Her fingers lay delicately, like a piece of lingerie in my hand, making me feel strangely masculine.

"Mrs. Matthews, I'm very pleased to meet you too. I am a local representative for your husband's company." I froze. Did that mean she was with the CIA too? "I have been working with him on this trip," she continued. Her English was perfect, with just enough of an accent to make it interesting and exotic. "I'm terribly sorry to bother you so late. Discreetly she glanced around the room. "I was hoping to find Peter here." She smiled. Of course, her teeth were flawless too.

"He's not back yet," I said, and her expression clouded. "In fact Peter told us he was going to meet with you tonight."

Cao frowned. "Yes, well, that was what I thought too, but he never showed up. I've been waiting for him at the office since seven o'clock. Perhaps he misunderstood, or perhaps I did," she added quickly. "Did he say where he was going to meet me?"

"I don't think so. Did he, Lily?"

She shook her head. "He just said to go ahead and have dinner without him. We were supposed to go to Gaddis."

"You don't have any idea where he went?" Cao asked.

I looked at Lily. Should we tell this stranger what we'd witnessed? I had no way of knowing what her relationship was with Peter. But if Peter was in trouble we would need help. "As a matter of fact . . ."

Cao listened to my story with rapt attention. When I got to the part about stumbling over the corpse, she delicately averted her eyes and did not raise them again until I stopped talking.

"I am very disturbed by this," she said gravely, "but I am not surprised. Your Peter is most confident of himself and his methods. Sometimes he does not stop to question if the risk he is taking is merited by the reward he might gain."

"What risk, and what reward?" I asked.

She looked at me intently. "Mrs. Matthews, may I speak frankly? This is a matter of the utmost urgency."

The fist of anxiety in my stomach tightened. "Of course," I replied.

"If Miss Pullen would excuse us —"

"Anything you have to say to me, you can say in front of Lily," I said firmly.

Cao looked from me to Lily, then back again. "Very well. I presume you are aware of your husband's affiliation with the CIA." She said it as a statement. What could I do but nod?

Lily was less restrained. "You're joking, right?" She looked from me to Cao and back to me. "You're not! The CIA! Holy shit, Karen, Peter's a CIA agent and you never told me? Oh my God, this is incredible!"

I shot Lily a look that said shut up, and she did. "Are you with the CIA too?" I asked Cao.

"I work with your government, yes, but in a different capacity than Peter," she replied evasively. "Did he tell you why he came to Hong Kong?" I shook my head.

"His assignment was to locate and retrieve some critical scientific data, which was passed by an American physicist into the hands of the Chinese several years ago. Through an informer in China, we were able to trace the location of the data to the city of Fuchow in the Fujian Province. The plan was for Peter to go there to get it. Because of the sensitive nature of the operation, he would be a blind asset, which means he would be unknown to local CIA. In other words, he would be working completely alone."

Cao stood and walked to the window, gazing out at the harbor. The riot of lights decorating the buildings across the water reflected on the smooth skin of her face, dramatizing her words. "He was to go by junk at night, tonight, to be specific, so he would not be detected."

Her words rang ominously in my head. So Peter was not coming back tonight, had never intended to come back to the hotel. Once again he'd disappeared without telling me where he was going or when he would return, and only hours after he'd promised never to lie to me.

Cao continued. "This afternoon I received an emergency communiqué from our informer in Fuchow. He told me that word of our plan had been leaked and the operation was in jeopardy. You see, there are some who want this data to remain in China. They would go to any lengths to keep us — the U.S. government — from taking it back. When I called Peter late this afternoon, I told him we had a problem, and he agreed to meet me this evening to discuss it. But he never showed up. Now, after what you have told me, I know why, Mrs. Matthews," she sat next to me on the couch and looked into my eyes, "Karen, if Peter has gone ahead with the plan, he is surely in grave danger, and most certainly he isn't even aware of it."

"These other people who want the data, what will they do to Peter if they catch him?"

"You saw a man shot tonight in Aberdeen because of this." Cao bowed her head. "There are many other unspeakable ways to die."

The word 'die' ricocheted round the room, expanding and sucking all the oxygen out of the air. I coughed, a shallow, dry wheeze, and gasped, "I need some water."

I went into the bedroom, closed the door and sat on the bed, my mind reeling. At least some of the facts of Cao's story coincided with what Peter had told me, which meant there was a possibility that her story was true, and his life was in danger. But it felt so unreal. Things like this didn't happen to people I knew. But then where was Peter? Why had he been on that junk in Aberdeen, and why hadn't he told me that he wasn't coming back to the hotel tonight?

I opened the bar refrigerator to get some bottled water, and staring me in the face was a folded piece of hotel stationery with a Chinese character drawn on the front. I opened it and read,

> *Dear Kar,*
> *This is REN, the Chinese word for 'people.' As you can see it's made up of two leaning strokes, mutually supporting each other. If either stroke is removed, the other will collapse. What I'm trying to say is I need you. I have to go into the PRC to finish what I started. But I will be back. Believe in me. Wait for me. I love you.*
>
> *P.*

Lily padded into the bedroom. "You don't really believe her story, do you?"

"Yeah, I do."

"Then you're more gullible than I thought."

I handed her the note. She read it quickly. "So maybe he is in China. But come on, the CIA?"

I shrugged. What could I say?

We returned to the living room and sat down. Cao looked at me expectantly. "If Peter is in danger, why doesn't the CIA intervene?" I asked. "He's only acting on their behalf!"

Cao lowered her eyes. "There is a saying, 'When the oyster and the heron fight, the fisherman benefits.' In this case the CIA is the fisherman."

"You mean Peter is expendable, as long as they get what they want?"

"I would not put it in exactly those words."

"Karen, I think we should call somebody, like the American Embassy or something," Lily said.

Cao shook her head. "I am afraid they will disavow any knowledge of him. In any event they would not be able to help because Peter is not traveling under the auspices of the U.S. government. Once he goes beyond the boundaries of Hong Kong into China, American laws and customs will cease to apply."

"There's got to be something we can do to warn him." Lily looked from Cao to me.

"I agree," Cao said earnestly. "Please understand, I would go to Fuchow myself, but I cannot return to China. I did not leave my homeland under the best of circumstances." She did not elaborate.

"Is there anyone else who could go?" Lily asked. "Some other agent?"

Cao shrugged. "It would have to be someone who knew Peter, someone he trusted, someone who could cross the border and travel within China without arousing undue curiosity. That's why

Peter was assigned to us in the first place, because he was not known in China." She sighed. "Apparently, that is no longer the case."

The three of us sat in silence, gathering our thoughts.

"How hard is it for an American tourist to go into China these days?" I asked cautiously.

Cao cocked her head. "There used to be many restrictions on tourism, but now it's only a matter of getting a visa, which can be accomplished in several hours."

Lily had read my thoughts "You want to go?" I nodded. "Oh, no. Karen, come on!" she stormed. "Don't you think it would be just a little bit dangerous?"

I didn't say anything.

"I agree with Lily," Cao said firmly. "This is a treacherous business. It would be foolhardy for you to attempt it." She pursed her lips. "You have no experience in these matters."

"But you just said it should be someone who wouldn't arouse curiosity. No one would suspect me."

"If they're after Peter, they'll know you're his wife."

"Not if he's using the name P. Linden," I reminded her. "Is he?" I asked Cao. Reluctantly, she nodded. "Well, my passport says Karen Matthews." Cao said nothing.

"Look, somebody has to warn Peter. Why not me? I can't just sit here twiddling my thumbs, knowing my husband's life is in jeopardy when there's something I could be doing to help him."

"There are a billion people in China," Lily pointed out. "How on earth do you expect to find him?"

I looked at Cao. "If he followed our plan, finding him would not be so difficult," she conceded. "An aunt and uncle of mine live in a tiny village outside Fuchow, and Peter was going to them, to use their home as a safe house while he made arrangements to collect the data. It would be a fairly simple matter to meet him there and warn him, unless . . ." her voice trailed off.

"Unless what?" I demanded.

"Unless it's already too late."

3

FUCHOW, CHINA

Sunday, January 8, 1986

"YIEEI!" Chun Sok Lee jerks his hand out of the nest of his largest Qing Yuan hen. She is a mean one, this old girl, constantly warning him away from her eggs with vicious pecks of her scarred beak.

The other hens, though wary of his presence, allow the removal of eggs from their nests, as long as he replaces them with the smooth, rounded stones he collects from the stream and warms at his hearth, a technique passed down through generations. But this particular hen seems to know the difference.

By raising chickens, the Chun clan survived the cyclical famines that decimated China's population through many dynasties, and prospered when times were better. But during the Cultural Revolution, Chun's parents were forced to turn over their poultry business to the state, and three of their sons and one daughter were taken from them and reassigned to work cadres in the far corners of China.

Only Chun, who had been an infant at the time, was spared. He had learned the trick of the warm stones when he was six years old. The family had only a few Qing Yuan hens left, and they were scraggly and poor. But the cock, a black-skinned Zhusi, who marched proudly across the dry dirt farmyard, seemed not to know the difference, and his presence inspired the hens to profligate laying.

Chun's current rooster is a relation to that proud bird, but like Chun, he is tortured by the obstinate Qing Yuan hen. Often he must fight with her for his share of grain, and his ragged feathers bear testimony to many lost battles. Denied his rightful place in the pecking order, the cock has little use other than as a sentry.

Now he crows a warning as an automobile scuttles up the rutted road, raising a cloud of dust. Motorized vehicles of any sort are rare in the neighborhood, and Chun recognizes this one immediately. It is a Red Flag sedan, a luxury car produced in a truck factory in Changchun, in the northeast. Since a mere two hundred are built each year, they are sold only to high officials and to those few individuals who have the personal wealth and the guan-xi — connections — to obtain them. There is but one of these automobiles in the whole of the Fujian Province, and it belongs to Chun's employer, Wo Fat, owner of the Superior Eel Hatchery, and Dragonhead of the T'ung Yu Triad.

Chun ducks into the shadowy gloom of the hen house and peers through a crack in the earthen wall, watching two of Wo Fat's massive bodyguards emerge from the Red Flag. His heart pounds wildly. Are they coming for him? There is nowhere to run; Chun can only wait, and pray for mercy.

But the two thugs do not approach his hut. Instead they swagger to Wan Lo's side of the courtyard. Without warning, one kicks at the flimsy wooden door with his booted foot, breaking it off its hinges. Although his vantage is obscured, Chun manages to glimpse the expression of surprise in Wan Lo's eyes as he turns away from his scientific equipment to face the intruders.

Afraid to move, barely able to breathe, Chun watches and listens. One thug pins Wan Lo against the wall while the other ransacks the room. Chun's heart sinks. He saw Wan Lo hide the black box in a shallow hole under the wisteria tree. If Wan Lo tells them it is there, Chun will lose his chance to profit from the old man's discovery.

Moments later the thugs emerge from the hut and drag Wan Lo across the courtyard to the Red Flag. Wan Lo resists weakly, tossing his head in defiance, and his prized Trojan cap falls to the ground.

Chun watches the Red Flag disappear in a cloud of dust. He is relieved to be spared, relieved that Wan Lo did not yet reveal where the black box is hidden. But he must move it to a safer place quickly, in case the thugs return. As he crosses the courtyard, he bends to pick up the cap. When the car is out of sight, he puts it on his head, pulling it down low over his eyes. A perfect fit.

HE IS STILL WEARING THE HAT later as he works his shift at the hatchery. Wan Lo is not in his customary place in the line, but work goes on as though the old man never existed. Like the eels, workers seem to be in constant supply, new ones rushing in to take the place of the missing. And they are equally expendable.

Before long he sees the two thugs coming down the aisle in his direction. He is not surprised. Meekly he steps away from the tank and allows them to lead him through the hatchery toward the stairs to the catwalk leading to Wo Fat's office.

But a tram piled high with sacks of feed blocks the quickest route, so they are forced to go another way. One of the thugs unlocks a metal door with no handle and leads Chun through a small room he has heard about but never seen before. It is an electrical center, filled with important looking machinery — computers, he thinks they are called — equipped with buttons and switches, and electrical wires passing in and out in all directions. They are rusted with disuse.

He remembers last year, overhearing two of the supervisors grumbling that like other factories in China, the eel hatchery had tried to modernize by purchasing this expensive equipment. But to save money, they had not hired the experts to operate it. Within days of its delivery the equipment had jammed and no one knew how to fix it. The supervisors had been glad, preferring the traditional methods they understood, rather than try to cope with change.

Chun extends his hand to a panel intricately laced with silvery wires, now turning orange with corrosion. "Do not touch anything," one thug snaps, and pushes him up through a hatch in the corner, a secret passageway.

Then, once again, Chun is brought to stand before the white-clothed table in Wo Fat's private office. The obese man ignores him, but Liu smiles a greeting. On the table is a raised pot, lapped from below by flames. At a nod from Liu, a waiter approaches and pours vodka into the dish. The liquid hisses angrily as it meets the hot metal, and billowing steam obscures Wo Fat's cabbage face.

"You did the proper thing, Brother Chun, to inform us of the existence of this magical invention," Liu says, his voice calm and low. "But it appears that you were tricked to think the invention is in Hong Kong. Much time has been lost."

The waiter reappears with a basket of live eels. They thrash about, as though anticipating their fate.

"What have you done to Wan Lo?" Chun blurts out, his voice little more than a whisper.

"See how robust the eels are? We are trying a new type of live feed which they seem to prefer," Liu says.

Wo Fat points to one of the eels. It snaps at his hand, and Chun realizes that they are not the harmless variety the hatchery packages for sale, but the deadly morays that can sever a man's hand in two bites. The message of Liu's statement becomes clear. Chun steps back, trembling.

"They have learned to love the taste of it," Liu continues. "It's amazing, really, how efficient the eels are, devouring every morsel so not a trace remains."

"Wan Lo . . ." Chun mutters softly, realizing the fate of his neighbor.

Using a plier-like tool that he clamps just below the eel's fierce jaws, the waiter removes the eel Wo Fat requested from the basket. Another waiter slits the dangling body from jaw to tail, then strips the skin from the flesh in one swift jerk.

Then he drops the skinned eel, still alive and wriggling, into the boiling alcohol. It thrashes about in a violent dance of death, splattering the burning liquid on the white cloth. As it succumbs to the barbaric ritual, the turbulence in the pot gradually subsides.

"You know the saying, 'The weak become food and the strong eat them,'" Liu says.

He lets this thought sink in as the waiter plucks the now-limp eel from the pot and places it in front of Wo Fat. Using silver-tipped chopsticks the Dragonhead picks it up, and bites through the head. The juice runs down his chin, and through it he smiles at Chun, a predator who has cornered his prey.

Silent, speechless, Chun watches the grotesquely fat man devour the fish, thinking how the essence of his neighbor now flows through its flesh. Liu lifts the platter containing the remains of the eel. "Wo Fat offers you food off his plate, in return for information about the location of the invention." He looks at Chun expectantly, but Chun is silent.

"We know the invention is here in Fuchow. The old man hid it, and now, unfortunately, he cannot tell us where it is."

Still Chun does not speak.

"You must know where it is, or you would not have come to us in the first place, correct?" Wo Fat says, holding another bit of quivering fish to his mouth. "Unless you have been so foolish as to display a lamb's head and sell dog meat."

"But —"

"We have little time," Liu prods him. "Word has reached the capitalist running dogs from the West, and they are on their way to Fuchow even as we speak."

中國象棋

TWELVE

Like all of Hong Kong the Kowloon-Canton Railway station was teeming with life. In addition to the tourists — rosy-cheeked Germans with white-blonde children trailing in their wake, honeymooning Japanese couples with matching Nikons, Australians singly and in packs, toting knapsacks and sleeping bags, regiments of blue-haired Americans in Reeboks and windbreakers following guides with color-coded placards — there were hordes of Chinese transporting all of their earthly possessions in enormous crates and shopping bags baled with twine.

Lily had agreed to come with me. I'd known all along she would, because she hated to be left out of an adventure, and because Mainland China offered her a whole new world of culinary experiences.

I'd assumed we would fly to Fuchow, but the daily flight was booked solid for four days and Cao was afraid that if we waited it would be too late. So there we were at the train station, even though the trip would require about eighteen hours and a change of train.

We were required to hold tickets back to Hong Kong in order to get visas, so Cao had booked the two last seats on a flight out of Fuchow back to Hong Kong on the evening of the eleventh. "It's the day before Chinese New Year," she told us. "Everything will be shut down completely for the holiday, and all the planes and trains are fully booked. So if you miss that flight it will be impossible to get a reservation for quite some time."

We had one suitcase between us with a change of clothes apiece and our toiletries, and Lily's enormous tote bag for everything else. 'Everything else' consisted of her three Chinese cookbooks, a jar of peanut butter, canned tuna packed in water, Lipton's cup-a-soup mix, and a box of saltines, all of which Lily had purchased at Hong Kong's version of a supermarket, justifying it by saying, "I've heard the Chinese douse everything with MSG. That can't be good for Baby Matthews."

I was glad Cao had come with us to the station, because even though there were signs translating the boarding procedures in many languages, English among them, their meanings remained quaintly obscure, such as 'Tickets Only from Passengers,' or my personal favorite, 'This Way to Boarding Gate, No Entry.'

The cavernous building was like an open market, with food vendors and small storefront shops selling everything from T-shirts to luggage, cameras and computers to jewelry. Lily stopped at a cart offering Rolex watches for "Cheap Bargains!!", and was immediately swarmed by a horde of vendors who smelled the perfume of American dollars.

While she negotiated her purchase, I asked Cao how she came to live in Hong Kong.

"It's not a very interesting story, I'm afraid," she said modestly. "I was born and raised in Soochow, a smallish city in the Jiangsu Province near Shanghai. But I lived at my aunt and uncle's home — your destination — while I attended Wing On University, which is nearby."

"After that I came to Hong Kong on a two-year work/study program. But when the two years were up, I did not want to go back. China was still so far behind the rest of the world then, and I'd become used to the modern life in Hong Kong. So I decided to use *quan-xi* to remain in Hong Kong illegally. It was those connections who brought me into . . . my current work."

She shook her head. "Now, of course, I am prohibited from returning to my home. So I will be very eager to hear your report, not only of Peter, but of Auntie and Uncle as well."

"Check this out!" Lily crowed, triumphantly extending her wrist. She was wearing a Rolex oyster watch. "Only $300 Hong Kong," she said. "What's that in U.S. dollars?"

"About $40," Cao replied.

"Such a deal! It would have cost twenty times that at home."

"Yeah, for a *real* Rolex," I pointed out.

"This is real. See, it's even got the little inventory number on the back. The guy showed me."

She looked at Cao for validation, but Cao shook her head. "Karen is right. It's highly unlikely that it's authentic. But think of it this way, you can still fool all of your friends. Only you will know that it is not real."

It was a strange thing to say, and it made me wonder just a little bit if what our new friend had told us was real.

As we walked to the boarding platform, Cao handed me an envelope. "I've written a letter to my aunt and uncle to explain who you are."

"Didn't you call them?" Lily asked.

"They don't have a telephone. Few people in China do, outside of the cities."

"But the people I know who've been to China say it's become so Westernized — discos, fast food, rock'n' roll," Lily pointed out.

"Western culture has had a profound impact on our large cities, it's true. But in the countryside, peasants still live as they have for centuries. It is quite amazing, really, the contrast between the lifestyles of a villager and a city dweller, whose homes are only a few miles apart."

My concern must have shown, because Cao continued, "Don't worry. They do have running water, not hot though, and electricity, when it works, which is perhaps an hour a day."

"How do they refrigerate their food?" Lily asked.

"They don't. In the country, Chinese generally grow what they eat, and if they do purchase food, they shop only for what they will eat that day. Leftovers is a very Western concept. Nothing gets leftover or wasted in a Chinese household."

I was still worried about the phone situation. "How are we going to let you know what's happening if they don't have a telephone?" I asked.

"There are public phones, in the train station and at the post office," she assured me. "Call me when you arrive in Fuchow. I may have heard something by then. I've written my home number on the map to Auntie and Uncle's house. It's a secure line."

She handed me the map, a carefully drawn grid with a dotted line meandering through it.

"Don't the streets have names?" Lily asked.

"Some do," Cao said, "but unless you can read Chinese characters, I don't think they would be of much use to you. You will have to rely on your taxi driver. Give the map to him."

A staticky voice boomed over the loudspeaker in Chinese. The English translation that followed was equally unintelligible.

"That's the announcement for your train," Cao told us. "You should be prepared to board because it will not stop for long."

We followed her to the edge of the platform where the passengers were massed at a red line painted on the cement floor, like runners at the start of a 10K race. A uniformed conductor patrolled the line, pompous as a general reviewing the troops. Despite the jostling, no one defied his authority.

To my surprise, the train looked like it had *choo-chooed* straight off the pages of *The Little Engine That Could,* one of my favorite children's books. It had an old-fashioned locomotive with a grille on the front (did they call them cow catchers in China too?), a smoke stack and an engineer, nothing like the streamlined Amtraks we had in California, or Japan's bullet trains. This was something out of a past era, nostalgia incarnate. Yet it wasn't an antique, but a newly built fully operational replica of an antique. And it was as clean as a ride at Disneyland.

"I should explain to you about money," Cao said as we waited to board. "Credit cards and travelers' checks are not widely accepted, especially in rural areas like Fuchow. You can use either Renminbi, the People's Money, or Foreign Exchange Certificates. Supposedly RMB and FEC have the same value, but only foreigners can buy FEC. And since they are the currency needed to purchase most luxury items, the local people are always eager to trade for them. So if you trade your FEC for RMB with people on the street rather than in a bank you'll get about twice as much."

"That sounds illegal."

"Let's just say the black market is alive and well in China," Cao smiled. "Much business is done this way."

"How do we find someone to change with us?" Lily asked.

"Oh, they'll find you," Cao replied brightly. "Wait and see."

The train belched a long blast of steam, and finally the guard made a gesture with his hand. When he did, the waiting passengers surged across the line and began to board.

"They won't let me on, so I'll have to say good-bye here," Cao told us. "You're in car number twelve, seats 5A and 5B. On this train, the numbers are written in English as well as Chinese, so you shouldn't have any trouble finding them. At the border you'll change trains to Fuchow."

A whistle blew and the last passengers hurried to board the train. I'd known Cao for less than a day, but she was the sole link I had to Peter at this moment, and the only tie we would have to the rest of the world once we got on the train. I took her hand in both of mine.

"Thank you for everything you've done for us," I said, hoping I sounded as grateful as I felt.

"Please," Cao replied, modestly lowering her eyes. "If you find Peter, you will be doing a great service to me and to your country."

We stepped aboard the train. "I'll meet your plane at Kai Tak on the eleventh," she called. "Give my love to Auntie and Uncle."

I waved, holding up the letter as a signal that I would, then I followed Lily into the car. It was as clean and serviceable inside as it was outside. The seats had blue velvet upholstery which was plush and brushed free of dust, and brass accoutrements polished to a high sheen. Even the floor carpet was spotless.

Young girls costumed in starched gingham aprons and white gloves stood at the door to each compartment to check tickets and direct passengers to their seats. They were well-groomed and personable, but the anomaly of their Asian features and all-American uniforms didn't compute — it was as though some inspired railroad official had gotten his hands on a *Good Housekeeping* magazine, circa

1954, and had tried to achieve that look. But the girls seemed proud of their uniforms and wore them with the earnestness of soldiers in parade dress. They spoke only enough English to direct us to our seats and urge us to "Have a safe and auspicious journey to China."

Lily and I got to our row just as the train jerked into motion. I peered out the window to let Cao know we'd found our seats and wave one last good-bye, but her back was to the train. She was deep in conversation with a handsome man with slicked-back hair, wearing wraparound sunglasses and a shiny suit. A friend? Someone needing directions? At the last possible minute, they bowed to each other and parted, and he jumped onto the moving train several cars back from us.

I sat down and found myself facing two middle-aged men, both stern-faced and skinny, wearing military blue caps and baggy blue uniforms, embellished with no insignia or signs of rank. The odor of garlic was so intense it rose off of them like steam.

They stared at us with childlike curiosity, puffing on short, unfiltered cigarettes and talking in a guttural, atonal singsong. I was curious about them too, but I found it impossible to stare at them while they stared at us. Since Lily was already reading one of her cookbooks, I did my best to ignore the secondhand smoke, and turned my eyes back to the window as we chugged out of the station.

Endless blocks of high-rise tenements slipped past us. From each small balcony a window pole extended, airing laundry, rugs, and bed linens like banners of poverty. The tenement rows were punctuated every so often with a construction site sheathed in bamboo scaffolding, the framework of another identical apartment house going up. All the buildings, even these unfinished ones, looked old and defeated, like hollow-eyed survivors of famine or war.

I watched for a few minutes, but the monotony of the urban landscape and the gentle motion of the train rocked my mind back to Peter and the CIA. There were still so many unanswered questions. Why had he chosen this time to confess? What if Cao was wrong about where he was going? What if it was already too late? Was this mission to save him a fool's errand?

When I'd made the decision to fly to Hong Kong to confront Peter — was it only two days ago? — I'd been proud of myself; to travel to a distant country on the spur of the moment was a boldly assertive step for a meek and mild dental student from Santa Monica. But if that was a bold step, this was like bungee jumping into the Grand Canyon. I had no idea what to expect; there had been no time to read a guidebook, to study up on Chinese culture, climate or social conditions. I spoke a smattering of French and Lily could read menus in several languages, but neither of us spoke a syllable of Mandarin or Fukienese, the dialect of the local province. Why had I gotten us into this?

Because Peter's life was in jeopardy, I reminded myself. And whether or not he had lied to me in the past or might be lying now, I couldn't sit back and do nothing while he walked into a death trap, anymore than I could watch him step out in front of a bus on Wilshire Boulevard, for the very good reason that I loved him.

My thoughts were interrupted by a low, sucking sound, like the noise of a milk steamer on a cappuccino machine. I glanced up, then stared in disbelief as the older of the two soldiers sitting across from us drew in his thin cheeks, positioned his lips in a mockery of a kiss, bent forward, and loudly let loose with a gob of foamy mucus.

He didn't so much spit as dribble a colossally long, frothy string of saliva into an urn on the floor under the window. Automatically, my eyes followed the trajectory of the spittle from his mouth to the urn. It was a sickening mistake. My stomach heaved at the sight of the swill brimming the pot, a brownish liquid, grotesque with snot and stray particles of food.

"Oh, gross! Do you have to do that!?" Lily cried. The soldier blinked at her and said something to his companion. They laughed, displaying mouths full of teeth ravaged by neglect and poor hygiene, a sight that sickened me even more.

A cart rattled up the aisle, and a woman in a smock began dispensing hot tea in beautiful covered porcelain mugs. The tea smelled delicious, and I hoped it would calm my stomach, so I took one.

"I'd love a Diet Coke," Lily said to the tea server. "Do you have caffeine free? With ice, please, and a straw. Oh, and some lemon too, if it's not too much trouble. I don't mind lime, but lemon would be better if you have it."

The tea server nodded curtly, and handed Lily a cup of tea, then pushed her cart up the aisle. Grudgingly Lily took a sip and winced. "Why does this make my tooth hurt?" she asked.

"Teeth can be heat sensitive," I hedged.

"They never were before you put the crown in."

"It's only a temporary," I reminded her. I still didn't know exactly what I'd done wrong in Lily's mouth, but whatever it was, I couldn't fix it here. "Where's the oil of clove?"

"In the suitcase." She motioned to the rack above us.

"I'll get it for you." It was the least I could do. I stood up and stepped into the aisle. But as I jerked the bag off the overhead rack, someone grabbed my jacket from behind, throwing me off balance. I went sprawling face first onto the floor.

I wasn't hurt, just stunned and annoyed. I turned to face my assailant, prepared to convey my anger with a graphic gesture that would transcend the language barrier, but he was already disappearing through the door to the next car.

"Have a nice trip?' Lily teased.

"He pushed me on purpose," I grumbled. "He practically ripped my jacket right off my back."

She frowned. "Better check your pockets."

A quick pat-down revealed my passport and wallet on one side, and some gum and Cao's letter on the other. I breathed a sigh of relief. "It's all here," I said. I took the oil of clove out of the suitcase and handed it to Lily. The bottle was nearly empty. Pretty soon I would have to come up with some other magic potion to relieve her pain.

I sat down and took the gum and Cao's letter out of my pocket. Although the envelope was sealed, it could easily be opened. I nudged Lily and held out the pack of Juicy Fruit. "Don't chew on the side with the crown," I warned her. We both chewed in silence, staring at the letter. "I wonder what she said about us," I mused.

"Yeah," she said, "What if this is some kind of a scam? For all we know she might be shipping us off to white slavers."

"You're forgetting she works with Peter," I said.

"Yeah, as a *spy*." Her voice dripped sarcasm. "How come you never told me you were married to James Bond?"

"I didn't know it myself until yesterday."

"Yesterday! Let me get this straight. Peter's been a spy since college, but you never had a clue until yesterday? It doesn't say a whole hell of a lot for your marriage, does it?"

It was true, but it hurt to hear it. Tears stung my eyes. "How do you think I feel? I really believed he was selling insurance all this time. Our whole life has been a lie."

"What makes you think he's telling the truth now? I hate to say it, but if he *is* having an affair with Lauren, maybe he's just trying to throw you off track."

"Then how do you explain Cao?"

"Good question." Lily narrowed her eyes. "She never gave us any proof that she worked for the CIA. How do we know she does?"

"It would be quite a coincidence if they both made up the same story."

"Well, she just didn't seem like a CIA agent to me."

"Neither does Peter."

"My point exactly." Lily studied me, trying to intuit my thoughts. "I think we ought to read the letter and see what she said about us."

"It doesn't seem right."

"Who do you think cares? Them?" She nodded at our seatmates. "Give it to me," she commanded.

I handed her the letter. Without hesitation she slid her index finger under the lip of the envelope and deftly forced it loose. Then she unfolded the thin, white paper inside, pinching it awkwardly between her thumb and forefinger as though she were trying not to leave any fingerprints.

She stared at the letter for a second, then started to giggle.

"What's so funny?" She handed it to me.

The page was covered with those neat little Chinese pictures! Of course it was written in Chinese. How could I expect two old people who didn't even have a telephone to read English?

The more we looked at it the more ludicrous it seemed. Here we were, trekking into a country whose culture was so alien that its language wasn't even written in words. We didn't know a soul for thousands of miles, and no one knew we were coming. We had no guidebook, only a map we couldn't read, to lead us to a place we'd never heard of, on the hope that we would find my husband *the spy* and save him from a sinister enemy we hadn't even identified. It was sheer lunacy.

Our companions across the way watched, fascinated, as our hilarity mounted to near hysteria. Lily started to gag, laughing and coughing at the same time.

"What?" I managed to choke out.

"I'm laughing so hard I sucked my gum up my nose," she gasped, and that set us off again.

Then we felt the train begin to slow, and the slower it got, the less we laughed. We both stared out the window at the approaching station. *Lo Wo* the sign said, *China Border.*

"We're crazy to be doing this," Lily said.

"You don't have to come. You can still go back."

"You think I'm going to let you go without me? Not on your life," Lily said. "We're going to Fuchow together." She looked at the men in uniforms. "Fuchow?"

"Fuchow," they replied, nodding sagely, as though this made everything perfectly clear.

中國象棋

THIRTEEN

At Lo Wo, we were shuttled off the train and invited to walk over the Shum Chun River Bridge, the boundary between Hong Kong and The People's Republic of China. Although the far side of the river looked much the same as the side we were on, armed guards at either end of the bridge, however nonchalant, added a serious dimension to the crossing: we were entering a Communist country, leaving our intrinsic personal freedoms behind.

Once over the bridge, we were herded into the first of several long, slow lines — health, immigration and baggage inspection, the last requiring us to fill out an exhaustive form, itemizing our possessions: the books and magazines we were carrying, jewelry, clothing and electronic gadgetry, undeveloped exposed film, drugs, plant and animal matter, weaponry. It was a far cry from the apathy of customs in Hong Kong.

We watched an agent inspect the contents of Lily's tote bag. He was a slender man wearing a uniform that looked like it hadn't been laundered since Mao died. His face was fleshy and flat, scarred by a rash of acne. His teeth protruded mulishly, and were streaked with brown stains.

He rifled carelessly through Lily's stash of food, and pulled out a bag of Snickers bars I hadn't known was there. "In China you eat Chinese food," he scolded her. But instead of putting the candy with other officially confiscated goods, he slipped them into his drawer.

"Hey, what are you doing?" Lily demanded. "I need those in case of emergency! I have low blood sugar!"

The agent just stared at her, his hand resting on his gun.

"It's all right," I said firmly. "We're not going to starve to death in three days." The last thing we needed was to start an international incident over a bag of candy bars.

I thought we were out of trouble, but the agent went into orbit when he found my Swiss army knife. He called three of his comrades over to inspect it. The knife had been a graduation gift from my brother Mitch. It was a traveling tool kit, complete with scissors and corkscrew, magnifying glass, and even a tiny flashlight. The agents passed it among themselves, flicking the light off and on, examining each of its gadgets with the kind of rapt fascination young men usually reserve for *Penthouse* magazine. They seemed convinced I meant to use it to overthrow the Communist Party; it took our two cans of tuna and a packet of Lipton cup-a-soup mix to prove otherwise.

While we waited for the train to Fuchow, we exchanged our American dollars for FEC. And true to Cao's explanation, we had no sooner stepped out of the bank office than a man tapped me on the arm. "Shang mory?" he asked, with a gap-tooth smile, pointing to our bundles of rumpled bills.

"I think he's saying 'change money,'" Lily translated.

He gave us nearly double the amount in RMB, so it appeared

we made a pretty good deal, considering our negotiation was strictly nonverbal.

To celebrate the transaction I bought an orange soda from a vending cart, the only beverage for sale. It was heavily carbonated and syrupy, with a sour metallic flavor, but I drank it even though I'd sworn off soft drinks when I started dental school. My mouth was parched and gritty, and I knew it would be madness to drink the water which bubbled out of a public faucet into a trash-filled basin.

Lily declined a soda, but bought us red Popsicles that she said were made of mashed red beans and frozen sugar water, and a snack that looked like elongated sticks of Yorkshire pudding, which the vendor was frying in a wok. People all around us were eating them by the greasy bundles, the way Americans eat cookies, so I gamely nibbled at one. It was bland, like deep-fried foam rubber, a far cry from Mrs. Field's best. But Lily wolfed hers down anyway, and urged me to do the same. "Who knows when our next meal will be?" she pointed out.

When we finally boarded the train, it was nearly 8 P.M. Cao had told us the trip from Lo Wo to Fuchow would take about fourteen hours, an excruciatingly slow way to travel five hundred miles in this modern era. But we had no choice. There was no Avis Rent-a-Car in China, and we'd been told that the highway system was practically nonexistent.

In contrast to the last train, this one was beat to hell, rusty, dented and dilapidated. It shuddered to a stop, emitting a death rattle and a puff of acrid smoke, tinting the air sepia and making breathing a health hazard. We hurried aboard trying not to inhale.

The air inside was not an improvement. As we made our way down the corridor past curtained sleeping compartments, the stench of dry rot and decay choked my nasal passages. The train looked like it had not been cleaned since the Ming Dynasty. The corridor was littered and the floor was sticky. Incongruously, a bucket filled with live crabs had been plunked down in the middle of the aisle. Someone's luggage? Leftovers from dinner? Excess baggage?

"What's our compartment number?" I asked Lily, carefully skirting the bucket.

She looked at the tickets. "If it says, it's not in English," she replied.

We peered into the compartments as we passed, looking for seats. As far as I could see we were the only Americans on board, and the train was packed.

We finally found two empty seats near the end of the car, and quickly staked our claim. The other occupants were a young Japanese couple and a Chinese family of four — mother, father, grandfather and teenage girl — with all their worldly belongings bound in twine. Granddad clutched a small cage in which perched a green bird the size and shape of a kiwi, with a curved yellow beak and brilliant red eyes. The old man was nonchalantly dismembering a live grasshopper and feeding it to the bird, limb by quivering limb.

"What a beautiful bird!" I bent down to admire it.

The old man glared at me and jerked the cage away, causing the bird to drop the tendril in its beak. It hopped frantically from perch to perch, squawking in rage.

"Sorry," I said, and took my seat.

Still staring at me, Granddad dredged up a wad of spit, and like a dog marking his territory, deposited it in the omnipresent spittoon. He wasn't a very good shot; I watched the foam run like candle wax down the side of the urn, puddling on the floor. No wonder my shoes stuck to the floorboards.

As soon as we pulled out of the station, an attendant came up the aisle distributing coarse blankets and stained, lumpy pillows. I wanted to ask her for a cleaner pillowcase, but her expression stopped me cold. This was not a person who would be likely to grant special favors.

"Excuse me, what time do they start serving breakfast in the morning?" Lily asked, on her best behavior.

"Aiie?" the woman grunted, glaring at Lily.

Whatever 'aiie' meant in Chinese, the woman made it sound like 'Shut up you arrogant foreigner.'

"What time does the dining car open?" Lily repeated, stubbornly exaggerating each syllable.

The attendant threw Lily's blanket at her, screeched something unintelligible and stomped out of the compartment. "Good thing we ate at the station," Lily said, and opened one of her cookbooks. I turned my attention to the window.

My first glimpse of the People's Republic was disappointing. The scenery was unchanged from what we had seen in Hong Kong — row after row of bleak, high-rise tenements, crowded in amongst smoking factories, traffic-clogged roadways and bustling humanity. Cao had told us that this area near the border was a so-called Special Economic Zone. In an effort to benefit from the commercial sophistication of Hong Kong, China had begun allowing the Colony to bring industry and its accompanying modernization up to and across the border. Already you couldn't see where one ended and the other began.

Then, quite suddenly, as though we'd crossed an invisible line, the wall of buildings ended, and we were swept back centuries into the China of Confucius and Lao Tse. The landscape unrolled past my window like a dark scroll, allowing fleeting glimpses of rural life: the full moon shimmering mirrorlike on a flooded field; wisps of smoke rising like incense from a distant farmhouse; young peasants, their backs hunched under swaying bamboo shoulder poles with buckets at each end, making their way home in the dark after a long day of work in the rice paddies.

But mostly what I saw through the window was a vast and impenetrable land veiled by night, and my own face reflected back at me in the glass. China looked foreboding and inscrutable. Would I be able to find Peter hiding beneath her dark cloak?

I turned away from the window. Lily and the Chinese family were asleep, their snores as discordant as a New Age symphony. But I was still wide awake, and so was the young Japanese couple. They were in their early twenties, sporting identical Buster Brown haircuts and color-coordinated Fila windbreakers. They looked enough alike to be brother and sister, but I guessed by their luggage — a matched five-piece set covered in nubby blue and yellow flowers — that they were newlyweds. Either that or third-prize winners on the Japanese version of "The Dating Game."

"Just married? I whispered to the bride, and pointed to her wedding band.

She blushed, averted her eyes. "This day," she said softly, casting a worried glance at her husband who was ignoring her.

"Congratulations," I beamed, touched to share this intimacy, and pleased to have broken the language barrier. I poked Lily. She stirred sleepily. "It's their wedding night."

"How romantic and memorable to spend it sitting up on a train with us," she mumbled, and turned toward the wall.

I watched the bride. She was very shy of her new husband, and sat carefully so no part of her body came into contact with his. He was turned toward the window, leaning on it, staring out, completely oblivious to her, as though they were strangers. Had their marriage been arranged through a go-between, supposedly still a common practice in Asia? If so, this was probably the first time they had ever been together without a chaperone, the equivalent of their first date. No wonder they were shy of each other.

Smiling inwardly, I settled back and closed my eyes, remembering my first date with Peter.

SOON AFTER OUR ENCOUNTER at El Rancho Park, he had invited me to go with him to a USC football game. I wasn't a sports fan, but I accepted for the simple reason that I was attracted to him. Also, even a football game was better than my usual Saturday afternoon occupation, 'picking the whites' at my father's oriental rug store. This was the tedious job of poring over every square inch of a carpet with a magnifying glass, finding tufts of wool that hadn't taken the dye properly, and using appropriately tinted felt tip marking pens to fill them in. The memory of Saturdays spent crouched over a foul-smelling Heriz in the back room of a musty rug store made an afternoon at the L.A. Coliseum sound most enticing.

Peter didn't reveal much about himself on the way to the game, a reticence I later learned was consistent with his reserved nature. So I was shocked when we arrived and he whipped out a gold pass, allowing us access to the parking lot closest to the stadium. Unschooled though I was in the etiquette of athletic events, even I knew that a good parking pass was the ultimate sign of status — the closer to the stadium, the more important you were. Our proximity to the playing field put us in a category with movie stars, politicians, and local billionaires. I was impressed.

"I went to SC," Peter said simply, by way of explanation. And when he saw by my face that I was expecting more, he added, "I played ball for them."

That was all he said about it until we got to our seats. They were on the fifty-yard line, so close to the field that I had to stand to see over the heads of the cheerleading squad. The people on either side of us greeted Peter with the solicitous awe usually reserved for the famous and the infamous. Peter acknowledged the attention politely, but seemed unimpressed by it, another plus in my book.

"Everybody seems to know you," I said to get a conversation going.

"I've had these seats since I graduated," he explained. "Most of the people in this section have had theirs even longer than that."

"It's a pretty upscale group," I commented, for everyone around us looked like they were posing for *Town & Country*, with their cashmere blankets, hi-tech binoculars, and silver flasks. Peter didn't comment.

"I never sat so close before," I continued to babble. "What did you have to do to get these seats? Win the Cy Young Award?"

"Wrong sport," Peter replied, hiding a smile by turning to wave at someone a few rows up. "I've got to say hello to a guy before they . . . throw out the first pitch. Will you be okay?" And he was gone.

"You must not know Peter very well," said a man in a fedora next to me. Had he heard my stupid remark?

"Not very," I confirmed.

"Didn't you ever hear of Peter 'The Pied Piper' Matthews?"

I shook my head no, but muddled in a decade-old haze of memory, I vaguely recalled that *Life* magazine photo of Lauren Covington and some guy nicknamed 'The Pied Piper' — was that *Peter*?

"He was probably one of the two or three best athletes who ever threw a pass for the Trojans," the man went on, "right up there with Pat Hayden. He got the nickname because he always had half the opposing team trailing after him when he ran for a TD. God, it was beautiful to watch him move."

As Peter moved up the aisle now, I tried to imagine him streaking down the field with the rest of the players in hot pursuit.

"Too bad about his shoulder," the man continued. "He would've gone pro for sure."

"What about his shoulder?"

"They said it was a hiking accident. He fell or something just a few days before the draft. He held a press conference, made a statement that he was retiring from football, and never even took a shot at the big time. It was a real tragedy for the sport, I'm telling you."

Everyone was rising for the national anthem when Peter slipped back into his seat beside me. I guess the expression on my face betrayed some awe, because he looked past me to the man in the fedora. "Has George been giving you an earful?"

George winked at me. "I didn't tell her the half of it, Matthews. Not about the Heisman Trophy nomination or the Phi Beta Kappa key."

"Don't believe everything you hear," Peter cautioned.

"Don't believe everything you don't hear," George shot back with a wink.

As we dated over the next few months, I was able to worm precious few facts of Peter's football fame out of him. He was reluctant to talk about it, saying it was a time in his life that had passed, that he had moved on to other things and it wasn't important any more.

His attitude surprised me. At some point he'd metamorphosed from a nationally known jock celebrity into an anonymous insurance agent, what most people would consider stepping down a rung on the food chain. You'd have thought he would remember the good old days with fondness and pride. But he never mentioned one anecdote from his football years. Except for that old picture in *Life*, I never saw a picture of him in football gear, no framed mementos or drawers filled with press clippings. Nor were there any drunken nights reminiscing with 'the boys.' When I probed, he was typically cryptic.

"I live my life day by day. I don't think about the past and I don't wonder about the future. What's the point?" And we left it at that.

At the time, I decided that he must have been bitterly traumatized by the injury that had ruined his football career, and was probably still in denial. It would be like winning the lottery, then having the lucky ticket snatched out of your hand before you could collect your prize.

But something had always bothered me about the story. Peter's body bore no physical evidence of the hiking accident that had supposedly derailed his career in sports, no scars on either of his broad shoulders, no disability or upper body weakness which could be attributed to an old injury. Now I wondered if there had even been a hiking accident. Had he made up this excuse to get out of the public eye so he could go off unnoticed to join the CIA? It seemed likely.

Why had I never pressed him to open up to me? Why had I always accepted what he'd told me at face value, stifling my doubts and questions? Was it because I loved him, or because I sensed something was wrong and I was afraid to learn the truth?

中國象棋

FOURTEEN

Just as dawn was breaking, for no perceivable reason, the train began to shudder. Then it screeched to a halt, emitting a sound about as soothing as fingernails on a blackboard. The Grandfather awoke and cleared his throat loudly, and the little green kiwi bird squawked in outrage, hopping from perch to perch. I peered out the window. We were truly in the country now. Rice paddies in various stages of cultivation, outlined by mud dykes, stretched across the flat land as far as the eye could see.

The train lay like a snake airing itself in the crisp morning breeze, steam rising from it. Immediately passengers began pouring out of it like children released from school. They acted as though the delay were cause for celebration instead of an inconvenience.

"We should find out what's going on," I said.

"What about our stuff?" Lily asked. "Should we leave it with them?"

We looked at our traveling companions. The Chinese family was still sleeping, but the Japanese couple was awake. Sometime during the night they had bridged the intimacy gap — her head was on his shoulder, and both of them were watching us.

I smiled at them. "You'll watch our things?"

The bride looked to her husband for permission, but he remained stony-faced. She looked back at me and shrugged.

When I stood up morning sickness hit me like a ton of bricks. It was too late to do anything but stick my head out the open window and let heave. The Japanese couple watched me make a spectacle of myself.

Outside the air was cool and electric with the threat of rain. In the distance, a front of nimbus clouds hung so low in the sky that they seemed to be rolling toward us across the field like billowy white tumbleweeds. "Is it a mechanical problem?" I asked the first porter I saw. He shrugged and walked away. "Why have we stopped?" Lily asked another. He ignored her. "When will the train start again?" I inquired of a passenger. Her reply was not in a language I could identify.

We crossed the tracks and found a narrow dirt road leading into the field. Several military-style jeeps were parked on it. Were they the cause of the delay? None of the other passengers seemed to care. They just milled about, sucking in great gusts of fresh air and doing T'ai Chi to pass the time.

"Let's find a place for a picnic," Lily suggested.

"Okay, but we shouldn't go too far."

Even at this early hour and with rain imminent, farmers were wading into the unplanted paddies, sinking ankle deep into the red mud, and dumping out buckets of foul smelling slop.

Lily's expert nose gave it the sniff test. "Fertilizer," she announced, "probably human waste. I bet they save the animal dung for cooking."

"Thanks for sharing that," I replied. If pregnancy didn't rob me of my appetite, Lily's discourse would certainly do the job.

"Think of it as nature's way of recycling," Lily continued, "Just like Cao said, in the Chinese ecosystem nothing is wasted."

"Lily, enough!"

As we walked, we watched peasants bent double at the waist, moving backwards step by step, transplanting rice seedlings into the mud. Teenage girls, in loose-fitting black pants rolled knee high, were working on long, wooden treadmills to pump water into a field that men hitched to lumbering water buffaloes were plowing.

"I wonder if they make bufala mozzarella," Lily mused.

Mostly the people were intent on their efforts but once in a while a solitary worker would look up from his labor and stare at us in dazed bewilderment. Perhaps they had never seen a Caucasian up close before. Geographically, they weren't that far from Hong Kong's cosmopolitan civilization, but practically speaking, they lived in another world.

"Come on, let's eat." Lily plunked herself down on a small, dry patch of dirt and began to pull out the provisions she'd brought from Hong Kong. "Aren't you glad I shopped?" she asked, pleased with herself.

"Actually, I'm not all that hungry," I admitted, sitting down beside her. "I think I left my appetite in California."

"This is no time to go anorexic on me," she scolded. "Pregnant women need extra protein and fiber."

Grudgingly I took a few crackers and used my finger to spread them with peanut butter. When I looked up, I saw that my meal preparation had drawn an audience. Two children, a boy and a girl both under five were standing ankle deep in the muddy water in front of us, staring up in wonder. Behind them, other farmers, old and young, were gathering.

"Now I know what Michelle Pfeiffer feels like," Lily said, licking peanut butter off her fingers. This caused a murmur of exclamation to ripple through the audience.

"E.T.'s more like it."

"Do you think they're hungry or just curious?"

"Probably both. Here, would you like some?" I asked the children, eager to make friends. But when I thrust out my hand, they drew back. I'd moved too fast, and they were smart enough to be cautious.

"It's called peanut butter," I said to them, mouthing the words slowly, "peanut butter and crackers. Good to eat. Mmmm." They seemed as interested in me as they were in the food, watching my mouth as I took a nibble of cracker to prove that it was edible. Finally the boy stepped close enough to pluck the crackers from my hand. He gave one to the girl, and with gleeful smiles they splashed through the mud, holding their prizes aloft.

Now the rest of the audience pressed in. We gave them each a cracker spread with peanut butter, but I didn't see one person actually eat. They sniffed and poked at them; one old man even held his cracker up to his ear. But mostly they treated them like precious tokens of Western civilization — if you could call peanut butter civilized.

As fascinating as it was to provide cultural entertainment to these people, I was antsy — every minute we were delayed in transit was a minute in which Peter might be drawn into danger. So I was relieved when the train whistle blew and everybody hurried to board. Lily gathered what remained of our food and stuffed it in her bag. My bladder was full again, and I decided I'd be happier emptying it out here where I could be responsible for my own hygiene rather than on the train where an eclectic variety of international bacteria was no doubt breeding. "I'll meet you on board," I told Lily."

"You'd better take this." She handed me a packet of Kleenex and went on ahead.

The train was jerking into slow motion by the time I'd finished, and I had to run to get on. Just as I swung myself up, three men were getting off. Two were in uniforms but the other one wore a suit. He was the man with the slicked back hair I'd seen talking to Cao in Hong Kong! I watched him get into one of the jeeps on the dirt crossroad and drive off. Who was he? Someone important, no doubt.

The corridor was crowded and it took me a while to push through the congestion. By the time I reached our compartment we were moving at full speed.

"Thank God you're back!" Lily cried, leaping to her feet. She was chewing gum with her mouth open, making little popping noises with each chomp, the way she did when she was excited. The green bird had picked up her anxiety and was squawking loudly, again hopping from perch to perch in its cage. The Chinese family and the Japanese couple were all staring at Lily with undisguised hostility, which they transferred to me when I entered.

"What's wrong? What happened?" I asked.

"When I got here, some soldiers were ransacking our side of the compartment! At least I think they were soldiers, because they had uniforms and guns. Long ones, you know, like rifles. They yelled at me in Chinese and grabbed my bag. They ripped one of the straps, see? I started thinking of that movie, 'Midnight Express,' the one where the guy gets put in a Turkish prison for ten years."

"That was because he was selling dope. Lily, you're not trying to tell me that you're carrying drugs, are you?"

"Of course not." She held out the ripped bag for me to inspect, the way a child does with a cut finger. "The oil of clove fell out and broke," she finished sorrowfully.

I looked at the Chinese family who were huddled together staring at us. Clearly they had seen this drama unfold, and knew what the soldiers had wanted since they spoke the language. "What about them?" I asked. "What about their stuff?"

"All they cared about was our stuff."

"Then what happened?"

"Another guy came in. He wasn't like the other two. He was very cool, dressed in a suit. And I don't even think he was Chinese. He looked Italian, or Spanish maybe. He got really angry, shouting at the soldiers, pushing them away. But to me, he was smooth as silk. He told me he needed to see my passport, if I didn't mind."

"He spoke English?"

"Yeah, perfectly."

"Then what?"

"I showed it to him, and he said thank-you, and left. And the soldiers left too."

"Wait a minute. He left with your passport?"

Lily was immediately defensive. "It's not as though I had a choice. I didn't say like, here, would you like to have an American passport, be my guest. I'm telling you, they had guns!"

"Lily, for God's sake! Didn't you try to stop him?"

"Of course. I said, 'Wait, I need that.' And he said, 'You'll get it back at the appropriate time,' whatever that means. There was nothing I could do."

This was not good news. I groped for my own passport. It was safely zipped in my pocket. "What did the guy look like? Did he have black hair, slicked back like this?" I showed her what I meant. "And wraparound shades?"

"Yeah, and a kind of shiny suit. Why, did you see him?"

I nodded. "He was getting off the train when I got on." I don't know why, but I didn't mention that I'd also seen him at the Hong Kong train station, talking to Cao. For some reason I thought it best to keep that little nugget of information to myself.

"Good."

"Good?"

"Yeah, I'm glad he got off the train because he can't harrass us anymore."

"But what about your passport? You can't just stroll through China without a passport," I said in exasperation. "How do you think you're going to get out of the country? That's why they have those little immigration booths at the border, so people without passports can't get through."

"I know that. I lost my passport once in London. But it was no big deal. I went to the American Embassy and got a temporary replacement in a couple of hours."

"Yeah, but London isn't a Communist city. I don't even think we have an Embassy in China. In any event, it wouldn't be in Fuchow. I don't get the feeling it's a major metropolis."

"When we get there, we're going to call Cao anyway. We can tell her what happened. She'll know what we should do to get out of this mess."

That was true, unless she was the one who'd gotten us into it.

THE DELAY had upset the schedule and the theft of Lily's passport had upset me, so I did nothing but watch the station signs at each stop throughout the rest of the morning, agonizing over the lost time, panicked that we'd somehow missed the Fuchow stop, and desperate to figure out why someone would take Lily's passport.

But just before three o'clock I saw a sign that said "FUCHOW" in English letters. Soon after, we entered a nondescript, mid-size city of drab, low-rise buildings, with an occasional ten- or twelve-story 'skyscraper' jutting up here and there. At first glance Fuchow had nothing to recommend it, save the chance that we would find Peter here.

The Japanese couple and the Chinese family were apparently

continuing on this train, because they all watched in silence as we gathered our belongings, clinging possessively to their bales and boxes to be sure we didn't try to take anything that didn't belong to us. When we walked out the door even the Japanese bride refused to return our departing smiles. Only the green bird chirped a farewell.

A woman was having trouble negotiating the stairs down to the platform with her two twine-wrapped parcels, each nearly the size of Rhode Island, and all the rest of the detraining passengers were helplessly crushed together, trapped between the blockaded stairs and the press of people.

I was so close to the man in front of me I was nearly asphyxiated by the smell of his perfumy cologne. He was bald on top, with the wisps of straight, black hair at his neck gathered into a ponytail. His stature was small and sturdy, and he was wearing the kind of Western clothes you buy in a third world country — badly cut denims and a synthetic knockoff of a Ralph Lauren sweater that missed in the translation. Something about him was familiar, but I didn't know what. Then he took a tasseled knit cap from his pocket and pulled it down over his head. That was when I recognized him. He was the man I'd seen on the boat tour to Aberdeen!

Suddenly the bottleneck at the foot of the stairs cleared, and we surged forward, caught in the momentum of the crowd. Knit Cap seemed in a hurry to disembark, but when he tried to hoist his bag onto his shoulder, its handle strap caught and the bag was jerked out of his hands. To my horror, a knife the size of a machete fell out of it and clattered down the stairs onto the platform.

Knit Cap muscled his way through the descending horde to retrieve it. "Look out! Look out!" he cried in English.

"Look out!" I cried too, unintentionally echoing his warning.

"Yeah, he already decked you once," Lily said. She was

shorter than I, and from her vantage point she couldn't see the knife, only the commotion. "What a troublemaker."

"That was the guy on the other train? But he was on *The Dragonlady* in Aberdeen too," I told her. "He was behind me on the deck right before we saw Peter. Don't you think that's weird?"

"So he's hitting all the tourist traps, just like us," Lily replied, looking around. "Although I must say, this place doesn't look like much of a tourist trap."

We stepped onto the platform, and my curiosity about the man and the machete was forgotten. We had arrived in the People's Republic of China.

The train station was cavernous and drafty, filled with travelers and luggage, snack stands and ticket counters. But unlike the Hong Kong depot, which gave the appearance of a monumental shopping mall, this one was stripped down to the basics, functional and drab. There was none of the razzle-dazzle of neon signage, no glut of gaudy doodads for sale, no hawkers, no beggars, no nonsense. And for that matter, no rubbish, no graffiti, no human detritus of any kind. Everything and everybody seemed to have a utilitarian purpose.

There were no other Caucasians either, which made Lily and me something of a novelty. People stared at us as they passed, not unkindly, but with great curiosity. One elderly lady, a maintenance worker of some sort to judge by the rag and straw broom she carried, stopped two feet away from me and gaped, her jaw hanging open, her eyes riveted to my face. She could not have been more enthralled if I'd had three noses. I smiled at her, but she did not return it. Her expression remained solemn, intent, unrelentingly curious.

"What do you think she wants?" I asked Lily.

"An autograph? A handout? Who knows? Let's see the map."

I got out the map Cao had made and we both looked at it, trying to make sense of the grid of lines.

"I think we're going to need some help with this," I said.

"Ask her." Lily inclined her head toward the old woman who was still agog. "Maybe she speaks English."

"Right, and I'm fluent in Swahili."

Still, it was worth a try. I gave the woman a winning smile. "Hello, can you help me?" I held the map up so it faced her. "I'm trying to find — oh God, I don't even know the name of the street."

"Just show it to her," Lily prodded.

I pointed to the written symbols on the page. "We're trying to get here. Is there a taxi, or a bus?"

The woman waved the map away and grunted, "Cuky." She pointed a gnarled finger at me then waved off to the left, motioning around a corner. "Cuky," she repeated. End of conversation.

"Maybe 'cuky' is the word for taxi or telephone," Lily said.

"I'll go see," I replied. "If I find the phone, I'll call Cao. If I'm not back in five minutes . . . I will be back in five minutes," I amended. I pushed the bags together and Lily straddled them like a lioness protecting her young.

I turned to the old woman. "Cuky?" I asked.

She nodded vigorously and beamed at me, her smile revealing a mouthful of misshapen, decayed teeth. "Cuky, cuky," she said, and grasped my arm to drag me out of the station. "Cuky," she repeated one last time, jabbing the air with her finger. Then, abruptly, she turned and walked away.

I looked in the direction she had pointed. There, nestled between a shoe repair stall and a bank, was a familiar white neon sign decorated with red dots and the English words, "Mrs. Field's Cookies."

Nothing could have been a more incongruous or a more welcomed sight. Cookie, I thought, the woman must have put two and two together, and assumed that I, an American, would want to know where I could get American food. She didn't know how right she was. I was starving.

I pressed my nose to the glass and a wave of homesickness engulfed me. Inside there were the familiar aluminum baking trays, weighing scale, marble topped counter and cash register. Mrs. Field's cookies were more than just a taste treat to me, they were a symbol of my connection to Peter. Surely finding the shop was a sign that I was on the right track to find him.

But the store was closed. I checked my watch. It was only three o'clock in the afternoon, yet there wasn't a chocolate chip in sight, not even a hint of the fragrance of baking cookies, only a teenage boy, mopping the dirty floor with an even dirtier mop. I rattled the door to get his attention. He glanced up once, then turned his back, pointedly ignoring me. That put me over the edge. I began pounding on the door with my fists. If he wouldn't open it, by God I was going to beat it down.

"Karen, get a grip!"

Lily's voice brought me back to reality. I turned around and was shocked to see that a crowd had gathered. "I guess they've never seen a foreigner making a fool of herself," Lily scolded. She dumped our luggage on the ground and smiled at the onlookers. "It's just a hormonal surge," she explained to the uncomprehending Chinese. "She's pregnant." The crowd just stared in rapt curiosity.

"Why is it closed?" I implored them, pointing to my watch. "It's only three o'clock. What kind of a store closes at three o'clock?" They stared at me dumbfounded.

"Excuse me," said a gentle voice, and a nicely dressed young man stepped forward. "The cookie shop is closed because cookie is finish. They open ten o'clock, finish one o'clock," he explained in fractured English.

"A three-hour work day?" Lily mumbled. "Don't let the Free World hear about that!"

"Tomorrow?" I asked.

"Tomorrow same," he said. "Every day, same." He pointed to a rack of advertising flyers on the door. The English translation touted, 'The Famous Cookie from Mother's Skillet.' Then it listed the various types of cookies and the shop hours — ten o'clock until one o'clock, Monday through Saturday.

I put a flyer in my pocket. It was apparently as close as I was going to get to satisfying my craving for Mrs. Field's milk chocolate, no nuts.

The young man must have seen my disappointment because he said, "Maybe you try Chinese sweet. Many shop in Fuchow open now."

I cracked a feeble smile and opened my mouth to explain that it wasn't just any cookie I wanted, but Lily interrupted. "What we could really use are a telephone and a taxi. Could you help us, please?"

Our new friend Wallace Ho was a godsend. He had only ten minutes before his train departed, but he seemed pleased be able to help us and to have a chance to practice his English. "I study six year at my school in Shanghai," he told us proudly. "Someday I hope to visit America and have sex with Madonna."

"I suppose he's got as good a chance as anyone," Lily said under the breath.

"You know about Madonna?" I asked, hiding a smile at his oddly appropriate statement.

"Oh, yes," he replied enthusiastically. "At school my teacher played Western music for my class. We hear Madonna, Michael Jackson and Barry Manilow."

"Barry Manilow?" Lily and I grimaced.

"Very nice music," Wallace said as he dialed Cao's number on a telephone older than me. "Very much romantic." He handed me the phone and took Lily to find a taxi.

"Don't forget to tell her about my passport," she called over her shoulder.

"KAREN!" Cao's voice crackled through a bad connection. "I've been so worried. Was the train late?"

"Yes, we just got here. We had an unscheduled stop."

"Otherwise, how has the trip been?"

"Mostly okay. But Lily got hassled on the train. Somebody took her passport."

"Oh, dear. I must apologize for my people," Cao said, as though the burden for the actions of every Chinese citizen rested on her shoulders. "Crime against foreigners in China used to be unheard of, but in the past few years it's gotten very bad. You can imagine the value of an American passport on the black market. These thieves are like your purse snatchers in New York City."

"Should we report it to the police?"

"There wouldn't be much point. After the fact, there is little Public Security can do but make a report and fill out forms. Besides, whoever took it has no doubt disappeared."

"But Lily got a good look at him. He had slicked back hair and wraparound sunglasses. She said he looked European. And I think I saw a man like that get on the train in Hong Kong. A handsome man, tall, wearing a shiny suit. Did you see anyone like that at the station?" I probed, hoping she would offer an explanation. Any explanation.

"No," she said. "After you got on the train, I left immediately. I didn't see or talk to anyone."

My heart fell. I was positive I'd seen her talking to the man Lily had described. Why would she lie to me? "Maybe we should contact the authorities. Is there an American Embassy in China?" I asked.

"Unfortunately no. I will start the machinery at this end to see if I can get a replacement passport, or some kind of temporary document for Lily, and have it waiting at immigration at Kai Tak when you return," she was saying. "In the meantime, let me tell you the good news. We can be fairly certain Peter is in Fuchow," she said.

My heart leapt. "How do you know?"

"The police in Aberdeen have released the name of the dead man you saw on the junk. He was a professor from Wing On University, there in Fuchow. His name was Dr. Zhou Ping. Did Peter ever mention him?"

"No," I said, "but he never told me anything about his business in Hong Kong." Or about a lot of other things, I thought, but didn't say. "What do you think this professor had to do with Peter?"

"I don't know, but I want to warn you to be very careful. It's likely that the police in Fuchow are investigating the murder from that end. So they are looking for Peter as well. This is a candle that is burning at both ends."

"But Peter didn't kill anybody, the men in the power boat did! Why would the police be after Peter?"

"They took the owner of the junk into custody," Cao said. "Perhaps he gave them a description of Peter so things would go easier for him. In any case, this is a dangerous situation. If you and Lily don't find Peter at my aunt and uncle's, you should come back to Hong Kong immediately."

LILY WAS WAITING for me at the curb outside the station.

"What did she say?" she asked as soon as I found her.

"She says she'll try to have a passport waiting for you at the airport in Hong Kong, and to be careful," I said, giving her an abbreviated version of our conversation. "Where's our friend Wallace?"

"He had to catch his train."

"Did he find us transportation?"

Lily nodded. "Our chariot awaits." She motioned toward a vehicle at the curb. It had three patched, bald retreads the size of bicycle tires, one centered in the front and two more at the rear. The car's body looked like it was made out of recycled tin. It was unpainted, squared off at the nose and open in back like a miniature pickup truck. The tiny covered cab held one comfortably, two in a pinch. But after we dumped the luggage in the back and covered it with a tarp, all three of us squeezed in. The sky was overcast; I hoped we wouldn't get caught in a downpour.

"Does he know where to take us?" I asked Lily.

"Wallace showed him the map." She held it up. "You take us here, right?" The driver nodded vigorously and started the engine. It groaned like a dying cow, then, to my relief, chugged to life.

"Pontiac," the driver said with pride, and put it in gear.

"You speak English?"

He smiled and nodded. "Pontiac," he said again, and stepped on the gas. We roared out of the station at five miles an hour.

Were we nuts to get in this deathtrap of a car, with a complete stranger who didn't speak English, on the assumption that he understood where we wanted to go, let alone could be trusted to take us there safely? Lily must have been thinking the same thing. "Can you imagine doing this in L.A.?" she asked nervously.

I shook my head. No one in their right mind would get into a stranger's car in L.A.; it was risky enough getting into your own car.

"Do we know how far it is?" I asked Lily.

She shrugged. "It couldn't be too far. Eugene got him down to three Yuan — he said it's about six U.S. dollars."

"What's your name?" I asked the driver. He looked at me questioningly. "Name?" I repeated. "I am Karen. This is Lily. You are . . ." I tapped his arm. "What is your name?"

He smiled broadly, and as he replied, Lily and I said with him, "Pontiac."

Our first glimpse of Fuchow was through a dirty windshield. It was difficult to distinguish much because of the built-up crud, but what we did see was bleak, made even more so by the inversion layer of dark, threatening clouds pressing down on us.

The train station was located in an industrial zone, amidst sprawling factories, whose smokestacks vented billows of putrid-smelling black fumes into the already gray sky. Each factory was surrounded by a wall topped with curls of barbed wire, whether to keep workers in or visitors out, I couldn't tell. But they gave the area the ominous look of a militarized zone, an ambiance heightened by the absence of pedestrians, trees, ornamentation, or color.

But as the small truck bounced along the wide, rutted road, the imposing factories gradually gave way to retail businesses — tailors, wool spinners, bicycle repair centers, restaurants, all open to the street. I nudged Lily and pointed as we passed a streetside cafe named in English, "Mr. Beef Seafood Restaurant."

"Something for everyone," she mused.

The further into the city we went, the more populated the streets became. There were hordes of people on foot, and thousands of bicycles, each with a basket front or rear, and a piercing bell. Brrng! Brrng! The sound could be heard even over the cacophony of the traffic.

There were few private cars, but many trucks, jeeps, and buses, all the worse for wear, due no doubt to the dreadful condition of the road. Every so often the pavement simply stopped and turned into gravel or dirt, leaving rocky mounds of excavated rubble dotting the road like molehills. CalTrans would have had a field day.

In the absence of private automobiles, people used their bicycles like minivans. I saw one stacked ten feet high with building materials, another hauling mattresses, perhaps a dozen piled one atop the other. Every so often, a small, puffing tractor moving at three miles per hour, or a team of draught mules hauling a wooden-wheeled cart, would bully its way into the middle of the street, causing motorists to brake, bicyclists to swerve, and walkers to step into the line of oncoming traffic in order to get by. There were no traffic police.

The rain that had been threatening finally began, further muddying the windshield. Pontiac had to stick his head out the window in order to see, so progress slowed. We rolled up the window on our side in order to keep the rain from blowing in. The glass was crisscrossed with duct tape to hold the broken pieces together, so we could not see out at all. The feeling of isolation I had had since we'd gotten on the train was getting stronger every minute.

I noticed that Lily was holding the small peach pit cameo her great-grandmother had given her, rubbing its carved surface with her thumb as she stared out the window.

The taxi suddenly began to buck and bounce like a disgruntled mule. I rolled the window down and stuck my head out. To my surprise, we were no longer in the city. Urban development had ended abruptly and the countryside had begun. And just as suddenly, the wide, paved road had ended, funneling traffic into a rutted one-lane dirt road.

It was rough going. With every bounce of the small truck, my spine pogo-sticked into my skull. And I had to pee again. I'd heard pregnant women complain about constant pressure on their bladders, but I was only two months along. Did I have seven more months of this to look forward to?

Our pace slowed to a crawl as we passed through small villages, rabbit warrens of houses tightly clustered about a few winding alleys and surrounded by broad belts of fields. Every once in a while we passed people walking or riding bicycles, and then a few minutes later they'd pass us as we tried to maneuver out of a muddy pothole.

At last we turned onto a still narrower road, barely more than a path, which wound up a hill. Here the rains had washed away the loose topsoil, sluicing out the ruts into snaking gullies, exposing the rocks below. It was a tremendous effort for the taxi to make it up the incline. We skittered forward and slid back, sometimes losing more ground than we gained.

But eventually the road leveled off, and soon after we came to a wheezing stop in front of a tiny earthen house, one of three huddled at the end of the road. I stuck my head out the window to get a good look. It was built solidly, like a log cabin only of earthen brick instead of wood, with small, high windows flanking each side of the front door and a symmetrically curved tile roof, embellished by eaves which seemed to sweep upward at the ends like birds' tails. A rusty bicycle was propped up against the wall. A mangy looking dog made a half-hearted foray into the rain to check us out, then thought better of it and retreated around the corner.

Pontiac handed the map back to me, pointed at it, and then at the house. This was it? The little adobe building looked unremarkable. The facade was decayed, but the walk was swept and the surrounding courtyard orderly. Through small windows on either side of the door we could see light. Someone was inside. Was it Peter?

I looked at Lily. She looked at me. "I guess this is it."

"I guess it is." We were both reluctant to get out.

"What if it isn't? We'll be stuck here out in the boondocks."

"You stay in the car so he doesn't leave," I said. "I'll make sure we've got the right place."

"Done."

I climbed over Lily and got out.

It was still drizzling, so I ran across the muddy courtyard to the house. The dog's barking and the muffled wail of a baby pierced the monotony of the rain, but I neither saw nor heard anything sinister to warn me away. The thought that I might see Peter any second gave me courage. I stepped up to the door.

中國象棋

FIFTEEN

It was thick, and bolted from the inside. There was no doorbell, so I rapped sharply on the wood. Almost instantly the bolt slid back, and a diminutive gray-haired woman peered out. She was dressed in what I now recognized as standard dress — a pajama-style blue jacket buttoned to the neck, and trousers so baggy I could have stepped into them with her. The diary of a hard life was written on her face, and her eyes were devoid of emotion. I tried to look past her into the house — was Peter inside?

"Hello," I called loudly in case he was, and bowed the way I'd seen people do since we'd arrived in Asia. Even though I knew she didn't speak English, I assumed she would sense friendly intent in my body language, but she didn't bow back or offer any hint of welcome.

There was nothing to do but give her Cao's letter. She took it with a tiny hand, crippled with arthritis. Without looking at it, she slammed the door in my face.

I turned to Lily and shrugged. Then I waited. What else could I do? The rain had soaked through my jacket and pants, so I drew up my collar and hunkered close to the wall. Were eyes peering at me through the tiny slat windows of the other houses, or was it my imagination?

Finally the door creaked opened. This time the woman was accompanied by a man who looked to be her twin in age, height, weight and dress. They bowed and, to my relief, smiled — he had a mouthful of crooked teeth, hers were small and pointy. I bowed and smiled back, relieved, and they stood aside for me to enter.

I knew immediately that Peter was not there. In retrospect I realized it had been incredibly naive of me to have assumed that he would be sitting inside discussing current events with Cao's aunt and uncle, but honestly, I had expected it. I was disappointed, but there was still a chance that he hadn't arrived yet, or perhaps he had stepped out for a moment.

I remembered Lily, still waiting in the cab. Bowing again to the old couple, I went to the door and motioned to her to join me.

"Should I have him wait?" she called as she pulled the luggage out from under the tarp.

"Yes," I called back. But it was too late. Pontiac was already backing down the rutted path to the main road.

"Stop him! We'll never get back to town!" I cried.

I ran a few steps trying to flag Pontiac down, but he was oblivious. The road was muddy, and the rain was increasing so I gave up and walked back to the doorway where Lily waited.

"This is it?" she asked.

"I think so, but Peter's not here."

We stepped inside the door and stood there, awkward and shivering. The man motioned to us to take off our wet jackets and move closer to the fire, which gave off warmth and acrid smoke.

"Not exactly mesquite," Lily sniffed. "Like I told you, they use —"

"Don't mention it," I cut her off.

While we dried off and warmed up, I looked around the room for signs of Peter, any clue that he had been there or was expected soon. We were standing in a small room which had a sleeping alcove on the left, and a portal on the right that led to an outdoor communal kitchen connecting our hosts' house and the two other living areas in the compound. The floor of the house was earthen, and neatly swept, the walls made of adobe-style bricks. Inside the walls was an exposed wooden framework which rose from the ground to support the weight of the roof beams. In any house I'd ever seen, the roof was supported by the walls, with the wood framing hidden inside them. But from the looks of it, these walls merely enclosed the space; the wooden scaffold inside did all the work of holding up the roof.

The main room was proportioned to the two diminutive Chinese, so with the addition of Lily and me, our wet luggage and the foreign aura around us, it became claustrophobic. The furniture was spartan — a canvas-covered sofa big enough for two, a folding table propped against the wall, and four hard chairs. In one corner a sink was filled with wilting vegetables, and above it, shelves held a few pots, pans and dishes.

The walls were bare, except for two photographs, one of a Chinese man in uniform, not Mao Tse Tung, but probably his more recent incarnation, whose name I'd forgotten, and one of former U.S. President Richard M. Nixon. On a sideboard, there was a red plastic vase holding a bouquet of faded plastic flowers. It provided the only color in the drab room.

The old man arranged the four chairs in a circle and beckoned us to sit while the old woman busied herself at the sink. He opened a drawer in the sideboard and pulled out a photo in a rough wood frame. He thrust it at me.

"Cao, Cao," he said, stabbing the picture with his finger. These were the first words he had spoken.

In the photo I recognized Cao, much younger, in a group shot with about twenty unsmiling men and women in uniforms. They were standing on a stage, somberly holding a banner with red Chinese characters on it. Around them were men in uniforms, soldiers holding guns.

"Cao, Cao," the old man said again, and took the photo away before I could look at it too closely.

"Yes," I said. "And we are her friends. This is Lily," I gestured to Lily, "and I am Karen." I touched my own chest. "Friends."

The old man nodded vigorously and pointed to his wife. "Xi," he said, and then to himself, "Li." We sat in silence for a moment, mutually pleased to have breached the language barrier, and exhausted by the effort it had taken.

I unzipped my jacket pocket and took out my wallet, sifting through it to find the photo of Peter I carry. We'd taken it at the beach. Peter was standing with Hermie at the water's edge, wearing a tank top and knee-length jams, his hair tousled by the wind, his mustache bristling in the salt air, a squint-eyed grin on his face. Would I ever see that grin again?

I held the photo out to Li. "This is my husband, Peter," I said.

Li studied the photograph carefully. "Petel?" he tried to imitate the sound.

"Okay, Petel," I replied. "You see Petel? Here? He visit here?" I pointed at the picture, then walked to the door, pretended to open it and come in. "He come here? Tall, blonde hair, mustache, green leather jacket?" It was like playing charades, only how do you describe blonde hair and a green jacket without words?

Li looked at the picture and grunted, then carried it over to Xi and showed it to her. They chattered in rapid Chinese as though we weren't there. Then, finally, solemnly, Li handed the photo back to me, presenting it to me with both hands as though it were a thing of great value. He shook his head and shrugged his shoulders, clearly indicating that he did not recognize Peter. Shattered, I put the picture back in my wallet. Had we reached a dead end so soon? Where would we go from here?

I stole a glance at Lily. She was looking through the portal to the outside kitchen, watching Xi attack a pile of vegetables with the gusto of a master chef. Lily smiled at me. "It looks like we're invited to dinner."

LATER, sitting at the tiny table laden with food, Lily was in her glory, salivating over the stringy greens and gummy fungi, tasting, drawing pictures, and cataloging her impressions in her journal. As for me, I couldn't stop thinking about the Mrs. Field's cookies at the train station.

Xi bustled in from the kitchen with one final platter for the table, and hovered behind us, watching. From the expression of pride on her face I could tell she'd saved the best for last. It was some stringy meat that looked semi-digested, the color of a bruise. For all I knew it could be the regurgitated cud of water buffalo. At least that's what it looked like.

Lily transferred a heaping portion from the new dish onto her plate and pushed the platter toward me. "It won't kill you to try it."

"Depends on who ate it the first time around."

"With Chinese food, the texture is even more important than the taste," Lily said, ignoring me. "There are four major texture groups."

"Is slimy one of them?"

She gave me a dirty look. "You're being rude. Just eat it. Baby Matthews needs the nourishment."

"But I'm a vegetarian. This is meat. At least I think it's meat."

"Eat!"

"I just wish I knew what it was." Grudgingly, I picked out a sliver and bit it in half, gulping it down without chewing. It didn't kill me, even if it did smell like a wet espadrille. I took another nibble.

"Hey, I've got an idea!" Lily reached for her bag and pulled out one of her Chinese cookbooks. She held it open in front of Xi, pointing to the pages, then to the dishes of food on the table. The recipes were named in both Chinese and English. Once Xi saw the Chinese characters she seemed to get the idea, and thumbed through the pages until she found what she was looking for. Then she handed the book back to Lily, gesturing proudly to the page.

"This is it? This is what we're eating?" Lily eyes skimmed the list of ingredients excitedly. Then her enthusiasm curdled.

"What is it?"

"You don't want to know." She slammed the book shut and slumped back in her chair.

"Lily!"

"Trust me, you'll have a stroke.

"It's too late now, I've already eaten it. And to tell you the truth it tasted like dog food."

"Well, you're half right," Lily said, and paused, waiting for me to understand. I covered my mouth with my hand, gagging involuntarily. "Hey, come on, everyone knows they eat dog in Asia. It's a delicacy. You should feel honored."

I thought about the dog I'd heard barking earlier. All was ominously silent now. "Well, maybe not," she said. We both put down our chopsticks and pushed away our plates.

THE RAIN HAD NOT LET UP by the time we'd finished

dinner, so it appeared we had no choice but to spend the night and try to find a way back into town in the morning. Xi and Li showed us into the tiny alcove off the main room where the bed was. It was an unpadded wood pallet, kind of like a wide picnic table, covered with a worn pad the thickness of a placemat. There were no pillows or sheets, but two threadbare quilts were neatly folded at the foot. Above the bed was a tiny window, about six inches square.

Li indicated that this was where we were to sleep.

"Oh, no, we couldn't," I protested. "This is your bed." But Li gestured insistently, urging me to sit. And when I did, he swung my feet up onto the bed, forcing me into a prone position.

Lily sat down beside me and tested the firmness by trying to bounce up and down. It had the buoyancy of a slab of marble, but she stretched out on it anyway, and sighed with fatigue.

Our hosts backed out of the alcove, drawing a thick drape across the opening, which gave us some privacy.

"I feel terrible that we're taking their bed," I whispered.

"Me too," Lily replied. "But on the other hand, the floor couldn't be much harder than this."

We lay side by side in our clothes, staring at a stain in the ceiling as though it were a Rorschach test.

"I see an eggplant," Lily said, squinting at it.

"I see a pregnant woman," I said.

For a while we could hear Xi and Li moving around in the living room. Then it was quiet. We lay in silence, lost in our own thoughts.

"Karen?" Lily whispered finally.

"Hmmm?"

"I think Xi understands more English than she lets on."

"Great, you mean you think she understood all the nasty things I said about the food?"

"I'm serious."

I turned toward Lily and propped my head up on my elbow. I'd become accustomed to the dark and now I could see the outline of her body. "Why do you think so?"

"Well, you know when I gave her that package of Lipton's soup mix?

"Yeah."

"She was showing it to the neighbors, and I distinctly heard her say the words, 'instant onion soup.'"

"Come on. How do you know she didn't just say some Chinese words that sounded like that?"

"Because as soon as she said it, she looked away and started running off at the mouth, like she was trying to cover up her slip. Don't you think it's weird?"

"Yeah, maybe. But let's worry about it in the morning," I said. "Sleep well."

"You too."

BUT OF COURSE I couldn't sleep at all. I lay awake listening to the unfamiliar silence, thinking about what Lily had told me and wondering what we were going to do next. I had been so sure Peter would be here that I hadn't come up with an alternative plan. What if I didn't find him? Had he already walked into a trap?

My mind went into overdrive, conjuring up a succession of tragedies: I'd never find Peter because he was lying in a ditch somewhere, dead. Or the police had arrested him for the murder in Aberdeen and shipped him off to prison where he'd spend the rest of his life painting Chinese fans. Or maybe Peter wasn't anywhere near Fuchow. Maybe he'd run away with Lauren Covington and they were in some Tibetan Shangri La at this very moment, making passionate love on a yak fur bed.

Then I heard a very faint creaking sound coming from the front room. As quietly as I could, I got out of bed and pulled the curtain aside. It was too dark to see much, but I could distinguish a quilt-covered lump on the floor right in front of the door, Xi and Li's makeshift bed.

Suddenly I realized there was someone standing at the door. A scream choked in my throat and I nearly fainted from fright. A thief? An assassin? Peter?

It was only Li. He opened the door and stepped outside, gently shutting it behind him. Why was he leaving the house at 2 A.M.?

I looked back at Lily — she was dead to the world — then at the door. I wanted to see where Li was going. Could I possibly get from the alcove to the door without waking Xi? I could hear her soft, snores rhythmically punctuating the stillness. But her body was between me and the door. No, better to go through the outside kitchen and over the wall.

I fumbled around in the darkness, trying to remember the floor plan and the placement of the furniture — the sofa, pushed out of the way to make room for the dinner table, the sideboard with the vase of plastic — oof!

My body bumped the sideboard just as my brain remembered the vase, and instinctively I grabbed for it, fortunately catching it before it fell. As I carefully put it back in place, my hand brushed something soft. My jacket. I picked it up and took one last giant step through the portal and out to the kitchen yard connecting the three houses. Then I climbed over the wall.

I was glad for the jacket. The night air was cold and moist. The rain had finally stopped, and the sky was clear and starry now, with a full moon that threw off enough light for me to see a human shape moving across the field. It had to be Li, but where was he going? I stepped into the courtyard to get a better view. The ground was spongy beneath my feet and my shoes made sucking sounds with each step. I hoped Li was too far away to hear.

Then I saw the other man. He stepped out from beneath a tree, thirty yards from the house. When Li reached him, they spoke at length. I waited, unable to understand what they were saying and getting colder by the second.

Finally, Li handed the man a small packet the size of an envelope. The man put it inside his jacket and hurried down the path, to where I now saw a jeep idling. As he moved out of the shadows the moon shone off his slicked back hair. It was the man who'd stolen Lily's passport! What was he doing here? How had he found us? My heart was pounding so loudly against my ribcage that I wrapped my arms around my torso to silence it and watched helplessly as he got into the jeep and drove away.

Suddenly I realized that Li was walking toward me. Ducking low into the shadow cast by the overhanging roof, I slipped around the corner and flattened myself against the wall, praying I was out of his line of vision. When he got to the door, he stopped and slowly pulled off his boots. I held my breath. He was only a few feet away from me. If he came around the corner, how would I explain my presence?

But he only picked up his boots, opened the door, and went in. Relief made me weak in the knees. I was safe! But I was also outside, and I'd have to wait until Li was asleep before I could attempt to sneak back in.

Hopping from foot to foot trying to keep warm, I zipped up my jacket and stuffed my hands in the pockets. Something was missing. My wallet was there, the gum, the Mrs. Field's flyer . . .

My passport! I turned both pockets inside out, and just for good measure, checked the pockets of my pants, although I knew it had been in my jacket. Then it hit me like a ton of bricks. The passport was just the size of the packet I'd seen pass between Li and the man with the slicked back hair. Li must have stolen it! But why?

And how had the man found us here? I hadn't been aware of anyone following our cab; there'd been practically no other cars on the road. He had to have known we were coming here. And the only person who could have told him that was Cao.

Which meant that Cao must have told Li to steal the passport to give to him. She'd probably given him explicit instructions in the letter. I caught my breath. What else had she told him to do?

I wasn't going to wait to find out.

Going back into the house to get Lily was out of the question, so I crept around to the rear and tapped lightly on the glass of the small window over the bed. I visualized her panicking when she heard the noise. But I kept it up until finally her face appeared. "Jesus, you scared the shit out of me," she breathed, squinting to peer out of the tiny window. "What are you doing out there?"

"Come on," I whispered urgently.

"Why?" she whispered back.

"We have to go now. It's an emergency. Just leave everything and come!"

"You're crazy . . ."

"Just do it, Lily, please? Go through the kitchen and over the wall. I'll be there to help you. Xi and Li are on the floor by the front door. Make sure they don't hear you, and whatever you do, don't step on them!"

中國象棋

SIXTEEN

Lily slipped over the wall and fell to the ground with a thud. I suppose it was lucky the dog who'd barked at us when we'd arrived was no longer around to sound the alarm.

"What's going on?" Lily whispered, bouncing on her toes to keep warm.

"We have get out of here now. Come on!" I wheeled the bicycle I'd 'borrowed' away from the house.

Lily trotted after me squinting at her Rolex. "Now? It's not even — " She shook her wrist and held it to her ear. "Shoot, it stopped."

"Just get on the bicycle, please? I'll explain when we're away from here."

"What about our stuff?"

"We have to leave it. There's only one bicycle."

"We'll come back for it, won't we?"

"Please hurry, Lil. This is serious."

"It better be," she grumbled.

The bicycle was an old three speed with squishy, wide tires, a high, curved handlebar, and a basket on the front. "How do you propose we do this?" Lily asked.

I'd wrapped my jacket around the bar that connected the seat to the handlebars. "You sit here. I'll pedal."

"Mary Lou Retton I'm not," she murmured, but climbed on anyway.

The first bit was downhill, so I didn't have to pedal, and could concentrate on getting my balance. But the road was deeply rutted, and the awkwardness of Lily's weight made it hard to turn the handlebars.

Finally we got into a rhythm. I kept us moving forward, and Lily pointed out the obstacles ahead so I could steer a wobbly path around them.

"What's the deal?" she asked when we hit even ground. "Why are we leaving like thieves in the night?"

"Talk about thieves. Li stole my passport out of my jacket pocket. I saw him sneak out of the house and hand it off to someone."

Lily was silent for a moment. I could imagine the wheels turning in her mind. "Did you see who?

"Kind of. It was dark."

"It was the guy who took mine, wasn't it?"

"Yeah, it looked like him," I admitted. "My guess is that he got yours by mistake, or he meant to get mine then too. So he probably followed us here and . . ." I shuddered, realizing that we had probably been followed since we left Hong Kong.

"How did he get Li to steal it for him?"

"I don't know. Unless . . ."

"Unless what?"

"Unless Cao told Li about him in that letter. I have a sneaking suspicion Li and Xi aren't on our side." I paused a beat, regretting what I had to add. "Or Cao either."

"What do you mean?"

"I mean maybe she's not with the CIA."

"That's what I've been saying all along!"

"Well, so I guess you were right and I was wrong. There's something else I haven't told you. I saw her talking to the guy in the train station in Hong Kong."

"What? Are you sure? What did she say to him?"

"I don't know. It was when we were already on the train."

"Why didn't you tell me?"

"I don't know. I guess I didn't want you to freak out and decide not to come."

She mulled that over for a second. "Why would anyone want our passports?"

"All I can think of is that if we don't have passports we can't leave China."

"And we won't be able to prove who we are."

"In other words we don't exist."

"Oh, this is just great! Here we are stranded in the middle of a Communist country, with no passports and no one to call for help." Lily's voice was shrill. I could hardly blame her. "What are we going to do?"

I'd gotten us into this mess — me, the pragmatist who never took chances, who followed the straight and narrow path no matter what — it was my job to get us out. "We'll go back to the train station and I'll call the American Embassy in Hong Kong."

"And then we should get on the next train out of here."

"What about Peter?"

"Karen, face it, we don't have a clue where Peter is. This has all been one giant fiasco!"

She was right, but still, if something happened to Peter, it would be a tragedy I would live with the rest of my life, and I would be reminded of it every time I looked at my child's face. "Let's just take it a step at a time."

By the time we reached the main road the sun was rising, and people were coming out of houses, heading toward Fuchow on bicycles and on foot. We joined the throng. Around us the sleeping countryside was hilly, with crops terraced up steep slopes. Not one foot of land was uncultivated as far as I could see. In the unearthly light of near dawn, the hills rose like green humpbacked dragons, which we would have to slay to find Peter and get back home.

It took all my strength and concentration to negotiate around the deep ruts in the road, and soon I'd worked up a sweat. Pedaling for two was exhausting, and my bladder was starting to complain again. "Time for a pit stop," I announced, and pulled to the side of the road.

"Good thing. My butt is beginning to feel like chicken palliard." Lily slid to the ground.

I laid the bicycle down against the ground. Once I stopped moving, my sweaty body started to feel the chill in the air, so I unwrapped the jacket from the handlebars and threw it over my shoulders. Getting sick was the last thing I needed.

We started to hike up the slope for privacy. It was slippery and steep, and we were about halfway up when Lily said, "Do you think we should have left the bicycle there? They took our passports, what's going to stop them from taking our bicycle?"

She was right. "You go first. I'll stay with the bike."

I had to concentrate to keep my footing as I made my way back down the hill, so I was almost to the bottom before I saw that I was being watched — but not by the man with the slicked back hair who'd stolen our passports. It was the man in the knit cap I'd seen on *The Dragonlady*, the one who'd gotten off the train with the machete! Now he was holding a remote control of some sort, clumsily moving it left and right like a divining rod, finally pointing it right at me!

He looked up and our eyes met. But instead of running away as he'd done on the train, this time, he started running toward me. My adrenaline kicked in and I began to run.

"Wait!" he cried in English.

But I wasn't waiting. I scrambled back up the slope, trying to put some distance between ourselves and Knit Cap. Lily was sitting on a rock, untying her shoe. "We've got to run," I panted.

"Chefs don't run," she protested. "Not this one, anyway."

"I don't mean run like in jog, I mean run like in run, fast!" I cried, tugging at her arm. "Look who showed up!" I pointed at Knit Cap struggling to climb up the slope.

"What's he doing here?"

"He's not taking a leisurely stroll in the country, you can bet on that. Come on!"

Leading the way, I headed up the rise. Lily followed as best she could, but she was terribly out of shape. The only exercise she ever got at home was lifting a fork, so her energy quickly began to flag, and at the top of the hill I had to stop to wait for her. The far side was terraced all the way down to a valley, through which a swiftly flowing river ran. A grid of train tracks snaked around the hillside and up to the river, crossing it by means of a narrow bridge. In the distance, I could see steam from the smokestack of a lazily approaching train. If we picked up our pace, maybe, just maybe, we could jump onto the train as it passed. But once the train got to the bridge it would be too late. It was a long shot, but it was our only chance to get away.

"Lily!" I panted, "We've got to get on that train!" I turned toward her and lost my footing, sliding down the soggy incline. I scrambled to my feet, but my jacket snagged on a low shrub, and it pulled off when I stood. As I reached for it, in a flash I remembered how Knit Cap had grabbed my jacket when he'd bumped me on the train. Could he have planted some sort of tracer on it? Was that how he'd followed us? But why? Was he working with Cao and the man who'd stolen our passports?

There was only one thing to do. I left the jacket lying in the mud and scrambled up the slope to Lily.

"Come on!" I shouted.

She didn't move. She just stared at me, her face the color of a ripe peach. "I just realized my journal's at Xi and Li's house."

"There's nothing we can do about it now."

"I can't leave it there. It's my life's work."

I tried to make my voice calm. "Lily, if you don't hurry, you won't have a life. This guy's carrying a knife you could butcher a cow with. We've got to get on that train!"

"You aren't serious." Then, seeing my face, she said, "Oh shit, you are."

Pulling her upright, I pushed her ahead of me down the hillside, following the narrow footpaths between the plots of land to the tracks. The train was moving slowly to negotiate the hairpin turns. We jogged alongside it, trying desperately to keep from sliding down the steep slope.

"Watch what I do, then jump when you can," I shouted, as we neared the train. "I'll give you a hand up."

"No!" She was breathless, frantic, trying not to stumble. "Don't leave me here!"

"Then you go first."

"I can't."

"Then I'm going!"

The nearest car was a boxcar whose door was open wide. Gathering my courage, I flung myself at the opening, but my foot slipped and I had to claw for purchase on the raw wood floor. Splinters dug into my fingers and in panic I felt myself falling. The metal wheels of the train whined only inches from my dangling legs, their motion drawing me down. I hung there helpless, floundering, without the strength to save myself.

But then, suddenly, I was being pulled up by unseen hands, strong hands that deposited me safely on the flat wood floor of the car.

Panting, I looked up and found myself staring into the somber face of a young Chinese boy. He gazed at me with unabashed curiosity. I was curious too, and grateful.

"Thanks! Can you help me get my friend?" I scrambled to my feet and leaned out the door. Lily was trying valiantly to jog alongside the train, but we were fast approaching the narrow bridge and she was falling behind. "Karen!" she called, gasping in desperation.

"Come on, come on!" I braced myself against the door and reached out to her. "You've got to jump now!"

The boy grabbed the boxcar door with one hand and swung his body around so he was dangling outside the train. He reached out his hand to Lily as the locomotive clattered onto the bridge. In seconds our car would reach the trestle, and it would be too late.

"Come on, Lily, grab hold!"

In a final burst of energy she flung her body at the car and landed with a belly flop thud, half in and half out. The boy caught her by the belt and held her steady until I could pull her the rest of the way into the car.

As the train trundled noisily over the bridge, I looked back and saw Knit Cap standing at the top of the slope. He was holding my jacket, watching the train. I doubted that he could see us, but surely he would deduce that we were on board, and try to beat us to the Fuchow station. But it would take him longer to get there than it would take us, so for the time being, we were safe!

"Thank-you, thank-you!" I said, bowing to the boy. He nodded his head curtly, moved back into the shadows of the car and squatted there, picking his teeth with a piece of straw, staring at us.

I wanted to hug Lily, to share the triumph of our escape, but she was concentrating on something in her hand, staring at it as though she were going to cry. "What's wrong? Are you hurt?" I asked.

She opened her palm and held it out to me. She was holding the temporary crown I had put on her tooth.

I groaned. "Oh, no. Let me see."

Lily opened her mouth and tipped her head back obediently. Fortunately the nugget of cement was still in place, blocking the hole I'd drilled to the root. If she was careful — and lucky — it would stay there for a while. But if it fell out, the root would be exposed and the pain would be intense.

"Don't worry," I said to her. "I can fix it. Just don't lose the crown." It was true, I could fix it, but not without the proper equipment, which was a long way from a boxcar on a train chugging across a river in the Fujian Province of The Peoples' Republic of China.

TRYING TO CALL the American Consulate in Hong Kong from the telephone at the Fuchow train station proved to be an exercise in futility. There was no telephone book, and no way I could make myself understood to the operator. Unless I found someone to translate for me, I was out of luck. Who else could I call? The police? No, they were already looking for Peter. I couldn't risk it on the off chance that they'd make a connection between us. Cao?

No, definitely not, until I found out who she really was and what part she had played in the theft of our passports.

I racked my brain. Who else did I know on this continent? The list was nonexistent. Except . . . my sister-in-law Jae. I suddenly remembered that Mitch had given me the number of his estranged wife. I hadn't talked to her since she'd left him more than a year ago, but she was my only hope. Wouldn't she be surprised to hear my story?

LILY WAS WAITING for me in front of Mrs. Field's. The shop wasn't open yet, but the smell of baking cookies had drawn a small crowd.

"What did they say?" Lily asked.

"I couldn't get through."

She deflated like a day-old helium balloon.

"But I thought of someone else to call."

"Who?"

"Jae."

"Jae? You mean Mitch's Jae? How on earth did you get her number?

"Mitch gave it to me before we left. I guess they've stayed in touch since she's been in Hong Kong."

"Can she help us?"

"She said she knows someone at the Consulate in Hong Kong and to call her back at the end of the day."

"What are we going to do until then? We can't stay here. That maniac with the machete might show up."

Suddenly the doors to Mrs. Field's swung open. We looked at each other. "Maybe we can stay here for a little while," Lily conceded. And for once I didn't disagree. We went in.

I pointed to the tray of milk chocolate, no nuts, still melting from the oven, and held up three fingers. Lily pointed to the double chocolate with macadamia nuts and held up both hands. "Ten," she said, "to take the edge off until we can get some real food."

I plunked down what was left of my Renminbi, assuming the server would take what was needed to cover the bill. Instead, he set the bag of cookies out of my reach and stared at me. I pushed the money towards him and reached for the bag. He moved it away and shook his head. It was inconceivable to me that the cookies would cost more than the handful of bills I'd splayed on the counter.

"We're in a hurry, please," I snapped, feeling my frustration about to spill over. "Take what it costs, take it!"

He called over his shoulder, and an older man came out from the kitchen. He was bandy legged and stooped, and his cheek bulged with chewing tobacco. He spat a disgusting brown gob on the floor before looking at me.

"Cookies," I said, pointing at the bag sitting tantalizingly out of my reach, "and money." I pointed to the pile of bills. Then I struggled to convey my confusion as to why this simple transaction had gone awry.

He chewed thoughtfully for a moment, spat again and spoke to the clerk in rapid Chinese. Then he looked at me. "We no take Renminbi to pay," he said. "Take Foreign Exchange Certificates."

"You speak English!" Lily cried.

"Little bit," he smiled, revealing more gums than teeth. "University of Miami, 1982."

"You went to school in Florida?" I asked.

"No go school," he replied. "I go learn American business. Work as cook in dormitory."

Lily's ears perked up. "You're a cook?

"Sure! I cook cuky!" he bellowed, grinning broadly.

HIS NAME WAS Sun Ye, and he invited us to come back into his kitchen to 'talk English' over a pot of tea and the cookies, which we finally bought with FEC. There was no sign of Knit Cap. So we decided to risk it. Anyway, the kitchen of Mrs. Field's seemed like a fairly safe hiding place.

All but one of the workers were sitting on crates, huddled around a dented aluminum pot filled with noodles, despite the fact that there were freshly baked cookies at hand. Sun Ye found crates for Lily and me to sit on, and set the tea in front of us. Lily reached for a cookie, took a bite, and swore under her breath.

"You no like?" Sun Ye asked her.

"She has a toothache," I explained, holding my own jaw to illustrate.

Sun Ye nodded sagely. "Green tea help tooth." He fished some leaves out of the pot and held them out to her. "You try?"

She looked at me for a professional opinion. I shrugged. "I've heard that green tea contains chemicals that supposedly weaken streptococcus mutans, the bacteria that start cavities. Used as hot compresses I suppose they might ease the pain as well."

Gingerly, Lily plucked a few leaves out of the pot. She was pressing them to her guns when we heard a man's voice calling impatiently from the front of the store — I peered around the corner and saw Knit Cap pounding on the counter, demanding service.

"How did he find us?" Lily whispered.

The answer was in his hand: the crumpled Mrs. Field's flyer I'd had in the pocket of my jacket.

"Please," I whispered to Sun Ye, "We do not want that man to know we are here."

"Why for?"

I wished I knew the answer myself. "He wants to hurt us," I said. It was probably true.

Sun Ye peered out at Knit Cap, then scrutinized me and shrugged.

"I have more money," I said, and withdrew a handful of FEC.

Sun Ye pocketed it and went to the front of the store.

Knit Cap spoke, and showed him the crumpled flyer. Sun Ye shook his head. There was more conversation, and Sun Ye continued to shake his head. But Knit Cap was suspicious. He craned his neck trying to see into the kitchen and would have come around the counter to look for himself if Sun Ye hadn't blocked his way. I grabbed Lily and pulled her back against the wall, burying us both in the workers' coats and day clothing hanging there.

At last Sun Ye reappeared. "Coast clear," he said.

But I hardly heard him, because I'd realized I was leaning against a green leather jacket! Although it was stiff, the way leather gets when it's been wet and smelled like a four-day-old fish, it was Peter's, I was sure of it. How many green leather bomber jackets do you see wandering around the Fujian Province of The People's Republic of China? I gasped and grabbed it off the peg, hugging it to my body.

The smallest of the workers leapt to his feet and tried to pull the jacket from me, speaking in frantic Chinese.

"This is my husband's jacket," I said, refusing to let go.

Sun Ye spoke to the boy, and the boy replied, gesturing extravagantly with his free hand. Sun Ye turned to me. "He say American man come behind store two day ago. First he buy many cuky."

"Milk chocolate, no nuts?" I asked.

Sun Ye looked at the boy. He nodded. "You right!" he said with surprise. "Man want to buy bicycle. This boy offer trade bicycle for jacket."

"Was he a tall man, blonde, with a mustache?" I asked, curling my fingers up at the corners of my mouth to demonstrate. And then I remembered the picture in my wallet. I showed it to the boy and he nodded vigorously.

"I knew it! He was here!" I hugged Lily. She seemed almost as surprised and excited as I was.

"Wait a minute. You said the man talked to the boy. In Chinese?" Sun Ye translated Lily's question and the boy nodded.

"Ask him please, if the man said where he was going on the bicycle."

Sun Ye translated and the boy shook his head.

"I know this bicycle," Sun Ye said. "This boy make very good trade, American coat to bicycle. Tires no good, chain broke, bad here." He motioned to his rump, indicating, no doubt, that the seat was uncomfortable. "He not go so far."

"I want to buy the jacket back," I said firmly.

Sun Ye translated, and the boy shook his head, trying once again to wrest it from my arms. But I held tight. "I'll trade him anything I have — my watch! I held out my wrist, displaying my cherished Movado. Sun Ye and his workers crowded around me to look at it. "Take it. It's almost new. That jacket is old, and the leather is practically ruined."

The boy looked doubtful, staring at the jacket, then at the watch. Without relinquishing my hold on Peter's jacket, I unbuckled the watch and held it out to him. It was too tempting. He finally reached for it and let go of Peter's jacket. I quickly put it on.

It was huge on me, and stiff from being wet. But emotionally, it felt like a big bear hug from Peter. I stuffed my hands in the outer pockets hoping against hope for a clue to Peter's whereabouts. Nothing. I tried the inner pockets one by one.

Something flat and thin was in the left side. I pulled it out. It was a damp envelope with a Chinese symbol on it. The letter inside was also damp, much of the writing too waterlogged to read. I held it out to Sun Ye. "Can you translate this?"

"Sorry, no," he said, "eyes too bad."

"Well, do you know this symbol?" I asked.

He looked at it and showed it to the boys, then said, "Symbol from Wing On University. Very important place for doctor and science."

"How far is that from here?" I asked.

Sun Ye shrugged. "By bicycle, four, five hour. By car, one hour, maybe more. You want go? Maybe we make another trade," he said looking at Lily's Rolex.

"No way," Lily cried, pulling the sleeve of her jacket down over her wrist.

"Give it to him," I whispered to Lily. "What do you care, it doesn't even work."

"That's not the point. I don't want to go on some wild goose chase. We should wait here to call Jae tonight."

"Lily, Peter is in Fuchow! He's nearby! This is the clue we've been looking for. There's still time to find him."

Lily pursed her lips tightly, the way she did when she was angry. "With a maniac chasing us and no passports? Don't you think it's just a little bit dangerous? That guy is probably waiting right outside."

"So we'll go out the back. Lily, this is Peter we're talking about. Peter, my husband, your friend. I'm not giving up trying to find him until I've exhausted every possibility. I'm going to find him even if I have to walk from here to the damn University."

"You're not being rational."

"Love isn't rational. It's emotional. If you'd ever loved someone you'd understand that you have to take risks for love." That sounded strange coming from me, the one who had always played it safe.

Hurt flared in Lily's eyes, then anger. "I'd like to remind you who took the risk of offering herself up to a student dentist for major oral surgery she didn't even need, just to help out someone she thought she loved."

"Okay, you're right. So you can understand why I have to try to find Peter. If you want to wait here, fine. You wait. I'm going." I looked at Sun Ye. "I'm ready. Let's go."

"She come too?" He pointed to Lily's watch and smiled hopefully.

"No, I'll have to trade you something else. How about this?" I took off my wedding band and held it out to him. Lily's jaw dropped. "It's all I have."

"Watch better," Sun Ye said.

To my surprise, Lily suddenly unbuckled the strap of her fake Rolex and handed it to Sun Ye.

"Here, take it," she said. And then she turned to me. "I still think you're crazy to think you can find Peter. But I can't let you go alone."

4

FUCHOW, CHINA

Tuesday, January 10, 1986

THE DAY HAD DAWNED like any other for Chun Sok Lee — the crowing of his cock announcing the rising sun, the evaporating mist rising like a veil off the face of the sleeping land, his stomach growling to be fed. By habit, he had risen from his bamboo mat and gone to the doorway to check on the old man across the courtyard before he had remembered that Wan Lo was not in the hut, nor would he ever return to it, except as a spirit. The old scientist was dead, killed by the Dragonhead Wo Fat.

Sickened by the part he played in this tragic drama, Chun had gone back to bed. Now, hours later, he walks across the courtyard and steps over the wooden door to Wan Lo's hut which still lies broken off its hinges, as the thugs left it two days ago. Although he has peered in the window before, this is the first time he has actually set foot inside the hut, and he is astounded to see so much laboratory equipment. In awe, he runs his hands over the fine caliber tools, the heating chamber and the centrifugal pump, having no idea of what they are or how they are used. He realizes how little he understood his old neighbor.

The rooster crows, and Chun peers out the high window. A man on a bicycle is peddling up the hill. He must be strong, for the bicycle is approaching rapidly despite the incline and the sorry state of the road. Could he be a messenger of death sent by Wo Fat?

Aware that it is too late to run, Chun ducks back into Wan Lo's hut and watches as the bicycle slows, then stops in the middle of the courtyard. The rider is not Chinese, he has the round eyes and thick yellow mustache of a foreigner!

He looks towards Chun's hut and then towards Wan Lo's, as though undecided where to go first. Finally he walks to the open doorway of Wan Lo's hut. Chun ducks under the table and huddles close to the wall, fearing even to breathe.

"Hello?" The foreigner calls out in English. "Anybody home?" And then he repeats words in Mandarin. "Ni hao!"

Chun remains very still, hoping the man will go away. But he calls out again, and then the soft tread of rubber soles announces his entry into the room. From his low vantage point Chun can only see the man from the knees down, as he walks around the laboratory table, stopping to run his hand over the pump and the burners as Chun had done. He is wearing trousers of a coarse blue material, and colorful shoes that have the English letters 'N-I-K-E' on them. Chun has heard that all Americans wear such clothing and shoes, but this is the first time he has seen such quality up close. An acquaintance from Nanjing told of a factory there where thousands of pairs of the shoes called 'N-I-K-E' were manufactured. Most were stamped for export; only the imperfect pairs were kept for sale within China. But, although the price was dear, nearly three months' pay, at the end of each day there were twice as many people lined up to buy the defective shoes as there were shoes for sale.

The rooster crows again. This time Chun does not need to look out the window to know that an automobile is coming up the road, for he can hear the hum of the Red Flag's engine. Apparently the man with the rubber shoes hears it too, for he drops to the floor and slips under the table — within inches of Chun. Chun huddles against the wall, flattening himself to it like a lizard on a warm rock.

And then two things happen at once: the man in the rubber shoes turns and sees Chun crouched not six inches from him, and Wo Fat's two burly thugs burst into the hut.

Somehow, this second action draws Chun into conspiracy with the man in the rubber shoes, as apparently they are both hiding from a common enemy. And since Chun realizes that his own chances of remaining undetected depend on his new companion, he raises his finger to his lips indicating silence, then motions to the man to slide further back against him.

The man does not hesitate. He scoots backward so his body presses against Chun, as though they are two drops of oil in a pan of water. He has a strange, strong odor that tickles Chun's nose, and it is all Chun can do to keep from sneezing. The man stares at him, his round eyes clearly begging Chun to remain silent.

Then both men are distracted by a crash and raucous laughter. "Watch me!" one thug crows, and with a piece of pipe he delivers a thundering wallop to the table. Both Chun and the other man hunker down as the wooden planks over their heads reverberate with the blow. Liquid drips through the slats of the table onto Chun's face and down the collar of the other man's shirt. Chun does not dare move to wipe the droplets from his eyes; he can only hope that it is water and not some dangerous scientific concoction.

"No," the other thug shouts. "Stand back and let a master finish the job. Aieei!!" he screeches, and the table groans under his bludgeoning, its rear leg splintering. It will not withstand much more abuse.

Like a mouse cornered by a cat, Chun is frozen to the spot. But the foreigner seems calm. His back to the wall, he edges away from the center of the table, motioning to Chun to follow him.

"Look, I pretend it is Wo Fat. I beat him in his belly, full of lard," the first thug grunts and pounds the table.

"No, hit him in his pocket full of gold!" his companion cries.

While the thugs are intent on their destruction, the foreigner crawls out from under the end of the table, and crouches in plain sight by the wall. Again, he beckons Chun to follow, and afraid to be left behind, Chun does. Now they are both exposed, easy prey if the thugs so much as turn their heads.

But miraculously, they do not. At the moment the table collapses in a loud crash, Chun and the foreigner dart out the open door. They press themselves against the wall of Wan Lo's house, breathing heavily with the exhilaration of their escape. The foreigner hesitates, looking left and right, not knowing where to run. Chun nods at the small structure attached to his own hut and runs across the yard towards it. This time it is the foreigner who follows.

They squeeze through the small hatch of the hen house, and the birds squawk, flapping their wings like fat, feathered bats, furious at this invasion of their territory. Using her sharp beak like a rapier, the mean Qing Yuan attacks the foreigner, pecking mercilessly at his hands and eyes.

Swatting her away, Chun helps the man cover himself with soiled straw. Although the light is dim, Chun sees that the foreigner's face is contorted in a grimace of disgust. Chun forgets his fear for a moment and smiles. The rancid stench of the hen house is as familiar to Chun as his own body odor, not nearly so objectionable as the foreigner's strong scent.

The Qing Yuan hen is still squawking, and Chun fears the noise will attract the attention of the thugs. So he grabs her and throws her out the small entry hole into the yard. Flapping her ruffled feathers she stalks indignantly toward the rooster who is pecking at a maroon and gold object on the ground.

Wan Lo's American cap! It must have fallen off when Chun ran to the hen house. What if the thugs see it? Will they remember that it wasn't there when they arrived? Chun doesn't dare retrieve it now. Already he hears the voices of the two thugs emerging from Wan Lo's hut. Please, he prays silently, let them go away!

"Look there," the first thug says, gesturing to the hen and the rooster. Chun's heart sinks. But when the thug lunges, instead of grabbing the hat, he captures the rooster in his bare hands. The hen stalks away.

"What do you want with that scrawny cock?" the other thug asks. "He is old, you can see by the darkness of his claws and his many wrinkles."

"Even so, his comb and testicles will make a fine treat for our master. If we satisfy Wo Fat's belly, perhaps he will overlook our failure to find the key to the black box."

The two thugs get into the Red Flag and drive back down the road. As soon as they are out of sight, Chun steps out of the hen house. The foreigner is right behind him, brushing straw from his clothes and chicken droppings from his rubber shoes. Chun picks up Wan Lo's cap. It is soiled and tattered now, but still the pin on its brim glows brightly. He puts it on his head.

The foreigner extends his hand and speaks in careful Mandarin. "Thank you for showing me where to hide. My name is Peter. I am looking for a man of science named Wan Lo. Are you Wan Lo?"

Chun stares in disbelief. He has never met a round-eyed foreigner, let alone one who could speak Chinese. The dialect is strange, but the meaning of the words is clear.

"I have been sent by the United States of America, by Dr. Leo Kensington, to see your invention," the man called Peter continues. "Dr. Kensington received your letter, but he could not come himself because of the danger." He nods toward the road. "Obviously others are also interested in your discovery and want to take it from you. Believe me, I mean you no harm. My government will ensure that your invention is used as you wish, as you stated in your letter, for the betterment of mankind."

It is beyond the scope of Chun's imagination that news of Wan Lo's invention has so quickly penetrated the wall of silence that surrounds China and reached the exalted government of the United States of America. Even so, it is too late. The black box is gone.

"Come in and I will prepare a pot of tea," Chun says at last. "We will talk."

中國象棋

SEVENTEEN

"This 'Yang Chang Xiao Lu,'" Sun Ye called to us. "Goat Intestine Road. Because it have so many windings." He chuckled at his own words.

"How much further is it?" I shouted back.

"Not so many," he answered.

He'd also said it was only an hour's drive to Wing On University, but we'd been driving more than three, even neglecting to take into account the stops we had to make for gas and directions, and the detours due to highway repairs on the narrow, twisting road. Time was our enemy. We only had thirty-six hours left to find Peter. But there seemed to be no way to hasten the pace, since we were riding in the back of Sun Ye's truck, a decrepit remnant of World War II, and he had decided to play the part of driver/tour guide, and bring us on the scenic route.

As we passed through the heart of the city we saw local people sitting on bamboo chairs and even on beds they'd pulled onto the sidewalk, to enjoy the passage of life before their doors. There were old men hunched over games of cards, sipping tea from tin cups, and women chatting over bowls of long beans, cleaning and cutting them with dull knives. Children played with sticks and balls and pieces of junk, and every so often a young mother held her infant out a doorway to urinate onto the street.

I thought of my own child, growing inside me. Could he or she feel the 'windings' of Goat Intestine Road, or my sense of excitement that we were finally on track to finding Daddy? As if in answer, I imagined I felt a slight tug in my belly, an embryonic foot pressing against the wall of my womb or a still webbed hand reaching out to test the limits of its world. Pretty soon, little one, I will introduce you to my world, *our* world.

And suddenly I was suffused with joy. I was going to be a mother! My body was performing a sacred miracle, creating a new life from my union with Peter. I wrapped my arms around my middle to let my child know that I had felt its presence, silently promising to do everything within my power to find its father.

I turned to Lily, eager to share my renewed determination with her. But she was withdrawn, her attention focused inward. I watched her fidget, alternately kneeling, squatting, and lying on the slatted floor of the truck, trying to get comfortable. To distract her I pointed to a rickety three-decker van carrying a load of enormous pigs with the floppy ears of beagles and the wrinkled faces of shar-peis. "Hey, Lil," I called, "check out the pigs."

"Huh?" her grunted response unconsciously imitating them.

"Don't they look like what would happen if Sheila Malone's dog got lucky with a rhinoceros?"

Grudgingly, she hoisted herself up and twisted to look in the direction I was pointing. But the truck turned sharply and she was thrown off balance and fell against me.

"When are you going to ditch that jacket?" she grumbled, recoiling. "It smells like a rancid fish."

I pulled the green suede closer around me. It was all I had to assure myself that Peter was still alive. "Whoa! Give this girl a rabies shot," I teased her with a nudge in the ribs.

"Back off," she spat with surprising venom.

"What is wrong with you?"

"What's wrong with me?" Lily's eyes spat fire. "Let me see, there are just so many possibilities to choose from. Could it be that I'm tired or hungry or cold? Or how about the fact that my entire body is black and blue from all this bouncing around? I feel like I've been through a meat tenderizer." I tried to interrupt, but she was on a roll now, and there was no stopping her.

"Or, I could mention the shock of being robbed of my identification by a guy on a train, or the debilitating fear of being chased through a field by some psycho with a cleaver. Or how about having to leap onto a moving train and getting half my tooth knocked out?"

I thought she'd finished, but then she added, "And to top it off I have one hell of a toothache that is making my ears ring like the Liberty Bell. It's worse now than before you botched the damn root canal. In fact, I'm starting to have fond memories of that pain, like, you know, those were the good old days."

She'd sucked all my prenatal joy into the black hole of her nasty mood, and that got me angry too. "Look," I snapped. "I'm sorry you're so miserable, and I'm sorry your tooth hurts. You know there's nothing I can do about it right now. Lily, this is bigger than us."

"You mean because it involves the CIA?" She shook her head derisively. "Do you actually believe your beloved husband is a spy disguised as an insurance agent?"

"As a matter of fact, I do believe what Peter told me."

"Really? Then there's a piece of property in downtown Fuchow I'd like to sell you."

"If you're so damn smart what do *you* think's going on here?"

"I don't have a clue, and I don't think you do either."

"Well, I know this much: All I've got right now is my faith in Peter. I lost it for a little while, I admit, but now I've got it back. And God damn it, I'm not going to let you talk me out of it."

We sat staring at each other, our hostility fermenting into a miserable silence. Finally I broke it.

"Okay, it's outrageous, I know. But can't you give him the benefit of the doubt? You care about Peter practically as much as I do."

Lily's voice was softer now, conciliatory. "I just don't see how he could have kept it from you all this time. I mean, you sleep with this guy. You wash his underwear. Geez, Karen, no offense, but talk about being blind, deaf and dumb. If it's true, for all you know, Peter has been involved in two murders, first, that guy in L.A., Fernando —"

"Only it turns out it wasn't Ferdy, just someone set up to look like him. And Peter had nothing to — "

"Did you say 'Ferdy'?" Lily interrupted.

"Yeah. That's what they called him. Fernando. Ferdy. Why?"

Her voice was quieter, almost lost in the street noise. "I don't know, it might be nothing."

"What might be nothing? Tell me."

"The first night we were in Hong Kong, at the Peninsula, you went to bed, and I couldn't sleep, you know? So I decided to take a walk around the hotel, maybe find Gaddis, see if I could check out the kitchen.

"I walked around downstairs for awhile, but the restaurant was closed. So I came back up to the room, and there was Peter, sitting on the couch with his back to the door, talking on the phone. I guess he didn't hear me come in. I didn't mean to eavesdrop, but you know, I was standing there, waiting to say hello, and I couldn't help but hear."

"What did he say?"

"At first he was talking this gibberish I couldn't understand. But now that we know Peter speaks Chinese . . ."

"He was speaking Chinese to someone on the phone in the middle of the night?"

She shrugged. "I guess so. I don't know for sure. It was so late, and with jet lag and all, my head was screwed up. I thought I wasn't hearing right, but now, I suppose that was it." She stopped to look at me. "And then all of a sudden he switched to English."

"What did he say?"

She sighed. "He said, 'You've got to help me get them out of here.'"

"Get who, out of where?"

"Us, I suppose. You and me."

I mulled this over. "Who was he talking to?"

"How should I know?

"Did he say a name or anything?"

Lily lowered her head so she wouldn't have to look at me. "That's the thing. I think I heard him say the name Ferdy. 'You've got to help me get them out of here. Get Ferdy to take care of them."

We both sat in stunned silence, letting the wind carry Lily's words away from us.

"Lily, why didn't you tell me this earlier?"

"It didn't mean anything to me, until we found out that Peter speaks Chinese. And then, just a second ago when you called Fernando Ferrar 'Ferdy', I kinda put it all together." She took a deep breath. "You don't think Peter is a double agent, working with the Chinese, do you?"

"No, of course not! It's impossible. You must have misunderstood." But I knew it *was* possible, at least as possible as anything else Peter had told me. But would he turn on his own wife?

Suddenly, we pulled to the shoulder of the road and the truck screeched to a halt next to the iron gate of a walled compound, another factory. Was something wrong with the truck?

Sun Ye got out of the cab and came around to the back. He unlatched the rear siding and lifted out a portion. "Okie dokey," he said cheerfully. "We here."

"This is a University?" I asked, gaping at the bleak, yellowed walls topped with curls of barbed wire. What I could see through the gate hardly looked like an institute of higher learning, all cracked concrete and dirt, no grass at all, and only a few weathered shrubs to break the monotony of the buildings, without an ivy-covered wall in sight. I began to worry that maybe Sun Ye had taken us for a ride, figuratively as well as literally.

But he bobbed his head up and down in response to my question. "Wing On University. Good school for scientist and doctor."

He pointed to the arched metalwork over the gate. In the crotch of it was an insignia. I took the envelope out of the pocket of Peter's jacket and compared its seal with the design on the gate. They were identical.

"It must be a hell of a place if they have to use barbed wire to keep the students in," Lily muttered.

We climbed down from the truck. Sun Ye pointed to his watch — Lily's Rolex. "Time to go," he said, and gave us one of his toothy smiles. He seemed eager to be on his way. "*Zaijian*," he called.

"That must be Chinese for 'sucker,'" Lily muttered.

中國象棋

EIGHTEEN

The guards ignored us as we passed through the gates of Wing On University, as though their presence were ornamental rather than functional — instead of trees and flowers, it seemed the Chinese used people to embellish their architectural facades. Probably in a country of more than a billion, people were cheaper.

"So, we're here. Now what?"

"Okay, here's what we know." I ticked the points off on my fingers. "Number one, the man who was killed in Aberdeen was a professor at this school. Number two, since the letter we found in Peter's jacket had the school's crest on it, chances are the professor gave it to him. So number three, if we can find someone to translate the letter for us, it will probably give us an idea of why Peter was coming here, and who he was coming to see."

"But how do we find someone to translate it?"

"Look for someone with an English textbook. We'll follow them to class and ask the teacher to look at it."

Wing On University was designed like a factory which, instead of making radios or toasters, manufactured doctors and scientists. The campus was barren and timeworn, and lacked architectural dignity. Even the newer buildings looked ravaged, like cancer patients in the last throes of chemotherapy. There was no grassy quadrangle or tree-lined commons where students could congregate and be nurtured by nature, only rack after rack of bicycles in front of the buildings, and hundreds of students, black-haired and serious, clutching their books with fervor and reverence, the way musicians carry their instruments.

As we walked among them we craned our necks to read the names off the spines of the books they were carrying, in hopes of seeing *English as a Second Language*, or *Webster's Complete Chinese/English Dictionary*. But it was easier said than done. The students we tried to talk to gave us wide berth, and met our friendly smiles with wary stares.

A truck slowly rumbled by us. It was filled with vegetables — cabbages the size of basketballs, bok choy, long green beans, and carrots. We moved out of the way and Lily leaned against a bicycle rack to extract a rock from her shoe. "Are there any more cookies? It's got to be lunchtime and I'm starved."

"Lily, that's a great idea!"

"Huh?" It had been a while since I'd shown an interest in food, and Lily was surprised, if not wary.

"Lunch. Let's do lunch. There should be some English students at the cafeteria."

"*If* we can find the cafeteria."

"That's easy. Follow that truck!"

I jogged ahead and saw the truck turn right, then left, then it trundled towards a long, low building. I waited for Lily to catch up to me.

She sniffed the air. "Ginger, garlic," she sniffed again, "and onions, lots of onions. I'd kill for a hamburger."

THERE WERE NO HAMBURGERS at the Wing On University cafeteria, no pizza or wobbly wedges of strawberry jello, but in the presence of food, even the serious and unsmiling Chinese students were lively, almost as boisterous as U.S. coeds, chattering loudly, teasing, laughing, reaching, and stuffing themselves. It was very encouraging.

We got into line behind a girl with a pelt of the most exquisite hair I'd ever seen. It was so black it had a purple cast to it, and hung to her waist, a thick curtain that swished like the grass skirt of a hula dancer when she moved, then fell perfectly into place again.

As I moved my tray forward, I kept her in sight. Not because of her beautiful hair, but because she was wearing a pair of Levis, the first I'd seen in Fuchow. If she wore Western clothes, she might be more receptive to our plight.

"My God, this is incredible!"

Lily was gaping at a wok the size of a hot tub, in which part of the meal was being prepared. One chef had a spoon that resembled a paddle. He stood on a crate, and leaned over the enormous vat, stirring with both hands. Four more chefs used bowls to scoop the cooked food into serving containers, from which it was doled out to the line of students.

The portion glopped onto my plate was a glutinous mass, desultory lumps of vegetables and shreds of anonymous meat smothered in a sticky sauce. Steaming noodles were next in line, and then dumplings, greasy spinach, and bowls of brothy soup. Almost as an afterthought, a square wrapped in waxy paper was tossed onto my tray.

"Sweet bean curd," Lily answered my unasked question. "Dessert."

"Not exactly Mrs. Field's, is it?"

We'd reached the end of the food line, but there were no napkins, utensils or beverages, nor was there any place to pay.

"At least there are some perks to the Communist system," Lily said, cheered by the thought of free food. "Where shall we sit, comrade?"

I looked around for the girl with the long hair and spotted her across the room at a round table with two other girls and a boy. "Over there," I said and led the way.

There were two empty seats on one arc of the table and we took them. The girl and her friends gave us sidelong glances, continuing to talk and laugh among themselves, covering their mouths with their hands when they giggled so I couldn't see their teeth.

Nor could I see their books, which they held on their laps or in plastic backpacks hanging on their chairs. This would take some strategy.

A waitress came by pulling a wooden keg on a trolley. She stopped by our table, held a pot under the spigot and let some tea pour in. Then she carelessly dumped some cups and the pot on the table, sloshing hot water onto my plate of food as she reached over me.

"Could you please bring us some napkins and some chopsticks?" Lily asked politely. She pantomimed spreading a napkin on her lap and eating with imaginary chopsticks, but the tea server ignored her too, and shuffled on to the next table. Our tablemates tittered behind their hands, keeping their eyes averted.

"How are we supposed to eat, with our fingers?"

"Use your toes for all I care. Just try to blend in."

"Thank you, Emily Post." Lily poked at the liquidy stew with her fingers and tried without success to maneuver a fingerful from the plate to her mouth.

Watching Lily out of the corner of her eye, the long-haired girl across the table called sharply to the tea server. The woman shouted back without turning, but the girl repeated herself, more firmly this time. Still, the server didn't answer, but she reached into her pocket and withdrew two pairs of chopsticks, tossing them unceremoniously into the center of the table.

The girl gestured to the chopsticks and looked at us, somehow without raising her eyes.

"Great," Lily said, reaching for a pair. "How do you think you say 'thank-you' in Chinese?

"You smile and nod your head," I said, and did so myself.

I picked up the other pair of chopsticks to be polite, but I had no intention of using them. They weren't the disposable balsa wood kind wrapped in paper. These were made of sturdy reusable plastic, permanently stained by the meals and mouths that had come before. I'd seen too many diseased gums in China to even consider putting them in my mouth unless they came with a finger bowl of hydrogen peroxide.

"You like eat Chinese food?" the girl asked Lily. She pronounced the words as though their sharp edges might cut her mouth. But her English was music to my ears.

"Mmmm, very good," Lily replied, deftly using her chopsticks to pinch a shred of meat and carefully place it on the right side of her mouth, away from her damaged tooth.

"She likes all kinds of food," I explained, to keep a dialogue going.

"Hamburger," the boy said. Only it sounded more like "*ambugil.*"

"Pizza pie," one of the girls said.

"Hot fudge Monday," the other girl added.

"Sundae," I corrected, "we call it a hot fudge *sundae.*"

"Sundae," she repeated, and then they all giggled, hiding their mouths behind their hands.

"You speak very good English," I praised them. "Did you learn it here at school?"

"Oh yes, we learn it here at school," the boy mimicked me. Obviously he'd been taught by the repeat-after-me-method.

"You must have a very good teacher."

"I must have very good teacher," he repeated, nodding.

"English teacher," the other girl added.

"Aach!" Lily dropped her chopsticks and pressed her hand against her jaw. We all watched her root around in her mouth and very gingerly pull out a white blob the size of a peppercorn. She handed it to me. It was the cement which had been covering the exposed nerve of her damaged tooth.

"Now what?" she demanded.

"Let me take a look," I said, and when she opened her mouth, I saw what I'd feared: a nasty hole gaped in Lily's damaged tooth. The nerve was completely exposed. Without the temporary cap or the filling in place, Lily was in for serious pain.

The students were watching us with cautious curiosity. "Bad tooth. Me, dentist. Me fix" I explained.

"In your dreams," Lily said and pulled away. She took another bite of food then moaned and quickly clamped her hand against her jaw to stem the rush of pain. Tears filled her eyes.

"We just need to replace the temporary," I assured her confidently. "Here, this will help for now." I dug a piece of Juicy Fruit out of my pocket, stuffed it into my mouth and quickly chewed the sugar out of it. Then I removed it with my fingers and rolled it into a ball. "Open up."

"No way," Lily hissed through clenched teeth.

"It'll stop the pain for a while, I promise. Gum is made with chicle, which is almost the same as gutta percha, the stuff dentists used before plastic was invented."

"You're making that up."

"I'm not!"

Lily was unconvinced, but wavering. "What about germs?"

"There are less germs on this gum than there are on those chopsticks," I whispered. "Trust me on this."

"That's what got me into trouble in the first place!"

But she opened her mouth a fraction of an inch and let me stuff the masticated wad of gum into her distressed tooth. The Chinese students watched intently, as though I were performing brain surgery. When I was done Lily jerked her head away and ground her jaws together to set the gum in place. She didn't speak, but I could tell from the look in her eyes that just covering the hole helped ease her agony.

"Better?" I dared ask.

"A little," she conceded, sniffing.

A bell rang, and the students rose in unison, gathering their belongings. The girl with the long hair smiled shyly curling her lips up without showing her teeth, and nodding her head in a modified bow. It was now or never.

"Please," I said to her. "Could I ask you a favor?"

"A favor?" she repeated, and cocked her head. "What is 'a favor?'"

I groped for the words. "A favor, it's a, you know, I need something, I ask you to help me, so you do me a favor."

She looked perplexed, and turned to her companions for clarification. They whispered among themselves in Chinese, glancing at us worriedly.

"It's not a *big* favor," Lily put in, "it's no big deal."

"A big deal? Sorry, I do not understand good English," the girl said. "I student, only two year."

Perfect, I thought. "Please," I asked, adopting her halting dialect. "We go English class with you now?"

"We go?"

"Yes," Lily said. And then gesturing with her hands, "We go, class, all, with you."

"Ah," said the girl, and she smiled with understanding, at last letting me see her teeth. They were straight and strong, but the color of old straw. What wonders a little bleaching could do for her. "We go class, all," she said.

THE ENGLISH CLASS met in a low-ceilinged second-story room built to accommodate fifty students, but it was jammed with three times that number. We were among the last to enter, and there were no chairs left, so we followed the example of the majority of the students and sat on the floor. Except for the chairs, the classroom was bare — no desks, blackboards, or computers, not even an electric pencil sharpener. The lighting was poor and the floor was unswept. But the students were quiet and well-behaved, almost reverent; you could have heard a diphthong drop.

The bell rang. A man I hadn't noticed before closed the door and strode to the front of the room, mounting a small platform.

He was Chinese, in his early thirties, and wore round spectacles with lenses as thick as Coke bottles. But instead of traditional Chinese dress, he was outfitted like a good ol' boy from Texas in sharp-toed cowboy boots, a plaid snap-front shirt, and Levis cinched at the waist with a tarnished silver-buckled belt.

He looked out over the sea of students, then smiled. "Howdy, y'all!" he drawled in a hokey imitation of a cowboy.

"Howdy, y'all," the class echoed, perfectly mimicking his accent.

"Today we'll review the parts of the body," the teacher said. "Very important when you go on your first American date."

Nobody cracked a smile until he repeated what he'd said in

Chinese. Then the class broke up. Pleased with himself, he unscrolled a chart and tacked it to the wall. It was an anatomical drawing of a human body, with bits of paper tastefully taped over its genitalia. The class giggled again.

"Okay, cowpokes. Are we ready to ride the range?"

"Ready to ride!" they cried.

"What do we say?"

"Yippie-ki-aye-ki-yo," they shouted distinctly.

The teacher looked pleased. "We'll start at the tail end of the herd today. Yo, cowboy."

He nodded to a student leaning against the wall in the back row, uncomfortably close to Lily and me, and then pointed to the hand on the anatomical chart.

The student called out, "Hand."

"Good." He pointed to the wrist. "Next?"

"Wrist?" a timid female voice asked, only it sounded more like "wist."

"You got it," the teacher replied. And he proceeded to point out body parts, which were identified by the students on down the row. Their answers were all correct, but the words were pronounced in clipped Chinese with a Texas twang.

Then he was pointing to the figure's upper leg. "Next," he said. It was my turn.

I hesitated, then softly answered, "Quadriceps."

The teacher spun around glowering at the class. "Who spoke?" he demanded. Timidly, I raised my hand. "See me after class," he said sternly and went back to the lesson. "Next."

Lily was sitting right beside me, so she was up. The teacher pointed to the genital area.

"I *knew* I'd get that one," Lily whispered. "He doesn't really want me to . . ."

"Of course he does," I whispered back. "Where else are they going to learn it if they don't learn it here?"

The teacher tapped the chart again. "Next."

Finally Lily blurted out, "Is it a man or a woman?"

The teacher turned again, and took off his glasses, staring hard at Lily and at me. "Both of you, after class. Next cowpoke, gimme both barrels."

The boy next to Lily called out, "Groin."

"Sure, take the easy way out," Lily grumbled.

中國
象棋

NINETEEN

His name was John Lee. He had been born in Oklahoma City, a third-generation Chinese American who, at the age of twenty-six, had shocked his wife, friends, and family by announcing that he had decided to return to his ancestral roots in the Fujian Province. He had been teaching English in China for five years, at Wing On University for the last two.

"When Nixon opened the door to China in '78, I charged through the chute like a bull with a burr in its behind," he explained to us. "I wanted to help my people learn about democracy, teach them 'the American way.' But it didn't work like that. Instead of my changing China, China changed me. Case in point."

He lit a cigarette, drawing on it with obvious pleasure. "I wouldn't have been caught dead with one of these cancer sticks back in the States, but here it's one of the few affordable vices. And not so affordable at that. A pack of Marlboros sets you back thirty Yuan. That's the equivalent of fifteen American greenbacks. And that's if you can find them on the black market." He offered the pack to us and seemed relieved when both Lily and I declined.

"If you're unhappy here, why don't you go back to the States?" I asked.

His expression turned serious, and when he spoke it was without the cowboy colloquialisms. "This is where I live," he said. "It's home now, whether I like it or not." And then, after a pause, "The truth is, I had to renounce my U.S. citizenship in order to stay."

"What about your wife?" Lily blurted out with her usual disregard of tact. "Did she come with you?"

"She's dead," John said, and our conversation died as well. He looked away for a moment to regain his composure. Finally he asked, "What brings you ladies to this outpost of civilization?"

"We're looking for my husband," I explained. "He came here on business and disappeared."

"How long ago?"

"Three days."

"That's not very long in Chinese time. Maybe his plane got delayed. They shut down the Fuchow airport for a week if the sun so much as goes behind a cloud."

"He's not traveling by air," I said.

"Well, maybe it's just taking him longer than he expected to finish his work. Chinese bureaucracy is notoriously slow. They haven't learned that time is money. How did you end up here at the University?"

"We found this in his jacket." I pulled out the letter. "We were told that this is the Wing On University seal, so we thought maybe Peter was doing business with somebody here. Could you translate it for us? It got wet, so some of it's a little smeared," I added apologetically.

John took the letter and read it slowly, his eyes moving from right to left behind the thick lenses of his glasses. Finally, he looked up at us, his expression somber. "You have no idea what this says?"

"Not a word. Can you read it?"

John Lee rose. "It's mostly equations, from what I can make out, some kind of formula. With your permission, I'd like to show it to the head of the Science Department."

"What for?"

"The man who wrote this letter was named Zhou, Dr. Zhou Ping. He was a professor here. And I do mean 'was.' He went to Hong Kong about a week ago to attend an energy symposium, and he never came back."

I recognized the name Zhou. It was the name of the man Cao said had been killed on the boat in Aberdeen.

John went on. "He was murdered. I don't know the details, the police have been dealing with Dr. Liang. That's why I want to show him the letter."

I remembered Cao's warning about the local police. If they were already looking for Peter, whatever was in this letter might tie him to the murder. How could I have so stupidly handed it over to a complete stranger? I stood and took the letter out of John's hand.

"Thanks, but I think we've troubled you enough. Come on, Lily."

Lily was perplexed. "What?"

"I don't see how it will help to show this to anyone else. We'd better just go on back to Fuchow."

"But we don't even know what it says."

"Come on, Lily!"

Lily looked at John. "Do you mind if we just have a word?" He shrugged, and Lily and I walked out of earshot.

"What's wrong with you? This perfectly nice, *single* American man offers to help us, and after all we've gone through to get here, you tell him 'no'?"

"What if it ties Peter to the murder, did you ever think of that? Supposedly the police are already after him. Suppose this is the clue they're looking for. It was stupid to assume a stranger would help us. I should have been more careful."

"You're jumping to conclusions. Why would Peter have been carrying around evidence that tied him to a corpse? Don't you think he would have destroyed it? Anyway, it's too late now. John's already seen it. And he seems trustworthy. Plus, he's cute."

"Yeah, I noticed you thought so."

We went back into John's classroom. "All right, we'll go with you," I said. It was against my better judgment, but it seemed to be the only option. "I'll hold this, though." I folded the letter back into its damp envelope.

"Suit yourself."

John took us across campus to a building that was even older than the English Department. I recognized the acrid stench of chloral hydrate, and sure enough, as we walked past an open door, we could see a class huddled around a lab table.

"Why are they wearing black arm bands?" Lily asked.

"Out of respect for Dr. Zhou. That was his classroom," John explained. "It may take months, even years, before the university completes the paperwork and finds someone to take his place, even though there are dozens of qualified applicants. It's not a very efficient system."

He led us up a stairway — there was an elevator shaft, but no elevator — to a second floor classroom. I couldn't believe my eyes — it was a dental laboratory! Although the equipment was shabby and dated, it was still recognizable: the tilting chairs, the adjustable lights, the cuspidors, the drills. Class was in session; every station was filled. Both the patients and the student dentists wore white lab coats.

"Oh no, he's a dentist?" Lily gasped, and involuntarily clenched her jaw.

"Trained in the U.S.A., as a matter of fact," John said. He tried without success to catch the doctor's eye. "Wait here," he said, and wove through the chairs to the front of the class, where Dr. Liang was demonstrating how to file plaque off a tooth.

"You know, I could patch your tooth right here if I could get my hands on some white zinc oxide powder and a few drops of liquid eugenol," I told Lily.

"Thanks, but no thanks. That equipment looks like it came off the set of 'The Bride of Frankenstein,' she said. "I'd just as soon wait until we get back to Hong Kong, or better yet, L.A."

"It's your mouth."

John motioned to us to enter, and I dragged Lily across the room."Dr. Liang, may I introduce Mrs. Matthews and Miss Pullen," John said.

Liang was a portly man, one of the few overweight people I'd seen in China. His face was so puffy that his red-rimmed eyes looked like infected cuts. The mole on his chin was the size and color of a lentil. From it sprouted two three-inch hairs.

He offered a stiff bow and then spoke in Chinese, gesturing to a doorway at the far end of the classroom. John translated, "He wants us to wait in his office until class is over."

"How long will that be?" I asked. "We don't have much time."

"Maybe ten minutes."

There were only two chairs in the tiny cubbyhole, so John

stood while Lily and I sat. I looked around. There were several diplomas on the wall, a B.S. from the University of Michigan, and a D.D.S. from the USC School of Dentistry.

"We have the same alma mater!" I told John.

"Can we talk about something other than dentistry, please?" Lily asked. She turned to John. "I hope you're not going to tell me that you worshipped at the temple of the tooth back in Oklahoma."

"No, I had a restaurant," John said. "I was a chef."

She perked up instantly. "No kidding! I'm a chef too! What kind of food did you cook?"

"In my hometown, everybody was into BBQ," John told her. "But at home we ate Chinese. So I combined the two. I called the place, 'The Chinese Cowboy.'"

"I've heard of it!" Lily sputtered excitedly. "It was written up in *Gourmet*, wasn't it?"

John looked pleased. "In May of '77. But that had to have been before your time."

Lily laughed. "When I was in high school I used to read *Gourmet* and *Bon Appetit* the way other girls read *Seventeen* and *Glamour*. Didn't you get a four-star rating?"

John nodded. "The irony was, a month later we had to file for Chapter 11. See, in Edna, Oklahoma, the only kind of stars that count come in a six-pack, on the labels of Lone Star beer."

Lily smiled sympathetically. "I know what you mean. Even in L.A., practically the only restaurants that make money are the fast food franchises and the sports bars. So few people really care about real food."

John and Lily commiserated about the perils of the restaurant business and chatted animatedly about their mutual passion for cooking. When Lily told John about Ah-So Schwarma, her concept for cross-cultural cuisine, he was impressed. "I'd eat there," he said. And Lily blushed with pleasure.

At last the bell rang, and as though by mutual agreement, we sat in silence until Dr. Liang entered. He bowed to us. Lily and I both stood to return the greeting, but he motioned to us to sit again. So the two men stood while we sat.

John spoke to Dr. Liang in Chinese, motioning to us every so often. The doctor nodded and asked a few questions, but he did not look at us until John was finished. And then he turned to me and spoke in excellent English. "May I see the letter, please."

Reluctantly, I handed it to him. What choice did I have? He took a magnifying glass from his desk and studied the letter, reading it slowly. Then he turned to John. Once again they began speaking in Chinese. I could see John's expression darken, and his voice crept up a notch.

"Could you please speak in English?" I asked anxiously. "I'd like to know what you're saying."

The doctor looked at me sternly, then twisted his mouth into a patronizing, tight-lipped smile. "This letter was written by Dr. Zhou Ping, a professor here until his recent and, I might add, untimely death. It is addressed to a scientist named Dr. Leo A. Kensington, a most famous personage in the West, and it speaks of a local man named Wan Lo. Do you know these people?"

Lily and I shook our heads. Dr. Liang stroked the hairs growing out of his mole, watching us closely. "At one time, before the Cultural Revolution, Wan Lo was head of the Department of Science here at the University. As far as I can tell from the letter, he now purports to have invented a magnetic device that he calls 'an alternative to electricity.' Dr. Zhou feels — felt — it has an application in the area of super conductivity. There are some equations to justify his theory," Dr. Liang brushed his hand at the letter dismissively, "however, they are too blurry to read. Apparently this is an invitation to Dr. Kensington to come to Fuchow to see the invention. I am afraid I do not understand the connection between these men and your husband, Mrs. Matthews."

Nor did I, so how was I going to explain it? Peter hadn't mentioned an invention, nor had Cao. Were John Lee and Dr. Liang being truthful about the content of the letter? Once again, I was in the frustrating position of not knowing what was fact and what was fabrication.

"My husband was sent here on behalf of Dr. Kensington," I blurted out.

"I thought you said you didn't know Kensington."

"I . . . I don't really. I just heard the name," I finished weakly.

Despite my earlier request that they speak English, Dr. Liang and John again began conversing in Chinese. Their exchange grew heated, and I could see that John was becoming angry.

"Does Mr. Wan Lo still teach here?" I burst in. "Because maybe if we could just talk to him . . ."

Dr. Liang sneered. "Oh no, he is no longer at the University. At one time he was highly esteemed, but he was discredited during the Purge of the Four Olds and stripped of his rank. He is no longer a teacher at all, of that I am certain."

"Well, maybe he still lives or works nearby. If I could I would like very much to speak with him, to find out if he has seen my husband."

"I do not know Wan Lo's current *danwei*," Dr. Liang said, "but I will consult with the party cadre in charge of records."

John cut in, "Mrs. Matthews, Miss Pullen, I think we should

not take any more of Dr. Liang's valuable time." He motioned to us to stand.

There was urgency in his voice, and though Lily and I were confused, we rose. I reached for the letter, but Dr. Liang held it away from me.

"No, Mrs. Matthews, I must give this to Public Security. It may be the final correspondence of my former colleague, Dr. Zhou. Perhaps it contains evidence that will lead the police to the person or persons who were responsible for his death."

My heart stopped. This was exactly what I had been afraid of. I looked at John pleadingly.

He spoke up. "But Dr. Liang, that letter is all Mrs. Matthews has to guide her to her husband. I think –"

"Nobody has asked what you think, Mr. Lee," Dr. Liang snapped. He turned to us. "Regrettably, I cannot return the letter to you until I have shown it to the Fuchow Municipal Department of Public Security," he said. "I will take it to them in the morning." And then as an afterthought he added, "Perhaps they can make a copy of it for you, Mrs. Matthews."

"But we don't have time to wait." I groped for a convincing argument, anything to get the letter back. "We must leave China very soon. Tomorrow night. And I must find my husband first."

"We are not in the West, Mrs. Matthews. You Americans must accept how our system works. The authorities will discuss this when they meet tomorrow. Now, if you will excuse me, I am late for a staff meeting."

I watched Dr. Liang put the letter inside the pocket of his lab coat. I couldn't let him keep it, but how was I going to get it back?

The four of us filed out of the office and into the dental lab, which was now empty. I racked my brain for an idea, and in my desperation, a thought came to mind. "Dr. Liang," I said politely, "Miss Pullen has a very bad pain in her tooth. You are a dentist. I wonder if you would take a look at it, as long as we're here in your classroom."

Lily shot me a look of sheer horror and started to back away. I grabbed her. "She lost a temporary crown earlier today and I'm worried she'll get an infection if it's not attended to. She is in great pain. Right, Lily?" I dug my fingernails so savagely into the flesh of her palm that she gasped. "Could you look at it?"

He hesitated, his reluctance evident. But as acting head of the department, he would lose face if he refused, here in his own dental laboratory. I had him over a barrel. "Very well," he said.

"Show him, Lily," I prodded her. "Open your mouth and show him, Lily, please."

The look she gave me was full of fury at my betrayal. But she unclenched her jaw, opening her mouth a fraction of an inch.

Now having no choice, Dr. Liang took her chin in his free hand and guided her face up to the light, prying her mouth open wider by cruelly hooking his thumb around her jaw. He drew back in surprise. "What is this?"

I peered over his shoulder. "Oh, we stuffed a piece of gum in the hole as a temporary solution," I explained. "Juicy Fruit."

He frowned. "I cannot see this way. Please, if you will sit in a chair." He pointed to the nearest station. Lily's shoulders slumped resignedly, and she eased into the seat as though it were the electric chair.

"Open, please."

Using a pair of tweezers, Dr. Liang swiftly plucked out the chewing gum and set it on the nearest bracket tray. He peered back into Lily's mouth. "Yes, I can see the hole," he said.

Now fully committed to his role as dentist, Dr. Liang used both hands to position the light over Lily's head. I could have grabbed the letter then, but I waited. And I was glad I did, because suddenly he swung around, obviously just to make sure I wasn't trying anything funny. To reassure him, I took another step backwards. The letter taunted me from his pocket. How was I going to get close enough to grab it?

"Why don't you stand over here so you can hold her hand," John said to me. His eyes shifted ever so slightly from me to Dr. Liang's pocket and back again. Was it a sign that he was on our side? I had to believe it was. I moved closer and took Lily's hand. It was clammy and stiff. Beads of sweat stood out on her forehead, and her eyes were glazed in terror. If I could just make her understand what she needed to do . . .

"It's okay, Lily, just relax, kiddo." I looked at Dr. Liang. "She's probably remembering the last time she went to a dentist, a friend of her brother."

Lily's eyes found mine. I stared at her as I continued, praying she would grasp my meaning. "He was champing at the bit to do an extraction. But she didn't let things get out of hand. Remember that day, Lily?" Remember how you *bit* his hand, I added silently.

Apparently she did, for as Dr. Liang probed her tooth with the Explorer No. 7, she screamed bloody murder and clamped her jaw shut, capturing three fingers of his right hand between the molars on the good side of her mouth, grinding them just the way I'd hoped she would.

John moved forward to help the good doctor extricate his hand from Lily's mouth, effectively blocking his view of me, and in an instant I whipped the letter out of Dr. Liang's pocket. Then I slipped the letter out of the envelope and slid the empty envelope back in the doctor's lab coat. Mission accomplished, as effortlessly as if we'd practiced the moves.

"It's okay, Lily," I assured her. She'd played her part admirably and now we needed to make a swift exit. I shook her arm gently and slowly she loosened her jaw. Dr. Liang jerked his hand away. "I'm so sorry Doctor Liang," I said, "I hope you aren't hurt."

"No, no, it's nothing," he snapped, cradling his right hand in his left like a wounded sparrow. But I could see that Lily's bite had been strong enough to break the skin.

"Maybe it would be better if we waited until we got back to Hong Kong to get this taken care of," I said.

"Yes, definitely," said Lily, bounding out of the chair.

"I think we should go now." We started for the door.

Mistrusting our sudden change of mood, Dr. Liang patted his pocket to reassure himself that the letter was still there. Feeling the papery weight of the envelope, he relaxed slightly.

"You're going to the hotel?" John asked.

"The hotel — " I began.

John interrupted, "Didn't you say you were staying at the Peace and Friendship Palace downtown? After the letter is copied tomorrow, I will see that it is delivered there."

He was giving us our chance to escape. Pretending to mull this over, lest Dr. Liang get suspicious, I said, "Oh yes. Well, okay. I hope you can get it to me before checkout time."

"You will have it by tomorrow evening at the latest," Dr. Liang growled.

We bowed our good-byes to Dr. Liang and hurried out of the classroom. John accompanied us to the staircase.

"Thank you," I breathed. "But where do we — "

"Do you have transportation?" We shook our heads.

"Then grab some bicycles outside. Nobody locks them here. Follow the main road away from Fuchow, left out the gate, about twenty kilometers to the Gilded Lotus Guest House. You'll see a sign painted with lotus blossoms by the bridge at the Ming River. Stay there tonight and I'll meet you at dawn tomorrow. I may be able to help you find your husband."

中國象棋

TWENTY

The twenty kilometers to the Ming River stretched interminably, lengthened no doubt, by my fear that any second we'd be apprehended by a Chinese SWAT team. Every few minutes I looked over my shoulder, sure we were being followed, but there was little traffic on the narrow road, only bicycles and an occasional truck. Still, my imagination was running at full tilt. Would we end up in a Chinese Gulag reform camp, laboring by day in rice paddies and shackled together in a windowless cell by night? Would my baby be born in a nursery filled with rats and roaches and disease? Was Peter in one already?

But we'd committed no crime. Outside of 'borrowing' a couple of pre-owned bicycles that were surely untraceable, we had merely taken back a piece of paper that was rightfully ours. And as much as Dr. Liang wanted the letter, he would have no way to trace it to us, except through John Lee, who, it seemed, had chosen to throw in with us instead.

But that brought up another question: Why did Dr. Liang want the letter so badly? What did it really say?

After a few miles of frantic peddling, I allowed myself to relax. If no one had followed us yet, they probably weren't going to now. Lily was riding beside me with her head down, concentrating on the road passing beneath her wheels. She was breathing deeply from the exertion and I could tell she was in pain. "Why don't we walk for a while?" I called to her. Without a word, she dismounted and fell into place beside me.

We were out in the country again. In the late afternoon light, the rows of newly planted crops slashed the hills like white and gray claw marks. Here and there a woman was bent, weeding her plot of land. Men yoked like oxen carried buckets of water up hillsides where the laws of gravity made natural irrigation impossible. Children, who looked at first to be playing were, on closer inspection, actually scaring away birds by waving sticks and streamers. And somewhere out there Peter was looking for a mad scientist named Wan Lo who had devised a way to create power without electricity, a magic formula which could catapult these hard-working people out of the dark ages and into the twenty-first century.

Lily removed her scarf and tied it around her jaw in a pathetic attempt to alleviate the pain in her tooth, or at least get my sympathy.

"Do you want me look at it?"

"No!" she grunted without opening her mouth.

"Lily, I'm so sorry. I'll make it up to you as soon as we get home, I promise."

"Assuming we get home," she managed to mumble through clenched teeth.

At the crest of a hill, we paused and looked over the valley. There were no trees in sight, only mile after mile of undulating countryside. A river, the Ming I assumed, wove through the crosshatch maze of fields, which became progressively greener near its banks. It was wide and fast-flowing, spanned by a single bridge. Near the bridge a cluster of buildings hugged the riverbank, a small village. I couldn't see the Gilded Lotus Guest House from where I stood; I could only hope we would find it there, as John had promised.

"We're close," I said brightly. "It's got to be just down this hill."

Lily eyed me in silent reproach, anger no doubt compounding her exhaustion and pain. We mounted our bikes and fairly flew down the road, letting the slope do the work. Then, at the edge of the village, increased bicycle and foot traffic forced us to again dismount and walk. Apparently it was market day, because the street was clogged with vendors and shoppers. Mahogany-skinned men in black pajamas and lampshade hats hawked their wares, everything from kites, to fans, to handmade eyeglasses, food and clothing, bags of seed, and crude farming implements. Old women sat behind trays of odd household items — a dark, bristly toothbrush, a used cake of Ivory soap, a dented saucepan. Children scampered between the stalls.

Nearer the river, a group of shirtless young men stood behind baskets flopping with fish. On their shoulders perched long-necked black birds, each wearing a silver ring about its neck. As we watched, one man released his bird and it dove into the river, thrusting its long neck deep into murky water, surfacing with a large fish in its beak. The ring around its neck made it impossible for the bird to swallow the fish. Instead it was forced to relinquish its catch to the handler, who rewarded it with a tiny scrap of flesh.

"There you have it, a perfect metaphor for the Communist system," I murmured to Lily. But she was no longer walking beside me. She had stopped before a low pallet strewn with a bizarre assortment of fauna and flora: dried, splayed lizards, fuzz-covered deer antlers, dead snakes and frogs, birds' beaks, furs, bony skulls, tortured barks and mildewed plants. The old woman selling these wares rose and began her sales pitch, disregarding the fact that Lily obviously understood not a word of what she was saying. She was less than four feet tall, and couldn't have weighed more than seventy-five pounds. Her withered muscles wound over the bones of her thin body like copper wire over an armature. But even more startling were her feet. As she hobbled forward, I saw that they were stunted knobs of flesh, maybe four inches long, stuffed into tiny pointed slippers that would have fit a doll.

Lily and I stared, speechless. Ignoring our rudeness, she continued to talk to us in a high singsong voice, extending a vial of brownish goo.

"Look, she wants to give us something."

"Give, or sell?"

The old woman pointed to Lily's jaw and then at the vial. She stuck her finger in the vial, brought it out coated with a glob of the potion and thrust it in Lily's face.

Lily stepped back, shaking her head, 'no.' Undaunted, the old woman opened her own mouth and patted the medicine onto the place where a molar should have been, but which was now only blackened periodontal tissue, not a very convincing testimonial as far as I was concerned. But she smiled with what teeth she had left to let us know that it felt good, then she held out the vial to Lily, looking at me, urging me to encourage Lily to try it.

"She must be some kind of healer," Lily said in awe. "How did she know I had a toothache?"

"The scarf around your jaw is a dead giveaway. Come on." I started to roll my bike away, but Lily didn't move. She sniffed the vial. "Herbs, chicken fat. Maybe I should try it. A lot of people swear by Chinese medicine."

"Yeah, look what it did to her teeth."

"And look what Western medicine did to mine."

"I'd be careful," I warned her.

"I'm sure you would." More out of defiance, I think, than a true belief that the mystery medicine would help, Lily pulled out her remaining FEC and offered them to the old woman. She picked out three bills and handed Lily the vial.

Lily unscrewed the lid and peered into it.

Putting an unknown medication directly on an exposed nerve was risky at best. Infection was only one of the possible consequences. "I doubt if that's F.D.A. approved," I said, trying to make light of my concern.

In reply, Lily dipped her finger into the gel and rubbed it onto her tooth and gum as the vendor had done.

"Well?"

"It feels like . . . nothing, but at least it doesn't feel worse."

No sooner were the words out of her mouth, than her knees buckled and she slowly collapsed onto a fruit display. Instantly a crowd gathered, forming a semi-circle around us. The fruit vender began shouting at the top of his lungs, pulling Lily's arm and at the same time gesturing to his friends to help him lift her off his precious fruit. I knelt beside her. She was lying on a bed of lemons, and small orange fruits which were clustered on pieces of branch. She didn't look hurt, in fact she was grinning like an idiot.

"Are you okay? What happened?" I asked, shooing the fruit vendor away.

"Nothing," she giggled. "I was just standing there, and the next thing I knew I was lemonade."

I pulled her to her feet and helped her pick up her bike. She took a wobbly step and nearly toppled again, so I kept one hand on her handlebars and the other on my own until we got out of the market.

"Boy, that's strong stuff," she said. "Do you think it's herbal?"

"You don't want to know what I think."

"Hey, I've eaten Labrador retriever. It couldn't be worse than that."

"My guess is that it's got some opium in it."

She stopped dead. "Opium! Oh my God. Am I going to be addicted?"

"Don't panic. It would take a lot more than one topical application to make you an addict. But it can cause the numbness and fainting." Nausea was another definite possibility, but there was no sense in putting ideas into Lily's impressionable mind.

Sobered by my words, Lily tried to walk faster, but her legs were uncooperative. "Where is this hotel? I've got to lie down."

Bed sounded good to me too. The sun was behind the mountains now, and already the evening chill was cutting through my clothes. The stress of the past few days was beginning to take its toll. I couldn't remember ever feeling so tired.

When we reached the bridge, the road narrowed to one lane. And to my relief, I saw a small wooden sign with a lotus flower painted on it, just as John had described it. We turned up a path to the Gilded Lotus Guest House.

I was expecting a Chinese version of a bed and breakfast, or a quaint mom and pop operation in a renovated farmhouse. But the Gilded Lotus was a multi-level stone longhouse painted a drab green, like an army barrack. Indeed, after we paid our money, seventy-five cents each, the desk clerk led us to a dormitory-style sleeping porch, with cots separated by thin muslin curtains. Between our beds a rickety table held a pitcher and a bowl of beige water, a thermos, and a tea mug. Several misshapen wire hangers clung precariously to a rough hook on the wall. The bed was made, but the linens were wrinkled and smelled of mildew. A coarse towel the size of a dishcloth was neatly folded next to a small, hard pillow. I pulled back the curtain separating our two beds and found Lily sitting on hers, holding her head in her hands.

"Remember how sick I got after Antonio and Margie's wedding reception at El Torito? This is worse," she groaned.

"You can't imagine how hard I'm trying not to say 'I told you so.'"

"Passport?" the desk clerk asked in English.

I caught my breath. What would he do if he found out we didn't have them?

"Passport," he repeated, holding out his hand.

I looked helplessly at Lily. She rolled her eyes and promptly threw up into the basin. The clerk stepped back to avoid being spattered. When she began to retch a second time, he made a derisive gesture. "I come later," he said, and fled.

Watching Lily get sick, my own stomach responded with a sympathetic tug. But since I'd hardly eaten for two days, it was a dry heave, thank God. I didn't relish the idea of competing with her for the one basin.

I tried to keep Lily comfortable, holding damp tendrils of hair out of her face as she bent over the pot again, mopping her neck and brow with the towel. "At least my tooth doesn't hurt any more," she managed to say before heaving up what was left of lunch.

"Lil, what do you give someone who's dehydrated? Bananas? Tomato juice?"

She put her hands over her ears. "Don't mention food!" And she leaned over the bowl again.

It took an hour before it was all out of her system. When she finally dropped off into an exhausted sleep, I lay back on my cot and closed my eyes, trying not to wonder who had lain there before me. We had only twenty-four hours left to find Peter. We were getting closer, but finding him hinged on John Lee, a stranger. True, he had helped us retrieve the letter from Dr. Liang, but then he had taken us to Dr. Liang in the first place. Could we trust him? If there were only some way to check him out.

Then I remembered Jae. I was supposed to call her back to see if she'd been able to get us help from the Embassy in Hong Kong. Maybe the Gilded Lotus had a phone. But if it did, I would have to confront the desk clerk to use it, and run the risk he'd demand our passports. No, it wasn't a chance I could afford to take.

5

FUCHOW, CHINA

Tuesday and Wednesday, January 10 and 11, 1986

CHUN WATCHES with wonder as the round-eyed foreigner with yellow hair who calls himself "Peter" eats the meal Chun has prepared, a thin gruel poured over steaming noodles, with a fried egg on top. He seems very hungry, and although he handles the chopsticks with ease, his manner of eating is sloppy and inefficient. Instead of holding the bowl properly under his chin and shoveling the noodles and broth into his mouth so not a drop is wasted, this Peter eats with his bowl on the table, lifting each strand separately, without even a polite slurp to signal his enjoyment. Often the slippery ribbons fall back into the broth, splashing it wastefully on the table.

"I would be most grateful if you could tell me about Wan Lo's invention. Have you seen it?" Peter asks in Mandarin, but he speaks with difficulty, as though the words get lost finding their way from his tongue to his lips.

Chun leans back in his chair, and his eyes take on a dreamy glow. "Ah, yes, it was a truly wondrous sight. A miracle! The morning was as dark as my Zhusi rooster. There was much fog and damp. Wan Lo severed the electrical wires and attached them to his box, and suddenly, all of the lamps for a thousand miles lit the night like the celebration of the Moon Festival." He makes a sweeping gesture with his hand. "Never have I seen such magic!"

"Do you know where the black box is now?" Peter asks. "I must find it."

Chun removes the Trojan cap from his head and sets it on the table. "The invention is in the hands of Wo Fat."

Gravely he tells Peter how the Dragonhead threatened him, how he retrieved the black box from where he had hidden it and took it to the eel hatchery in order to save his life. "We put the box in a special room where the electricity is kept, but although I attached the wires to the box just as Wan Lo did that night, nothing happened. I could not make it work." Distractedly, he picks at the metal chip pinned to the brim of the hat, remembering the rooster whose beak did the damage, soon to have his testicles fried in Wo Fat's wok. "I was fortunate the Dragonhead did not kill me there and then."

Peter's eyes fasten on Chun's hands. "What is that?"

"This? It belonged to Wan Lo, a souvenir he brought back from America years ago. He wore this cap every day, even to sleep, I think."

"May I see it?"

Peter examines the glowing metal pin and unfastens it from the hat. Then, to Chun's surprise, he breaks it into two equal pieces, revealing another piece of metal inside, the size of a grain of rice. Peter studies it on the flat of his palm, then looks up at Chun and smiles.

"What is it?" Chun asks.

"Have you ever heard of microcircuitry?" Chun shakes his head. "It's like a key, a tiny, tiny key, that operates a computer. It is what those two were looking for."

Chun thinks of the black box. "I don't understand. The box had no lock."

"It's not that kind of key. This is what makes Wan Lo's invention work."

Once again Chun is awed by the scope of Wan Lo's magic. He thinks for a moment. "The box is useless without it?" he asks. Peter nods. "Then we need not be concerned that it is in Wo Fat's hands."

"That may be true for the moment, but if he has the box, sooner or later he may be able to duplicate the key. It's like two pieces of a puzzle. If you have one, the shape of the other is clear. We must find the black box before Wo Fat is able to solve the puzzle, and destroy it."

"But it is protected by men like the two who came here this morning. To try to get it back would be like climbing a tree to catch a fish. It cannot be done."

"If you can tell me where the box is kept and help me get into the eel hatchery, I will do the rest."

Chun shakes his head. "You underestimate the ruthless cunning of the Dragonhead of the T'ung Yu Triad. You would be killed."

Peter smiles. "As you saw this morning, I am lucky like a cat who has nine lives."

"It will take more than luck, it will take magic to get past the guards," Chun tells him.

"I have magic," Peter says, and pulls out a ballpoint pen. "With this I can stop an attacker."

"It is not possible," Chun frowns, thinking how foolish this Westerner is.

"I can show you, but I'd need something to use it on, something alive."

Chun thinks a moment. "The Qing Yuan hen," he says.

"It won't kill a person, it will only make them sleep. But a hen, I'm not so sure."

Chun shrugs it off, because he does not believe a writing pen could kill a hen, especially the tough old bird. "If it kills her I will make my Kung Pao Chicken for dinner tomorrow," he says.

He captures the hen and holds her still while Peter uncaps the pen. Showing Chun how he is pressing on a tiny button just under the place where his finger wraps around it, Peter touches the feathery neck of the hen with the point, leaving a small dark stain.

To Chun, it looks like any writing ink. But in an instant, the hen stops struggling in his hands. Within seconds, she hangs as limp as an air-dried duck.

Peter looks into Chun's eyes. "It is a risk, but if you will help me get the black box, my government will reward you richly. In America, we say, 'You can write your own ticket.' In other words, you tell me what reward you want, and that is what you will have." And he hands Chun the magic pen.

Chun stares at it, and before he even knows the idea is in his mind, he blurts out, "I would like to go to America."

中國象棋

TWENTY-ONE

I was up before the sun, knowing I had only fifteen hours to find Peter and get out of Dodge. Lily was still sleeping heavily as she had been all night, undisturbed by the nocturnal stirrings of our dormitory companions, whose coughing and snoring and spitting had kept me awake. I scrounged up the few remaining saltines from her bag and ate them to settle my stomach, thinking about John Lee. Would he prove to be friend or foe?

I wrote a note to Lily, to tell her I was going to meet John, and went downstairs to wait for him. But he was already there waiting for me. Alone. No police. So far so good.

We walked to a food stall overlooking the river and sat at a small table covered in gingham oilcloth. Around us shop owners were sweeping the walkways in front of their stores, opening shutters and doors, and preparing for the day's business.

John ordered us a pot of tea and some cold noodles. "Where's Lily?" he asked.

"She has stomach problems." The aromas wafting up from the sizzling woks behind the counter were threatening my own gastrointestinal equilibrium as well. "She took some medicine she bought in the market yesterday. It was a bad idea. She vomited for hours last night."

John looked worried. "She shouldn't have tried the local stuff. It can be very potent."

I smiled. "No one tells Lily what she can and can't put in her mouth."

"Do you think she should see a doctor? I know a fairly clean clinic in Fuchow."

"She seems to be past the worst. I'll take her to see someone in Hong Kong."

"You're leaving tonight?"

"Hopefully. We're booked on a nine o'clock flight, but we may have some problems getting out of the country. It's a long, complicated story. I won't bore you with the details, but, well, our passports were stolen."

"I have some *quan-xi* at the airport. Maybe I can help."

"Thanks, but right now I'm more concerned about Peter." I couldn't wait any longer to ask. "Have you found Wan Lo?"

John nodded. "He was reassigned to the Superior Eel Hatchery in 1972." He handed me a photo. "This was taken in 1978, on a trip to the U.S.A. See, when Deng Xiaoping took over the government, he wanted to prove to the world that China's scholarly leaders had survived the false purges of the revolution. So he sent a delegation on a world tour. Wan Lo was part of the scientific team. But when the tour was over, after his moment of glory, he was sent back to the boondocks, back to the eel hatchery, and he's been here ever since."

I studied the photo. The old man had weathered skin, which was dark, but with a powdery pallor, the way a chocolate bar gets when it's left unwrapped. He had a wisp of a goatee and a long gray braid which dangled over his shoulder. He was wearing a USC Trojans baseball cap.

"May I keep this?" John nodded. "Thanks. You've been really great." I paused. "You risked a lot for us yesterday, and coming here today. Can I ask why?"

John shrugged. "Isn't it obvious? One American helping another. Three cheers for the red, white and blue."

"But you gave up your American citizenship," I pointed out.

John looked away. When he spoke again, his voice was somber. "When I came to China, I left my wife Leslie behind. We were very much in love, but she'd been born and raised in Oklahoma, and she refused to leave. We fought about it. I'd been brought up with traditional Chinese values: the man is the head of the household, and the wife is expected to obey his wishes. But she wouldn't bend. Finally, I came alone."

He shook his head. "I was absolutely certain she'd follow me sooner or later. It never crossed my mind that it could be any other way.

"To put it mildly, I was miserable. China wasn't remotely what I'd thought it would be, and I missed Leslie like crazy. She wrote to me and said she was miserable too. More than anything I wanted to go back to Oklahoma, but I was too damn stubborn." His tone was self-mocking. "I would have lost face. She had to come to me. And, I told myself, when she did, we would return to the U.S.A. together. That thought was what kept me warm at night."

He took off his glasses and concentrated on cleaning them as he continued. "I'd been here about four months when I got the call from her father. She'd been in a car wreck. Killed instantly. I never even got to say good-bye." John stared into his teacup. "That's when I renounced my citizenship. Maybe it was a way of punishing myself. Maybe I was just afraid of going back and realizing all I'd lost through misplaced pride. There's still an empty place in my heart where she was."

Our noodles arrived. John nodded thanks to the waitress and waited until she'd walked away. "Did I mention that Leslie was a chef too? In fact, Lily reminds me of her." He smiled shyly. "She didn't come here to find a lost husband too, did she?"

I thought about the peach pit cameo and what her great- grandmother had prophesied. "Not a husband per se. But let's just say she hopes to find someone just the same, if that makes any sense."

John nodded, and I caught a gleam in his eye.

"But speaking of my lost husband, there's one more thing you can do to for me."

"Name it."

"Help me get into this eel hatchery."

John shook his head. "It would be very dangerous for you to go there. It's owned by the Dragonhead of the T'ung Yu Triad. Do you understand what that means?"

"I understand that Wan Lo works there," I said firmly. "And he's the only person who might know where Peter is. So I'm going, whether you help me or not." I put my hand over his and looked into his eyes. "John, maybe you can live with an empty place in your heart, but I can't. I have to find Peter."

THE FIRST ORDER OF BUSINESS was changing my appearance so I would look like a Chinese worker. I didn't have to go far to find clothes; our waitress was just about my size, and although she balked at first when John explained that I wanted her cotton trousers and jacket, when I let her feel the soft fleece of my sweat pants and the thick wool of my socks and offered to trade, she readily changed her mind.

Her clothes were clean, if threadbare and shapeless. But what they lacked in style, they made up for in essence: when I stepped into her pants and tied her scuffed sandals about my ankles with twine, I felt that I had assumed the mantle of her Chinese heritage, as though I were not just stepping into her clothes, but into her skin. For the first time since I'd arrived in China, I felt that I had been allowed to slip behind the Bamboo Curtain.

The right clothes were a start, but I still had a long way to go before I'd pass for Chinese. John Lee took me to a barbershop off an alley. He had a long conversation with the owner before the man finally motioned to me to sit in the chair. He covered my shoulders with newspapers.

"What did you tell him? I asked.

"That you wanted a cut like Lin Bao." He pointed to a photo taped to the wall, a publicity still of an Oriental seductress with bobbed black hair and bangs, exaggerated red lips and a mole above her right nostril. "Asia's answer to Madonna," he said.

Using the photograph as his guide, the barber parted my shoulder-length hair in the middle, and with five snips of his dull scissors, sheared it to a blunt line just below my earlobe. I'd always worn my hair long, and I cringed as it fell like chaff on my shoulders. But, too, there was something liberating in the rush of air on the back of my neck. I was no longer clinging to my old identity. I was anonymous, free to blend with the local culture.

While I admired myself in the mirror, the barber took out a tiny silver spoon and held it ready.

"What's he going to do with that?" I asked John.

"Clean the wax out of your ears. It comes with the price of a haircut."

"I've heard of a silver spoon in the mouth, but in the ear? Thanks, but no thanks," I said, and set the peasant girl's conical straw hat on my head, tying it under my chin. I turned a slow circle for John. "Well?"

He studied my appearance, buttoning the jacket up to the throat, pulling the hat down over my eyes. "I think you'll pass, as long as you don't open your mouth. Your teeth are a dead give-away."

He had a point. Straight white teeth were a rarity in rural China. "So what should I do?"

"If someone asks you a direct question, just lower your eyes and say 'duile.' It means 'yes, you are right.' Try it."

"Duile."

"Good. And when you smile, remember to hold your hand over your mouth. Chinese women do that anyway because it's considered vulgar to let anyone see your teeth."

"I wonder what they'd make of a woman dentist."

WE RODE our bicycles along the river on the same road Lily and I had been on the day before. It was a beautiful morning. A pale mist was shimmering over the mountains, and farmers working in distant fields appeared as faint brush strokes in a delicate watercolor. Because there were so few cars, there was very little noise, only the sounds of rural life and the rush of the river. Finally I was on the right track to find Peter, I was sure of it, and I was surprised how calm I felt.

The Superior Eel Hatchery was another enormous, anonymous walled institution with a guarded gate, this one stretching along the banks of the Ming River. The setting looked strangely familiar. Was it just that I'd seen so many similar walled compounds during my two days in China?

"What do you know about eels?" John asked.

"Only that they aren't in any food group on my personal nutrition chart," I said.

A caravan of four tarpaulin-covered trucks rumbled up the road and pulled to a halt at the entrance gate. The guards sauntered up to the lead truck and made a cursory inspection, then circled back around to the cab to speak with the driver. The three other drivers turned off their engines and climbed out of their trucks, and all the men stood in a circle, passing around stubby brown Chinese cigarettes.

"The Fukienese are proficient at breeding and farming eels, but their success depends on special feed which comes from Japan. So the two old enemies have put aside political differences and now work together to maximize profit."

"Sounds like creeping capitalism to me."

"Don't let anyone tell you there's no such thing as capitalism in China. The partnership has been amazingly successful. This factory was one of the first in all of China to be privatized, and it's highly profitable. Of course, with the Triad connection, that may be due to more than just eels."

We hid our bicycles and stole close to the last truck in the convoy. John lifted a corner of the tarpaulin. The cargo looked like bags of grain, but it smelled like decomposed flesh.

"John, I'm going to hitch a ride in."

"It's too risky, Karen. Even if they don't catch you, the smell will kill you."

"I'll be an instant hit with the eels," I replied, hoping I sounded braver than I felt. "Will you go back to the hotel and fill Lily in? Tell her I'll be back tonight, hopefully with Peter."

Before John could stop me, I pulled myself up onto the back of the truck, swung my legs over the side rails, and slid onto the pile of feed bags. I had expected them to be hard and granular, like sacks of unpopped popcorn, but they were spongy to the touch, and gave under me, pillowing my body.

But the stench! I pinched my nostrils closed and tried to breathe through my mouth. Even so, the acrid aroma caused my eyes to tear. Gagging, and praying I wouldn't throw up, I pushed aside a couple of the feed bags and wormed my way into the pile so I would be hidden.

I felt a sense of movement under me, but it was too dark to see, so I tried to ignore it. I peeked through a tear in the tarpaulin in time to see the guards toss their cigarette butts into the road and push open the gate. The drivers sauntered back to their vehicles, and one by one, the trucks accelerated, belching diesel fumes into the air. I heard the stripping sound of a heavy hand at the gearshift, and the truck I was in jerked forward.

"I'll borrow a car and bring Lily back with me to pick you up," I heard John whisper, and then I couldn't hear him any more.

A moment later, the truck wheezed to a stop and the door of the cab slammed. I heard men talking, their voices getting fainter and fainter, so I snuck a peek out from under the tarpaulin.

We were backed up to a loading dock. Workers were already crawling onto the first truck, peeling back the tarpaulin and handing down sacks of feed. There was no way I could climb out undetected, so I waited. And when the tarpaulin was thrown back on my truck, I picked up a sack and got off the truck as though I were part of the unloading squad. Some of the workers looked at me curiously, but no one spoke. In fact, there was no conversation at all. They kept their heads bent to the work, silently going through the motions like human cogs in a giant machine.

The sack wasn't heavy, but it was mushy and awkward to carry. I hoisted it onto my shoulder as best I could and followed the line of bearers into the building, dropping my contribution onto a gurney next to the other sacks. Then I followed the line back to the truck to pick up another round. I felt a tickle at my neck, and I scratched at it, trying to be inconspicuous. To my horror I dislodged two squirming, maggoty slugs!

Recoiling in disgust, I lost my balance and dropped the sack. It split open, spewing the gross, slimy creatures all over me, all over the dock. They crawled obscenely, a mucousy mass of fat, white worms.

A supervisor shouted and directed two other workers to drop their loads and help me clean up the spill. Without hesitation, they knelt and began scooping up the worms by the handful. But I couldn't, I just couldn't.

The supervisor looked at me through narrowed eyes and started shouting, a shrill barrage of words that was terrifying, especially since I had no idea what she was saying. I could feel her hot breath on my face, her verbal abuse punctuated with bursts of spittle. I lowered my head as John had directed, and said, "Duile, duile." But still she continued to shout at me, jabbing her finger at my chest, plucking at the pocket of my jacket, then gestured to the other workers. Finally I saw what the problem was — all of the others had red identification badges clipped to their coats. I, of course, had none.

There was nothing else to do. If I didn't cooperate, she was going to make trouble for me. With great reluctance I bent to the ground to help my comrades. It took all of my self-control to stifle my revulsion; I knew I'd be having nightmares about this the rest of my life.

Finally every last worm was collected, and we all fell back into line, hauling the feed bags to the waiting gurneys. When a gurney was full, it was wheeled away and another put in its place. As the truck gradually emptied of feed bags, my anxiety grew. Time was passing and I was no closer to finding Wan Lo or Peter. But what could I do?

A voice crackled unintelligibly over a loudspeaker and everyone in my crew dropped the bags they were carrying. I dropped mine too, but very carefully this time. The formidable woman supervisor directed us to file through the entrance to the building, a tall sliding panel like a barn door. I kept my head bowed low, imitating the shuffling gait of the other workers. But even so, she gave me a hard shove on the back as I passed.

When we were inside, she clapped her hands and motioned to us to follow her. The building was roughly the size of a football field, with long rows of shallow aluminum tanks running the length of it. Workers were positioned on both sides of the tanks, some using nets, some using their hands, pulling eels from the water and depositing them in smaller containers. It was cold, and the air was thick with the fetid odor of fish and mildew. The floor under my sandaled feet was sodden, and in a few steps my feet were soaked.

With my straw hat pulled low over my face it was difficult to see, so I pushed the hat back just a little, and looked around, hoping for a glipse of the Trojan baseball cap and the scientist Wan Lo. To my astonishment I saw the hat, or one like it, on the head of a man not twenty yards in front of me. As we passed him my heart surged. Then it fell. It was the right hat, but nothing else about the man fit. There was no gray pigtail snaking down his back, and he seemed too tall and muscular for a sixty-five-year-old Chinese. But still, the cap was right, and it was the only one in sight.

We halted. At a command from the supervisor, the workers at the tank in front of us stepped back, and we took their places. I tried to steal a glance back at the worker in the cap, but there wasn't time. The instant we were in place a sluice was opened, and a current of water, thick with slithering green-black bodies, gushed into the tank.

I stepped back involuntarily. But a hand from behind shoved me forward. The tough lady supervisor, of course. So I plunged my hands into the frigid water and went to work like everybody else.

We were sorting the eels, pulling out the smallest ones and putting them in Styrofoam containers. The slimy bodies were disgusting and elusive; sorting them was like putting your hands into a writhing mass of snakes — not as vile as the maggoty feed, but running a close second.

With precious little help from me the tank was emptied and, as I waited with my co-workers for the sluice to be reopened and the tank to be refilled, I took the risk of turning all the way around to look for Wan Lo. The man in the Trojan hat was still there, with his back toward me. I had to see his face, to talk to him, to ask about Peter. How could I get his attention?

My back ached from leaning over, and my hands were waterlogged and numb with cold. I pursed my lips and blew a little warm air on them, but I felt nothing.

Suddenly I had an inspiration. My whistle, my famous whistle, the one I used to call Hermie at home. Surely that would make Wan Lo turn around.

Without fanfare, and without stopping work, I let loose with a shrill blast which echoed impressively throughout the cavernous room.The workers on either side of me fell back, gaping in astonishment at this loud breach of routine and etiquette. I turned to face the man in the Trojan hat. At just that moment, he turned as well, and —

It was Peter!

Peter! Even without his mustache, and in the worn, ill-fitting clothes of a Chinese peasant, I recognized him. And he recognized me, gaping at me with the startled expression of an animal caught in the headlights of an approaching car. I wanted to cry out and run to him, but at that moment a thunderous explosion rocked the building, and the lights went out. I was knocked off my feet. As I went down, I grabbed at the flimsy metal siding of the tank, wrenching it loose. A tidal wave of frigid water, viscid with slimy bodies, cascaded over me.

Smoke was filling the warehouse. I was flat on my back in the unbreathable dark, under a waterfall of clammy water which churned with eels. I clawed them away from my nose and mouth, and covered my face with my hands, gasping and coughing for breath. A second blast erupted and hysteria echoed off the walls, as workers panicked, slipping and screaming and choking, scrambling to get out of the building. Wouldn't that be the final insult, to be drenched, slimed, and then trampled just seconds after finding Peter?

I slipped further under the bent siding of the tank and hung on for dear life, trying desperately to accustom my eyes to the darkness. Then, through the confusion, I heard Peter's familiar voice, calling my name. "Karen?"

"Peter!" I screamed, and leaned out from my sheltered place, straining to see through the smoke. I couldn't make out faces, only bodies scrambling over each other, eerily mimicking the eels slithering on the floor. A tall figure was pushing towards me. "Peter!" I called again. "Here!" I crawled out from under the tank and shoved my way to him.

When I felt his arms close around me I forgot the fear, the dark, the damp, the disgusting slime of the eels. And when he bent his head to kiss me, I nearly fainted with joy and relief, even without the familiar tickle of his mustache.

中國象棋

TWENTY-TWO

We clung to each other, buffeted by our emotions and the frenzy around us. A third explosion boomed, knocking us to the floor. The Trojan cap tumbled off Peter's head, and he let go of me to lunge for it. Irrationally, I felt a stab of resentment — how could some hat be more important to him than holding onto *me* at this crucial moment?

But then Peter had the hat in hand, and he was helping me up, pulling me against the chaotic flow of humanity, moving deeper into the smoke-filled warehouse.

We finally reached a door, but it had no handle. Peter looked left and right. A gurney piled high with bags of feed had been abandoned nearby. "Stand back," he commanded, and wheeling the gurney in line with the door, threw his weight behind it. All those years of playing football paid off; the door burst open, no match for his brute strength.

"Come on," Peter said, and I followed him, praying to see the light of day. But we were in a room the size of a large closet. It was musty and claustrophobic, and fear swirled around me like a heavy fog; I couldn't help but suck it in and gasp with panic. "No!" I cried when Peter shut the door behind us.

"Don't worry. We'll be safe in here for a while," he said.

"What if the building blows up?"

"It won't." His voice was confident. "They're just smoke bombs, to cause a little diversionary chaos." He lit a match but it fizzled out before he could get a look around. "Shit," he said.

"Will this help?" I asked, handing him my Swiss army knife.

He flicked on the flashlight. "You would have made a great Boy Scout."

"Or a great spy?"

We were in a mechanical room, filled with electrical wiring, fuses, controls, and computers. Out of the corner of my eye I saw a black shape scuttle through the shadows hugging the wall, a rat, no doubt, the perfect macabre touch. I shivered with cold and disgust, and scrunched closer to Peter.

He shone the light on my face. "Karen," he said, and wrapped his arms around me. "What in God's name are you doing here?"

"Looking for you," I replied. "To warn you."

"What are you talking about?"

It dawned on me that Peter had no idea of all that I knew, of all that Lily and I had been through in the past three days. I hardly knew where to start.

"Cao told us —"

"Cao? You spoke to Cao?"

I nodded. "She told us you were in danger, that you were walking into a trap."

"She ought to know," he mumbled, "she set it."

"She told us *she* worked for the CIA. Like a dope I believed her." And then, "She doesn't, does she?"

"Not ours, she's *Cheng Pao K'o*, the Chinese CIA. They're

after what I came for. Her job is to keep me from getting it. God, Karen, do you have any idea how much danger you've been in?"

"I had to come. I just had to."

Peter hugged me hard, crushing my words. "Obviously Cao's been using you to get to me. She must have had you tailed."

"There was a man following us for a while, but I think we lost him. And someone else stole our passports. Do you think they're all working together?"

"Yes and no. It's complicated. The Chinese security network is made up of three divisions. There's the Central External Liaison Department, *CELD*, that's foreign intelligence. Ferdy. Then there's *Cheng Pao K'o*, External Security. That's Cao. Ferdy reports to her. The third branch is *Chi Pao K'o*. They're Public Security, the police. They all work together, but they each have separate interests as well. And they each want what I came for."

"What about the T'ung Yu Triad?"

"Right now they've got it."

Peter's attention flickered and his face softened. He touched the ends of my chopped-off hair. "You look different. You cut your hair," he said tenderly.

"And you shaved your mustache."

He ran his finger over his naked upper lip self-consciously, and I felt a stab of love for this proud, strong man, my own shorn Samson, now looking so vulnerable.

"I've never seen you without it," I said. "It seems there's a whole side of you I've never seen before."

"Karen." Again, Peter's voice stroked my name like a caress. "I'm sorry — "

"No, *I'm* sorry. I'm sorry I didn't believe you about the CIA. And I'm truly sorry I jumped to conclusions about you and Lauren.

I should have trusted you. But I still don't understand what's so important that you'd risk your life for it?"

"Think how the world would change if energy were as accessible as light and air." He moved the flashlight along the next bank of shelves until it shone on a black box the size of a toaster. He picked it up. "Imagine running all the appliances in our house — the lighting, appliances, heat, plus the cars, at a cost of about twenty-five bucks a year. Think about it. This is the modern equivalent of the discovery of the wheel. Code name: Chinese Checkers. And they sent me here to get it."

"To steal it, you mean? Doesn't it belong to the inventor, Wan Lo?"

Once again Peter looked surprised at how much I knew. "Wan Lo visited the U.S.A. with a communist delegation in the late '70s, and someone from our side slipped him a microchip of data. Then he built the apparatus. But it was ours to begin with. We've been trying to track it down for seven years!"

"Does it really work?"

"We don't know, but it's possible. And on the off chance it does, we can't let it get into the wrong hands." Using the screwdriver on my Swiss army knife, he pried open the black box and began ripping the guts out of it.

I didn't understand. If he'd been sent to *get* the box, why was he destroying it? It seemed like the solution of a selfish child: if I can't have it nobody can. But before I could ask for an explanation, a volley of gunfire sounded. Peter cracked opened the door. The overhead light had been restored, and the workers were returning the tanks. But now police were patrolling the aisles to keep order, scrutinizing each worker's face in turn as they passed.

"It's the *Chi Pao K'o*, Public Security," Peter said. "Who tipped them off?"

I was pretty sure I knew the answer to that. Dr. Liang

A voice over a loudspeaker began barking out commands in Chinese.

"What did they say?" I whispered.

"They're looking for the *yang-guy-zi* — foreign devil. Three guesses who that is. We've got to get out of here. How'd you get in?"

"In the back of a feed truck," I said. "Behind the building, to the right, there's a loading dock and a ton more of these gurneys."

He was already pulling sacks of feed off the gurney he'd used to break down the door. "Lie on this and I'll cover you."

I didn't move. "What about you?"

"I'm going to wheel you out."

"But they'll see you!"

"It's the only way I can get you out of here."

"No it's not. *You* lie down and I'll cover you. They're not looking for me."

At least I hoped they weren't.

I opened the door and pushed the gurney out into the main building. Mercifully, the cement floor was still wet and slippery with eel slime, so it slid easily despite Peter's added weight. I peered out from under my straw hat to get my bearings.

The workers were back at their stations, and police now guarded each aisle and doorway. On the catwalk above us stood a hugely obese man in an embroidered coat, and a smaller man in a Western suit. With them were two bodyguards who looked like rejects from Gold's Gym back home. Apparently, the stairs leading up to the catwalk had collapsed when the workers panicked, isolating the men thirty feet above the floor — too far to jump or even climb down — and a crew was scrambling to construct some kind of a ramp to rescue them.

The loading dock was at the far end of the building. To get there we would have to pass a phalanx of workers and at least three policemen. I bent my head and threw my weight against the load.

As I moved past the first tank no one looked at me. Why should they? The feed gurneys were a common enough sight, and dressed as I was, I too was unremarkable. Then again, it could have occurred to someone to wonder why a gurney full of feed sacks was being pushed *back* to the loading dock. I held my breath as I rolled past the first of the three policemen, a burly man in a misbuttoned jacket.

He ignored me, too busy patrolling his section of the warehouse and verbally harassing the workers to pay me any heed. I relaxed a little and straightened up to get a better grasp on the gurney.

The next policeman was standing at the end of the aisle. I knew I'd have to be careful when I negotiated the turn so none of the bags would slide off, but at the same time, I didn't want to lose the momentum which was propelling us toward the loading dock, and escape.

I planted a foot on the cement for leverage to make the turn. Pulling back with my left arm, I pushed forward with my right so the gurney pivoted. Adding a little reverse torque I made it swivel neatly around the corner. But as I gave it a final shove, my foot slid out from under me on the slimy floor and I fell against the gurney. To my horror, the pile started to slip. Two, three, then four bags slid to the floor, and the gurney surged forward, rolling down the aisle by itself.

A policeman stepped into the aisle and body-blocked the runaway gurney. It came to a halt beside him. Out of the corner of my eye I glimpsed the blue material of Peter's pant leg exposed where the bags had fallen. I had to do something! Ignoring the sharp pain in my knee where it had cracked into the cement, I scrambled to my feet and hobbled toward the gurney, dragging a fallen bag of feed.

The policeman was between me and the gurney. With trembling hands I tried to reach around him and jam the bag into the space where the blue material showed through. But he grabbed my arm and swung me around to face him. He looked at me for a long, hard minute, and then, at the top of his lungs he screamed, "*Yang-guy-zi*!"

The workers crowded close around me, curious to see the *Yang-guy-zi*. So when Peter burst from the mound of feed bags screaming like a banshee, they scattered with gasps of surprise and fear. Grabbing a bag of feed, he heaved it at the policeman, knocking him to the ground. Then he wrenched the rifle out of his hand and swung it into the faces of the astonished workers. They backed further away.

"Come on!" he shouted, and led me through the crowd, which parted to let us pass. No one tried to stop us. We ran out the sliding door to the loading dock trailed by a few brave souls and the two policemen. It was USC star quarterback Peter 'The Pied Piper' Matthews living up to his nickname. But I was very aware that this wasn't college football, and there was more at stake than just a game.

"Help me!" Peter cried, and together we pulled the sliding door shut behind us. Peter jammed the rifle through the handle, securing it temporarily. It wouldn't stop them from following us, but at least it would slow them down.

There was one more policeman between us and the trucks. When he saw us coming he ran at us and fired without taking time to aim. But when we didn't stop, he took more careful aim and was about to squeeze the trigger when he was jumped from behind by a worker in a white coat. Both men fell, and the gun skidded across the floor.

The worker had no weapon, but to my surprise I saw him press a ballpoint pen to the policeman's neck. In an instant the policeman stopped struggling and lay still.

"Get the gun," Peter shouted at me and pulled the policeman's limp body off the worker.

"Are you okay, Chun?" he asked in English, and then said something in Chinese.

"*Hao*," the man replied in Chinese, grinning broadly.

"Good man. Don't let the bastards follow us," Peter said, then spoke again in Chinese.

"Okay," the worker said in English. "See you to America."

We raced to the nearest truck and climbed in. Peter threw the gun onto the seat. It was a pistol, military issue, old and not very fancy. I suppose a gun doesn't have to be fancy to kill people.

Luck seemed to be with us: the key was in the ignition. But when Peter turned it, nothing happened. Frantically, he stomped on the gas pedal and tried again. Nothing.

Behind us the door to the loading dock broke open and the two policemen ran out, with a crowd of workers behind them. Only one policeman still had his gun and he fired wildly. Peter cried, "Down!" and I hit the floor as a bullet ricocheted off the side of the truck.

At last the motor caught. I tried to sit up to see where we were going, but I was thrown down again as the truck surged forward, careening away from the dock.

A heavy thud dented the roof over our heads. Somebody had jumped onto the roof of the cab. Peter accelerated, then stomped on the brake. A body slid down the windshield, landing heavily on the hood. I gasped. It was the man with the slicked back hair, the man who'd stolen our passports. And he had a gun. "Peter!" I screamed.

With a savage cry, Peter flung open his door and lunged at the man, grabbing his leg and jerking him off balance. Without Peter's hands on the steering wheel, the truck swerved violently, and the man lost his balance, rolling to the edge of the hood, grasping wildly for purchase on the metal surface. Bracing himself at the last second, he tried to kick loose from Peter's hold on his leg and fired his gun. The shot went wild.

"Karen, the gun!" Peter shouted.

I didn't think about it. I just picked up the pistol, closed my eyes, and pulled the trigger. The bullet went through the windshield, causing it to shatter and rain shards of glass on the man. To my surprise and horror, he screamed and clutched an oozing wound in his thigh, an expression of shock on his face. Peter let go of his leg, and he rolled off the hood, landing on the ground with a dull thump.

"I don't think Ferdy's going to be sneaking up on anyone for a while," he said, stepping on the gas.

I was incredulous. "That's Ferdy? But he's the one who stole our passports. He's been following us since Hong Kong."

"That's what I was telling you. They're working together."

Peter headed the truck toward the gate. It was closed and the two guards stood in front of it, rifles drawn. He pulled out a pack of Marlboros and tossed some matches at me. "Light it!" he said, and I did.

He took one long drag on the cigarette, and checked to make sure it was lit. Then he took careful aim and tossed it at the guards, jerking the wheel around at the same time so that the truck spun like a clumsy polo pony. Behind us I heard a resounding BOOM! and smoke filled the air.

The people in the yard scattered as we fishtailed, sending up a spray of dry dirt. Grabbing the dashboard for support I pulled myself up high enough to see out the windshield.

Peter aimed at the iron grillwork of the gate, jammed the truck in high gear, and stomped down hard on the gas. As we barreled forward, the guards leapt out of the way. I braced myself for the collision, but the old warhorse took the impact with barely a shudder. We were through the gate and on the road. And, I thought, home free.

But Peter slowed to a stop. "Can you get back to the city?" he asked.

"Yeah. My bicycle's hidden over there. We can both ride it. Lily and I did it — "

"I can't go with you. I've got to go back and get Chun."

"Who's Chun? You can't go back. They'll kill you!"

He ignored me. "I'll do what I can to create a diversion and stop the *Chi Pao K'o* from following you, but . . ."

"Peter, don't do this to me!"

He took my face in his hands and kissed the teardrops on my cheeks. "Karen, listen to me. You're strong, you're brave, you've already proven how smart you are. Now I need you to do something very important." He took off the Trojan cap and unfastened a tiny glowing pin. He held it out to me. "Take this with you to Hong Kong."

"What is it?"

"It's a microchip, the energy formula." He carefully pulled the pin apart and showed me an even tinier piece of metal, about the size of a grain of rice. "They won't be looking for you, they'll assume I have it." He closed my hand around the little chip. "Hide it, don't let anyone know you've got it. Anyone! And when you get back to Hong Kong, go to the hotel, lock yourself in, and wait for me. I'll be there before you know it."

"How will you get there?"

"I'll have an escort."

"But —"

He put a finger to my lips. "Shhh. There's no more time." He found his pack of magic Marlboros and shook out a few 'cigarettes.' "You saw what these can do. Light them like real cigarettes. Then you have five seconds to get rid of them. Throw long and take cover. Okay?"

I nodded solemnly and put the 'cigarettes' in my pocket. Then Peter kissed me, and I clung to him.

"I'm afraid for you," I said in a husky voice.

"I'll be fine."

"You'd better be." I slid his hand from my shoulder down to my belly. "There are two of us counting on it."

I got out of the truck feeling frightened and very abandoned. "Good luck," he said. "I love you."

"Same goes," I replied. And with a backfire belch he was gone.

中國
象棋

TWENTY-THREE

I knew I could find my way back to the Gilded Lotus Guest House, because there was only one road, and I was on it. But the wind whipped around me, making my eyes tear and my ears ache with cold. My clothes, still wet from the flooded eel hatchery, were turning icy, and I began to tremble so hard it was difficult to keep hold of the handlebars.

A horn blared, and I realized a car was coming up fast behind me. When I turned I saw a woman lean out the window waving her arms frantically. I recognized the red hair before I saw the face. Lily! And John Lee was with her.

I jerked the bicycle to the side and the threadbare tires skidded across the muddy berm at the side of the road, dumping me into the ditch.

By the time I got to my feet the car had pulled to a stop and Lily was running up to me.

"I found Peter!" I cried, and fell into her arms.

She hugged me. "Oh, Karen, that's fantastic!" She looked

around. "Where is he? We saw the smoke and heard . . . are you all right?"

"I'll tell you while we drive. We need to get out of here fast."

"Fast isn't an option in this car, but at least it runs," John Lee said as he threw open the door of the ancient road-ravaged Ford. Lily climbed in first and slid close to John so we could all fit in the front seat. Her jaw was still swollen, but even in the half light of evening I could see that her pained expression was gone. In fact, she looked, well, beatific — not a word I'd ever before considered using to describe Lily.

John pulled back onto the road and we headed toward the Gilded Lotus. The car seemed to be moving in slow motion. Involuntarily, all three of us leaned forward, as though urging it to go faster. Lily reached over to probe the knot forming on my forehead, pressing on it as though she were testing a honeydew melon for ripeness.

"Ouch!" I jerked my head away.

"Where's Peter? Why isn't he with you? Is he okay?"

The microchip was burning a hole in my pocket, but I couldn't mention it in front of John. I wondered how much Lily had told him.

"He's fine. He'll meet us later in Hong Kong," I said evasively.

The car bounced on nonexistent shock absorbers, throwing Lily against John, and she seemed content to stay that way, her hand braced against his leg. "I don't get it," she said.

I turned, trying to see if we were being followed. It was too dark to see more than a hundred yards back, and that much of the road was empty. "Where are we going?" I asked John.

"To the airport. Your flight's at nine, isn't it?"

I looked at my wrist, forgetting I no longer had a watch. John glanced at his own watch. "It's early. We've got plenty of time," he said.

Lily wouldn't let go of it. "So tell us. What was going on in there? We thought we were going to have to come in and get you. Did you find what's his name, the inventor?"

"I'll tell you later," I said. "I just don't feel like talking about it now."

"Why?"

"Drop it," I said, rolling my eyes toward John and shaking my head.

"Well, wait 'til you hear *our* story," Lily said, looking at John with a conspiratorial grin. "We had a long talk over lunch. It was the best meal! We ate down by the waterfront, all the local specialties. What did you call that first dish?"

"Bêche-de-mer," John said, "sea slug."

"It was delicious! Sort of like abalone, only more tender. Anyway, tell Karen what you told me. Tell her who you work for." To me she said, "You're going to love this."

"I work for the government," John said.

"The *Cheng Pao K'o*?" I asked.

"The what?" Lily asked.

"The Chinese CIA," he told her. Then, looking at me, said, "That's what they think. But no, the good old U.S. of A."

"See?" Lily said with a note of triumph.

"You told us you renounced your citizenship."

"Technically, I did. I had to make my defection look real." He looked apologetic. "The thing is, I'm double undercover. For our CIA."

This was all sounding very familiar. Too familiar. It was exhausting to contemplate all the lies and half-truths swirling about us. Everyone we met seemed to have a double life. How was a person supposed to know who and what to believe? I couldn't keep the anger from my voice. "You mean that whole sob story about your wife dying was a bunch of bull?"

"No, it was true, as a matter of fact. That was why I signed up. Kind of like joining the French Foreign Legion, don't you think?"

"Tell her why you didn't tell us this in the beginning," Lily prompted him.

"Well, first I had to check out your stories. You could have been any kind of foreign agents, Japanese, German, Korean."

"Can you believe it?" Lily giggled. "Nobody ever told me I looked Korean," She ran her fingers through her red curls. "I don't even like kim chee."

"That's the point," John said. "You don't look it. Neither of you. At any rate, I had you both checked out. I didn't get the final word until late this morning."

"Checked out how?" I asked.

"Through sources," he replied cryptically.

"What about your Dr. Liang? Is he a good guy or a bad guy?"

"He's a relatively harmless mid-level bureaucrat," John said, ignoring the accusation in my tone. "An informer for the *Chi Pao K'o*. He's one of the people I keep my eye on."

"So you just handed us over to him on a silver platter?"

John frowned. "Remember the sequence of events here. At the time I didn't know if you were who you said you were. And I had to maintain a believable facade. Besides, he wasn't the main problem."

"Who was?" Lily asked.

But I cut off John's reply, suddenly realizing I hadn't asked the most important question. "How does all this relate to Peter? Are you saying you're working with him?"

"In the sense that we're all employed by Uncle Sam, yes. But I'm more of a general practitioner. He's a specialist, a blind agent. So I wasn't briefed on his operation until I called to check up on you. We're not always as organized as we'd like to be," he added apologetically. "Some people would say the left hand doesn't know what the right hand is doing. I prefer to think of it as being ambidextrous. Anyway, your husband was brought in for this one contract."

It was time for a test question. I had one ready. ""And that is?"

John chuckled softly. He knew I had him. If he verified what I knew to be true, I could be fairly sure he was for real. If he lied or hedged, it would be obvious he was playing for the opposing team.

"Sounds to me like you want to play a game of Chinese Checkers."

"Chinese Checkers?" Lily asked, puzzled.

"It's the code name for Matthews' assignment," John said. "The rules are simple, whoever has the microchip at the end of the game wins. And if I'm not mistaken, you've got it now. Am I right?"

Lily looked at me. "Is he right?"

I didn't speak.

"Still not convinced that I'm on your side?" John asked. "Lily, reach into my breast pocket. I have something for you."

Lily reached in and pulled out two U.S. passports. "Our passports! How did you find them?" she asked excitedly.

"Oh, these aren't yours. They're fresh from the laundry, courtesy of the American mission in Fuchow. See? There's an official stamp right on them."

Lily handed them to me. I looked at the pictures. One was of a nondescript middle-aged woman with dark hair, the other a redhead. They could have been almost anyone, even Lily and me.

"How did you get these?"

"Trade secret. So, did I pass the test?"

"As far as I'm concerned you did," Lily said. "See, Karen, we're all in this together."

"If we're all in this together, you've blown your cover," I said to John.

"I've done my stint anyway. To tell the truth, I miss the U.S.A., I wasn't kidding about that. I'm ready to go home, and this gives me a good excuse."

Lily brightened. "You're coming back to the States with us?"

"Not quite yet. Now that Mattnews is exposed I'm supposed to see that he gets out of China safely. Once I put you on a plane, I'll go back and get him and bring him out through Taiwan. There's a Nationalist-held island about a mile and a half off the coast called Chinmen. I've got a fishing boat lined up to take us there. Then a contact will meet us and fly us to Taipei. If everything goes as planned we should be in Hong Kong by this time tomorrow."

"We can have dinner at Gaddis to celebrate," Lily put in. "Which reminds me," she reached into the back seat of the car. "I brought us a snack. Now that you're an expert on eels, I thought you might like to taste the finished product, stir-fried fresh water eel."

"Thanks, but I've had more than enough eels for one day," I said. "You go ahead."

"John?"

"No thanks."

Lily opened a cardboard container and pulled out a sliver of eel, throwing her head back to eat it.

"Let's go back to the microchip," John said. "You do have it, don't you?"

"Yeah, I have it," I admitted.

•

"Where?"

"In my pocket."

"You can't carry it across like that, you know."

"I know."

"If you want me to — "

I interrupted. "Peter gave it to me, he trusted me with it. I'm going to take it. I just don't know how."

We drove in silence for a moment, pondering the problem.

Lily took another bite of eel and I watched her chew it with relish.

She saw me watching her. "What?" she asked.

"If you can eat, your tooth must feel better."

"As a matter of fact, it does."

"So much for the advances of modern science," I said sourly.

"You call stuffing a wad of chewing gum into my tooth modern science?" Lily countered.

A light went on in my brain. "John," I said sweetly, "is there any way you could get us into the dental lab at the University before we go to the airport? I want to take a look at Lily's tooth."

John looked at me, then at Lily. They both seemed to understand what I was thinking. "I can get you in, but it's risky. Dr. Liang and Public Security could show up any time."

"Forget it, you two! I'm fine now, I just told you." Lily's voice had an edge to it so sharp it could have cut glass. "No more gum gardening in my mouth!"

"I can do this pretty quickly," I assured John, ignoring Lily, "a shot of Novocain, a little gutta percha, I stick the crown back on — you do still have it don't you?" And when she didn't answer, I proded, "Don't you?"

"Yeah," she admitted reluctantly, "I've got it."

"It might work," John conceded.

"But I'm a chef," she pleaded. "My mouth is my instrument. Karen? John?"

THE UNIVERSITY GATES were open and a dozen buses were parked just inside, disgorging streams of people.

"Where's everybody going?" I asked John.

"There's a performance tonight of the National Gymnastics Team from Beijing to celebrate the start of the Chinese New Year. It's the local equivalent of a high school football game back in the States; the whole community comes out to watch."

We parked behind the science building and got out of the car. The entrance was unlocked, but there was no light inside, and we had to grope our way up the stairs to the dental lab. Inside, the darkness went beyond the mere absence of light; there was a foreboding in the air, and the deathly silence did nothing to dispel the feeling of impending doom. The hygiene and drilling fixtures at each station looked dated and sinister. I'd thought our lab facilities at USC were grim, but compared to this they were as cheerful as the set of Sesame Street.

"I'll turn on the generator so we can get some light," John said, and left us alone. As soon as he was out of earshot, Lily turned to me.

"I could kill you for this. And they'd never convict me on the grounds of justifiable homicide!"

"Lily, think of it as something important you're doing for your country. Think of the story you'll have to tell your goddaughter."

"Yeah, if I live long enough to meet her."

The lights flickered on, and a moment later we saw John walking towards us. "I'll never ask you for another favor, I swear."

"You'd better believe you won't."

"Help me close the blinds," John said to Lily. "If anyone sees the light, they're going to be suspicious." And while they wrestled with the venetians, I set about prepping one of the stations.

The equipment was old, but it appeared sterile and functional. I rummaged through a sparsely equipped cabinet and found some old Sweeny pluggers, a Kerr pulp canal sealer and some zinc phosphate cement liquid. It was reassuring to see a few familiar brand names among the Chinese-labeled supplies and medications; I felt myself relax a little and get into the familiar groove. Had it only been a week since I'd done Lily's root canal at home?

I knew I'd have to coat the inside of the hollowed-out tooth with something non adhesive so that when the time came to remove the microchip it would come out easily. Paraffin seemed the logical answer. I could mold it around the chip and press it into the tooth, allowing it to conform to the interior shape, then cover it with a thin layer of cement, and reattach Lily's crown. Then I'd pray that the whole apparatus would be inconspicuous and hold together for twenty-four hours.

"Lil, I'm ready for you," I said as calmly as I could. Joan of Arc could not have played the scene with more pathos. Although her chin was quivering, Lily held her head high. As she lowered herself into the chair, she gave John a martyr's smile, then closed her eyes and prepared to face her fate.

"Where's the mystery medicine?"

She opened her eyes. "Why?"

I had no choice but to tell her the truth. "I can't find any Novocain and I don't want to take a chance on anything with a Chinese name."

"But John can read Chinese," she whispered hoarsely.

I shook my head. "Sorry. It might not be called Novocain in Chinese. And we don't have time to translate all the chemical ingredients in all these bottles. Look, it shouldn't hurt anyway. I don't have to drill or anything. Just suck on that goo for a second to numb up the nerve and you'll be fine."

For a second I thought she was going to cry, but then she removed the bottle from her pocket and put a huge glob of the salve on her gums.

"How can I help?" John asked while we waited for it to take effect.

"Maybe you should keep watch, just in case," I said.

"Be brave," he said to Lily, and took up a post at the window.

I went to work.

It's a wonder Lily wasn't screaming with pain. The gingiva around her tooth was pink and hot with inflammation and the cementum around the root had turned black from exposure. I knew she'd need some serious reconstruction when we got home, but for now I concentrated on the job at hand: inserting the microchip into the open tooth cavity as gently as was humanly possible, and cementing the crown back in place.

I was about halfway into the procedure when I heard John swear under his breath. Lily heard it too and opened her eyes. "Liang's down there," John hissed. "With the head of Public Security and his band of merry men."

"What do we do?" Lily asked.

"We finish this and get out of here. I'm almost done."

"I'll see if I can distract them," John said. "When you're finished, go down the stairs at the south end of the building, and out the back. I'll meet you at the car." He bent over Lily and gave her a kiss on the forehead. "You did good, kid," he said, and he was gone.

Working quickly, I placed the microchip into the wax-coated cavity in Lily's tooth. Then I squirted a dollop of cement on top of it and pressed the crown into place. I held a piece of cardboard between her teeth. "Bite down hard, and count to two hundred. If this cement is any good, it ought to be dry in about three minutes."

While Lily bit and held, I tidied up the work station. It only made sense not to leave a trail.

"Eighty-seven, eighty-eight, eighty-nine, ninety," Lily mumbled as I peeked through the venetian blinds.

I watched John approach the semicircle of men in uniforms and speak to them. I couldn't hear what he was saying, and I wouldn't have understood anyway. But suddenly, as one, they turned and looked up at my window. Dr. Liang's eyes seemed to bore through the blinds, right at me. He motioned to the police and two of them ran into the building.

I stepped back. Had John betrayed us? There wasn't time to find out. "Lily." I shook her gently, "Come on, we have to get out of here."

"One twenty-seven, one twenty-eight . . ."

I dragged her to her feet and pulled her into the darkened hall, not knowing if we should follow John's instructions and head for the stairs at the south end of the hall, or if it was a trap. "Where are we going? I'm not to two hundred yet," Lily mumbled.

"The police — "

The only answer was to avoid the stairs altogether. But that left us two floors up without an elevator. Did Chinese buildings have fire escapes?

"I hear them," Lily whispered. And I heard it too — booted footsteps on the stairs.

"This way!" I charged through the nearest door, dragging Lily after me. It was a large storage room, filled with boxes and bottles and stacks of cotton surgical gowns, all neatly laundered.

My mind was racing. The used gowns had to be washed and

pressed somewhere on the premises; probably there was a facility in the basement of the building. Which would mean, if we were lucky, in a building of this vintage there would be a laundry chute somewhere. The footsteps were in the hallway now, and accompanied by the voices they stormed each room in turn. We didn't have much time.

I felt along the wall, pressing and probing until, to my surprise and relief, a panel gave way. It wasn't large, but large enough. I imagined the drop would be about twenty-five feet, which would be manageable if and only if there were a soft pile of laundry beneath it, and that was something I had no way of knowing.

"Lily, come here. This is a laundry chute, see?" I showed her the open panel. "We're going down."

"Are you nuts?"

"*Staying* would be nuts," I said. "Come on, it's just like a slide at Magic Mountain."

"I hate Magic Mountain!" she wailed.

Holding up the cover of the chute with one hand, I stuck one leg in and then the other. It was a tight fit, which was good, because I could brace myself against the fall. I shoved off. The three-second drop ended with a soft thud in a huge straw basket of sour smelling laundry.

"It's okay Lily, come on," I called up.

Then I rolled out of the way and waited. With a whooshing sound, Lily's body emerged and landed in the dent I'd just made. Then she turned her head to the side and threw up. That was all I needed. My stomach immediately answered with a retch, and I tossed my cookies too. We lay there for a moment, spent and smelling of vomit.

With the soldiers patrolling the upper floors, and John waiting in front with Dr. Liang, we had no choice but to slip through one of the basement windows at the rear and lose ourselves in the shadows behind the building. We crept along the wall as far as it went, then merged into the stream of pedestrians walking toward the auditorium.

"So, we get to watch the gymnastics exhibition after all," I said.

"Watch it?" Lily replied. "We could qualify for the world championship."

Suddenly, there was a crack of gunfire — or was it a car backfiring? I turned my head just far enough to see a policeman leaning out the second-story window of the dental lab, shouting and pointing in our direction. "Run!" I yelled to Lily. But she was already in high gear.

中國
象棋

TWENTY-FOUR

As we neared the auditorium, the huge crowd swelled around us and we were swept up in the undertow of festivities. I looked around to get my bearings. The auditorium building was festooned with long red banners waving cheerfully in the breeze. Here and there, vendors hawked fried dough and roasted chestnuts, their smoky aromas scenting the air. There were the usual uniformed guards posted at regular intervals; in typical Chinese fashion, they seemed to serve no function except decoration. But where the crowd funneled into the building, I saw something else that made me catch my breath: two huge men in Western clothes, the rejects from Gold's Gym I'd seen on the catwalk at the eel hatchery, were skirting the crowd like sheepdogs worrying their flock into the slaughterhouse.

I nodded toward them. "Those guys were at the eel hatchery. They saw me with Peter."

"Then they're after us too?" Lily choked on a sob of fear.

"Not both of us, just me. So if there's trouble, pretend you don't know me, and disappear."

"Sure, like I'm really going to leave you here."

"The point is you've got the microchip, and you've got to get it to Hong Kong no matter what."

We were only a few feet from the entrance gate. If we could just get inside we'd be safe, or at least safer, for the time being. I held my breath and pressed forward.

"Oh, no," Lily wailed. "They're taking tickets."

Sure enough, the attendants at the turnstiles were collecting thin slips of paper. If we tried to pass through, surely they would stop us; if we turned back we'd fall right into the hands of the police — or worse, the thugs from the eel hatchery. All we could do was slow our pace, letting the press of eager ticket holders surge around us, and pray for deliverance.

It came in the form of a nasal-voiced tour guide. "Travcoa Tours, Travcoa Tours," he shouted. "This way!"

He was shorter than I was, but compensated by hoisting a red, white and blue paper flag, and waving it like the Star Spangled Banner. A cluster of people formed around him. Americans! Instinctively, Lily and I pressed against the current to get to them.

The guide handed the ticket taker a wad of the thin slips of paper. "Thirty-seven of us," he said, and started pushing people through the turnstile. "Count off as you go through, people. One, two, three . . ."

Obediently, the members of the group began to file through, forming another cluster inside the gate.

"Hurry now, Mrs. Miller," the guide called to one of the stragglers. "You'll make us miss the show."

"I left my sweater on the bus," an elderly woman whined, "my white angora cardigan. Mary will get it."

"You'll be fine inside, Aunt Eleanor," a woman of about my age assured her.

"I won't enjoy it if I'm cold, Mary," the older woman insisted, rooting herself to the spot. "Land sake, you know how these people are about air conditioning, even in January!"

"Don't be a pain in the butt, Eleanor," a man inside the gate called. "You can wear my jacket." He started to take it off.

"There's no need to be vulgar, Mr. Howard." The elderly lady's voice quavered with indignation. "Mary will get mine. I'll wait here."

"Come, come, ladies, you're holding up the group." The guide turned away from the turnstile to deal with the problem.

As soon as his attention was diverted, I pulled Lily into the line flowing through the turnstile, as though we were members of the tour. The ticket taker didn't flinch. "Twenty-three, twenty-four," we counted, and he handed us each a stub as we pushed through.

"Good old Aunt Eleanor," Lily whispered as we let the crowd propel us into the auditorium. I chanced a look behind me. The thugs were plowing through the crowd toward the entrance, and one of them had his eye on me. But in a moment, we were inside the darkened auditorium, safe, at least for the time being.

We slid into empty seats in the middle of a row about a third of the way to the stage, and sat in stunned silence, waiting for something to happen. Despite the fact that the performance was beginning, all around us people were chatting and eating and shuffling in their seats. The woman next to Lily lit a cigarette and blew smoke in our direction.

Lily coughed, waving the smoke away. She gave the woman a dirty look, but the woman ignored her.

"You think John tipped them off, don't you?" she said.

"I hope not."

I watched the gymnasts contort their lithe bodies into impossible poses as they built a human pyramid on the high wire. I felt like I was up there with them. When the tiniest girl was hoisted to the top, she made the mistake of looking off stage. The wire vibrated, and the pyramid teetered precariously. I followed her line of vision into the wings. Standing just behind the curtain were the police. Four of them. And they were armed.

With horror, I watched them creep along the dark perimeter of the stage and file down the stairs into the audience. It was beyond imagining that they would be able to pick us out of this crowd, and even more absurd to worry that they would fire their guns and risk hitting innocent bystanders. But I couldn't get the phrase 'sitting ducks' out of my mind.

I nudged Lily and nodded at them. Her eyes followed mine and she gasped.

"We've got to get out of here," I whispered.

"How, run?"

"If we do, we might as well paint bullseyes on our backs. We need a diversion." I looked around, waving away the smoke from the cigarette of the woman next to Lily.

"Lily," I whispered, "see if you can grab her matches."

"What for?"

"Just do it."

"Okay, okay." She watched the woman inhale and breathe long ribbons of smoke out her nose. "Excuse me," she whispered.

"Ay?" the woman grunted, eyeing Lily suspiciously.

Lily pantomimed smoking, then extended her hand, almost into the woman's pocket where the matches were. The woman recoiled and scowled.

The police were nearing our aisle now. There was no time. I removed the magic Marlboros from my pocket and carefully tapped one out. Lily watched me, her mouth hanging open. "Since when did you start smoking?"

"Since now. Get the matches!" I whispered. Lily withdrew the crushed pack of Juicy Fruit from her own pocket. She offered it to the woman and pointed at the matches.

Still scowling as though she had been forced into this trade, the woman reluctantly held out the matchbook to Lily. Lily gave her the pack of gum, nodded thanks, and took the matches, handing them to me.

I held a cigarette awkwardly to my lips. What if there were some trick to it that Peter had forgotten to tell me? What if it exploded in my face?

But the police were only two rows away from ours, and I couldn't stall any longer. I struck the match on the arm of the chair, held it to the cigarette and sucked in, trying not to inhale or cough. Then I blew softly on the glowing tip the way I'd seen Peter do, to make sure it was fully lit.

"When I count five, run for that exit," I told Lily, pointing to a door near the stage. "I'll be right behind you."

"One, two, three, four —" I paused, taking careful aim, "five!" As I flicked the cigarette into the right aisle at the feet of the approaching policeman, Lily and I jumped up and ran for the left. Two seats from the end of our row, Lily tripped and went sprawling. Then I stumbled over her. We were prone when the blast detonated.

Since I was expecting the noise and the smoke, it didn't seem so terrifying to me. But the audience reacted as though the bomb had just fallen on Hiroshima. The place went wild. Every person in the auditorium was up and running for the exits through a thick, acrid haze. Someone shouted "Fire!" in English. Was there one?

It was lucky we were on the ground because, in the initial frenzy, the policemen fired their guns in the air to quell the mass hysteria. But the shots were much more terrifying than the smoke bomb, and the panic escalated. Around us people continued pushing into the clogged aisles. Beneath me, Lily struggled to join them, but I held her down.

"Stay. We'll be safer here."

"I can't breathe," she croaked.

I shifted my weight to give her some air and looked around. The smoke was clearing and I could see that the policemen who had been patrolling the aisles were now being carried inexorably toward the rear exits by the mass exodus.

Our only hope was to stay low and crawl to the front of the auditorium, and go out the stage door. It would be a tight squeeze, and the floor was a disgusting, sticky surface. But I was beyond caring.

"Lily, follow me!"

I pressed my body low to the floor and crept along the aisle, hugging the rows of seats, stopping every so often to wait for Lily.

"It's not that far," I encouraged her. "Probably only about twenty rows."

"Oof!" Lily grunted as someone accidentally kneed her.

A visibly shaken guard, who couldn't have been more than seventeen, was stationed at the stage exit. When we got close to him, I lit another cigarette, took a puff and threw it. It rolled to within inches of his booted foot and exploded with a loud smokey BOOM.

Screaming, he bolted through the door. Lily and I scrambled to our feet and ran after him. Outside at last we took deep gulps of air and hugged the shadows of the building, watching and waiting.

"If only we could find John," Lily whispered.

"Maybe it's better if we don't."

"What's that supposed to mean?"

"Come on, Lily, he practically led the police right to us. He probably called them when he went out to turn on the generator."

"You mean you don't trust him?"

"I want to, I really do."

"Travcoa, meet at the bus! Travcoa, meet at the bus!" The nasal-voiced tour guide was waving his red, white and blue banner a few yards away. Two of his elderly charges approached him.

"This is an outrage," the first one said. "I'd lodge a complaint if I weren't so glad to be leaving this place. Where is the bus?" the second one asked.

"It's parked right at the gate, where we left it," the guide said with strained patience. "Number 373. Hurry, hurry."

"I presume we're going straight to the airport," said the first.

"As soon as I find everyone," the guide replied, still waving his banner.

Lily and I looked at each other. "To Number 373?" she asked.

I nodded. I didn't know how we were going to do it, but we had to talk our way onto that bus. We melted into the crowd and walked as quickly as we could without being conspicuous. As we passed by the science building I saw that lights blazed on all three floors.

"Look, there's John's car!" Lily cried. "Maybe he's still waiting for us." She seemed torn for a moment. Then she said, "I'll go see."

"No, it's too risky," I replied, but Lily was already hurrying away from the safe stream of pedestrians toward the old Ford.

Out of nowhere, a gleaming black sedan drew up alongside her, blocking her path. One of the thugs from the eel hatchery reached out and cinched his brawny arm to her body, dragging her into the car.

"No!" I screamed, and lunged after her, but a vise gripped my shoulder. I spun around, instinctively striking out, and my fist connected with a wall of flesh, the stomach of the second thug. I kept on punching, but he ignored my blows as though they were the sting of some benign insect, and twisted my arm up behind my back, almost to the breaking point. I stopped struggling, and let him shove me into the car after Lily.

Seated inside were a grossly fat man in Chinese robes, and a smaller man dressed in a three-piece suit. I recognized them both from the eel hatchery: the two men on the catwalk. The fat man had a pearl-handled knife in his hand. He sliced through a section of pear, speared it, and thrust it into his mouth, watching us as he chewed.

The windows of the sedan were tinted black, so we couldn't see out and no one could see in. I felt the car accelerate.

"Good evening, ladies" the smaller man said in perfect English. "I am Liu. This is my cousin, Wo Fat. Please accept our humble apologies for the treatment you have received from our comrades. Unfortunately, they have never been taught more delicate means of persuasion."

"Where is Peter?" I demanded.

Liu smiled and looked at me intently. "We were hoping you might answer that very question for us, Mrs. Matthews."

My heart skipped a beat. If these men didn't know where Peter was, he must have escaped!

"How do they know your name?" Lily whispered.

"Ah, but I know yours as well, Miss Pullen, although we have not been formally introduced. Passport photos are never flattering, but they do serve their purpose." He held up two passports, presumably ours.

Lily gasped. I nudged her to be quiet. "What makes you think I know where Peter is? You've obviously been following us, so you know I left him at the eel hatchery."

"Yes, well, he seems to have disappeared with something very valuable that does not belong to him. And we thought, perhaps, if we had something to trade, something very valuable of his . . . such as his wife."

"How dare you, you despicable slime!" I sputtered. Liu gave me a patronizing smile and shrugged slightly.

The sedan screeched to a stop. Through the front windshield I could see that we were at the gate of the University. One of the guards approached the car with his gun drawn, and obediently the driver rolled down his window. The guard bent to look in.

"Help!" I screamed. "Let us out!"

Before the guard could react, Wo Fat flung the pearl-handled knife at him. It struck his neck, piercing his Adam's apple like a ripe fruit, and he slumped to his knees, blood spurting down the front of his uniform. As he went down his fingers seized involuntarily and his gun fired point blank into Wo Fat's belly. The giant man looked down in surprise at the red stain seeping through his immaculate embroidered coat, and then heaved his massive bulk forward, pinning Liu to the seat. The smaller man tried to extricate himself, but he was trapped beneath Wo Fat's enormous body.

"Lily quick!"

I flung open the car door and scrambled out with Lily close behind. We did not get far. The two thugs had been following in another car, and sped forward to block our path. We ran blindly away from them and through the assemblage of bus drivers who had been drawn by the sound of the gunshot, and through the rows of buses. In the distance I heard a police siren.

We found our way to a blue and white bus that had #373 written on it in bold letters, and got on, huddling low so that we couldn't be seen through the windows.

"You okay?" I asked Lily.

"I'm alive," she said. She looked around the empty bus, and

out the window. The tourist groups were beginning to board the buses around us. "They're going to know we're not part of the tour."

"Hopefully, they won't give us a hard time. We're Americans. We just need a ride to the airport."

"You've got a problem though."

"What?"

"Look at how you're dressed. You look Chinese."

I'd forgotten all about my clothes. Not only were they not the clothes of tourists, but they reeked of fish.

"Here." Lily pulled a sweater off the seat beside her. "Put this on." I tore off the Chinese jacket and slipped the sweater on. Buttoned over my baggy blue cotton trousers, the white angora cardigan made quite a fashion statement.

中國象棋

TWENTY-FIVE

It took a few minutes for the bus to fill. At first nobody mentioned our presence. Beaten down by weeks of travel and the late hour, not to mention the explosive interruption to the evening's entertainment, they acted like prisoners on the way to death row, ignoring us and collapsing into their seats.

The elderly lady, Mrs. Miller, and her niece Mary were among the last to board, and sat in the seats across from us. As the guide walked down the aisle counting heads, I felt the older woman's eyes charting a course up and down my body. Finally, in a loud voice, she demanded, "Young lady, where did you get that sweater? I have one just like it, don't I, Mary?"

I held my breath, but Mary turned to me apologetically and said in a loud whipser, "Don't mind Aunt Eleanor. One of her bags was lost for a few hours in Xian. She keeps forgetting we got it back." Then she added in a lower voice, "Alzheimer's . . ."

"Did you get yours at Filene's too, dear?" Mrs. Miller demanded.

"Hmmm," I said, not knowing whether a yes or a no would get her off the subject.

"May I ask what you paid?"

"Aunt Eleanor!"

"I'm only curious because they told me mine was on final sale, $29.95 I paid." She waited for me to answer.

"That's a very good price," I said. "I think I paid more." I was certainly paying for it now.

Aunt Eleanor smiled triumphantly at Mary. I looked away to discourage further conversation. No such luck. "You weren't on our tour, were you dear?" she persisted.

"Um, no," I said, "I wasn't."

"Of course you weren't," she chuckled knowingly, "or else I'd've noticed that we had the same sweater. What was the name of your group?"

I was at a complete loss. Should I make up a name? Would she know the difference? Would she scream bloody murder and blow our cover if she found out we were impostors? I looked helplessly at the people around me.

"What group *are* you with?" the Travcoa guide demanded, having just determined that his count was high. "This is the Trav-coa bus."

"We're with Superior. Superior Tours," Lily said. "But our bus left without us. Since you're going to the airport anyway, could we ride with you? Is it a problem?"

"Superior," Aunt Eleanor sniffed. "They're a bit cheaper than Travcoa, aren't they, Mr. Cleary, sort of a 'no frills' company?"

I held my breath.

"Superior," the guide sneered, "where did you say they were headquartered?"

From behind him a voice called out, "Oklahoma. We're headquartered in Edna, Oklahoma."

It was John Lee. He strode down the aisle in his best cowpoke swagger with his hand extended to shake with the Travcoa guide. "I've been looking for y'all," he said to us, in the hokey drawl he used with his English class. Then he turned to the Travoca guide. "Our wagon was ready to roll, except for three strays, so I sent it on ahead and stayed to flush 'em out." He held out his hand. "John Lee, Superior Tours."

The Travcoa guide eyed him with suspicion, but shook his hand. "Martin Cleary," he said.

John went on. "Good t'make your accquaintance, Marty. You mind lettin' these two hitch a ride with y'all?"

Martin Cleary thought about it. "I suppose we could manage it. What about you? D'you need a ride too?"

"Oh, thanks, but I got one more out yonder by the gate up-chuckin' her chop suey, and I gotta wait." He bent to look out the window as though looking for his charge. "Bad case of the tourista y'know?

He smiled at us and gave Lily a wink. She beamed back at him. "I'll meet you gals at the airport with the rest of the crew. Okay?"

"See you there," she said.

John shook the Travcoa guide's hand once again. "Thanks for the favor, Marty. I'll buy you a Lone Star at Jimmy's Kitchen when we get back to Hong Kong." And he was gone.

Lily couldn't stop smiling. "I told you he was on our side," she whispered.

"I'm glad," I whispered back.

"Me too."

THIRTY MINUTES LATER the bus turned onto the airport access road. In the distance I could see a low-slung terminal building with a flight tower that looked more like a campanile in an old Mexican village than a modern airport's control center.

There was only one runway, and one prop plane was on the tarmac.

"I hope that's ours," I said as we filed off the bus with the others. If it wasn't, we were in trouble.

The terminal was nearly deserted, the check-in counter closed at this late hour. Even the information desk was shut down. There were a few Chinese travelers clutching their shopping bags and twine-baled boxes, and several men dressed in shiny ill-fitting business suits. A mountain of luggage was heaped in the center of the room, bags of every size and description, all sporting jaunty Travcoa Tours identification stickers.

Lily nudged me and nodded at a man who was standing with his back to us next to the entrance to the immigration inspection area. It was the man in the knit cap. Only he wasn't wearing his hat now; his bald dome glistened under the harsh lights, the wisps of new fringe caught in the ponytail. How had he found us?

And who was he working for: Cao, the Triad, or the Public Security police?

"Travcoa Group, listen up," the tour guide was saying. "You know the drill. I need each of you to find your bags in this pile and move them over here," he said, indicating a row of luggage trams linked like railroad cars, "so we can make sure nothing is missing. After you've identified what's yours, go on through immigration, and then get right on the plane. It's the only one out there, so Mrs. Lafayette, you can't get on the wrong one like you did in Xiamen. We'll be departing as soon as we're all aboard, so the faster we get through this process, the sooner you'll be back in the bar at the Hong Kong Hilton."

The Travcoa group pounced on the pile of luggage. Lily and I waited until a few people had identified their bags and moved toward the immigration area, then we followed. Knit Cap still stood at the door to Immigration, scrutinizing each person who passed through the door. Our only hope was to keep our heads down and hope he wouldn't recognize us.

Suddenly there was a commotion at the terminal entrance, and to my horror, Liu entered, followed by his two swaggering thugs. How had they gotten away from the soldiers? How had they known we were here?

Knit Cap was alert now. He unbuttoned his jacket and reached to the back waistband of his trousers. I'd seen enough Clint Eastwood movies to know that he was going for a hidden weapon! I looked around for airport security, but for the first time I could remember since we'd arrived in China, there was not a guard in sight.

Liu motioned to one thug to stand at the entrance, and he and the other approached our line from the rear, swiftly checking each person in turn. Oddly enough, no one in the Travcoa group seemed the least bit concerned. I suppose after three weeks of being scrutinized by the Chinese, they were used to it.

"Karen, what do we do?" Lily whispered.

"I don't know. Just be calm," I said through gritted teeth. "Act natural."

"That's easy for you to say, you don't have a microchip cemented into your mouth."

Someone tapped my shoulder, and I jumped. It was a bespectacled Chinese woman in an immigration officer's uniform. "May I have your travel documents, please?" she said in accented English.

We held out our bogus passports, and she opened them, quickly comparing our pictures to our faces. Apparently satisfied she said, "Come with me," and put the passports in her pocket.

Had she seen the discrepancy between our faces and our passport photos? Were we going to prison? Right now anything sounded better than waiting for Liu or the man in the knit cap to find us.

She led us to the front of the line and straight past the immigration booth without stopping.

"Why do they get special treatment?" grumbled someone in the Travcoa group.

"They must know someone," his companion replied. "That's how it works here."

Of course Liu had to have seen us being escorted out of line. And we had walked right by the man in the knit cap. Any second, I expected to hear gunfire, screams, and heavy footsteps behind us.

But nothing happened.

The immigration officer led us down a dead-end hallway, and stopped in front of the last door. She fumbled with the keys. "Hurry," I urged her.

"Eh?" she said, looking annoyed. And then she turned the key in the lock and opened the door. Lily and I hurried in past her, not caring what was inside.

The room was tiny and claustrophobic, barely large enough to hold a small desk and a single chair. It had no windows, no other doors. It was a cell, or maybe an interrogation room. "You wait here," the immigration officer barked, and swung the door closed. I heard it lock. We were prisoners.

What could we do? Hide under the desk? Blockade the door? "Lily, help me," I said, throwing my weight against the small metal desk. But it was bolted to the floor. I tried to loosen it with my Swiss army knife, but the blade snapped in my hand. There was nothing to do but wait.

Time passed, and the exhilaration of fear gave way to the frustration of not knowing what was going to happen next. "We're going to miss the plane," Lily said.

"That's the least of our worries," I was saying when the door swung open, startling us both. It was Knit Cap.

I stepped in front of Lily, ready to defend her mouth with my bare hands if necessary, but he only bowed and said softly in English, "Follow me, please."

He unbuttoned his coat and reached to the back waistband of his trousers. We hurriedly put up our hands and rushed out the door before I saw that he hadn't been reaching for his knife after all. He'd pulled out his knit cap. He put it onto his head, and motioned to us to follow him.

"No need to worry," he said. "You are safe now. The airport has been secured."

He walked us straight through the terminal and out a door onto the airstrip. Our way to the plane lit by stars and a single beam of light emanating from the control tower, we hurried across the tarmac. It was eerie. There were no other passengers around, just the airport mechanics, pulling the blocks away from the plane's tires, and the immigration officer with the glasses waiting at the base of the stairs up to the plane. Where was Liu? And how did it happen that the man who had been chasing us all over China had saved us from the very people I thought he worked for? Was this just another trap?

At the foot of the stairs, the immigration officer handed us our bogus passports. "Have a pleasant flight to Hong Kong," she said, and turned and walked away. Knit Cap gestured to the stairs. We started up them, and he followed behind us.

The CAAC flight attendant was waiting for us at the top of the stairs. She bowed a greeting and beckoned us to follow her to two empty seats in the first row. We sat down and strapped ourselves in. Knit Cap spoke a few words to her in Chinese, then bowed to us.

"There will be someone at the airport to meet you when you arrive in Hong Kong," he said. "Safe journey."

Then he stepped off the plane and the flight attendant closed the door behind him. Immediately the aircraft began its taxi onto the runway.

I beckoned to her. "Excuse me, could you please tell me, who was that man?"

"I think he is a good friend of yours, a very good friend with very much *guan-xi*, eh?" she said, and walked away.

中國象棋

TWENTY-SIX

The plane hit the runway with a thud and bounced several times before coming to a firm landing.

Unlike on our previous arrival at Kai Tak, the small CAAC prop plane taxied to a stop about a quarter of a mile from the terminal. A stairway was wheeled up, and a bus pulled to a stop at its base. Around us the other passengers began to gather their belongings.

I looked at Lily. Was it just my imagination or was the left side of her jaw beginning to swell again? "How's your mouth?" I asked in what I hoped was a neutral tone of voice.

"Hurts."

"How bad?"

"Bad."

"You know you're going to have to pretend it's okay until we get to a safe place."

She nodded wearily. "Just don't expect me to recite the Gettysburg Address."

"It would be better if you didn't say anything at all."

"Good."

We were in no hurry to get off the plane and meet our fate, but we were in the first row, and the flight attendant held the others back. "We must deplane by row," she announced. "Please proceed."

So we were the first off the plane. I stood for a moment at the top of the stairs, feeling the cold midnight air whip around my body. In the distance I heard an explosion, then saw a burst of light high above me. Fireworks.

"Happy New Year," the flight attendant said.

"Happy New Year," I replied.

I was too nervous to watch the colorful display overhead, too frightened to feel the chill of the wind, my mind conjuring up lurid images of the scene that was about to transpire. If we got through immigration, that is.

Cao would be waiting for us; it was obvious that's what Knit Cap had meant when he'd said someone would meet us here. If she tried to force us to go with her we would have to refuse, even if it came to violence. It was my duty to my husband and to my country to protect the microchip in Lily's mouth. But how I was going to do it, I did not know.

Actually, it was funny in an ironic sort of way — the dental student risking her life to save a tooth! Maybe the American Dental Association would give me an award. Hopefully, it would not be posthumous.

THE STAIRS SPAT US into the immigration area and I saw that the terminal was completely deserted. My relief at not having to stand in a long line was tempered by fear of being fully exposed with nowhere to hide. Where was everybody?

"Where is everybody?" asked Lily, eerily echoing my thoughts.

"There must not be many flights this time of night," a man said to no one in particular.

"We should thank our lucky stars," said another Travcoa traveler, hurrying to an empty booth and proffering his passport to a yawning immigration officer. "In Singapore we were on line two hours, and another forty-five minutes at customs. And that was at 3 A.M. We barely got to the hotel in time for breakfast."

"Next person in line," the officer said, and I motioned to Lily to go ahead of me. She hesitated, and I gave her a little shove. "Go on. I'll meet you on the other side and we'll go through customs together."

There were police patrolling the baggage claim area behind the immigration booths, guns and clubs strapped to their sides, little microphone mouthpieces like telephone operators use attached to their hats. Had they been there last time we came through the terminal? I hadn't noticed. But then it hadn't mattered. Tonight it mattered a great deal.

Another immigration officer motioned to me and I stepped up to his booth. Lily was still waiting to be cleared, anxiously shifting from foot to foot. I handed my bogus passport to the man in the booth and yawned to give myself an excuse to cover my face with my hand as he checked my picture with the one in the passport. He glanced at me, then idly riffled through the rest of my passport.

"How long you stay Hong Kong?" he asked, flipping through the thick book of numbers on his desk.

"I don't know for sure," I said.

"How many days?" he insisted.

"Not many. One or two."

"Where you come from?"

"China," I said. "Mainland China."

He was flipping through the volumes to find my number, asking questions by rote. "How long you there?" he asked. "What cities you visit?" "You tourist or business?"

"Karen!"

Lily's scream startled me. I looked up in time to see her being forcibly led away by two policemen. Her bogus passport had failed!

"Stop! Don't hurt her!" I cried. I grabbed my passport out of the immigration officer's hands and ran after her.

"You cannot go! I not finish yet!" my officer called. He must have pressed a silent alarm, because a horde of policemen converged on me, holding me at bay as Lily was escorted through a doorway at the side of the building. "Lily!" I screamed. It occurred to me that I might never see her or the microchip again.

But in a matter of seconds, I was escorted through the same door. To my relief and surprise there was Lily, smiling broadly. In fact she was actually laughing, along with two men and a woman whose backs were to me.

Then she saw me. "Karen! Look who's here!" And they all turned around to face me.

It was my brother Mitch, his ex-wife Jae, and another man I didn't know. I ran to Mitch and threw my arms around him, tears of relief now flowing freely.

"What are you doing here?" was all I could choke out.

"It's a long story, I'll tell you about it in the car."

"But — what about out passports? What happened?"

Mitch smiled and gestured to the strange man. "This is Les Stevenson, from the American Consulate," he said. "Les has already signed a waiver for you and Lily. It's all taken care of."

"We don't have to go through customs?"

"You're all clear," Les said. "I hope you're not attempting to smuggle anything over the border," he said with a wink.

Could he possibly know?

We exited through a hallway that opened behind the main thoroughfare where the locals met arriving passengers. I nudged Lily and nodded. There was Cao, anxiously peering into the customs inspection area each time the automatic doors opened to disgorge a passenger.

Some instinct caused her to turn as we passed, and I saw surprise register in her eyes. Then the surprise turned to anger, the anger to fury. She wheeled and started to run in our direction. As she did several men stepped out of the crowd, also converging on us. But at a nod from Les Stevenson, our little entourage was instantly surrounded by a protective circle of police. Cao stopped dead in her tracks. Her men halted as well.

Safe and more secure than I'd felt since I left Santa Monica, I gave Cao a little wave and walked out of the terminal, into the night.

MITCH WAITED until we were inside the U.S. Consul General's Lincoln Town Car to begin his story. "The day after I talked to you, what was that . . . four, five days ago . . . I got a call from my contact at the morgue. You were right. The corpse they'd found in the car on St. Andrews Place wasn't Fernando Ferrar, but someone with his clothes and I.D."

"If it wasn't Fernando, who was it?" Lily asked.

"The point is, if it wasn't Fernando, and we were supposed to *think* it was Fernando, where *was* Fernando? And what did his disappearance have to do with Peter?" Mitch said.

"I figured the only way to find out was to talk to Lauren Covington, so I went up to her house. That must have been, let me see,

I talked to you on the seventh, Hong Kong time, that was the sixth in L.A."

"You talked to Lauren Covington?" I asked incredulously.

Mitch nodded. "I told her who I was, and she was actually very civil, I was surprised. She had only nice things to say about you, Karen."

"We never even met," I said drily. "What could she possibly know about me?"

"More than you think."

"Such as?"

"Never mind. I explained why I'd come, what I'd found out about Fernando, and I told her I needed to know what was going on. At first she was reluctant to talk to me. But she made a couple of calls, then asked me to take a ride with her. To make a long story short, we met a man named Sam, or at least that was what he said his name was."

"At the Santa Monica Pier?" I asked.

"How'd you know?"

I just smiled.

"Anyway, without going into specifics he told me about Peter's connection to the CIA and the work he'd been sent over here to do. When I realized what you'd stumbled into, I called Jae immediately."

We all looked at Jae. I hadn't seen my sister-in-law since she'd left my brother, and I was pretty sure Mitch hadn't either. But the two of them weren't acting like two married people who had been estranged for more than a year. They looked like a couple, a happy couple. What was going on?

Jae picked up the story. "Mitch had already called me and told me you were coming to Hong Kong and asked me to keep an eye on you. This can be a pretty dangerous city for two girls alone . So

I made arrangements with a black belt from my Shing Yi class to follow you, just to make sure you were okay."

"Not a bald guy in a knit cap?" I asked.

Jae nodded. "His name's Freddy Ko. At first Peter thought it was unnecessary. But when he found out they wanted him to go into China . . ."

"Wait a minute, Peter knew about Freddy? You and *Peter* have been in touch?"

Jae smiled at Mitch. "I'd better back up," she said."Mitch told me you were meeting Peter at the Peninsula, so I called there. This had to be the sixth. They said they didn't have a Peter Matthews registered, but I left a message that you were arriving."

"So that's how Peter knew we were coming," I murmured.

Jae continued, "In the middle of the night — it was the night you arrived I think — Peter called me. He sounded anxious about your being there. He told me he was involved in some work that could be dangerous, and he felt it would be best if you two were out of harm's way. I told him about Freddy, and he said —"

"He said, 'Tell Freddy to take care of them,'" I finished for her.

"Something like that," Jae agreed. "How did you know?"

I looked at Lily. "That must have been the conversation you overheard. Peter was talking about *Freddy*, not *Ferdy*."

"I told you I wasn't exactly sure what I'd heard," Lily said.

"That reminds me." Les Stevenson took a photograph out of his jacket. "Recognize this man?" He handed the photo to me.

It was an enlarged copy of the photo that Cao's Uncle Li had shown us of Cao and the group of students. One man's face was circled in red. He had strong, hawk-like features and a crew cut.

"I've never seen him before, but I've seen this picture. Cao's uncle showed it to us in Fuchow! How did you get it?"

Les smiled. "Our files are pretty extensive. And he isn't her uncle, by the way. How about this one?"

He handed me another picture. It was a picture of Cao at the train depot, saying good-bye to the man with the slicked back hair — Fernando Ferrar. But before I could speak, Les Stevenson said, "It's the same man, before and after reconstructive facial surgery. Pan Shu, a.k.a. Fernando Ferrar."

I held the two photos side by side and gradually saw the similarities, disguised by a surgeon's knife. "I can't believe it's the same man."

"Believe it," Les said. "He's a master of disguise. He'd do anything to preserve his identity. Even fake his own murder by killing an innocent person and substituting the body for his own."

"He thought of everything," Mitch added, "except the fact that he and Lauren had had blood tests so they could get married, and the guy in the car crash was type O. Pan Shu was A+."

I looked at the third and final picture. It was of Cao, talking to Lily and me before we got on the train. "You were watching us all that time?"

Les nodded. "But once you crossed the border, we were stymied. All of our local people are known and if we'd sent them in to get you it would have made you obvious targets. Cao knew that; it's probably one of the reasons why she orchestrated your trip. We decided to use Freddy to keep tabs on you since he was already in place, and could cross the border without arousing suspicion. Unfortunately, he proved to be rather inept, as you know."

"But luckily, an hour after Freddy reported in that he'd lost you, you called me to ask me to help find out about Cao," Jae said."

"Why didn't you tell me about Freddy then?" I said to her.

"Orders from Mitch," Jae said. "He thought it would frighten you to know we'd sent a bodyguard to follow you."

Mitch shrugged. "I thought I was doing the right thing. Who knew?"

"What happens to Cao and Ferdy now?" asked Lily.

"Nothing," Les said. "They lost this game. Next time, who knows?"

"What about us?" I was thinking about Lily's tooth. I needed to get the microchip out of her mouth.

"We'll take you to the safe house where we've got Dr. Kensington stashed – we've had him under wraps ever since Cao and Ferdy blew up his energy seminar. Then we'll wait for Peter."

"Is he all right?"

"John Lee radioed from Chinmen. They should be getting on a plane for Taipei within the hour."

中國象棋

EPILOGUE

JUNE 10, 1996

Peter and I were late for the wedding. Again. It seems to be a habit with us.

But this time it wasn't our fault. And it wasn't because of the traffic on the 405.

Lily and John had asked our daughter to be the flower girl in their wedding. And independent spirit that she was, ten-year-old Ming Xin — named after the river in Fuchow — had decided to *pick* flowers to carry from our neighbor's garden.

Which was fine in and of itself. But the Corbett's flower beds were on an automatic watering system, and at 5:30 P.M., while Ming picked daises and delphinia, the sprinklers activated.

Hermie's frantic barking alerted me to the crisis, but it was too late: Ming Xin was drenched, and her beautiful Laura Ashley flower girl dress was ruined. So by the time I'd gotten her dried and redressed — realizing she had me over a barrel, Ming had insisted on wearing her favorite outfit, the little embroidered green silk pajama set we'd bought her on our last trip to Hong Kong — we were late.

But it didn't matter. When we finally arrived, fifteen minutes after the ceremony had been scheduled to begin, Lily was still in the kitchen, apron over her wedding dress, putting the finishing touches on the wedding cake.

"I can't get her out of the kitchen," John complained, but said it with a smile that told us he understood and approved.

"Maybe you should have the wedding back there," Peter joked.

And that's how it happened that Lily and John were married in the kitchen of their restaurant, The Gilded Lotus, with a flower girl dressed in traditional Chinese silk pajamas, and all of the guests crowded in around the ovens, the built-in woks and the prep counter. It was one of the best, most touching and unique services I've ever attended. It even made the cover of *Nation's Restaurant News*.

While I listened to my dearest friends repeat their vows, I reflected on the years that have passed since our adventure in China, and how all of our lives have changed.

As soon as we got back home, I met with Dr. Noritoki and explained my absence from school. With generosity and understanding of which I wouldn't have thought him capable, he allowed me to make up the tests I'd missed, and I graduated from dental school with my class at the end of January.

As he'd promised, Peter retired from the CIA, and, while I worked three days a week at Lily's uncle's Pacific Palisades dental office to pay the bills, he went back to UCLA to get a master's degree in Mandarin Chinese, and then signed on with a trading company headquartered in Hong Kong, which imports textiles from Mainland China. He's worked for them ever since. This gives us the opportunity to travel to Asia twice a year on buying trips — hence the little green silk pajamas Ming Xin wore to the wedding.

Often we have company on these trips. Lily and John come with us when they can get away from their restaurant, to pick up ideas in the culinary wonderland of Hong Kong. But now that they're expecting their first child — which is why they decided to legalize their relationship and get married after all these years — it may be awhile before they come with us.

Mitch and Jae came with us once, four years ago, after Jae finished her surgical residency and went into private practice. Although they seem blissfully recommitted to their marriage, Jae needs, and Mitch understands that she needs, time alone to study her Shing Yi. I give Mitch a lot of credit for accepting Jae's independence, and I'm happy that they have found an approach to marriage that works for them both.

At my urging, Euphrates and Gordon made the trip with us in 1990. With Peter's business ties in China, he was able to introduce Gordon to some trustworthy sources for Chinese rugs, and open up a whole new avenue of sales for my dad. Thanks to the world's focus on the Pacific Rim in the '90s, my father's knowledge of rugs and Peter's business contacts, *Kalderian's* has expanded into a successful wholesale carpet business.

Gordon will probably retire in a year or so; he is eighty-five, after all. I never thought I'd see the day that he'd walk away from the business he built, but in the past ten years he's come to trust and rely upon his assistant manager, Chun Sok Lee, who oddly enough has an aptitude for the rug trade. And he is happy enough living in the apartment over the warehouse in Sherman Oaks. Out in back, he keeps a dozen or so chickens, eleven layers and one black rooster he imported from China, who keep us all supplied with eggs.

And what happened to Wan Lo's miraculous energy producing invention? Well, it turned out to be not quite so miraculous after all. Once they had the microchip in hand, the Plasma Physics

Laboratory at UCLA was able to recreate the black box Peter had destroyed back at the Superior Eel Hatchery. And they actually got it to work. But it seems the theory was flawed. When the researchers tried to scale up the formula, injecting 15 million watts of energy into the reactor and producing a temperature nearly ten times as hot as the core of the sun, the fusing atoms produced only 1.7 million watts of power — enough to energize a mere 17,000 100-watt lightbulbs — before the reaction fizzled. In others words, it spent more energy than it made. But they're not giving up. Apparently Wan Lo's device has given them some new ideas to tinker with.

As for Peter and me, I think it's safe to say that we've built a solid foundation for our marriage, based on trust, honesty, and shared experiences. The old Peter, who used to build walls around himself, has learned that a relationship is stronger if two people are working to hold it together. We are no longer two solitary souls facing in different directions. Rather, like the Chinese character REN, we are two strokes joined together to create a greater entity which is our partnership. I guess Ming Xin is a living manifestation of that bond.

Last Christmas, after Ming had her first cavity filled, by Lily's father of course, as a special treat I took her to *Toys R'Us*. And while she was test-driving the Barbie dolls, I wandered into the game section. There, on an upper shelf, was a new miniaturized version of Chinese Checkers. I bought it and stuck it in the refrigerator on our eleventh anniversary, to remind Peter of our adventure in China ten years ago, and to let him know how glad I am that we're playing on the same team.

The End

AFTERWARD

i have thoroughly enjoyed many trips to Hong Kong and The People's Republic of China. But like Karen and Lily, in my journeys, i have only skimmed the surface of these fascinating cultures. Thus, in order to create a credible work of fiction, i read extensively and with great enjoyment the writing of authors whose knowledge of Asia is far deeper than mine. The following list is a partial bibliography. By including it here, i wish to thank these authors and institutions for their inspiration, and encourage others to read their books.

Across China
by Peter Jenkins (New York, Ballantine Books, 1986)

The American's Tourist Manual for The People's Republic of China
compiled by John E. Felber (Newark, NJ, International Intertrade Index, 1974)

At the Chinese Table
by T.C. Lai (Hong Kong, Oxford University Press, 1990)

Beyond the Chinese Face, Insights from Psychology
by Michael Harris Bond (New York, Oxford University Press, 1991)

The Breakthrough, The Race for the Superconductor
by Robert M. Hazen (New York, Summit Books, 1988)

China Alive in the Bitter Sea
by Fox Butterfield (New York, Bantam, 1982)

China Business Strategies for the '90s
by Arne J. deKeijzer (Berkeley, CA, Pacific View Press, 1992)

Children of China, Voice from Recent Years
by Ann-Ping Chin (Ithaca, NY, Cornell University Press, 1988)

Chinese Forms
translated by Peter Eberly (no bibliographical information available)

The Chinese House
by Ronald G. Knapp (Hong Kong, Oxford University Press, 1990)

Chinese Lives, An Oral History of Contemporary China
by Zhang Xinxin and Sang Ye (New York, Pantheon Books, 1987)

Chinese Sayings
Compiled and translated by William M. Bueler with the assistance of Chang Hou-Pan (Tokyo, Japan, Charles E. Tuttle, 1972)
Chinese Shadows
by Simon Leys (New York, The Viking Press, 1977)
CIA Special Weapons & Equipment, Spy Devices of the Cold War by H. Keith Melton (New York, Sterling Publishing Co. Inc., 1994)
Culture Shock! China
by Kevin Sinclair with Iris Wong Poo-yee (Singapore, Times Books International, 1990)
Digging to China
by J. D. Brown (New York, Soho Press Inc., 1991)
The Execution of Mayor Yin and Other Stories from the Great Proletarian Cultural Revolution
by Chen Jo-hsi (Bloomington, Indiana, Indiana University Press, 1978)
If Everybody Bought One Shoe, American Capitalism in Communist China
by Graeme Browning (New York, Hill and Wang, 1989)
Iron and Silk
by Mark Salzman (New York, Random House, 1986)
Journey to the Forbidden China
by Steven W. Mosher (New York, The Free Press, 1985)
Legacies, a Chinese Mosaic
by Bette Bao Lord (New York, Alfred A. Knopf, 1990)
Magic Walks, Volumes 1 and 2
by Kaarlo Schepel (Hong Kong, Alternative Press, 1990)
Mountains and Streams of Inexhaustible Splendor
translated by Peter Hill (no bibliographical information available)
Night Train to Turkistan
by Stuart Stevens (New York, Atlantic Monthly Press, 1988)
Riding the Iron Rooster
by Paul Theroux (New York, G.P. Putnam's Sons, 1988)
Seven Years in Tibet
by Heinrich Harrer (Los Angeles, J.P. Tarcher, Inc., 1953)
The Spirit of the Chinese Character
by Barbara Aria with Russell Eng Gon (no bibliographical information available)
The Triads
by Martin Booth (Hammersmith, London, Graton Books, 1991)
The Work and Life of Chinese Young People Today
(Beijing, China, China Reconstructs, 1986)

ACKNOWLEDGMENTS

This book would not be without the support of my family. Thank you all for your love and encouragement. it sustained me through days when the end seemed far from sight.

Friends from many places also helped this book evolve:

My dentist, Dr. Tom Jones, and hygienist, Frances Boyajian, taught me more about dentistry and dental school than i ever thought i'd want to know.

Good friends in Hong Kong, China and Taiwan graciously contributed facts and fictions, without realizing that some of their wit and wisdom would end up in print.

John and Nicky Barber, John Deep and Michele Liberti-Lansing generously lent their sure vision and precision to this book, as they did to the last; Judy Hilsinger and Milo Frank, with surpassing patience and warmth, guided me through the stages of being an author which follow publication.

And most especially, Angela Nichol, who inspires me and conspires with me, taking care of business so i can write, taking care of me so i feel like writing.

The text of this book was set in Bembo,
a facsimile of a typeface cut by one of the most
celebrated goldsmiths of his time, Francsco Griffo,
for Aldus Manutius, the Venetian rinter, in 1495.
The face was named for Pietro Bembo,
the author of the small treatise entitled *De Aetna*
in which it first appeared.
The present-day version of Bembo
was introduced by
The Monotype Corporation, London, in 1929.
Sturdy, well-balanced, and finely proportioned,
Bembo is a face of rare beauty
and great legibility.

By contrast,
secondary portions of the book
were set in Duchamp, a typeface designed
by P22 type foundry of Buffalo, New York,
and based on the handwriting of
artist Marcel Duchamp.
While lacking the refinement
and legibility of Bembo,
Duchamp is a face of great
whimsy and personality.
It is the publisher's hope
that it will add a visual dimension
to the reader's impression
of the character of the narrator of
"Chinese Checkers."